A DETECTIVE CH █████████████ ▪ ▪ ▪▪▪▪▪ ▪▪▪▪▪▪

STAND AND DELIVER

NEW YORK TIMES #1 BESTSELLER **TONY LEE** WRITING AS

JACK GATLAND

Hooded Man
MEDIA

———————

Published by Hooded Man Media.
Cover photo by Paul Thomas Gooney

First Edition: April 2025

PRAISE FOR JACK GATLAND

'Fast-paced and action packed, Jack Gatland's thrillers always deliver a punch.'

'This is one of those books that will keep you up past your bedtime, as each chapter lures you into reading just one more.'

'This book was excellent! A great plot which kept you guessing until the end.'

'Couldn't put it down, fast paced with twists and turns.'

'The story was captivating, good plot, twists you never saw and really likeable characters. Can't wait for the next one!'

'Totally addictive. Thoroughly recommend.'

'Moves at a fast pace and carries you along with it.'

'Just couldn't put this book down, from the first page to the last one it kept you wondering what would happen next.'

LIQUIDATE THE PROFITS

FOLDED HANDS

Declan Walsh. Ellie Reckless. Tom Marlowe. Liam Harper. Ryder Waites. Damian Lucas.

COUNTER ATTACK

STEALTH STRIKE

BROAD SWORD

ROGUE SIGNAL

SNIPER ALLEY

SHADOW THREAT

ELLIE RECKLESS BOOKS

PAINT THE DEAD

STEAL THE GOLD

HUNT THE PREY

FIND THE LADY

BURN THE DEBT

LIAM HARPER BOOKS

FINAL STRIKE

BLOOD RIDGE

DAMIAN LUCAS BOOKS

THE LIONHEART CURSE

STANDALONE BOOKS

THE BOARDROOM

As Tony Lee

STANDALONE

TWELVE TASKS

THE PLAYING CARD WAR

KNAVE OF SPADES

QUEEN OF BLADES

For Mum, who inspired me to write.

For Tracy, who inspires me to write.

*And to Fosco, who sat or walked beside me as
I wrote all of these, but does so no longer.*

CONTENTS

PROLOGUE

IT WAS AN HOUR PAST MIDNIGHT, AND THE LONDON NEW ROAD heading out from London stretched before them like a silver ribbon in the moonlight ... empty, save for the occasional car driving past, or fox darting across the road to the verge.

Lord Adrian Carmody watched one of the little brown bastards enter the woods to the side, imagining a hunting rifle at his shoulder, following the blur until his car had continued way past, shifting in the back seat of the Range Rover, his hand resting possessively on Sophia's thigh. Well, that was the name she'd told him anyway, although he doubted its authenticity as much as he doubted the shade of her hair. The platinum-blonde colour reminded him of his wife's attempts to stay eternally youthful, although Sophia carried it with considerably more style, possibly due to the fact that she was half Carmody's wife's age.

The evening had started normally enough; a fundraiser at the Dorchester, all crystal glasses and polite conversations about nothing in particular, the sort of event where the proper business happened in corners and corridors, away from the clicking cameras and hovering waiting staff. Carmody had noticed Sophia early on – hard not to really, she moved through the crowd like a shark through shallow water, all graceful curves and predatory intent, bundled together in a champagne-coloured cocktail dress that hid nothing. Anyone who'd seen her there would know she wasn't there as a guest, there was a certain "sixth sense" you gained at these events; she was one of many women at the event who were "for hire".

It hadn't taken much to arrange things either, a discreet word with the right person, a number passed on a business card, and here they were. His wife was safely occupied at some dreary charity function in Chelsea, surrounded by the sort of people who thought giving money to the poor was a good thing, and as far as she was concerned, giving money to the poor made up for taking it from them in the first place. She'd said before leaving that she'd stay the night in one of the clubs that they were both members of, rather than drive back to a cold bed and an equally cold husband.

And that was fine by Lord Adrian Carmody.

The Dorchester's fundraiser had interested him, not because of the charity being promoted – unlike his wife, Carmody had gone because this event provided women like Sophia to convince people *like* Carmody to attend. It was a clever decision, really, although amusing, considering the fact that the amount of MPs and high-ranking ministers who were there probably made it quite a concerning place to be seen picking up escorts. After all, you never knew who you'd be photographed next to – ask anybody who hung around at parties in the late nineties with Jeffrey Epstein.

Carmody had never attended Epstein's parties. The fact

Carmody had never been *invited* was carefully forgotten, especially after realising he'd dodged a bullet there.

In the front seat, Matthews – Carmody kept forgetting his rank, just knew he was Special Escort Group, a department within the Royalty and Specialist Protection Group – kept his eyes fixed firmly on the road, his jaw clenched tight enough to crack walnuts. The SEG officer's disapproval as to what was happening behind him radiated from him in waves, and Carmody could practically hear the man's teeth grinding. Twenty years in the protection service had given Matthews an unwavering moral compass, one that Carmody found both admirable and deeply irritating in equal measures, especially as he knew that while he was in a cubicle in the men's washroom earlier that evening, he could hear Matthews snorting a line of cocaine in the cubicle at the end. Or at least, that's what he assumed had happened. There was definitely snorting, and definitely a wide-eyed, pupil-dilated look to the hypocrite when Carmody emerged, ready to leave the party.

Carmody stretched back, forcing himself not to growl in satisfaction. He was in his early sixties, short and with the build of a rugby player, mainly because he'd *been* a rugby player during his youth. He was aware his muscled frame still caught the occasional interested glance as he walked through the House of Lords, and his hair, slightly peppering now, was a deep and natural black, thick and vibrant as well.

No thinning bald spots for Lord Carmody, no. You could tug and tug, and nothing would come out. In fact, he'd even tried this frequently with many women. There'd even been one who had tugged from behind when they were trying something new –

He didn't like that encounter. It wouldn't be happening again.

Matthews' likely drug-addled moral compass had been unhappy with *that* one, too.

'You seem tense, Matthews,' Carmody remarked, enjoying the way the man's shoulders tightened at his words. 'Perhaps you should consider a career change. I understand the private sector's much more, well, relaxed about these things. Maybe you should have something to relax you? I can definitely recommend some recreational options.'

Matthews didn't respond, but his grip on his lap tightened. Harris, the driver – also SEG, but apparently a rank or two lower than Matthews – shot his colleague a sympathetic glance. They'd been together for about three years now, long enough to know when to keep quiet and when to intervene. This was definitely a "keeping quiet moment". Lords rarely got Close Protection, but Carmody was a special case, having been brought in a couple of Prime Ministers ago to become the Financial Secretary to the Treasury. He wasn't a Member of Parliament, but it had been happening more and more of late. Carmody assumed it was simply a case of Westminster understanding, finally, that some wet-behind-the-ears twenty-five-year-old woman couldn't become something of note – but a Lord, someone who had spent his time working in business, in industry, building those connections ...

Well, it was the natural option, wasn't it?

He'd been dropped when that idiotic Michelle Rose had taken over, but she lasted about a week and change, and her replacement, the irritating and likely still centrist Charles Baker had brought him back, all teeth and smiles as he told Carmody "the country needed his service."

Balls to service. Who was going to service him?

'Another late night at the office?' Sophia purred, and Carmody fought back a smile.

Oh yes. As far as everyone's concerned, she'll be fulfilling that duty tonight.

Even her accent was practised, but just a little bit too perfect to be real; everything about her was designed to appeal to men like him ... powerful, wealthy and, more importantly, married. There was the slightest thought in the back of his mind that the last word there should have bothered him more than it did, but he shrugged it off.

'The life of a Minister is never easy,' Carmody replied smoothly, patting the small black briefcase beside him. It'd been thrust into his hands just as he was preparing to leave the fundraiser, the woman giving it explaining it was most likely some tedious documentation that Baker wanted reviewed before tomorrow's meetings, but reviewed it must be.

The Prime Minister's timing, as always, was impeccable. And the fact this wasn't the usual "red box" briefcase made Carmody wonder whether this was "on the record" or some clandestine "save my arse again, Lord Carmody" play.

Amusingly, Baker hadn't been at the event either, finding some excuse to be somewhere far away – clever man – so he wouldn't have known Carmody's plans for the remainder of the night.

But Lord Carmody did.

'You poor thing,' Sophia purred.

'It's fine, I can deal with the stress,' Carmody said, the martyr tone audible in his voice, and loud enough for the others to hear. 'Especially when certain important people, like the Prime Minister, insists that I need to work at all hours for the nation's safety.'

Sophia gave an impressed purr, and Carmody shot a meaningful glance at the briefcase. From the rambled conversation he'd had with Jennifer Farnham-Ewing, the messenger on this occasion – now an MP in her own right, somehow gaining her position with the right-wing crowd, and Baker, being very aware of how important those people were, had ensured that she was as close to him as she ever was – inside were papers that could reshape London markets if handled correctly, likely connected to upcoming major infrastructure plans Baker had been discussing, returning the country to the glory days of John Major ... if you could believe such a thing.

She'd pulled him aside just as he was leaving, pressing the case into his hands with a shark-like smile.

'Prime Minister needs your eyes on this before morning, Lord Carmody,' she'd said. 'Urgent business.'

The last Carmody had heard she had been dumped in some forgotten room, but some people knew how to get back into the good graces of their betters, it seemed. The timing wasn't accidental either, Carmody knew that much. Baker had probably waited until the very end of the evening before his assassin struck, when most of the guests had already left; no witnesses to the handover, no awkward questions from the press outside about what sort of documents required such secrecy. The bloody Prime Minister treated running the country like a game of speed chess, trying to pretend he was always three moves ahead, but constantly rushing to stay there. Sometimes Carmody wondered if the man ever slept, but more often he wondered when Baker would trip up, his rivals all waiting in the shadows, sharpening their knives like Brutus's buddies, waiting for Caesar to turn his back. He chuckled at the mock-headline.

Gaius Julius Caesar, popular Roman leader and author, dies at the age of fifty-five, surrounded by his friends.

'Perhaps I could help you relax,' Sophia suggested, her hand sliding slowly up his thigh. 'I could make the paperwork less tedious.'

Matthews cleared his throat loudly at this.

'Sir, we should review the route. There's been some concern about ...'

'About what, Matthews?' Carmody interrupted angrily. 'Some nebulous security threat, perhaps? Drones flying around? There's always a bloody threat, and there's always bloody drones. That's why we pay you little people so much money.'

'Actually, sir, there's been reports of ...'

'Motorcycle approaching from the rear, sir,' Harris cut in, his voice carrying the slightest edge of professional concern. It was enough to make Carmody sit up straighter, although it could have been Sophia's hand reaching high on his thigh that made him jump. Even after fifteen years in Westminster's House of Lords, and three in politics, the paranoia never quite faded; every photographer could work for the opposition. Every passing car or motorcycle could contain a journalist. After all, Carmody believed passionately it was what killed Diana all those years ago – paparazzi on bikes.

The tabloids would love this; *Lord Carmody, Conservative Minister, caught with a high-class escort while his wife attended a charity function.* The headlines would write themselves.

'Paparazzi?' he asked.

'Can't tell, sir, single headlight moving fast. Unusual profile.'

The bike rocketed past them at speed, and Carmody looked out of the window, something he shouldn't have done, but as he did so, he caught a glimpse of what looked to be a cape billowing behind the rider. Relaxing slightly at the lack of a camera, he pushed Sophia's head quickly down towards his lap with a throaty chuckle.

'You need to hide for the moment,' he said. 'But of course, while you're down there ...'

'That's inappropriate, sir,' Matthews muttered, his knuckles now white on his holstered weapon, his other hand already reaching for his radio.

'Everything's inappropriate to you, Matthews, unless you can take it nasally,' Carmody laughed, but there was an edge to it. 'It's only a bloody motorcycle. Some other poor sod trying to get home from London before he loses any more bloody sleep. How much longer is it till we get there, anyway?'

'Another twenty minutes to Theydon Bois, sir,' Harris responded, his voice professional but strained. 'Unless you prefer we drop off your "guest" first?'

The slight hesitation before the word *guest* spoke volumes. Harris, although having been part of the protection detail for three years, was ignoring rule number one – *what happens in the car stays in the car.*

Rule number two was always *never refer directly to what happens in the car.*

But before Carmody could answer, and as they crested a rise near Lincoln's Lane car park, the ancient woodlands of Epping Forest on either side of them, the car's full beam lighting them up like guardians on either side of the single-lane road, Carmody saw Harris' eyes widen.

The motorcycle had parked itself sideways across the road, the front wheel facing towards them its single headlight painting their Range Rover in a harsh white. In front of it, silhouetted by the light, stood a figure that seemed to have stepped out of a history book.

The rider had removed his helmet and replaced it with what appeared to be a tricorn hat, and, as they pulled closer, they could see an ornate black mask covered the upper half of his face, an opaque scarf covering the bottom, leaving only the upper nose and part of the cheeks visible, his eyes shadowed by the hat, and in one gloved hand he held what looked to be an antique pistol. The figure's clothing was a modern interpretation of historical garb; motorcycle leathers cut to suggest an eighteenth-century Highwayman's coat and cloak, with silver buttons catching the moonlight.

'He's blocking the way, sir,' Harris spoke casually, already slowing the Range Rover down.

'Speed up,' Matthews snapped. 'Run the bastard over! It's the middle of the sodding night and he's got a weapon in his hand –'

Before anything could happen, though, there was the sharp crack of an explosion, and the Range Rover lurched to the side as the front tyre exploded, forcing Harris to brake.

'He shot out the bloody tyre!' the driver exclaimed, and the car slid slightly – but luckily for the people inside the Range Rover, Harris' training kept them steady as they came slowly to a stop.

'I should warn you that traditionally, Highwaymen didn't actually shoot out carriage wheels,' Harris muttered.

Matthews was already reaching for his weapon but froze as a bright-red dot appeared on his chest. Looking to the side, he saw that another had appeared on Harris, also freezing, and Carmody looked around wildly, as both officers in the front realised they were trapped in the middle of nowhere, with at least two sniper rifles aimed at them.

'What do I do, sir?' Harris asked.

'Stay where you are,' Matthews replied. As Carmody looked around, he could just about make the shapes of two vans at each end of the stretch, blocking the road from anybody coming in, the vans pretending they'd skidded to a halt, breaking down.

'This is professional,' Matthews said quietly. 'Multiple shooters, coordinated blocking vehicles. This isn't some random Highwayman, sir, this is a planned operation.'

'Well, of course it isn't a random bloody Highwayman, Matthews! Random bloody Highwaymen don't exist in the twenty-first century!'

'I think you should tell *him* that,' Matthews said, as the figure approached with an unhurried grace, boots clicking against the tarmac. As they drew closer, both Matthews and Harris could see that the pistol wasn't truly antique; although it looked like a duelling pistol, it had been modified, modernised even, while maintaining its historical appearance. It wouldn't be the same one-shot-ball style of the original one; there was probably an entire cartridge within it, and it had already showed it was effective.

'Best not to piss the man off, then, perhaps?' Carmody suggested. The craftsmanship was exquisite, however, but somehow that made it more terrifying, and Matthews quickly snapped off a photo with his phone, before bringing it back down, almost as if he knew he'd never be believed if word of this got out.

Sophia, meanwhile, had paled, her eyes wide.

'I can't be killed by a Highwayman,' she said, her voice suddenly very much northern. *A grating accent, possibly Oldham?* Carmody spent little time up north. All he knew was that the voice had completely stopped his libido with a single phrase.

'I don't think the Highwayman's here for you,' he said. 'Don't worry though, the windows of the Range Rover are bulletproof, so I think his popgun won't breach our defences any time soon.'

'The Highwayman isn't our main problem, sir.' Matthews was still assessing the situation, and Carmody wondered how the cocaine still in his system would play out here. 'There's maybe three shooters, high ground positions. Thermal scopes maybe, given the darkness and the accuracy of taking out the tyre.'

'I thought the Highwayman did that?'

'He fired at the same time, but there could have been back up. The vans could suggest a team of six minimum.'

'But they can't get through the glass though, right?'

Matthews shrugged, giving a "I have no idea" response.

'Depends what they have,' he eventually replied. 'The windows are bullet *resistant*, not bullet *proof*. If they have a larger round, like a full metal copper jacket ...'

He didn't need to continue; the point was made.

'Can we do anything?' Carmody asked.

'Not without casualties, sir. They've blocked us in perfectly.'

Once beside the Range Rover, the Highwayman rapped on the window with the barrel of his pistol, and Carmody could see that the mask on his face was expensive looking and intricate, very much a black version of the Venetian masks that you could buy during the carnival. He'd been there once, and he enjoyed parties where people wore masks. But this really wasn't the time to consider such things, as the

Highwayman rapped again, and when nobody moved, the Highwayman spoke, his voice carrying an affected theatrical quality that somehow made the situation a little more surreal.

'Come now, good sir, lower your carriage window, lest I be forced to shatter it,' he said, his accent sounding very upper class and almost mechanical. It took a moment for Carmody to realise it was some kind of voice modulating microphone, most likely hidden behind the scarf. 'I assure you; the clean-up would be most tedious.'

Matthews instinctively reached for his radio, but the Highwayman tutted, motioning his pistol at the window; not to shoot, but to remind Matthews of the red dot on his chest.

'I pray thee, cast out thy devices of communication, phones and radios both, if you please. We would not want anyone interrupting our transaction here. Also, please cast out thy own pistols, lest we find ourselves duelling in the Essex darkness.'

'Do it,' Carmody hissed. He had seen enough red dots in action movies to know what they meant, and Matthews' earlier comment about the windows had chilled him. This wasn't an amateur looking for quick cash. This was an orchestrated, planned, and precise heist.

Sighing, Matthews opened the window, passing out the radios and both service revolvers – although the latter he tossed to the floor rather than passing to the Highwayman, who didn't seem to care, as long as they were out of the Range Rover.

'And phones, don't make me repeat myself,' the Highwayman added, turning his attention to Carmody. 'My lord, I see you travel in interesting company tonight. How fortunate that Lady Carmody is otherwise engaged with her charitable pursuits. The papers would be most interested in your choice of evening entertainment.'

Sophia now pressed herself against a far door, all pretence of seduction forgotten. Her carefully constructed persona had pretty much cracked now, revealing genuine fear beneath the polished surface.

'I ain't being paid enough for this kind of shit,' she muttered.

'For sure,' the Highwayman chuckled.

'What do you want?' Carmody demanded, trying to keep the tremor from his voice.

'Your valuables, naturally. Watches, wallets, jewellery; anything you have on, and more,' the Highwayman's voice carried a note of amusement, as though they were an actor in some kind of elaborate street theatre. Carmody's hand tightened on the handle of the briefcase – he couldn't let this go. Hypothetically, it could contain more than just market sensitive information; inside could be information on shell companies, offshore accounts, arrangements that could destroy careers. Charles Baker's bloody inner circle operated in shadows within shadows, and this briefcase contained enough matches to set them all ablaze.

'Now, that's a very interesting item you seem very concerned about,' the Highwayman said, noting the briefcase, and Carmody cursed back at him.

'Look, I don't care what you want. Take anything else. Take our wallets. Take our jewellery. Take her bloody stuff, although it's probably paste. The briefcase stays.'

At this, the Highwayman's laugh was cold and sharp.

'My dear Lord Carmody, I fear you misunderstand the nature of this transaction,' he explained, as if talking to a three-year-old. 'This is not a negotiation, although I must admit your reluctance to part with this pretty trinket only amuses me. Perhaps I know more about its contents than you do?'

The Highwayman turned to Matthews, the window still down.

'I know you have ballistic-rated glass,' he said. 'The rifles aimed at you are prepared for this. Believe me when I say that if you were to return thy window to an upwards location, believing yourselves safe within, your carriage's windows would explode inwards with such ferocity that you would be sliced apart, at the simplest flick of my hand.'

He returned his attention to Carmody.

'The briefcase, if you please. Do not make this evening any more uncomfortable than necessary.'

Slowly and with great reluctance, Carmody handed it over with trembling fingers. The Highwayman accepted it with an elaborate bow, and Matthews tensed, ready to move, but suddenly, two more red dots appeared, dancing across his and Harris' chests like deadly fireflies.

'Shit, there's more of them out there.' Harris remained perfectly still, controlled breathing and steady hands on the wheel. Only his eyes showed he was terrified.

'It has been an absolute pleasure doing business with you,' the Highwayman grinned, sweeping off his hat in a mocking salute, before holding it out, revealing what looked to be dark hair in the night's vision. 'And now I would like your jewellery, your wallets, and anything else you feel you should be passing me.'

Quickly, Carmody threw his wallet into the tricorn hat, watching as Sophia removed her earrings and necklace, tossing them through the window, and at a tut from the High-wayman, he reluctantly removed his watch. It was an Omega

Seamaster; expensive, at least five grand, and Harris and Matthews also reluctantly gave their wallets across, dropping them into the hat, and the Highwayman gave them a mocking salute before picking up the fallen revolvers and walking back to his motorbike.

'Do give my regards to the Prime Minister,' he said over his shoulder. 'I'm sure he'll be most interested in hearing how you lost his private papers while entertaining such charming company.'

Placing the helmet on and attaching the briefcase, placing the stolen items into his panniers, and taking time to toss the weapons into the woodlands, the Highwayman clambered back onto the motorcycle as its engine roared once more to life, and within moments both bike and rider had vanished into the night.

The moment he did so, the red dots disappeared and in the distance, Carmody could hear vehicles moving away. The entire operation had taken less than five minutes and was incredibly professional, efficient and devastating.

'Sir,' Matthews turned in his seat, already assessing the situation, 'are you alright?'

Carmody barely heard him. His mind was racing through the implications. His wife, the papers, bloody Charles Baker's reaction when he learned the documents were gone, it was going to be a public disaster.

'Sir,' Matthews pressed, 'we need to call this in.'

'Oh God, do we have to?'

'Yes.'

'Fine, do it,' Carmody said distantly. Climbing out of the Range Rover, Harris ran over to the phones, picking them back up. Luckily, the screen hadn't broken on one of them, and he dialled 999, standing beside the car.

'This is Detective Sergeant Harris, Special Escort Group. We've been robbed on the London New Road, west of Loughton. We need immediate assistance.'

There was a pause as he listened to the operator's questions, and Carmody could hear his own heart pounding in his ears, wondering how much of his carefully constructed life would survive the coming day. Behind him, Sophia had stopped crying and was now moving as far away from him as she possibly could. Carmody was about to comment about this, saying loudly for the cheap seats how *she seemed quite happy to be stroking his thigh when he had money,* but before he could, she pulled open the door and, with a scream, ran off into the night, heading away, through the woods.

'Should I go after her?' Matthews asked, with a reluctance in his voice.

'No, if she wants to run, that's fine,' Carmody actually smiled now. 'It means she's not with us when the police arrive, and it saves a ton of questions. Let her bugger around in Epping Forest in the dark.'

Harris, meanwhile, was finishing his call.

'The suspect? Well, you're not gonna believe it ... it was Dick Turpin,' he said down the line. 'Yeah, Turpin on a bloody motorcycle.'

In the silence following this, Lord Adrian Carmody looked out through the open window at the empty road. Behind them, he could hear sirens approaching – too late as usual ...

And somewhere in London, someone was about to break open a very important briefcase.

1

POLITICAL CURRENCY

THE FENCHURCH STREET VAULTS PROBABLY HADN'T SEEN THIS *much excitement since World War Two,* Detective Chief Inspector Declan Walsh considered as he pressed himself against a century-old support column, listening to the echoes bouncing off the Victorian brickwork as, somewhere in the darkness ahead, Patrick Cullen was running out of options. The former bank manager had led them on a three-week chase through shell companies and offshore accounts, but it was about to end in the very vaults he'd once hidden his ill-gotten gains.

His radio crackled.

'North-west corner secured,' Detective Inspector Anjli Kapoor's voice fought through the static. 'Billy's got eyes on the systems.'

'Copy that,' Declan kept his voice low. 'De'Geer?'

'In position at vault exit,' came the response, barely audible through the interference from the thick walls. 'He's not getting past.'

They'd spent weeks building this case – missing pension funds, desperate retirees, and a paper trail that led straight to Cullen's private accounts in Geneva. It would have been the perfect crime if one of his junior associates hadn't developed a conscience, mentioning the off-books rental of this long-forgotten location.

A scraping sound echoed from his left; Declan moved carefully, his shoes silent on the old stone floor. There was something satisfying about catching someone in the act, although Declan hadn't appreciated Anjli's comment, as they arrived, that "at least they didn't have to listen to him go all *Poirot* this time."

His radio hissed again.

'Guv,' Detective Sergeant Billy Fitzwarren's voice cut through, 'laptop's giving up all sorts of secrets. Full spread-sheet record. He's labelled everything as "management fees".'

'You're only making it worse, Patrick,' Declan called out, his voice bouncing off the arched ceiling. 'We've got everything. The transfers, the fake accounts, even that rather creative spreadsheet you kept on your personal laptop.'

'You don't understand!' Cullen's voice cracked with desperation. 'They made me do it!'

'They?' Declan edged closer to the source of the voice. 'The same "they" who helped you buy that villa in Tuscany?'

A crash of metal on stone suggested Cullen had knocked something over in the darkness. Declan smiled – the man was getting sloppy.

'Those pensioners trusted you, Patrick,' he continued, gesturing silently to Anjli as he spotted her approaching from a side tunnel. 'Forty years of savings, and you treated it like your personal lottery win.'

'They were going to lose it anyway!' Cullen's voice echoed

from behind a stack of old filing cabinets. 'The market crash was coming. I just ... redistributed things!'

'To your own accounts?' Anjli's voice rang out, her closeness making Cullen curse. 'That's an interesting definition of redistribution.'

Declan could hear the suspect's ragged breathing now. The vault complex was a maze, but they'd examined the blueprints before following him down. Cullen had nowhere left to run.

A metallic clang followed by rapid footsteps told Declan that Cullen had heard enough. The bank manager burst from his hiding spot, nearly colliding with a support beam in his panic. He was running towards what he thought was an exit, but Declan knew better.

'De'Geer,' he called out. 'Get ready for company.'

'Standing by, guv.'

In the shadows, Declan could see Cullen as he rounded the corner at full speed and bounced off Sergeant Morten De'Geer's chest like a tennis ball hitting a wall. The massive officer caught him before he could fall, efficiently securing his hands behind his back.

'Patrick Cullen,' Declan began, approaching with his warrant card already out, 'I'm arresting you for fraud, embezzlement, and misappropriation of pension funds. You do not have to say anything, but it may harm your defence if you do not mention, when questioned, something which you later rely on in court. Anything you do say may be given in evidence –'

'This is all a mistake,' Cullen protested weakly as De'Geer began leading him towards the exit. 'I can explain everything.'

'Save it for the interview room,' Anjli suggested, falling into step beside Declan as they followed. 'Though you might want to work on a better story than "*they made me buy a villa*".'

Declan's phone buzzed in his pocket. It was an unknown number, so he ignored it. If it was truly important, they could call back. After a moment, it stopped.

Then, a minute later a second buzz showed a text message from Monroe.

Answer it.

Declan frowned at this, but then the phone started ringing again; the same mysterious number.

'Need to take this,' he told Anjli, stepping aside. 'Get Cullen processed and start the paperwork. I'll catch up.'

Answering the phone, he didn't have time to say anything before the voice on the other end spoke. It was a male voice; crisp, official, and didn't waste time with pleasantries.

'Detective Chief Inspector Walsh, your presence is requested at the Guildhall Art Gallery. The Prime Minister is hosting a private viewing and would like a word.'

Declan's eyebrows rose. Charles Baker didn't "request words" with Declan without good reason. And Monroe didn't send cryptic messages unless it was important.

'When?'

'Now, DCI Walsh. A car is already en route to your location.'

The line went dead before Declan could respond or even ask how they knew his location – Monroe must have told them. And for him to do so ...

He looked back at De'Geer, who was placing Cullen into a squad car with methodical precision.

'Something's come up,' he said. 'Can you handle this?'

De'Geer nodded, not breaking rhythm and Declan headed towards the main road, where, sure enough, a sleek black car was already pulling up. The driver, wearing the discreet earpiece that marked him as SEG, climbed out and opened the rear door without a word.

'Any idea what this is about?' Declan asked as he climbed in. The driver returned to the driver's seat and then turned his head to face Declan.

'Honestly sir, no,' he replied, shaking his head. 'All I can tell you is that Baker's in a foul bloody mood, and we had two of our guys held up last night. That's all I know.'

THE GUILDHALL ART GALLERY WAS ONLY A SHORT DRIVE AWAY, but morning traffic made it feel longer. Declan used the time to send a quick text to Monroe, updating him on the Cullen arrest, and informing him of his revised travel plans, but he was surprised to receive an immediate response:

Already here. Hurry up.

The gallery was technically closed for a private viewing, but the security presence suggested this was more than just the Prime Minister admiring some paintings. Declan counted at least six protection officers in the entrance hall alone, all trying very hard to look like they *weren't* protection officers. Detective Chief Superintendent Bullman was also waiting by the reception desk, her short white hair spiked in its usual fashion, over a charcoal suit and pastel-yellow blouse. She nodded at Declan's approach.

'Quite the morning?' she asked, referring to his slightly dishevelled appearance.

'Had better,' Declan admitted, straightening his jacket. 'Running around in tunnels is never good for tailoring. What's this about? The driver mentioned something about his colleagues being mugged or something?'

'Above my pay grade,' Bullman replied, but there was something in her tone that suggested otherwise. 'Monroe's inside with the PM. He's been practically bouncing off the walls – you know how he gets around Baker. We give him a few more minutes, we might find him becoming the first City of London copper to be placed in the Tower of London.'

'Nah,' Declan grinned as they started through the gallery's main hall, past priceless artworks that Declan knew would have had Billy's current beau, the one-time art forger Sam Mansfield, salivating. 'We've got too much on Baker for that.'

'For us to have something over on the Prime Minister does require him to still *be* Prime Minister,' Bullman replied ominously. 'Keep that in mind.'

———

THE PRIME MINISTER'S PARTY WAS GATHERED IN A SMALLER viewing room, the space dominated by John Singleton Copley's "Defeat of the Floating Batteries at Gibraltar". Charles Baker stood before the massive canvas; hands clasped behind his back like a schoolmaster preparing to deliver a lecture. In his late fifties, his lustrous white hair – usually in a quiff – seemed quite understated, as if his head was in mourning. He turned as they entered, and Declan was struck, as always, by how the man seemed to fill any room he occupied.

Detective Superintendent Monroe stood nearby, trying not to look too pissed off about being in such elevated company.

'Ah, Detective Chief Inspector Walsh,' Baker smiled, though it didn't reach his eyes. 'Thank you for joining us on such short notice. I trust whatever incredibly exciting case we dragged you from is concluded?'

'Yes, sir, in custody now. A banker, using his company's pension fund to feather his nest. We stopped him, as we do *all* such people who look to feather their own nests at the cost of the public.'

'Excellent. Though I'm afraid we have a somewhat more pressing matter,' Baker ignored Declan's obviously specifically aimed comment, and gestured to a nearby bench. 'Please, sit. We have rather a lot to discuss.'

Declan took a seat, noting how Baker still positioned himself with the massive painting at his back, like a general addressing his troops before battle. He also noticed that, as Monroe and Bullman joined him, the other officers, those of Baker's close protection moved away, as if giving the impression of moving out of earshot.

'Last night,' Baker began, 'or, rather, in the early hours of this morning, Lord Adrian Carmody was returning from an essential charity fundraising event at the Dorchester. He was carrying sensitive documents in a briefcase that required immediate review.'

'That doesn't sound like routine security procedure,' Monroe interjected, his voice carrying an edge of something that made Declan glance at him. 'Usually we advise against reviewing classified materials from a "red box" while in transit.'

Baker's smile tightened fractionally.

'Indeed. However, it wasn't the usual "red" box, it was a normal black leather briefcase, and time was of the essence.'

'No red box?' Declan frowned.

'It was sent late. My office missed the red box close out. Don't make it more than it was.'

'Was Lady Carmody with him?' Monroe continued, asking innocently. 'Only, I heard she was at some charity do in Chelsea.'

Bullman shot Monroe a warning look, but the Scotsman seemed to be enjoying himself. Declan had seen this side of Monroe before – the skilled investigator, hiding behind a role of casual inquiry, and following the beat of his own drum, likely in a direction that could possibly get him fired.

'Lord Carmody was accompanied by his security detail,' Baker said carefully. 'Detective Chief Inspector Matthews and Detective Sergeant Harris from his Special Escort Group.'

'Just the three of them?' Monroe pressed. 'In a Range Rover? Seems a bit spacious.'

Baker's fingers drummed once on the bench beside him – the only tell in his otherwise perfect composure.

'The exact passenger manifest isn't relevant to the current situation, Alex.'

Declan noted the casual use of Monroe's name and wondered if this was his attempt at being friendly, or rather an attempt at reminding Monroe that, as Prime Minister, he could call anyone what he wanted.

'Actually, sir,' Declan cut in, 'it might be. Any witnesses could be crucial, especially in the first twenty-four hours.'

'The situation,' Baker continued as if neither had spoken,

'involved a highly coordinated attack. The vehicle was stopped on the London New Road, in Essex, apparently between Buckhurst Hill and the *Robin Hood* pub.'

'Convenient spot,' Monroe mused. 'Quiet at that time of night.'

Baker ignored the comment.

'A motorcycle approached the vehicle. The rider was dressed ...'

He paused, as if the next words physically pained him.

'The rider was dressed as a Highwayman.'

'Like Dick Turpin?' Declan raised an eyebrow at this.

'Actually, I mean precisely like Dick Turpin,' Baker nodded. 'Complete with tricorn hat and period-appropriate costume. Though the weapon was modern, despite its antique appearance.'

'Just the one person?' Declan leaned forward. 'Against an armed ministerial security detail?'

'According to the officers, there were others, hidden in the woods on either side,' Baker admitted. 'Snipers, support vehicles. Highly professional.'

'Special Escort Group protocol requires immediate action in the event of a threat,' Declan said. 'Unless they were somehow prevented from responding?'

'Well, they had laser sights on their chests,' Baker said tersely. 'I'd say that bloody well meant the situation called for discretion.'

There was an awkward silence at the uncharacteristic outburst.

'The Highwayman,' Baker continued, his tone growing sharper, 'demanded valuables. Phones, wallets, the usual. And then ...'

'The briefcase,' Declan finished.

'Yes.' Baker's expression darkened. 'Lord Carmody was reluctant to part with it, naturally. As I said, the documents inside are ... sensitive.'

'How sensitive?' Declan asked.

'Sensitive enough that if certain parties were to acquire them, the resulting chaos could destabilise a large part of our entire financial system.' Baker straightened his already impeccable tie. 'The briefcase contained details of planned market interventions, pending policy changes, certain ... arrangements with our European partners in relation to an upcoming infrastructure agreement we were looking to implement.'

'And this was just casually handed to Lord Carmody at a fundraiser?' Monroe's scepticism was palpable.

'The handover was discreet.'

'Everything about last night seems to have been discreet,' Monroe muttered, and Baker's composure finally cracked, if only slightly.

'Detective Superintendent Monroe, if you have something to say, please say it directly.'

'Oh, I think we all know what happened last night,' Monroe smiled. 'Lord Carmody, alone in his car with his security detail, just happening to be on a quiet road when he's robbed by Dick Turpin himself. Very neat. Very discreet.'

'The facts of the robbery –' Baker began.

'Are that Lord Carmody was carrying documents he shouldn't have had been given in such a way, from a place he shouldn't have been given them,' Monroe finished. 'And now someone else has those documents.'

'Why was he given them at the dinner?' Declan asked.

'I didn't get them until late, and I wanted him to peruse them before a bill reading later today,' Baker admitted. 'And, if I'm being brutally honest, I wanted him to have to do some bloody work for a change.'

'And there we go,' Monroe smiled. 'You gave him his brief-case of shiny goodies at the end of a party you knew he'd be at, purely to piss him off, and make him work through the night, rather than whatever jollies he had planned.'

Charles Baker didn't deny this, simply shrugging.

'I had Jennifer do it,' he said eventually. 'She was going to be there, and we're regaining trust.'

'You let Jennifer Farnham-Ewing take sensitive documents to a party?'

'She didn't know the code to open the damned thing,' Baker snapped. 'And there were other aides around.'

'So why not let *them* give it to Carmody?'

'Lower levels talking to a Lord? Be serious,' Baker shook his head. 'Besides, by asking her to go there meant I removed her from another event last night.'

Declan sighed; the amount of bloody internal politics in Westminster outweighed the actual politics, sometimes. But something else niggled here.

'You made a mistake,' he said simply.

'Of course I made a sodding mistake,' Baker snapped. 'I was distracted, overworked and I listened to the wrong people again.'

'Aye, bloody Farnham-Ewing, for a start.'

'Who knew?' Declan asked. 'About the briefcase?'

'You think the robbery was for the briefcase rather than the person?' Baker shook his head. 'According to the officers, the Highwayman knew Lord Carmody by name, and didn't seem surprised at the briefcase.'

'So, Carmody had no idea he'd be getting the briefcase?'

'Oh, he probably had his minions tell him, and from the

meetings we all had during the day, he knew it was coming,' Baker was examining his nails now. 'But unless they worked with Jennifer, there was no way he could have known in advance. The whole point was to spring it on him.'

'And how did that work out for you?' Monroe grinned, no longer caring if it pissed Baker off.

Charles Baker glowered at the three officers facing him.

'Look, I need to get it back,' he said. 'Carmody had a bad evening, but I can't throw this all on him. I need to know if this was an inside job before the press gets hold of it and nails me to another bloody cross.'

'Then you need your own people to look into this,' Declan frowned. 'We're not even a Met unit, and the City's borders don't reach Westminster, or Epping Forest.'

Baker's smile tightened.

'Under normal circumstances, perhaps. But this particular situation requires a more ... specialised approach. Let's be honest, Declan. Your unit has a reputation for handling unusual cases with discretion, and you've all pulled my arse out of the fire on multiple occasions. I need you to do it one more time.'

'The Last Chance Saloon,' Bullman interjected, looking back at Declan and Monroe now, 'is being tasked as a special investigative force. Full resources, complete autonomy. We had the paperwork hit before I left my office, but it wasn't until now I understood why.'

'Full resources and complete autonomy within reason,' Baker added quickly.

Declan glanced at Monroe, who was practically vibrating with excitement at the possibility of pissing off more members of Parliament.

'There's something you're not telling me,' Declan said to

Baker, earning a sharp look from Bullman. 'Where's Commander Bradbury? Shouldn't he be here for this, considering we're being removed from his remit?'

The temperature in the room seemed to drop several degrees. Bullman's expression didn't change, but her posture stiffened slightly.

'The Commander is handling other matters,' she said flatly. 'I'm here as his representative.'

Baker cleared his throat.

'Well, I believe that covers the essentials. Declan, Alex, I cannot stress enough the importance of recovering those documents quickly and quietly.'

'Don't you worry, Charlie,' Monroe grinned, patting the Prime Minister on the shoulder in a casual and familiar manner. 'We'll save your arse again.'

AS THEY LEFT THE GALLERY, DECLAN NOTICED BULLMAN checking her phone, as Monroe fell into step beside him, still grinning.

'Special investigative force,' he said quietly. 'Baker knows he's deep in the shite, aye?'

'Something's not right about this,' Declan replied. 'Since when does the PM personally assign cases?'

'Since now, apparently. Don't look a gift horse in the mouth, laddie.'

But, as they walked back to their waiting cars, once more laid on by Baker, probably to stop them from being seen calling cabs back to the Unit, Declan couldn't shake the feeling that they were being handed a poisoned chalice. *The*

Last Chance Saloon might have just been upgraded, but at what cost?

'Back to Temple Inn,' Bullman ordered, already heading for the first car. 'Full team briefing in thirty minutes.'

Declan watched her go, noting the tension in her movements.

'What's her issue?' he asked. 'She's acting like the world's fallen in.'

'Maybe she hoped for more shite on Baker?' Monroe suggested. 'I know I did.'

2

BRIEFING

'RIGHT THEN, MY BAND OF LITTLE KIDDIWINKIES,' MONROE began, standing at the front of the briefing room. 'It seems that once again our valiant team has been placed in the jaws of danger, taken from our comfortable offices and thrown to the wolves. Will we solve this case? Who knows? Will we help our illustrious Prime Minister? Who cares?'

The room was as it always was for these briefings; Monroe, as per his original agreement with Declan, took the lead on the case, regardless of his rank. Declan sat to the right, Anjli beside him, with Doctor Marcos, Sergeant De'Geer, PC Cooper at the back, and Billy Fitzwarren to the left, working his laptop, connected to the plasma screen behind Monroe. Special guest for this briefing was Declan's seventeen-year-old daughter, Jess, effectively the unit's official mascot, sitting beside Billy, on half-term from her A-levels. But Declan had to remember she was a grown woman now rather than a stroppy teen, as she'd held her own in various cases over the years.

The only other addition was Detective Chief Superintendent Bullman, standing by the door in her usual position, looking slightly abashed.

'You seem quite chipper, Guv,' Anjli remarked.

Monroe turned and grinned.

'Aye, lassie,' he replied, 'I am indeed chipper, for this is a case involving Lord Adrian Carmody.'

'And we're supposed to know who that is?' Anjli queried.

Monroe seemed horrified by Anjli's lack of what Declan supposed was aristocracy knowledge.

'You don't know the Carmodys?' he exclaimed. 'The Carmodys were made lords in the fifteen hundreds.'

Declan felt a history lecture coming on.

'Originally from Berkshire, they were given lands up north –'

'Ah, here we go,' Doctor Marcos muttered from the back. 'Bloody Scottish independence again, isn't it?'

'The only Scottish independence you should worry about, darling,' Monroe said to his wife, 'is the fact that you're now tied to me by bonds of marriage seen by God above.'

'God above doesn't give a monkeys about your Scottish independence either,' Doctor Marcos leaned back on the chair, folding her arms. 'So, let me guess. The Carmodys – what – touched the people of Glasgow in a bad place? Would you like to show us on the teddy where it happened?'

Monroe straightened, and Declan could tell he was getting irritated by the conversation.

'Let's just say the Carmodys didn't help themselves during the Jacobite rising,' he mumbled. 'They're no friend to Scotland, and if I have a chance to bring one down –'

'Guv,' Declan held a hand up. 'I got the impression that Lord Carmody was the victim here and not the suspect?'

'Aye, that's a possibility,' Monroe accepted reluctantly. 'But it doesn't necessarily mean we can't ask him loads of wee questions now, does it?'

'If you start your investigation with "what happened on the night of the robbery" and then turn it into "tell us about your ancestors raping and pillaging their way across Edinburgh," I think we're going to have a problem,' Bullman spoke for the first time.

'Aye, I know,' Monroe grumbled, as he nodded over at Billy. 'Play the bloody slideshow.'

Billy tapped on the laptop and on the screen behind Monroe an image of a man, early sixties with thick jet-black hair, appeared. It was a professional-looking headshot of Carmody, in a dark-blue suit with a pale-blue shirt and tie and had been taken from his parliamentary page.

'Lord Adrian Carmody,' Monroe pointed at the picture mockingly, as if bowing to a Lord in front of him.

'He's cute,' Doctor Marcos smiled. 'Maybe I married the wrong side.'

Monroe glared at her.

'If you married Lord Carmody, you'd have had a far quieter existence,' he replied. 'Apparently, he's been married in name only for the last fifteen years.'

'Is his wife aware of this?' Declan asked.

'Actually, I'm not sure she is,' Monroe replied. 'Anyway, he was brought into the cabinet three years ago when Stephen Holland was Prime Minister, asked to become the Financial Secretary to the Treasury in his cabinet. In fact, he was in the state dinner that Helen Gane almost poisoned –'

'So, we saved his life,' Anjli looked up.

'Aye, that was a dark day for the Monroes ... but we move ahead. When Michelle Rose took over, for her very short period of time as Prime Minister, he was removed from his role, and I suppose sent back out to pasture – if pasture means standing on his immense estate and shooting things. But after that, Charles Baker brought him back in, same role, probably because of his experience hobnobbing with the relevant people. Last night he was at a charitable event at the Dorchester Hotel and apparently was returning to his accommodation in Theydon Bois in Essex, or somewhere around there.'

'I thought he had estates in the north of England?'

'He does, but they're more of a holiday home. Think of it like Balmoral, but for a slightly lesser gentry,' Monroe shrugged. 'Anyway, he was driving back about one o'clock in the morning with his police detail, and they were accosted by a man on a motorcycle.'

Standing behind the desk and facing the room, he placed his hands on the top of it, leaning forward.

'This is where it gets interesting,' he said. 'You see, the motorcycle? It was a Highwayman.'

'Which is a term you don't hear much,' Billy said, looking around.

'According to the officers who were there, the man in question wore motorcycle leathers that had been shaped to look like the clothing of Dick Turpin,' Monroe explained. 'He'd parked up in the middle of London New Road, headlights shining at the Range Rover as it approached, standing in front, and silhouetted like Batman. Also, during this point he had replaced his bicycle helmet with a tricorn hat.'

'Well, of course,' De'Geer stated. 'I would have expected nothing less.'

'So speaks our resident Viking who likes to dress as a Merry Man from Robin Hood in his spare time,' Monroe smiled. 'Anyway, in his hand was a duelling pistol which, according to Detective Sergeant Harris, Special Escort Group, was definitely modified to fit a more modern round.'

There was a moment as people took this in.

'So basically it was Dick Turpin with a semi-automatic?'

'Effectively yes. Wouldn't *that* have made a different story back then? Anyway, he divested Lord Carmody and his men of all items and then left.'

'And his protection just accepted this?' De'Geer asked from the back. 'I thought they were supposed to be a little bit more, well, gung-ho.'

'They would've done what they could've,' Declan said, turning around. 'But, according to Baker, they stopped when the sniper lasers appeared on their chests.'

'So it wasn't just a lone man on a road,' De'Geer nodded, noting it down in his own notebook. 'Gotcha. I'll give them a pass on that, then.'

'According to the Special Escort Group, there were at least two vans driven that blocked off both ends of the road while the heist was occurring and most likely two people in the woods on either side.' Billy had brought up a Google map of the location. On it, the London New Road could be seen, with the woodlands of Epping Forest on either side. 'There's nothing around here, apart from a few country houses and a car park for runners and dog walkers.'

'It makes sense that they somehow blocked him at a quiet choke point,' Declan commented. 'Two people in the woods, hidden under darkness with sniper rifles –'

'Or maybe even laser pointers,' Billy suggested. 'We don't actually have proof they had rifles.'

'They shot out a tyre,' Monroe offered.

'Someone shot out a tyre,' Doctor Marcos added. 'It could

have been "Turpin" himself, as he fired his pistol while they approached.'

'Even so, the wee laddie might've had a point with that,' Monroe remarked. 'No bullets were fired from the woods. The only weapon discharged was the strange duelling pistol.'

He glanced over at Doctor Marcos.

'And, as you have something to say...' he offered her the floor.

Doctor Marcos rose, nodding at Billy.

'My folder, first file.'

With a nod in response and a quick swipe of the trackpad, Billy uploaded and then changed the image on the plasma screen. Now it was a photo, taken through a car window, of the Highwayman, barely more than a silhouette, the bike's headlight behind him.

'This was taken by Matthews before everything kicked off,' she explained. 'It's not a great one of our Turpin, but it does show the pistol, which, as we can see is pretty authentic on the outside. However, the inside's definitely been played around with, as it fires a nine-millimetre round. We checked the casing found on the road, and with only one shot fired, it had to be from that.'

Billy examined the image, zooming in on the gun.

'I've got an automation running, seeing if I can gain anything better from this,' he said. 'Luckily for us, the copper who snapped this saves his photos as RAW files, which means we can play with the levels.'

'See if you can get something,' Monroe nodded as Billy returned to his laptop. 'So, anything else?'

'From preliminary interviews, it seems the Highwayman picked them because he knew who Lord Carmody was. However, the briefcase seemed to be a surprise,' Cooper read from her own notes now. 'The sergeant I spoke to, who'd been first on scene, said that Carmody and the men seemed a little, twitchy, shall we say, and one of the witnesses blocked by the vans said they'd seen someone leave the car, running off.'

'Maybe one of the officers, checking the area? Look into that. Maybe check into the witness, too.'

'It took ten minutes for the police to arrive on scene, so anything could've happened at that point,' Declan mused, tapping his tactical pen against his lip as he considered this. 'The fact of the matter though is this – a treasury minister was hijacked on a country lane, and time sensitive financial data was taken. Whether he was targeted because of this or because of himself, we don't know. Also, looking at this, there were possibly five people.'

'How did you see five?' Bullman looked at him.

'Two in the vans, one on the bike, two either aiming rifles or laser pointers,' Declan replied. 'However, that could be what we've been made to think. Maybe there were more, or maybe it was smoke and mirrors. We've seen more done with less before.'

'That matches,' Bullman nodded. 'Anything else?'

'Aye. According to the driver, Harris, the masked man spoke in the same tone and style of an eighteenth-century Highwayman.'

'What, *thees* and *thous* and all that kind of thing?'

'I assume so,' Monroe replied as he turned to Bullman. 'Do we have anything from your wee fella about what could be going on?'

'And who the bloody hell is my wee fella?' Bullman asked.

'You know, Bradbury, your boss,' Monroe gave a wink. It was an open secret that Bradbury and Bullman had been having a secret relationship for at least six months, if not longer. The rumours had come out when she'd been promoted, with talk doing the rounds that it was purely because she was his secret girlfriend she'd got the role, but Declan knew well that her experience and skill-set warranted the promotion.

At the comment, however, Bullman reddened and almost seemed to shrink back a little into herself.

'We're, um, not exactly talking at the moment,' she mumbled. 'We might've, well, we might've broken up.'

'Oh aye?' Monroe asked, and Declan could see the twinkling of a smile beginning, and hoped that he understood tact enough not to rub it in.

Bullman nodded.

'It's quite painful, and I'd rather not talk about it,' she muttered. 'My choice, not his ... and I'd prefer to leave it at that.'

'Don't you worry, lassie, we'll absolutely be the archetypes of discretion. We wouldn't, after all, want you to feel bad ... especially when you've been so patient with us over the times we've had our own issues.'

Declan winced. Bullman was known to prod at emotionally open wounds for fun; Monroe was stating that turnaround was fair play. He wondered whether he could claim illness and get out of this case until the smoke settled.

Billy was staring at the picture of the Highwayman, complete with a pistol, on his laptop screen.

'Guv, I might have something,' he said. 'About the gun.'

'Go on, laddie?'

' You mentioned it was a modified duelling pistol.'

'What about it?'

Billy looked around the briefing room.

'Well, we have an expert on hand for things like duelling pistols, don't we?'

'Oh, God,' Monroe shook his head. 'Are you talking about who I think you're talking about?'

'I'm afraid so, Guv,' Billy gave an embarrassed smile. 'I think I need to contact my uncle.'

'Fine, whatever we need to solve this,' Monroe said, at a shocked gaze from Bullman. 'I, meanwhile, will go visit the crime scene.'

'Actually, I've been asked to pop up there, too,' Doctor Marcos replied quickly. 'I'll take Cooper with me as she can sort out the uniforms who are still there, so I don't get disturbed.'

'Wait, I'm not being left here to see the Chivalry Fitzwarren show!' Declan exclaimed. 'I'll go with Anjli. I know the area.'

'We all know the area, laddie.' Monroe sighed. 'Fine. Let's all go look at the crime scene. From what I can work out, Essex police were told not to touch anything until we got there, anyway.'

Declan checked his watch.

'That's twelve hours of waiting.' he muttered.

'Aye, and that's fast for Government,' Monroe said as he straightened from the desk. 'Shall we all go on a day trip, then?'

3

HIGHWAY-MAN

THE LAST TIME DECLAN HAD BEEN DOWN THIS ROAD, HEADING deep into Epping Forest, had been a couple of years earlier, when the body of Angela Martin had been found. Derek Salmon had been his passenger back then, leading them near Ambresbury Banks. This, however, was slightly closer to London, before the Robin Hood pub, but the forest was still as old here as it had been when he last visited back then.

The road had been reopened for several hours now, so Declan had parked in the Lincoln's Lane car park to the side, mainly used by dog walkers, trail runners, hikers, and ... well ... Declan hoped that was all it was used for. He didn't really want to consider what this would be like late at night.

He was in his still-battered Audi A4; Anjli had suggested taking her far newer Hyundai IX 35, but she had issues with the sat-nav, so currently in his car with him were Monroe in the passenger seat and Anjli in the back, although Declan had felt this was a weak excuse. He'd even mentioned she had sat-nav on her phone, but she'd come back with the fact she'd have been staring at a phone and not the road, so eventually

Declan acquiesced. In the end De'Geer had pulled rank and had gone ahead with Cooper and Doctor Marcos, who'd already been complaining about Essex Forensics before she'd even arrived. Jess had been told to stay behind with Billy, while Billy had been happy to stay with the computers. He was never the biggest fan of going out into the field, especially as, several times in the past he'd almost died in the process.

Declan smiled, not at the thought of Billy almost dying, but at the fact that the last time they'd been here, it had been Billy, wearing his expensive Wellington boots, who'd suggested Declan invest in a pair – or else watch his usual shoes get destroyed in the mud.

This time, however, they weren't in the mud. The ground was dry, and the leaves had fallen, as Declan and the others pulled into the car park.

'So, the Highwayman was about fifty yards north of here.' Monroe was already checking his messages. 'And apparently, Rosanna arrived five minutes ago, and she's already managed to piss off anyone still around.'

They walked along the edge of the road; the cars creeping slowly past, their progress halted by one of the Essex Police squad cars which had effectively turned the road into a one-lane stretch.

Anjli pointed off to the right-hand side.

'Somewhere in there, and a mile north or so,' she said, 'is Turpin's Cave.'

Declan paused, looking at her, confused.

'What do you mean, cave?'

'It's where they believe he'd hide out after his highway robberies,' she replied, a slight smile on her face. 'This was one road he'd often attack. He'd then ride off towards

Loughton, which is off to the east, and in there's an old iron fort named Loughton Camp, which people claimed was also Dick Turpin's cave. Probably nothing more than a barrow he'd hide in when the authorities were looking for him.'

'And how would you know this?' Declan asked.

'When we were in Wanstead, visiting Nightingale Lane,' Anjli replied, 'I learned a lot about Dick Turpin back then. The pub had a bloody great big painting of him.'

She grinned widely.

'And if you carry on a few more yards, you'll find the bridge where the Black Knight fought King Arthur in *Monty Python and the Holy Grail*.'

'You could've started with that one,' Declan replied.

As they arrived, Doctor Marcos stood at the side of the road, looking frustrated.

'They've been allowing this bloody road to … well, just be a road,' she complained. 'They should've had this cordoned off.'

'It is one of the main routes out of London,' Monroe replied calmly, knowing this was a conversation he didn't want to get too mired in. 'They couldn't leave the road closed. All they could do was keep a lane closed, which is what they did with squad cars behind us and up there.'

He nodded over to a blue tent off to the left-hand side.

'If it helps, I believe Essex forensics took what they could and left it there.'

'What, the great big bloody blue forensics tent?' Doctor Marcos snapped irritably. 'Well damn, darling. I never considered that. This must be why people call you the Guv.'

'Do we at least know where the car stopped?' Declan asked, deciding he didn't want to watch a domestic at the side of the road right now. Doctor Marcos irritably pointed diagonally across the road towards an overturned tree that had fallen into the forest.

'Parallel with that,' she said. 'And they were coming out of London –'

'So, they'd have been on the left-hand side,' Declan said as he continued up, noting that ten yards further on from it, an Essex police car had stopped. With De'Geer and Cooper helping wave traffic through – such as it was, the morning rush long gone, and only the odd car appearing here and there – Declan could walk over to where the robbery occurred.

He stood for a moment, painfully aware that every minute he stayed here was causing problems for drivers. He fought the urge to examine the ground or surrounding area; he knew Doctor Marcos would already have done this, as would Essex Forensics, and he didn't want to make them think he was stepping on their toes.

But he couldn't help himself.

He looked across to the left and to the right.

'Anjli,' he called out. 'Do you have the witness statements?'

'What exactly do you need?' Anjli replied, walking over to him.

'The two officers said they paused when laser pointers appeared on their chests,' Declan said. 'Did they say where on the chests?'

'The impression I got was it was front and centre,' Anjli replied. 'Why?'

'Laser pointers hitting them centre would've come through the windscreen,' Declan said, 'rather than the side windows. Which means ...'

He held his hands out in a slightly wide arc, both arms pointing at different sides of the road.

'Somewhere around there, our Highwayman had his two snipers.'

He looked back at Doctor Marcos.

'Have we checked this area yet?'

'From what I can work out, no,' Doctor Marcos replied. 'They wanted to lock down the site for us – when Baker told them only we could look into this, they took it literally, bloody fools. Still, a sniper rifle can be a long-range weapon as much as a short one. With no exact area to go from ...'

She shrugged with a slight smile.

'Feel free to trample through the forest and have a look. If you find something, I'll happily take credit.'

Declan glanced to the left; there was a clear path into the woods. Smiling at Anjli, he started across.

'You *are* kidding me,' she said. 'We're going walking in the woods looking for magical snipers?'

'Humour me,' Declan said. 'I've got a hunch.'

'And your shoes?'

'It's not rained for a while, we'll be fine.'

As they walked into the forest, Anjli caught up with him, pulling at his arm.

'Well, come on then,' she said. 'Tell me your hunch before we start this bloody wild goose chase. Wait ... you're not trying to drag us in here for a quickie, are you? Because I'm too tired, and you're too old.'

'Thanks,' Declan scoffed good-naturedly. 'There's some-thing in what Baker told me that didn't feel right. The High-wayman would've known this was a Minister's car, and he already knew it was Lord Carmody. And, if he knew it was a

Minister's car, he would've also known the glass would be bullet resistant.'

'So?'

'So the sniper rifle lasers were likely for show, because to use them would leave a body count and a larger force than just us chasing them,' Declan said. 'Sure, he mentioned armour-piercing bullets and all that ...'

'But all he really needed was a red dot, to sell the story.'

'Exactly,' Declan smiled. 'Now, a sniper rifle *could* fire from a fair distance away, and a red laser pointer attached to a rifle can pretty much do the same, as long as there's nothing in its way. But, what if our Highwayman was playing a game of smoke and mirrors, and just messing about with laser pointers, like Billy suggested? They don't have as much of a range –'

'Which means they'd have been a lot closer,' Anjli nodded as Declan turned, facing back to where he'd stood a moment earlier. Monroe was standing there, watching him with a confused expression on his face. Walking backwards and checking regularly to make sure he wasn't about to trip over a tree branch, Declan carried on until he could go no further, a thin tree blocking his way.

'This is roughly as far back as we get with a clear sight,' Declan said as he turned and started examining the trunk. He didn't have to spend long searching as attached to the branch, on a gimbal of some kind, were three thin black tubes which, when he pulled on a blue latex glove and pressed a button on one of them, shone a very bright red light, likely a laser pointer of some kind. Something confirmed a second later--

'Christ, laddie!' Monroe shouted from the line of sight,

holding his hand up in front of his eyes. 'I wish you'd bloody warn us!'

'Sorry,' Declan said quickly, turning it off. 'Didn't mean to blind you.'

Anjli had walked over and was examining the contraption.

'It's remote-controlled,' she said. 'Look.'

Above the three laser pointers was what looked like a small camera, some kind of knock-off GoPro.

'Each of the pointers is attached to gyroscopic gimbals,' she continued, 'which have wires leading to a power pack strapped to the trunk. Clever. You could connect to this and probably change where you're aiming, maybe even turn it off and on remotely as well. Also, they could wobble on cue, make it look less automated. Like someone was dancing about on your chest.'

Declan looked back to Monroe, who, hands still shading his eyes just in case, was now walking towards them.

'Guv!' Anjli shouted. 'Get De'Geer to check the other side. Same distance, same angle.'

Declan turned back to the tree.

'There were no snipers,' he said matter-of-factly. 'In fact, the guys blocking the road at either end could've done this themselves. Hell, for all we know, the Highwayman himself could've pressed a button and turned them on. This isn't a five-man job any more. This could've been done with just three people.'

He looked back out at the road.

'It also wasn't opportunistic,' he added. 'These had to have been angled, set up, tested. There was only a short amount of distance that car could stop in before it went out of range. This was very well planned.'

'Inside job?'

'Maybe. Harris was driving, we'll start with him.'

By now, Doctor Marcos had followed Monroe, hurrying in front of him.

'You'd better not have bloody touched that,' she said.

Declan waggled his blue-gloved hand.

'I only touched the on-off button,' he said.

'Which means you've probably smudged a bloody fingerprint.'

'I'm sure there are others,' Declan sighed. 'And at least I found the bloody thing, unlike your forensics.'

He saw Anjli wince aside, but he couldn't resist –

Doctor Marcos stopped as if hitting a wall. Her eyes narrowed.

'Oh, so we think we're forensics now, do we?' she asked coolly.

Declan internally groaned.

'I'm just saying –'

'No, no, DCI Walsh,' Doctor Marcos smiled coldly. 'I'm glad you found this. It makes our job easier. Thank you for taking the time to assist us poor forensic officers.'

With that, she stormed past Declan, already examining the contraption on the tree. Declan heard the faint shout of Sergeant De'Geer, having found the equivalent setup on the other side. Monroe gently took him by the arm, leading him away from Doctor Marcos.

'You've just dug your grave, laddie,' Monroe smiled. 'How does it feel to be a dead man walking, especially when the woman you've pissed off is superb at hiding bodies?'

'It felt like a good idea at the time,' Declan muttered.

'Well, how about we go look at other things?' Monroe

smiled. 'Perhaps keeping you away from Doctor Marcos until she calms down?'

THE BLUE TENT WAS INCREDIBLY BASIC, WITH NOTHING MORE than a couple of Essex forensics officers standing around looking bored, and a folding table with some bagged evidence in the middle. A 9mm magazine cartridge from the weapon that had been fired sat in one bag, but that seemed to be the bulk of the evidence found – apart from a second baggie set to the side. Declan held it up into the light, frowning as he examined what looked to be a gold earring.

'I didn't know Lord Carmody wore jewellery,' he said.

'Exactly,' the forensic officer said, looking up as if surprised anyone was even in the tent.

'Do we know anything about it?' Declan asked.

'No, sorry, Guv,' the officer replied. 'It was found right beside where the car was, but ...'

'But we've got a car with three male passengers, and you've found a female's earring.'

The forensics officer nodded.

'Therefore, it's not logged yet, as we don't know if it's related or not,' he said. 'All I know is that if I was held up by a Highwayman who looked like Dick Turpin, I wouldn't be telling people ... so maybe *everything* that happened wasn't reported?'

'Aye, it'd be like Carmody to keep quiet about a young strumpet in his car, the night the wife's in town,' Monroe muttered as Declan looked back at the jewelled earring.

'It looks expensive.'

'It's paste,' Doctor Marcos said, appearing behind him. 'You can tell just by looking.'

The forensic officer paled and scuttled out of the tent, into the woods.

Declan looked back out at the road, frowning.

'This was picked up where the car stopped?'

'Apparently so,' Monroe replied, checking the clipboard notes. 'We could ask the wee lad, but Rosanna scared him off.'

'Chances of this being there totally by chance?' Declan asked.

'Minimal,' Doctor Marcos admitted. 'Which means our little Lord Carmody is lying.'

'As are his protection officers,' Monroe growled, taking the bag with the earring in it and staring at it again. 'In more ways than one, as there's no way they could have stopped in that exact spot without someone planning it.'

'They shot a tyre out, so maybe that was done to make sure they were in the kill zone?'

'It's not really a "kill" zone if they're laser pointers,' Doctor Marcos smiled sweetly at Declan. 'More a "take that bloody thing out of my eyes" zone.'

'Either way, we need the Range Rover examined, Carmody investigated and the SEG officers spoken to again,' Monroe stroked his white beard, still staring at the earring. 'I'll go see Carmody. Declan, take Anjli back to Temple Inn and call in the SEG coppers. Rosanna, check that bloody car out. I want to know exactly what took out the tyre, if it wasn't laser pointed sniper rifles, it has to be this wee duelling pistol, and I don't believe the shot could be that precise.'

'All good plans, but how will you get to Carmody?' Declan asked. 'I drove you here.'

'I could take your car?' Monroe suggested.

'But then we wouldn't be able to get back to Temple Inn.'

'Aye, that sounds more like a "you" problem than a "me" problem, though.'

'Or you could wait for Bullman,' Doctor Marcos interjected, checking her watch. 'She's on her way now, and let's be honest, Carmody wouldn't speak to a lowly Detective Superintendent when there's a Detective Chief Superintendent around.'

She winked at Declan, and for a moment he hoped she'd decided not to kill him and hide the body.

'And I need clearer heads beside my darling husband, before he whacks on the blue face paint and starts yelling "freedom" at everyone.'

The smile dropped.

'Why are you still here?' she asked politely. 'Go be a copper, solve this case, show us poor mortals how it's done.'

'If I apologised, would it make any difference?' Declan winced.

Doctor Marcos considered this.

'I'd feel worse when I place your body in a shallow grave,' she said matter-of-factly. 'If that helps?'

Declan was already out of the tent and moving briskly towards his car, waving for Anjli to follow. He knew she was likely joking … that was; he *hoped* she was likely joking …

But he didn't want to check *too* closely.

4

THE DRIVER

DETECTIVE SERGEANT HARRIS LOOKED UNHAPPY AS HE SAT IN
the interview room when Declan and Anjli entered.

'I gave a statement already,' he said. 'I don't understand
why I'm here. And if I'm here, then Matthews should be as
well.'

'You gave your statements to a police officer on the scene,'
Declan explained, sitting down calmly. 'We weren't there. I'm
Detective Chief Inspector Walsh. This is Detective Inspector
Kapoor. You're also here because the Prime Minister himself
has taken an interest in your statement, and your boss ... well,
he works for Charles Baker, too. And don't worry, we want to
speak to both of you, so you're not being singled out.'

He looked at his notebook, as if checking facts before
speaking again.

'I understand you were the driver when the car was
hijacked –'

'There was no hijack,' Harris interrupted confrontation-
ally. 'There was a Highwayman.'

'Okay, sure, there was a Highwayman,' Declan said, closing the notebook and placing his hands on the table, the now closed notebook beside them. 'Look, Harris, I'm not taking notes. We're not recording. We're not the enemy here, I just want your opinion of what happened.'

Harris sighed, leaning back on the chair.

'We were doing the same as we always did; driving the Lord back to his house. We do it five, six times a bloody week. Sometimes it's a different driver. Often the protection team's the same. We've been working with him since he joined the Cabinet.'

'Did you know of him beforehand?' Anjli asked.

Harris shook his head.

'We only deal with Westminster,' he explained. 'And up to now, we've never had a problem. Well, apart from a fight between him and his wife about eight months ago.'

'About what?'

'About him being a massive bellend?' Harris shrugged. 'Look, he's an old-school Lord, yeah? Which means he's got a fancy title, some manor up north he goes to now and then, and a house in Theydon Bois that he usually commutes into Parliament from. If it wasn't for the job, he'd probably be broke. He doesn't make a great amount, you see, and he's not one of these cool new Lords who have billions and get their Lordships because they've donated stupid amounts to the party. His place up north is a money pit; I know that because he's used the term countless times while yelling at his accountant down the phone.'

He paused, realising he'd probably overshared, but seeing Declan and Anjli smile at this seemed to calm him a little, bolster him, even, and Declan felt that by airing Carmody's dirty laundry, Harris had relaxed now he'd believed he wasn't actually one of the people under investigation.

'Look, he's a nice guy,' Harris explained. 'I get on with him. He's a bit "boomer", but then he's Conservative, you know? I think if he'd had the option, he probably would've gone Reform, but they're not in power, and they're not giving him a paid job. Either way, he's a bit misogynistic, a bit racist, and genuinely everything you'd expect for someone of his type. Matthews and me, we're usually put together, and we find it best to ignore him.'

He looked up at Declan, making sure their eyes connected.

'And it's always been a case of what happens in the car stays in the car. Arguments, secrets, whatever.'

Declan nodded. He understood what Harris was saying. There were probably times when Carmody would've been taking a call or having a meeting with somebody in the back seat, where things that probably *shouldn't* have been spoken were.

'And how about last night?' he asked. 'Did Carmody talk to you about the briefcase he'd been given?'

'Only that it was a pain in the arse to have,' Harris replied.

He paused, as if rephrasing his statement.

'He had other plans for the night,' he continued, cautiously.

Declan caught a glimpse of something here, leaning forward.

'What exactly did he have planned, Detective Sergeant Harris?'

'It's not my place to say, sir.'

'I think it's very much your place to say,' Anjli added. 'If you've got something that Lord Carmody was up to, that could explain anything that happened –'

'This wasn't anything to do with that,' Harris said. 'It was more ... recreational.'

'Drugs?'

'Carmody didn't partake.'

'So, we wouldn't find traces if we checked?'

Harris said nothing, and Declan wondered if Carmody wasn't the one taking, whether either Harris or Matthews did.

Or could it be contestant number four?

He waited a moment, reached into his pocket, and pulled out the earring in the clear baggie.

'Could it be connected to the woman who wore this?' he asked. 'We've checked the records, and I don't believe it's owned by Lady Carmody.'

At the sight of the earring, Harris' lips thinned.

'Look,' he said, 'I don't talk about this, yeah? If it's found out that I'm telling people anything about what happens in that car –'

'I know,' Declan replied. 'But this is of national importance. Secrets that could bring down the country. You've signed the Official Secrets Act, right?'

He watched as Harris paled at the statement, unaware that even Declan wasn't sure exactly what was in the briefcase, or whether it related to the Official Secrets Act.

'Who was the woman?' he asked again.

After a moment, Harris gave a massive sigh of resignation and leant closer.

'Carmody picked her up at the event,' he stated reluctantly. 'I believe her name was Sophia, but I got nothing else. We weren't on a first-name basis, you know? I'm just a driver.

Matthews wasn't happy about it. He's a stickler for shit like that. Believes in the sanctity of marriage, and Carmody was intending to do a lot of things that breached that, if you get what I'm saying.'

'Lady Carmody wasn't back at the house last night, correct?'

'Yeah, she wasn't around that night. She was staying in London, had her own event. For all I know, she even had her own "Sophia" or whatever he was called. As far as Carmody was concerned, though, he had a night to go play. These charity events arrange for certain ... distractions, shall we say?'

'Carmody paid for it?'

'Oh, Christ, no.' Harris laughed. 'Carmody doesn't pay for anything. This would've been a gift from a friendly donor.'

Declan nodded, understanding. Somebody, somewhere, had wanted Carmody's ear and had made sure there was something of interest for the man.

'Do you know which donor?'

'You'd have to ask Carmody for that,' Harris shrugged. 'Look, I can't get involved in this. But what I can say is that she was organised at the event. There's a guy called Stefon.'

'Surname?'

'No, that *is* his surname. Mikhail Stefon. He's a big-time aide for some of the lobbyists, been around longer than I have. I saw him talking to Carmody last night, and I understand he's got form for this kind of thing. Perhaps if you find it through *him*, I don't ...'

He trailed off. He didn't need to continue. Declan understood very well what he was saying.

'We'll keep you out of the story,' he said.

Harris shifted in his seat, his earlier defensiveness fading into something closer to concern.

'Look, you seem decent enough,' he said. 'But there's something else, something that's been bothering me since last night.'

'Go on,' Declan encouraged.

'Lord Carmody ... he was weirdly calm about the whole thing. I mean, we've had incidents before – protesters, journalists trying to get photos, that kind of thing. He usually loses it. But last night ...'

Harris shook his head.

'Even with the gun pointed at us, even with the laser sights on our chests, he was just ... I don't know. Almost like he was acting.'

Anjli leant forward.

'Acting?'

'Yeah. Like when he was arguing about the briefcase, it felt rehearsed. And the route –' Harris stopped himself.

'What about the route?' Declan asked.

'He insisted we take that way home. Said something about avoiding traffic, but at that time of night? We would have gone up the North Circular, as the M11 would've been empty.'

Harris pursed his lips.

'Listen, we've driven him home dozens of times. He's never once asked to go that way before.'

Declan and Anjli exchanged glances.

'Did he give a reason?'

'No, and we assumed he wanted a more ... well, *secluded* trip, you see what I mean? And Matthews would usually have argued, but ...'

'But?'

Harris said nothing for a moment, then puffed out his cheeks.

'He wasn't … he wasn't himself.'

Declan went to concentrate on this, but Anjli, who'd been typing on her phone now tapped him on the foot with hers, and as he looked at her, she subtly showed her phone.

> Whatever this is – Harris doesn't want to grass. Drugs, perhaps?

Declan scanned his eyes across it, bringing them back to Harris who, staring at the desk, hadn't noticed the exchange.

'One last thing,' Declan said. 'This woman who ran – Sophia. Did she seem frightened by the Highwayman, or was she running from something else?'

Harris considered this.

'You know what's weird? When the shooting started, she didn't scream. Didn't panic. Just sat there, terrified, but quiet. It wasn't until after everything was over that she suddenly bolted. Ran off into the bloody forest. Matthews went to give chase, but Carmody stopped him. Didn't want the press finding out, and as far as he was concerned this made things easier.'

'You think she was waiting for her cue?' Anjli suggested.

'Maybe.' Harris leant back in his chair. 'Look, I've probably said too much already. Matthews would kill me if he knew I'd broken the bloody "code" and all that. But something about last night … it just doesn't sit right.'

Declan nodded.

'We'll need you to stay available. And Harris? Don't discuss this with anyone. Especially not Lord Carmody.'

'Don't worry,' Harris gave a sheepish smile. 'I was robbed

by Dick Turpin. I don't think my career prospects are that high right now if I go around talking about it.'

———

WALKING OUT OF THE INTERVIEW ROOM, DECLAN WAS ABOUT to speak to Anjli, ask her opinion, but paused as his phone rang. He scanned the caller ID, seeing what he'd named the contact when saving it.

Gutter Press

Declan frowned as he glanced back at Anjli.

'Think I should take the call?' he asked.

'What's the worst that can happen?' Anjli shrugged. 'Maybe he's got more bad news for us.'

Declan nodded, taking the call, placing it on speaker so Anjli could listen in.

'Declan,' said Sean Ashby, editor of *The Individual* newspaper sounding jovial, almost friendly. 'How are you today?'

'Confused,' Declan replied honestly, 'considering the fact that the last time I contacted you or your paper, you didn't want to be involved with me because of Malcolm Gladwell's tell-all novel.'

'Yes, sorry about that,' Sean replied, and Declan could tell from the tone that Sean Ashby really wasn't that sorry. He got it, though, he understood Ashby was a connection of Declan's from years earlier, and Malcolm Gladwell's tell-all book, whether or not it was lies, had been pretty damning for the people at The Last Chance Saloon, let alone people who knew them. The book, however, hadn't been released, Gladwell trying to use it as a bargaining chip for freedom, and folding at the last moment when he realised he'd likely come off worse than Declan did.

'And then, of course, there's the fact you tried to keep away from me when you thought I was benefiting from a serial killer's will.'

'No offence, Declan, but you *did* kind of benefit from a serial killer's will,' Sean replied. 'You can't say you didn't. What you *can* say is you turned it into a good cause, waiving the money, and I applaud you for that.'

Declan wanted to disconnect the call. Sean had helped him in the past and had been a friend of Kendis Taylor when she was alive. He'd actively assisted Declan on several occasions, and had even offered him a job when it looked like Declan was likely to be let go from the force, but for every moment of help, there seemed to be a moment where Sean had turned his back or washed his hands.

'So, what are you calling for?' Declan asked, all pretence at friendliness now gone. 'I'm in the middle of something.'

'I know,' Sean replied. 'Lord Carmody being held up by Dick Turpin.'

Declan didn't audibly groan, but it came out nevertheless as an expression of disgust. He knew it'd eventually come out, but he'd hoped he'd have a little while longer before the press knew.

'Is this call on the record or off the record?'

'Can it be on the record?'

'Sure. Thanks for calling, Sean. It'd be lovely to see you again sometime. Bye.'

'No, wait,' Sean quickly added. 'Off the record. Look, I know I've not been exactly the best of friends to you. But I'm wondering how much you know about what's going on here?'

'How much *I* know about what's going on?' Declan glanced across at Anjli. 'Go on.'

Sean Ashby cleared his throat.

'Look give me a "Marco Polo" whether I'm close or not, okay? I've been told by a reputable source that last night at the Dorchester, Lord Carmody was provided with a ministerial briefcase, and inside it was information he needed as Treasury Minister.'

'Polo'

'Okay, not the traditional red box ministerial briefcase, perhaps, but he was definitely given a case.'

'Marco.'

'I understand that the documentation was eyes only, and he was told to take it straight home and check it over.'

'Still Marco,' Declan said.

'And then at some point in the night, in the middle of Epping Forest, Dick Turpin appears and steals it.'

'And why would you think Dick Turpin had returned from the dead?' Anjli asked, and Declan gave a small smile. Her response had stopped him from having to "off record" confirm the statement.

'Oh, hi, Anjli, I didn't realise you were there,' Sean replied. 'I could say I used journalistic intelligence, or my expertise from over the years, even that we spoke to a few sources to gain it. But to be honest, we gained a recording of the 999 call. In it, your man Harris actively states that Dick Turpin robbed them.'

Declan grimaced. He'd known the words had been spoken, but he was really hoping the press hadn't gained it so quickly.

'Do you have a suspect yet?' Sean continued.

'Christ, we've only just left the crime scene,' Declan said. 'I know you think I'm good, but I ain't that good.'

'Can I give you one?'

'Do you think you know who did this?'

'No, but I know who's got form,' Sean replied. 'Have you started investigating the Essex Rider?'

Declan glanced with confusion at Anjli.

'What the hell is the Essex Rider?'

'So, you haven't,' Sean's voice took on a little tone, proud perhaps that he had something that Declan didn't have. 'Five years ago, actually probably closer to six now, there were a series of robberies. A bike rider, dressed up like Dick Turpin took out a few rich folks. Same M.O. as the man himself ... except he also outed the people he stole from, and didn't have a horse ... he rode a stunt bike.'

'What do you mean by stunt bike?'

'I mean it wasn't a normal racing bike, and it wasn't a dirt bike. At one point, the police chased him through Epping Forest. They said he went through it like a banshee. Did tricks and jumps that took out half the people following. Did you know they even had a police motorcycle crew patrolling, looking for him? It was kind of like a posse in a western, chasing a bank robber. But on bikes.'

Anjli was already texting Billy. 'I'm guessing we never caught the Essex Rider?'

'No, but you had suspects.'

'Are you going to give me them?' Declan asked, already knowing the answer.

'Oh, where's the fun in that?' Sean replied. 'Your boy Fitzwarren will have it all on his records, I'm sure. But here's the thing, and it's the reason I thought I'd call you. Your man, Carmody? This happened before he started working in the

Treasury, but when it happened he was brought in to assist his childhood friend Stephen Holland, who'd just been made PM. There was an inquiry into the Rider and what was going on, and Carmody was placed on it. As was a junior aide, seconded to him, Emma Thorne.'

'We've not met an Emma Thorne as of yet.'

'You won't have,' Sean replied. 'She's moved up in the rankings since then. Still works at the Treasury, but not directly under Carmody since his return, which, from what I hear, isn't exactly an uncommon experience.'

'I appreciate the heads up,' Declan said.

'Good,' Sean said. ''Cause you owe me now, and I will be calling it in.'

'And what kind of debt would you like me to repay with?'

'It'd be nice to know if the rumours are true.'

'What rumours?'

'I've got a source, and yes, I know that sounds a cliché, but I really do have a source, that claims they saw Carmody leaving the Dorchester event last night with his two close protection officers and a blonde woman in a champagne cocktail dress. I can tell you now, that woman was definitely *not* his wife. Yet the reports I've seen so far of the theft claim Carmody was on his own.'

'Maybe he was giving someone a lift,' Declan asked.

'Sure, that could be the case. Maybe you should have a conversation with the officers, and then come back to me, yeah?'

'If I find out anything new ... you'll be the first person I let know,' Declan said. 'Within the remits of my job, of course.'

'That's appreciated,' Sean said, and the call disconnected.

Anjli looked across at Declan, raising an eyebrow at his comment.

'Nice usage of the within the remits of your job,' she said. 'If I remember correctly, "within the remits of your job" means that you don't talk to the press.'

'I didn't say I would, I said I'd do what I could,' Declan grinned. 'Have you let Billy know?'

'Yes, and by the time we get downstairs, he'll be insuffer-able.' Anjli sighed, looking back at the Interview Room, and the man inside. 'This isn't the first time a Highwayman has crossed our paths? Right now he'll be bloody *cosplaying* him.'

5

LORDS AND LADIES

ONCE SHE'D ARRIVED AT THE CRIME LOCATION, BULLMAN HAD reluctantly agreed to accompany Monroe to Theydon Bois, where the commuting home of Lord Carmody was – and by "accompany", she meant "drive him there". As they approached, however, Monroe's eyes widened.

'Sweet Jesus,' he muttered, as they turned off the road towards the main gate. 'My dreams have come true. They've arrived with the pitchforks.'

'I don't think that's a crowd of pitchforks, Alex,' Bullman replied with the slightest of smiles as they approached the crowd of well-lit men. 'That's paparazzi and camera crews.'

'Really?' Monroe frowned, then growled. 'Oh, no. Who leaked it to the press?'

'Come on. It's been, what, twelve hours since it happened? Of course it was going to get out.' Bullman showed her warrant card to the police on guard, who waved her through. 'The question is, what exactly do the paparazzi think they're waiting for? Is it a Minister who lost secrets? Or is it a Minister who was attacked by a Highwayman wearing eighteenth-century clothing? I mean, either story's pretty good.'

'But one is career-ending,' Monroe finished.

Once they pulled up outside the house, exiting the car and making their way to the main entrance, a uniformed sergeant came out to meet them.

'Lord Carmody is in his study, sir,' he informed them. 'He's asked if we can keep it brief as he has some meetings.'

'Aye,' Monroe nodded. 'We'll do our best. Please tell the Lord that we'll be as quick as we can, as long as he answers the questions quickly.'

The sergeant smiled.

'I don't think you'll have a problem with that, sir,' he said. 'I think Carmody wants all this gone as fast as possible.'

They started walking through the large house.

'You know the Lord?' Monroe asked.

The sergeant shrugged.

'I'm local, based in Loughton. He's local, so to speak. We've had our run-ins since he's been here,' he explained. 'The problem is, when you're part of the aristocracy, you don't seem to understand that the little folk do still have a voice as well. There was a whole hoo-haa about it. I think it was called the Magna Carta.'

'Oh, I like this one,' Monroe grinned, looking at Bullman. 'Can we take him back with us?'

'No, Alex. You've collected your fill of misfit uniformed officers over the last couple of years,' Bullman replied. 'I've no more budget to give you any more new toys to play with.'

'You're just grumpy because –' Monroe went to continue but then stopped.

'Actually, could you give us a moment?' he asked the

sergeant, who, nodding, wandered off to check on another officer. As he did so, Monroe looked back at Bullman.

'Are you okay?' he asked.

'I don't know why people keep asking me that,' Bullman muttered. 'I'm a grown bloody woman. David and I decided it wasn't working. Too much stress. You know what it's like, working with somebody day in and day out. You either marry them or you walk away as quickly as possible.'

She shrugged.

'I got confused, maybe made the wrong call, who knows. Maybe I followed the rules of the Last Chance Saloon, which seemed to say that every relationship works.'

'Aye, well, you made a big mistake there, didn't you?' Monroe smiled. 'Bradbury isn't part of the Last Chance Saloon.'

'That doesn't give me much hope, though, does it?' Bullman grimaced. 'Who else is left? Sergeant Mastakin? If he's got five years left in him, I'll be stunned. The guy's one step away from angina and a heart attack. Billy plays for the other team. You're married; thank God it takes you off the page.'

She shook her head.

'Honestly, I appreciate the checking in, but you've got nothing to worry about.'

'Well, if anything does happen, please let me know,' Monroe replied.

'You're monitoring my dating life now?' Bullman raised an eyebrow.

'Of course I am!' Monroe shook his head. 'Look what happened with wee Billy! I turned my head for a moment, and suddenly he's dating a diplomat who turns out to be a

Colombian Cartel member, and now he's dating a bloody art forger!'

'Art restorer,' Bullman corrected.

'Only because we couldn't make the bloody charges stick,' Monroe grumbled. 'Anyway, even if you spend most of your time in Guildhall, you're still one of us. Which means, unfortunately, yes, I will be looking out for you.'

Bullman stared at Monroe for a long moment and then smiled.

'You remember when we first met?' she asked.

'Aye, it was in Birmingham. You wouldn't let me see what I'd come to see, until you'd confirmed my credentials,' Monroe chuckled. 'But I could tell you were just doing it to wind me up.'

'Actually, I believe I was doing it because you'd stormed into my police station demanding to see "the idiot that screwed up your case",' Bullman replied. 'And my desk sergeant later told me you'd loudly stated "I hate that bloody woman".'

Monroe winced at this, but Bullman rapped him on the arm.

'Look how far we've come since,' she said with a grin. 'We're almost family now.'

She gave it a moment's pause before adding.

'And I'm now your boss.'

She carried on through the hall, whistling, as Monroe rubbed at his arm.

'Aye?' he muttered. 'Well, maybe I'll date David Bradbury and become *your* boss.'

He paused, realising that although Bullman hadn't heard the muttered words, the sergeant to the side had, and was staring at him in confusion.

'At ease, laddie,' he mumbled, hurrying to follow her. 'We do things differently in the City.'

He paused, however, as a new arrival blocked their way.

'I'm afraid the Lord is incredibly tired,' the man who'd appeared said. He was in his mid-twenties, with a floppy hair-cut, akin to the "curtains" style from the nineties, and now back in fashion, over a Ralph Lauren Polo zip-neck jumper and jeans. His black hair and eyebrows however marked him as definitely a Carmody, maybe even Lord Carmody's son.

'And you are ...?'

'Lewis Carmody,' the man replied, 'and my father is incredibly busy, as well as traumatised, so I'd appreciate it if you came back at another point.'

'Aye, as much as we'd love to leave Lord Carmody to his own devices,' Monroe said, and Bullman wondered whether he was actually trying to be polite here, 'unfortunately, crime waits for no man, and justice doesn't care about feelings.'

He patted Lewis on the arm.

'You're a good son, though, laddie,' he added. 'Standing up in front of your father. I'm sure when the pitchforks come, you'll also stand in front of those.'

'What bloody pitchforks?' Lewis Carmody looked in confusion at Bullman. 'What's he going on about?'

'Scotland,' Bullman replied with a smile. 'Anyway, as much as it's lovely to meet you, Lewis, we're not here to speak to you, so could you please do me a favour and piss off so we can have a chat with your daddy?'

Lewis's eyes narrowed, and even Monroe was surprised at the intensity of Bullman's response, chalking it down to her own traumatic time over the last few days.

But Lewis simply gave a chuckle.

'About time you found some officers with some balls,' he said. 'Metaphorically speaking anyway.'

He stepped aside, allowing the two officers to walk through and, as they passed, Monroe noted Lewis Carmody had already wandered off, his entertainment now over.

Monroe glanced at Bullman.

'Not a fan?' he asked.

'Something about the boy I didn't like. Why?'

Monroe grinned.

'It's because he's a Carmody,' he explained as he patted her on the arm. 'And don't worry, I've got enough blue woad for both of our faces.'

Lord Adrian Carmody looked more unimpressed to see the police than the police were to see him. There was the most cursory of nods as he sat behind his study's mahogany and green leather writing desk as Monroe and Bullman walked into the room.

'Look, detectives,' he grumbled. 'I really don't have the time for this. I need you to get on this and get on this fast.'

'National security was stolen by a man dressed like Dick Turpin, I understand,' Monroe said, visibly enjoying the moment. 'Unfortunately, they don't seem to discriminate when attacking Lords.'

'I'm not just a Lord,' Carmody snapped. 'I'm the Financial Secretary to the Treasury. I'd appreciate you remember that.'

'Aye,' Monroe nodded. 'And if we're clearing the air, we're not just detectives, Lord Carmody. This is Detective Chief Superintendent Bullman, and I'm Detective Superintendent Monroe. Between us, there aren't many people higher up in the City of London police, so please be aware that we are giving you our utmost attention here.'

'But also, we weren't the ones who lost vital secrets in the middle of a London road, in the middle of a country lane,' Bullman added. 'Is your wife around?'

'My wife? She wasn't with me.'

'No, we believed that too, until we found the earring that had been dropped at the scene of the crime,' Monroe said pleasantly. 'We wondered if she could confirm whether she lost one or not.'

At the question, Carmody's face reddened.

'Now listen here, you jumped-up Scot,' he snapped. 'There was nobody else in that car. It was myself, the driver, and my CPO. We'd been to the Dorchester, at a charity party.'

'Where, according to several witnesses who've spoken to my DCI, who *does* so love to text me constantly with updates, probably due to abandonment issues or something, you were seen leaving with a young lady in a champagne-coloured dress,' Monroe interrupted.

It was enough to stop Carmody in his tracks.

'Lord Carmody,' Monroe moved closer, placing his hands on the desk between himself and the sitting Lord. 'I couldn't give a shite what you do in your marriage. If you want to play free with your wife, have at it, no skin off my nose, and I'm sure she'll be happy that you're happy for a change. But do not think that I or my colleagues are stupid people. We know there was a woman in your car. We also know that if *we* are aware of this, the nice photographers and journalists sitting outside will *also* become aware of this incredibly quickly.'

'If you're threatening to leak –'

'For Christ's sake, man!' Monroe shouted. 'We're here to save your sodding career! Charles Baker asked us *personally* to clear up your shite! You've lost important national documents to a guy playing Dick Turpin dress-up, and here you worry that someone might hear that you had a floozy in your bloody car? Get your priorities in order!'

There was a long, awkward moment.

Carmody glared at Monroe.

'What part of Scotland are you from?' he asked.

'Glasgow.'

'Fan of independence?'

'Shouldn't everyone be?'

Carmody sighed.

'Look, Detective Superintendent Monroe, I'm not an idiot. I know who you are and I know what you can do.'

'Oh aye?'

'Yes. You see, I'm aware of who you are, because you once saved my life.'

'The Queen's dinner. Aye, we know.'

'Yes. Which means I know you're very competent at your job, even if you are sometimes pushed aside by my own Government's aides in the pursuit of your duties.'

He sighed.

'Her name was Sophia, and I don't know anything more.'

'Luckily for you, we do,' Monroe replied. 'We're finding a way to contact Mikhail Stefon right now. I understand he's the man who orchestrated the relationship.'

He paused, frowning.

'Would you call it a relationship? Transaction, perhaps?'

'No money passed hands.'

'No, there never is,' Bullman now spoke. 'That doesn't necessarily mean there's not a trade, though, right? What did Mikhail Stefon expect from you?'

'Nothing,' Carmody flushed now; he hadn't expected the

conversation to go this way. 'Are you thinking that Mikhail was behind this?'

'Well, it does seem rather strange that on the particular day that you were hijacked by a Highwayman, a strange and unvetted woman was in your car,' Monroe replied. 'Did your protection officers check her over?'

'What do you mean?'

'Did they check her for trackers, for bugs, for anything?' Monroe continued. 'Our cyber guy, DS Fitzwarren, he has a little game he plays, where he sticks trackers on our cars so he knows where we are. Poor wee bairn has separation anxiety. Howls for hours when he's left alone in the office. But it means he can find us as quickly as you can find your iPhone when you lose it or use one of those wee little tracker thingies that Apple made.'

'Air tags?'

'Aye, that's the ones. Did she have something like that in her bag? Could the Highwayman have used her as a tracking beacon to plan out his attack?'

Carmody looked stunned.

'Are you saying that they deliberately targeted me for my secrets?'

Monroe shrugged.

'What I'm saying, Lord Carmody, is that it seems mighty suspicious that a complete stranger was in your car the night it happened. However, we also understand that you yourself weren't aware this was even going to happen tonight, that the briefcase was placed on you at the last minute?'

'Well, yes, that's exactly what happened,' Carmody said, nodding eagerly now. 'It was Baker's bloody woman. You know, the one that got sent down to the mines for being shit and then found a way to become an MP.'

'Jennifer Farnham-Ewing.' Monroe nodded. 'We know her well.'

'Look, the briefcase was passed to me well after I'd made contact with Mikhail and Sophia,' Carmody shook his head. 'There's no way he'd have known.'

Monroe rubbed his chin.

'When you met the Highwayman,' he asked, 'did he seem surprised by the briefcase?'

'Actually, I think he did,' Carmody replied. 'Perhaps he didn't realise it was going to be there. Maybe he thought he could just take some trinkets.'

'Most likely,' Monroe nodded. 'But to take out a Cabinet Minister with armed police in the front? To me, that says you don't just do that if you're opportunistic and hoping for a sweetie or two. You do it when you think you're going to get the whole bloody sweet shop.'

Monroe smiled.

'Did you give him the whole bloody sweet shop, Lord Carmody?'

'No, I sodding well didn't.'

'Do you know what was in the briefcase?'

'No, I don't. I didn't have time to look at the bloody thing,' Carmody said.

But Monroe observed him as he spoke.

That was a lie.

Monroe's eyes narrowed at the obvious falsehood. In his experience, Lords were terrible liars – they spent too much time having people agree with them to practice properly.

'That's interesting,' he said carefully. 'Because Jennifer Farnham-Ewing tells a different story.'

It was a shot in the dark, and as made-up as his earlier comment, but Carmody's reaction – a slight widening of the eyes, a tightening of his jaw – told Monroe everything he needed to know.

'I haven't spoken to Jennifer since last night,' Carmody replied, his voice steady but his fingers drumming nervously on his desk. 'And I certainly didn't open the briefcase.'

'Did you have the code to do so?'

'Of course.'

'And at no point you wanted a teeny wee peek inside?'

'I'm not a child looking for Christmas presents, man. I was told to look at them when I got home. I wasn't bloody well home yet, was I?'

'You know what I find fascinating about all this?' Monroe leant back, ignoring the statement. 'The timing is incredibly strange. I mean, there you are, given sensitive documents at the exact moment you invite a stranger into your car. You take a specific route home, one you've barely used before, according to your driving logs.'

Carmody's eyes widened again at this; once more, Monroe had shot in the dark and scored a bullseye.

'And then, miracle of miracles, a Highwayman appears.'

'Are you suggesting –'

'I'm not suggesting anything,' Monroe interrupted. 'I'm just pointing out some rather interesting coincidences.'

Bullman, who had been quietly observing, now leant forward herself.

'Lord Carmody, we spoke to Charles Baker this morning. He was quite specific about the contents of that briefcase.'

'Was he now?' Carmody's tone shifted slightly. 'Well, I suppose our illustrious Prime Minister knows best when it comes to PFI reports.'

'We can't say anything about that, or even whether he knows best or not,' Bullman replied. 'But interestingly, we never told you what was in it or mentioned PFI reports. Yet, you already know.'

The colour drained from Carmody's face.

'This is absolutely ridiculous,' he blustered, standing up. 'I made a calculated guess. We'd been talking about PFI and infrastructure that day. Anyway, I've given you my statement. I've cooperated fully. And now you're accusing me of ... what, exactly?'

'We're not accusing you of anything,' Monroe said pleasantly. 'We're just having a wee chat about some very interesting timing.'

'I want you to leave,' Carmody snapped. 'I have meetings. And when Charles Baker asks why you're harassing me instead of finding the real criminals, I'll be sure to tell him exactly how helpful you've been.'

Monroe smiled, touching his forehead in a mock salute.

'Of course, my Lord. We'll get right on finding those real criminals. Wherever they might be hiding.'

OUTSIDE, AS THEY WALKED BACK TO THEIR CAR, BULLMAN glanced at Monroe.

'You think he arranged it himself?'

'Not sure, although I'm wondering whether our Lord in there is more involved than he's letting on,' Monroe nodded. 'But the question is why? What was in that briefcase that was worth staging his own robbery? You mentioned PFI?'

'I was following the Monroe school of "quote random shite to see if it gets a result",' Bullman smiled. 'I'd seen on the news that Baker was looking into it, so Carmody would have known. The one thing I don't understand though is why use such a theatrical approach?'

'That's what's bothering me, too,' Monroe admitted. 'It's too elaborate. A man like Carmody, if he wanted something to disappear, he'd arrange a simple mugging. This is someone showing off.'

'Or sending a message,' Bullman suggested.

'Aye, but to who?'

Before Bullman could respond, Monroe's phone buzzed. He pulled it out, reading the message with a frown.

'Well,' he said finally. 'That's interesting.'

'What?'

'That was Billy. He's been looking into similar robberies.' Monroe looked back at Carmody's house. 'Apparently, this isn't the first time someone's played Highwayman in Essex. And guess who was on the investigating committee for the last lot?'

'Carmody?'

'Aye. Along with a Treasury adviser named Emma Thorne.' Monroe pocketed his phone. 'I think it's time we had a chat with Ms Thorne, don't you?'

'After you, Dick Turpin,' Bullman smiled, climbing into the driver's seat.

'I think,' Monroe said as they pulled away, leaving Carmody's house behind, 'that we're dealing with something a lot more complicated than a simple robbery. And I think Lord Carmody knows exactly what it is.'

6

GREAT HALLS

AFTER CHECKING WITH THORNE'S OWN AIDES, THEY FOUND HER at an incredibly familiar place, and, after parking outside the Last Chance Saloon, Monroe and Bullman took a short walk-through Temple Inn itself over to the Great Hall of Middle Temple.

The Great Hall had stood for over four centuries, stretching a hundred feet in length and more than forty in width. The lower half of its walls was clad in dark oak panelling, leading up to four towering windows on each side, each adorned with eight stained-glass panels. Above them, a magnificent double-hammer beamed roof, blackened with age, arched high overhead. In front of each window, a soldier's breastplate and helmet were displayed, though no weapons accompanied them. Beneath these, the oak panelling bore the coats of arms of Middle Temple Readers – always senior barristers – arranged three high along both sides of the hall. Each was accompanied by three lines of intricate text detailing the Reader's name, whether they held the Spring or Autumn reading, and the year they took it. These arms continued along to the far end of the hall, where a raised stage and the renowned "bench table" stood.

Above the stage, set between the shields of past Readers, hung six grand paintings of various sizes: Queen Elizabeth I, Charles I, and a towering portrait of Charles II loomed over the hall, alongside James II and, in their coronation robes, William III, Queen Anne, and George I. Three royal crests and an additional stained-glass window crowned the upper wall, giving the impression that centuries of monarchs gazed down upon the barristers as they dined below.

It was here, on the slightly raised stage where centuries earlier William Shakespeare was believed to have performed *Twelfth Night* for Queen Elizabeth I.

Emma Thorne was there as part of a panel on financial irregularities for the London School of Economics.

Monroe waited at the back with Bullman; they were aware the panel was running to a close when they arrived, and as the audience applauded the closing statements, Monroe and Bullman made their way to the front.

Emma Thorne was in her late twenties or possibly early thirties; slim and toned – a woman who looked after herself with short, dark-brown hair and minimal makeup, giving her an almost pale expression. Her brown eyes had picked up Monroe when he had first arrived, and he had noticed her glance at him several times, as if aware that they weren't just there for the conversation.

Although, judging from the age of the audience, Monroe wondered if she thought he was the grandfather of one of them.

'Miss Thorne?' he asked.

Emma Thorne nodded, rising from her chair, placing the

small plastic bottle of water she'd been drinking from to the side.

'Am I in trouble?' she asked.

'Why would you think that?'

'Because you look like police,' Emma smiled. 'And it's never good when someone comes up and asks you your name after you've done a talk.'

'Maybe we're scouts from a rival university, wanting to do our own talk on financial irregularities?' Monroe suggested.

'Then I'd say you're probably in a terrible job situation, and you should consider finding alternative employment,' Emma laughed. 'What can I help you with?'

'I'm Detective Superintendent Monroe, this is Detective Chief Superintendent Bullman,' Monroe introduced themselves. 'We're part of the Temple Inn unit, a few yards to the east of here. But we've been asked by Charles Baker to assist him with an altercation last night.'

'An altercation? Sounds exciting,' Emma remarked.

Monroe noticed several people were watching her talk to them, possibly waiting for them to finish so they could continue their conversations and he wondered whether it was best not to speak too loudly just in case they could be overheard.

And then a little voice in his head went *nah, sod it.*

'You might not have heard about it yet,' Monroe said. 'However, your previous boss, Lord Carmody, was robbed at gunpoint.'

'Really?'

'Aye.'

'Well, Carmody was never my boss,' Emma shrugged. 'Sure, I worked on the same committee as him, and he thought he ran the bloody thing, but he was just some jumped-up aristocrat. Thought he owned the bloody place. Christ, if he could have, he would have tried to claim Prima Nocte on us all.'

'Prima what?' Bullman asked.

'It was the ancient lord's right to sleep with a bride on their wedding day, before the new husband did,' Monroe smiled darkly. 'And having met the man, I can believe that.'

'Oh, you've spoken to Carmody?'

'We've just come back from his house,' Monroe grinned. 'You see, last night he was attacked by Dick Turpin.'

At this, Emma Thorne's eyes narrowed.

'Do you think the Essex Rider's back?'

'Aye. Maybe. You were part of the inquiry that looked into it, right?'

Surprisingly, though, Emma shook her head at this.

'We weren't police,' she replied. 'And we sure as hell weren't involved in hunting down whoever it was. We were more looking into the instances of what happened, the ramifications of the thefts.'

'What do you mean?'

Emma paused, cocking her head slightly as she stared at Monroe.

'What do you know about the Essex Rider?' she asked.

'Honestly, nothing more than the name,' Monroe replied. 'It's only just come up in our inquiries. But I understand you were on a commission with Lord Carmody that looked into it. If there's anything else you can tell me ...'

Emma considered this, checking her watch.

'Look,' she said, 'I'm supposed to be in Whitehall at another parliamentary meeting in just under an hour, so I don't have that long, unless this is an official questioning. But I can give you the crib notes if that helps?'

'Please,' Bullman replied.

'A few years ago – we're talking six years back now, we had a kind of *Robin Hood* character, dressed like Dick Turpin.'

'Well, that's just confusing the folktales, isn't it?' Monroe replied. 'Dick Turpin was never Robin Hood, he was a Highwayman, he was a rotten piece of work.'

'And if you spoke to the thirteenth and fourteenth-century kings and lords of Nottingham, you'd be told that Robin Hood was the same,' Emma replied. Monroe went to speak, but she held her hand up. 'And before you say anything else, I know that most people class Robin Hood as around the time of Richard the Lionheart and King John, but that only happened in Elizabethan times.'

'Believe it or not, lassie, we've had our run-ins with our own Robin Hoods,' Monroe smiled. 'Tell me more about the Essex Rider.'

'Well, he really was a "stealing from the rich to give to the poor" type,' Emma said, and from her expression, Monroe wondered whether she actually had a level of admiration for the masked man. 'He wasn't exactly providing money or anything like that, but what he was doing was stealing paperwork, data, information, passwords, you name it, anything that could get him into the financial records of his targets. And then he'd provide it to the press, show where they'd been performing insider dealings or where they'd been gaining money from unfair advantages, monopolies, stuff like that.'

'Right,' Monroe said, finally understanding. 'I think I remember this going on, but I was a wee bit busy back then. So this was effectively a whistleblower?'

'You could call him that,' Emma replied. 'Although most whistleblowers don't ride around on stunt bikes and steal things at gunpoint – or rather *pistol* point. While the police hunted him over a period of about ten to eleven months, he managed seven or eight times to "ply his trade", as they say. Although he was never publicly credited by the press with the work, the Essex Rider took out three corporations in the process, and half a dozen Tory MPs at the same time. In fact, it's one of these reasons Carmody was brought in. Parliament was, shall we say, *concerned* about what was happening.'

'Aye, I can believe that, lassie,' Monroe muttered, understanding now. 'So what, you were brought in just to look into the victims?'

'It was a tough one,' Emma explained. 'I mean, they *were* the victim, but at the same time, they were targeted because they *weren't* the victim, if you get what I'm saying. The problem was, I was brought in to represent the Treasury, whereas Carmody at the time was nothing more than a lackey for Stephen Holland. In fact, it's the work he did on this that got him into the Treasury a couple of years later. Luckily for me, by that point I'd moved upwards and away, so I didn't have to deal with the prick any more.'

'There was no love lost?'

'The guy was a massive bellend with a thing for younger women,' Emma said. 'He even made a pass at me near the end of the enquiry, but I'd just lost my partner in a terrible accident. It was ... well ... let's just say I wasn't in the mood for shit like that, and it wasn't well received. I actually raised a complaint.'

Monroe went to ask about this, but Emma Thorne was on a roll.

'Anyway, the Essex Rider did one more heist after that, and actually Carmody was the one they targeted, but Carmody was clever, or lucky rather, and got away with it looking not squeaky clean, but definitely less tarnished than the other people connected.'

'How so?'

'There were claims Carmody was feathering his nest with insider deals thanks to the commission, and the Rider tried to prove this, but they'd covered their tracks.'

'They?'

'Whoever Carmody did it with, and believe me, he definitely did it, even if it couldn't be proven,' Emma narrowed her eyes. 'With that, the commission was closed, with people complaining there was no impartiality any more – not that there was in the first place.'

She looked as if she was about to spit, like an unpleasant taste was in her mouth, but held it back.

'Then a couple of years later, he wormed his way back into the Treasury.'

'And what about you?' Bullman asked.

'I carried on with my job,' Emma replied. 'The commission was something I was told to do, not wanted to do. I thought it'd get my name out there. I thought it'd allow me to change the world.'

'Do you know how the Essex Rider gained his information?'

'On the targets to attack? We believed there was a leak inside the Treasury. Possibly one of the Financial Conduct Authority,' Emma replied. 'Somebody was definitely taking the information from the Rider and passing it to the newspapers. For all we know, the Rider themselves could have been part of the FCA.'

'Do you have any opinions on it?'

Emma smiled, and it wasn't a friendly one.

'My opinions on the Essex Rider are that he did a bloody

good job by weeding out some absolute scumbags,' she said. 'And I'm just annoyed that Carmody ensured that he and his crony friends didn't end up spending jail time as well.'

She glanced at her watch again.

'Look, I'm very sorry, if you need me back in, I can come and talk to you, but I really do need to –'

'The Prime Minister himself has asked us to get involved in this,' Monroe interrupted. 'Are you telling me that what you need to go and do is more important than the Prime Minister?'

'As much as I don't respect Charles Baker that much,' Emma shrugged, 'the fact of the matter is my upcoming meeting is *with* him, about a financial arrangement he's trying to create, bringing in external money into the country. So sure, if you want to tell the Prime Minister that you've taken away the woman who's advising him on his upcoming plans, right before he does them, feel free to.'

Monroe smiled.

'I'd hate to drag you away from such charming company,' he said. 'If there's anything you can think of, please let me know.'

'Of course,' Emma frowned as a new thought crossed her mind. 'So, do you think it was the Essex Rider?'

'We're not ruling anything out, and the news is quite new to us,' Bullman added quickly. 'But ask yourself this, how many people do you know dress like Dick Turpin and hold up ministers or bankers?'

Emma nodded, but she seemed off at the comment.

'Do you have photos? Footage?' she asked. 'He had a specific bike, a modified, custom Ducati, if that helps.'

'How would you know that?'

'I was part of a committee looking into him,' Emma Thorne replied with the slightest of smiles.

'Aye, of course,' Monroe replied. 'Well, I'm sure we'll be finding out about the bike in good time, but thank you for giving us the heads up. Is there anything else we should be aware of?'

Emma Thorne considered this and then looked back at the students who were still standing around in Middle Temple Hall.

'Just remember that Dick Turpin wasn't a good man,' she said. 'Sure, the legends of Dick Turpin, the ride to York and all the other stuff made him sound like a romantic hero, Heathcliff with a gun, but he was a murderous, vicious bastard.'

She smiled.

'In fact, very much like Lord Carmody.'

And with that, she gave them both a small bow and returned her attention to the organisers of the panel, who had been patiently waiting for her to walk over to them. Monroe nodded thanks and then looked back at Bullman.

'I like her,' he said. 'She doesn't like Carmody. Or Baker. She'll go far.'

Bullman couldn't help it – she laughed, shaking her head.

'So,' she said, 'I think it's time to find out more about this Essex Rider, and exactly what he did six years ago.'

'Aye, and then go shake his bloody hand,' Monroe grinned as they left the Great Hall together.

7
———

FINANCIAL ADVICE

BILLY'S DESK HAD SOMEHOW GAINED ANOTHER SCREEN SINCE Declan and Anjli had left. Four monitors now formed a wall of information around him and Jess, who was working the rightmost keyboard with intense concentration …

Or watching YouTube. Declan couldn't be too sure.

'Any luck with the mysterious passenger?' Declan asked as he approached, Anjli wandering over to her own desk.

'Still working through the event photos,' Billy replied without looking up. 'The Dorchester thing was some kind of charity fundraiser – lots of social media coverage, but nothing concrete yet. Annoyingly, Jess is better at this stuff than me.'

'Only because I waste more time on Instagram and TikTok than you do,' Jess muttered, scrolling through what seemed like an endless stream of party pictures. 'Although that said, I've seen your feed. You should really curate it down now you have a boyfriend.'

Billy reddened as Jess grinned at her father.

'Moustaches and muscles,' she winked. 'That's all I'm saying.'

'And the event?' Declan asked, really not wanting the image of Tom Selleck's *Magnum, PI* in his head. 'Social media has it sorted, I'm guessing?'

'Pretty much,' Jess was still moving through the images. 'It was a charity event and these guys really want the social media boost, so tons of influencers were brought in. Those people document everything.'

'Anything useful?' Anjli asked.

'Maybe,' Jess tapped a few keys, and an Instagram page appeared. 'There's this one socialite who kept posting all evening. Mainly selfies with Z-listers and reality TV stars. Carmody appears in the background of a few shots, though. Nothing exciting, just him talking to different people.'

'What about Mikhail Stefon?' Declan asked. 'Harris mentioned him.'

'That's where it gets interesting,' Billy said, pulling up another screen of data; on it was a list of dates and company names. 'He's technically a consultant for various lobbying firms, but he's richer than half the people he works for, and his name keeps popping up at these events.'

'So what, a spy?'

'Maybe. Although for whom, I don't know. Apparently he was in the Yugoslav army in 1992, before it, well, stopped, so there's every chance he could be working for Russia or the Eastern Bloc. But, according to a couple of Westminster contacts I know –'

'Since when do you have Westminster contacts?'

'Okay, according to Anthony Farringdon, then,' Billy muttered, annoyed he'd been caught out, 'he's always in the background of these events, and always when certain guests need certain … arrangements made.'

'Like escort services?' Anjli suggested. 'Or, you know …'

She made a scraping noise as she ran her finger across her throat.

'Among other things.' Billy frowned at his screen as it beeped. 'Ah. Uncle Chivalry is on his way over at speed.'

Declan couldn't help himself; he instantly glanced back at the door, in case the man himself had already arrived.

'Does he have information on the weapon?'

'Oh, he has ideas,' Billy seemed a little hesitant to respond.

'He doesn't usually hurry over,' Anjli was also picking up on this. 'Is there something we're missing?'

Billy looked sheepish, but it was Jess that replied.

'Billy might have told him that Bullman's now single,' she smiled. 'Apparently Chivalry Fitzwarren has unrequited love.'

'You what?' Declan shook his head. 'Jesus, she's just broken up with Bradbury, and now you aim your *uncle* at her?'

'It slipped out!' Billy muttered. 'I didn't realise he felt that way. He asked how she was doing, I said she seemed pretty desolate about it, the next thing I know he's telling me to let him know when she's back in the office.'

Declan went to continue, but all he could do was chuckle.

'Actually, watching Chivalry try to woo Bullman could be fun,' he eventually admitted. 'Did you get my message about the Essex Rider?'

'Seven confirmed hits over eleven months,' Billy explained, bringing up archived news articles. 'All around Essex, all targeting City traders. The papers were strong-armed by the Government to put a lid on it, so there was a bit of a media blackout where he was concerned, but when you dig deeper, there's footage of him leading police on chases through Epping Forest, pulling stunts that even the motorcycle squad couldn't match.'

'Sounds like someone who knew what they were doing,' Anjli noted.

'Had to be a professional rider,' Jess added. 'Morten once told me you don't just get on a bike and *bam*, you're a motorcyclist.'

She smiled, looking back at Declan.

'On that note,' she continued. 'Can I have a motorcycle, Dad?'

'No.'

'Anjli has a motorcycle.'

'That's because she's a grownup.'

Jess pouted as Declan looked back at Billy.

'The robberies just stopped?'

'Just like that,' Billy nodded. 'But here's the thing – I've been going through financial records from that period, and there's something odd about the timing.'

'How so?'

'Still working that out,' Billy admitted. 'The data's all public record but it's buried in company reports and market analyses. Going to take time to piece it together.'

'Well, you'd better work it out before your uncle arrives, because once he's here, he's your responsibility.'

Billy's expression brightened.

'I sent him the photo from Matthews' phone,' he added. 'He came back pretty quickly. Claims it's an obvious design, which I disagree with, but he's the expert, not me. He says it's a Griffin & Tow duelling pistol, circa 1730. They only made eight pairs, and this one's been modified.'

'We had that from earlier, but do we know how yet?'

'That's what Uncle Chivalry's coming in to explain. He's quite excited about it.'

'Great,' Declan muttered. 'Just what we need. Chivalry Fitzwarren giving us a lecture on Georgian firearms.'

'And chatting up Bullman,' Anjli added. 'So there's that.'

'And ... hang on,' Jess straightened suddenly. 'Dad, come look at this.'

She'd paused on a video clip – someone's shaky phone footage of the Dorchester's entrance. In the background, half-hidden by the crowd, a blonde woman in a champagne-coloured dress was talking to an older man, balding and stocky.

'That's got to be our mystery passenger,' Anjli said.

Before they could discuss it further, however, Cooper appeared at the door.

'Sorry to interrupt, but there's someone in reception asking to speak to the investigating officer?' she said, nodding back down the stairs. 'Says his name is Martin Reeves from the Financial Conduct Authority, and he's got information about similar robberies.'

Declan and Anjli exchanged glances.

'Quite a coincidence,' Anjli said.

'A bit too much of one,' Declan replied. 'Billy, keep digging into those financial records. Jess, see if you can find any more footage of our blonde friend. Something tells me these pieces connect ... we just need to figure out how.'

'What about Chivalry?' Billy asked.

'Text me when he arrives,' Declan said, heading for reception. 'And order in some popcorn.'

Martin Reeves looked exactly how Declan imagined a Financial Conduct Authority investigator should look: regulation dark suit, regulation severity, regulation frown lines etched into his forehead from years of peering at spreadsheets. The only thing missing was a calculator watch, and Declan was willing to bet that was only because smart phones had made them redundant – although there was definitely a retro revival going on.

Martin Reeves looked like he wouldn't know a retro revival if it stood in front of him.

'DCI Walsh?' Reeves held out his hand as Declan approached. His grip was firm but not challenging and almost felt like the handshake of someone who'd read a book about making good first impressions. 'Thank you for seeing me. I know you must be busy.'

'Part of the job,' Declan replied, motioning towards a bench at the side of the reception. Until he knew what this was about, he didn't really want to bring anyone in, especially with the clandestine nature of the case. And, as the reception was currently empty, this felt like the best location to talk. 'Cooper said you had information about similar robberies?'

'Not exactly,' Reeves smiled apologetically as he took a seat. 'More of a ... professional interest. I used to work for the Financial Conduct Authority.'

'Used to? I was told you were currently there,' Declan frowned.

'I'm on garden leave, so technically I didn't lie to your officer,' Reeves pulled out a slim leather notebook, but didn't open it. 'Tell me, DCI Walsh, what do you know about the victims of the Essex Rider?'

Declan rose, the distinct feeling that something was *off* now running down his spine.

'I don't think we can discuss this,' he apologised. 'I can only really talk to people about –'

'Actually, I was hoping you'd give me some more recent information,' Reeves's smile didn't waver. 'About last night's incident, specifically. The Treasury's being remarkably tight-lipped about the whole thing.'

'Again, I can't talk to you about this if you're no longer connected to the office,' Declan straightened. 'But I do have to wonder why an officer of the FCA is interested in a highway robbery?'

'Former FCA,' Reeves corrected. 'And I didn't say I was interested in the robbery.'

'No?'

'No. I'm interested in the timing,' Reeves finally opened his notebook. 'You see, a few years back, I was investigating certain … irregularities in the financial sector. Nothing concrete, you understand. Just patterns. The sort of thing that makes you curious.'

'Curious about what?'

'How some people always seem to be in the right place at the right time,' Reeves glanced down at his notes. 'Did you know there was a series of similar robberies six years ago? Targeting City traders?'

'We're aware of them,' Declan nodded.

'Aware or actively investigating?'

'Aware.'

Reeves seemed disappointed at the answer.

'Then you'll know about the investigation committee?'

'Should I?'

'Probably not. It was all very quiet.' Reeves looked up from his notebook. 'Much like this current incident, I imagine.'

'Mister Reeves,' Declan leaned forward. 'You're no longer

part of the FCA, yet you seem to be acting as if you are. I can't work out if you're finishing a case or trying to open a new one. What exactly are you trying to tell me?'

'I'm sorry, I think I may have overstepped my bounds here,' Reeves stood. 'But, if I were investigating this case, I might want to talk to Emma Thorne. She's a Treasury advisor, and she has an ... interesting perspective on theatrical robberies.'

'And why would a Treasury adviser know about theatrical robberies?'

'I really couldn't say,' Reeves was now heading for the door.

'Mister Reeves –'

'Really must go,' Reeves paused at the door. 'Amazing how many of those victims turned out to have secrets. Financial irregularities. The sort of thing that makes you wonder how they were targeted, doesn't it?'

There was a long, uncomfortable moment, and then Reeves smiled.

'Good luck with your investigation, DCI Walsh. I'm sure we'll talk again.'

After he left, Declan sat for a moment, thinking. Something about Martin Reeves' careful hints suggested he knew far more than he was saying. The question was, why come forward now ... and why leave before too much was said?

Declan sighed, stretched, and was about to turn back to the door leading up to the offices, when a deep booming voice echoed through the reception.

'Declan, my boy!' Chivalry Fitzwilliam bellowed as he stood in the doorway. In his sixties, tall and broad with brown curly hair and beard, both peppered with white, he wore his usual mismatched tweed suit, his ruddy face grinning as he held out his hand to shake Declan's. 'I hear I've got a case to solve, and a lady to woo?'

Declan didn't quite know what to say to that. Instead, he just led Chivalry Fitzwarren into the upper offices of the Last Chance Saloon.

———

MARTIN REEVES WAITED UNTIL HE WAS THREE STREETS AWAY, heading back towards Cannon Street station before letting out the breath he'd been holding. His hands were shaking as he pulled out his phone, checking for messages.

Nothing.

He found a coffee shop off Cannon Street, ordered something he didn't really want, and took a corner seat where he could watch both the door and the street outside.

Old habits.

The sort of habits that had kept him alive after he'd started asking questions about that bloody committee.

He hadn't told Walsh everything. If he was being honest, he couldn't tell him everything, not yet. Not until he was sure he had a way out of this predicament.

His phone buzzed. A text from an unknown number:

You visited Temple Inn.

Not a question. Martin carefully typed a reply:

Just making inquiries. It's my job.

The response came quickly:

You don't have a job. You've been removed.

There was a pause, and then:

Did you do what we asked you to?

I mentioned her name.

Good man. Now forget about this, and we'll forget about you.

Martin stared at the last message and then deleted all recent messages before he looked out at the street. He had less than twelve hours to decide how much he could risk telling the police; he'd done *their* bidding in naming Thorne, but now he had to find proof of what really happened, if only to clear his soul from any blame.

And there was only one place he could do that.

Checking his watch, he sat back. He'd have to go back to an office he was barred from and use a computer he'd been banned from using.

He'd wait until later, though. Until the others had gone.

He just hoped the Highwayman hadn't worked out his plan yet.

———

8

ROOKWOOD

THE MAIN OFFICE OF THE LAST CHANCE SALOON WAS EXACTLY as Declan had left it; screens glowing with Billy's research, Jess still stationed at the auxiliary keyboard – although she'd moved across to her phone currently, most likely finding it quicker to check social media this way – and coffee cups scattered across desks like archaeological evidence of a long day. The only difference was the sudden overwhelming presence of Chivalry Fitzwarren, entering beside him, who seemed to fill the space with his personality as much as his imposing frame.

'William, my boy!' Chivalry boomed at Billy, striding past desks with the confidence of a man who considered all spaces his natural domain. His deep-blue Harris tweed jacket and burgundy corduroy trousers marked him as distinctly out of place among the office's everyday attire, except for Billy, whose own three-piece bespoke suit was also Harris tweed on this particular day. 'I see you're still limiting yourself to these dreadful digital interfaces to check through the liturgy of weapons. You know, in my day we had to actually handle the bloody things to identify them.'

'In your day,' Billy muttered, 'people still fought duels.'

'Precisely!' Chivalry beamed, missing or choosing to ignore his nephew's sarcasm. 'And speaking of duels, you see, that's the fascinating thing about this particular case.'

'What do you know about the case?' Declan glanced back at Billy – the *last* person he felt should have all the details about this would be Chivalry Fitzwarren.

'That Dick Turpin has returned, and the powder in his pistol still fires!' Chivalry bellowed. 'And what's amazing here is the whole point about Dick Turpin ...'

He paused dramatically, ensuring he had everyone's attention.

'... is that he wasn't actually the romantic figure that everyone believed him to be. That particular characterisation came from *Rookwood*. Magnificent novel. William Harrison Ainsworth wrote it in 1834, and there's talk it's possibly the first ever Gothic Romance. Brilliant man, quite brilliant.'

'Can I buy it in Waterstones?' Declan asked. 'Or is this one of those dusty, out of print books that doesn't really help us?'

'Dusty and out of print, I'm afraid,' Chivalry said as he pulled an ancient leather-bound volume from his briefcase, handling it with the reverence usually reserved for religious artefacts.

'The actual Dick Turpin was quite the nasty piece of work,' he continued, barely drawing breath. 'Home invasions, torture, that kind of thing. But Ainsworth, now there was a man who understood the power of reinvention! He took this absolute rotter and turned him into a folk hero. Created the entire mythology we know today. Black Bess? Never mentioned before the book. The ride to York? Utter tosh –'

'Uncle,' Billy tried to interrupt, 'about the pistol –'

'The pistol!' Chivalry's eyes lit up. 'Yes, I'll get to that, but you can't understand the significance of the weapon without understanding its context. You see, in *Rookwood*, Turpin becomes this magnificent creature of legend. There's even a song, several actually, but this one ...'

'Please don't,' Billy muttered, but it was too late.

'*Look! Look! how that eyeball grows bright as a brand! That neck proudly arches, those nostrils expand!*' Chivalry's baritone filled the office. '*Mark! that wide flowing mane! of which each silky tress might adorn prouder beauties – though none like Black Bess!*'

'Is he ... singing?' Anjli whispered to Declan.

'*By moonlight, in darkness, by night, or by day, her headlong career there is nothing can stay!*' Chivalry continued, now fully committed to his performance. '*She cares not for distance, she knows not distress: can you show me a courser to match with Black Bess –*'

He stopped abruptly as Monroe and Bullman entered the office, and something shifted in his demeanour – the bombast dimming to something more measured, more controlled. His entire bearing changed from theatrical raconteur to quiet gentleman.

'Detective Chief Superintendent Bullman,' he said, his voice suddenly softer, more cultured. 'Allow me to state here and now, it is a fine pleasure to see you again.'

Bullman looked taken aback by this unexpected restraint, and Declan noticed Monroe's eyebrows rise slightly.

'Mister Fitzwarren –' Bullman began.

'Please,' he raised a hand, 'just Chivalry. We have no need for names and titles, do we?'

Bullman actually looked a little lost at this. Monroe walked over to Declan, leaning close.

'Is he drunk?'

'In love, it seems.'

Monroe glanced from Chivalry to Bullman, and then back.

'Capital,' he smiled.

'Now, about this rather interesting pistol your team has encountered ...' Chivalry reached into his briefcase, producing a series of photographs which he laid out across Billy's desk with careful precision.

'I saw the photo your man took during the robbery, and young Billy was able to use his technological wizardry to enhance the pistol itself. And, looking at the markings, I'm pretty much sure it's the Griffin & Tow 1730 duelling pistol,' he said, his earlier exuberance replaced by scholarly focus as he glanced up. 'Where's the Viking?'

'Helping Doctor Marcos.'

'Shame. I like the Viking. Anyway, this is an extraordinary piece of craftsmanship. They only produced sixteen in total, sets of pairs, you see, each one slightly different. The interesting part, though, is the modification.'

'You can tell it's been modified from the photo?' Anjli asked.

'My dear, I can tell you the entire history of this particular weapon from this photo,' Chivalry replied. 'The original grip was ivory, but it's been replaced with a composite material that looks identical but provides better stability. The barrel has been re-bored to accept modern ammunition, but the exterior maintains its historical appearance. Most fascinating, though, is the firing mechanism.'

He pointed to a barely visible detail in the photograph.

'The original flintlock has been replaced with a modern firing pin, but they've maintained the external hammer. Brilliant work, really. The kind of modification that requires not just technical skill, but historical knowledge.'

'You know who did this?' Declan asked.

'There are perhaps three gunsmiths in England capable of such work,' Chivalry mused. 'Though only one who would maintain such attention to historical accuracy while ensuring modern functionality. But more importantly –'

'Could it take out a car tyre at a distance, at night?'

'God no,' Chivalry shook his head. 'These were short range, mainly for twelve-step-and-turn duels. Add distance and your ability to aim clearly diminishes tenfold. Although I suppose the additions could compensate for this.'

He stared at the photo for a long moment, distracted.

'Uncle?' Billy prompted gently.

'Ah, yes,' Chivalry seemed to shake himself out of his contemplation. 'As I was saying, the modifications are only part of the story. You see, these pistols were originally commissioned by the Earl of Devonshire in 1730, intended as diplomatic gifts. But they were never delivered.'

'Why not?' Jess asked, drawn in despite herself.

'Because, my dear girl, they were stolen,' Chivalry's eyes twinkled. 'By a *Highwayman*.'

'You're joking,' Declan said.

'I assure you, I am very much not, young Walsh,' Chivalry straightened. 'The pistols vanished en route to London, and while two pairs eventually surfaced in private collections, the others remained lost until 1805, when one turned up in the possession of a notorious road agent.'

'Road agent?' Declan regretted asking the moment the question left his lips.

'Ah, now that's a fascinating bit of terminology,' Chivalry was on a roll now. 'You see, "road agent" was a peculiarly Victorian euphemism for a Highwayman. Rather like calling a burglar a "second-storey man" or a pickpocket a "fingersmith".'

'Did we actually do that, or is he making up words now?' Anjli looked around, seeing no motions to answer in either way.

Chivalry, ignoring the question, continued on regardless.

'The Victorians loved their elaborate nomenclature; it made everything sound so much more genteel,' he said as he warmed to his subject, gesturing expansively. 'The term originated in the 1820s, primarily used by broadsheet writers trying to make their stories sound more sophisticated. "Highwayman" was considered rather crude by then, you see. "Road agent" gave it a sort of professional air. Particularly popular in the American West – "Halt, sir, I am a road agent and this is a hold-up" sounds so much more civilised than "Stand and deliver!"'

Billy cleared his throat meaningfully.

'Ah, yes, perhaps I'm getting a bit off track,' Chivalry admitted. 'Though speaking of tracks, did you know that in Yorkshire they called them "moon cursers", because they cursed the moonlight that made them visible to their victims? Absolutely fascinating regional variations in criminal terminology ...'

'Uncle,' Billy interrupted firmly. 'The pistol?'

'Right, yes, of course.' Chivalry straightened his waistcoat.

'Back to the road agent in 1805. The authorities believed he was using it precisely because of its historical connection to highway robbery.'

'Perhaps we could jump a couple of hundred years, as we've had a long day and it sounds like we're going to be here for hours,' Monroe muttered, but paused as Doctor Marcos and De'Geer entered the office through the main doors, both looking grim.

'Hold that thought for a moment, Chivalry,' Declan said quickly. 'Doctor Marcos, I guess you've found something?'

'Oh yes,' Doctor Marcos replied, her usual sardonic tone somehow more serious than usual. 'That shot that took out the Range Rover's tyre? Wasn't a shot at all.'

She placed an evidence bag on the desk. Inside was what looked like a small metal disc, badly damaged.

'Micro explosive,' she explained. 'Attached to the wheel arch. Remote detonated with a very specific timing mechanism, and sent small nails into the tyre, destroying it instantly.'

'Which means,' De'Geer added, 'whoever did this could calculate exactly where they wanted the car to stop. We found traces of a wireless receiver; they could trigger it from anywhere within range.'

'So Harris wasn't in on it,' Declan realised. 'The car was stopped when they wanted it to be.'

'He didn't need to be. They just needed him to be driving at the right speed ...'

'And someone with a detonator could do the rest,' Chivalry finished, walking past Doctor Marcos, examining the remains of the explosive with professional interest. 'Quite elegant, really. Though not as elegant as the Griffin & Tow.'

'Why is *he* here?' Doctor Marcos glanced over at Monroe.

'Did we lose a bet? Oh, God, is he a hallucination and I'm having a stroke?'

'Did you know there's a theory that Dick Turpin himself once owned one of the missing pairs?' Chivalry continued unabated. 'Complete nonsense of course, the dates don't match up at all, but it adds a certain poetry to your current situation.'

'Poetry isn't going to solve this case,' Monroe muttered, but Chivalry was already reaching back into his briefcase.

'Ah, but that's where you're wrong, Detective Superintendent,' he said, pulling out what looked like an old journal. 'You see, when someone goes to this much trouble to recreate a historical moment, they're not just committing a crime. They're telling a story.'

'A story about what?' Declan asked.

'That's the fascinating part.' Chivalry opened the journal, revealing pages of handwritten notes. 'In the original Turpin legends – the real ones, not Ainsworth's romanticism – he often targeted people who had secrets. The wealthy, the corrupt, those who thought themselves above the law. He wasn't just stealing their valuables; he was stealing their dignity.'

'Like targeting City traders who were later investigated for financial crimes?' Anjli suggested.

'Precisely!' Chivalry beamed as he spread more photographs across the desk. 'The modifications to this pistol? They're recent. Within the last three to four years. And look at the craftsmanship – it's identical to another piece I encountered when we were looking into your re-enactor people a few months back. The maker has a very distinctive style.'

'That's after the Essex Rider case,' Anjli mused.

'You know who changed it?' Declan asked.

'Better than that,' Chivalry replied. 'I know where they work. Small shop in Greenwich, specialises in historical weapons restoration. The owner, Marius Blake, is one of maybe three people in England who could do this kind of work.'

Doctor Marcos, who had been examining the explosive remnants more closely, looked up.

'The timing mechanism on this,' she said, 'it's custom work, too. Precision engineering. This wasn't some amateur job. Whoever built this knew exactly what they were doing.'

'Do we know where the items came from?' Declan asked.

'What, you mean Tesco?'

'No, I mean if they're American, Russian, whatever,' Declan shrugged. 'If Stefon's the guy to get things, and he was in the Yugoslav army before they collapsed ...'

'That's a possibility,' Doctor Marcos admitted.

'So we have a modified antique weapon, precision explosives, and a theatrical robbery that mirrors historical cases,' Monroe summarised. 'All of it pointing to someone with both technical skill and historical knowledge.'

'Or a person in the woods with the laser pointers is doing that,' Anjli replied. 'They could be beside one device, have a clear line of sight, know exactly when to fire. And the Highwayman would be pretty close, they could easily think it was the same shot if they fired the moment they heard the tyre explode.'

'You're realising the most interesting part,' Chivalry said, his voice dropping slightly. 'In the original legends, highway robbers often worked in pairs. One to distract, one to strike. Perhaps your theatrical friend is keeping to historical accuracy in more ways than one.'

'We think there were more than two involved, though,'
De'Geer added. 'Two men in vans blocking the road for a
start.'

'Footpads, hired for the job,' Chivalry suggested, 'maybe
not part of the team itself. You know, there's something about
this modification that's bothering me, though.'

'What's that?' Billy asked.

'These pistols were made in pairs, sets for duelling and
suchlike,' Chivalry explained. 'No gentleman would carry just
one. So, where's its twin?'

There was a moment of silence as everyone considered
that. Chivalry, surprisingly, let the moment continue without
trying to fill it with talking.

Monroe checked his watch, noting the time.

'We're getting close to the end of the day now,' he
remarked. 'We're probably not going to hear anything back
before morning. Chivalry, as you seem to be part of the team
right now, tomorrow I'd like you to have a chat with this
Marius Blake chappie, see if there's anything more he can
give us. Doctor Marcos? Check into the explosives. I'm sure
you have people you know who could help here, I'd like to
know what could detonate the explosive.'

De'Geer, meanwhile, had been typing on his phone, and
Monroe noticed this, raising an eyebrow.

'Are we boring you, laddie?' he asked with a smile.
'Arranging dates with someone who isn't in this room?'

As Cooper turned and glared at De'Geer, he flushed,
embarrassed.

'Sorry, Guv,' he mumbled, 'but I might have an idea of
how to find out more on this guy.'

'We're all ears,' Monroe smiled.

'So, when I started in the police, I was a motorcycle cop,'

De'Geer replied. 'It's what I was in Maidenhead, when I first met then-DI Walsh.'

'Aye, we know that.' Monroe watched carefully, almost mockingly. 'You still ride the bloody thing.'

'Well, so I'm still friends with a lot of the motorcycle cops, and when I became one, I trained in Essex.'

'Why in God's name would a Maidenhead officer be training in Essex?' Declan asked.

'Because the guy who trained people was in Essex?' De'Geer smiled. 'And yes, I know I could have gone to one of the Thames Valley trainers, but the man I'm thinking of is Danny Freeman.'

'Why do I know that name?' Monroe asked.

'Because he's DCI Mark Freeman's brother,' De'Geer replied, and Declan wasn't sure, but at the mention of the name, there was a slight twitch at the edge of his lips. 'And if I'm right, he'd probably have been involved in the teams who chased the Essex Rider. Maybe he has something about what happened six years ago.'

'Do you know where he'll be tonight?'

'That's what I'm finding out right now.'

'Well, why are you bothering talking to us, laddie?' Monroe laughed. 'Contact DCI Freeman's brother and find out what you can.'

9

BIKE SCHOOL

DANNY FREEMAN'S POLICE MOTORCYCLE TRAINING SCHOOL hadn't changed in the years since De'Geer had learned to ride there. The same scuffed training cones dotted the practice yard, arranged in patterns that, in some deep corner, still haunted De'Geer's dreams from his training days, and the same smell of oil and rubber hung in the air, mingling with fresh tarmac and the last lingering traces of exhaust fumes. Even the old shipping-container office looked identical, although the motorcycles lined up outside were newer models than he remembered.

It was the end of the day, the floodlights now lighting up the car park. Freeman himself was outside the container office, working on a police-spec BMW, carefully checking the oil level with the bike balanced on its centre stand, as De'Geer pulled up on his Triumph Bonneville.

Sergeant Danny Freeman hadn't changed much. Stocky build, still wearing the same oil-stained polo shirt with the police motorcycle school's logo, the only difference was a little more grey in his close-cropped hair.

'Still riding that bloody thing,' Freeman called out without looking up. 'Thought you'd gone modern by now. Got you lot those nice Yamahas, didn't they?'

'Some of us appreciate the classics,' De'Geer replied, dismounting. 'Besides, she's never let me down.'

'Yet.' Freeman straightened, wiping his hand on a rag. 'Your message said this was official business.'

'Sort of.'

'Sort of?' Freeman's eyebrows rose. 'Either it is or it isn't, Mort. Come on, that's lesson one, precision in all things.'

De'Geer smiled at that. His old instructor had drilled it into him constantly; precision in all things: in riding, in maintenance, in everything.

"*A motorcycle responds to exactness,*" he'd say. "*It might be the difference between catching your target and eating the road.*"

'It's about an old case,' De'Geer said, but stopped as Freeman raised a hand.

'Before we get into all this,' he said softly, 'have you seen my brother?'

De'Geer forced himself not to flinch at the comment. DCI Mark Freeman was a man who had, at one point, been De'Geer's boss, especially when first hunting for Declan – when he was believed to be a terrorist – and then, second, hunting for the Red Reaper. After that, De'Geer had moved across to the Temple Inn unit, but he'd still kept in contact with DCI Freeman ... well, until a few months ago. When placed in an impossible situation and with his son kidnapped, Freeman had been forced to spy on the Last Chance Saloon, something that had caused De'Geer to be captured and tortured.

He could still remember when Steve Cummings, his eyes

wide with anger and insanity, had faced him; De'Geer tied to a chair, his shirt ripped open.

Cummings had stood with a pair of dice, rattling them in his hand.

'Evens, you're safe,' he had said to him. *'Odds, I hurt you.'*

An eight had rolled. De'Geer had forced a smile, commenting that it looked like he was safe, but Cummings had ignored the response, leaning forward with the straight edge of a folding razor, slicing down De'Geer's chest, creating a long red cut that bled heavily. The long, sharp line was now nothing more than a pink scar on his chest, but he still saw it every morning when he woke, and when he changed his shirt. And though he understood his onetime boss's reasons, there was still a part of him that feared that if he ever saw Mark Freeman – currently still on administrative leave from Maidenhead Police – he'd ram his *own* knife into the man's chest.

'No,' he eventually replied, calming himself back down. 'I haven't seen your brother, not since ...'

He trailed off.

'Have you?'

Danny nodded.

'He's not the same man he was,' he said. 'He's barely speaking to his family, but I understand that. Mark always wanted the exciting jobs. I was happy to ride a bike. You know he would have done nothing to actively hurt you, though, right?'

De'Geer bit back a response and forced a smile.

'Old history,' he said.

'And yet you'll hear about old history anyway,' Freeman grinned. 'I'm guessing you're here about the Essex Rider.'

As he said the name, Freeman's expression had shifted

slightly, the professional facade cracking just enough to show something underneath. It could have been concern, maybe interest. De'Geer couldn't quite read it.

'How would you know that?' he asked.

'Heard about last night, didn't I?' Freeman said. 'Dick Turpin on a motorbike? Brought back people talking about the Essex Rider. And that's a name I haven't heard in a while. Come on, let's get a brew. Still take it white, no sugar?'

'You remember that?'

'I remember all my students' tea preferences. Tells you a lot about a person, how they take their tea.'

THE SHIPPING-CONTAINER OFFICE SHOULD HAVE FELT CRAMPED, but somehow Freeman had arranged it to feel kind of cosy inside. Instead, it reminded De'Geer of the last time he'd been in there; motorcycle manuals lining makeshift shelves, spines cracked and worn from constant use, a wall of photographs showed various training classes over the years and, as he looked closer, De'Geer spotted himself in one, younger and slightly slimmer, standing proudly beside his first police bike ... although still a good foot taller than everybody else beside him.

'You were one of my best students, you know,' Freeman said as he gestured at the wall of photos. 'You had a natural feel for the machine. Most of them, they learn the techniques, but they never really get it. You know, the connection between rider and bike. You had that from day one.'

De'Geer shifted, uncomfortable with the praise.

'Well, you know, I had a good teacher, didn't I?'

'Had the right instincts,' Freeman corrected, dropping tea bags into two chipped mugs. 'Heard you're a sergeant now.'

'That's right.'

'Heard you don't ride the bike as much, that you prefer to play with bodies.'

'I'm moving slowly into forensics,' De'Geer smiled. 'It's a little more hands-on, but not in the horrid Doctor Franken-stein way you're probably thinking.'

Freeman grinned.

'So, go on then, this robbery out on the New Road, the one with the Highwayman ...'

De'Geer waited as the kettle clicked off and Freeman poured, his movements precise.

It was just like the riding he used to do, De'Geer thought. *There was no wasted motion, no spillage.*

'How did you hear about it?'

'I still keep in touch with the motorcycle unit. They're all talking about it, wondering if it's connected to the old case. Is it?' Freeman took his time answering now, stirring his tea with the same careful attention. De'Geer grinned at this; Freeman had once used to show proper counter-steering technique with the same expression on his face. It wasn't just the stirring of the tea that was taking up his capacity; he was probably remembering the moments.

'Do you remember that summer?' Freeman asked finally. 'When the Essex Rider was active?'

'Nah, I'd just started in the uniform then, regular patrol over in Maidenhead,' De'Geer smiled. 'I'm not as old as you.'

'Lucky you. We spent months chasing shadows.' With a mug in his hand, Freeman settled into his chair, the plastic creaking slightly. 'Seven pursuits. Seven bloody times we thought we had him, and seven times he made us look like bloody amateurs.'

He sipped at his tea, staring at the wall of photos, but clearly a thousand miles away, seeing something else entirely.

'The first one was up near Loughton. Got a call about a robbery. Someone in period costume on a bike, if you can believe it. We thought it was a joke at first, but by the time we realised it wasn't …' he shook his head. 'Never seen anyone handle a bike like that, though. Through the forest in the dark, pulling moves that shouldn't have been possible.'

'But something caught your eye.'

Freeman paused from responding, staring out of the container window for a moment.

'Yeah, there was this thing he did coming into the tighter corners, a particular lean,' Freeman demonstrated with his hand, tilting it at an angle. 'Picked it up around the fourth chase. Sometimes he used it, sometimes he didn't, but there was a closeness to it. Most riders, they're all about the technical perfection, you know, textbook moves. But this, it felt like he was showing off, you know? Pure style over substance.'

He stood, walking to a filing cabinet in the corner.

'A couple of months after it all kicked off, I'd been to one of those bike shows –you know the ones, stunts, demonstrations, that kind of thing, at an Exhibition Centre near Watford. A few of us were going to do a police uniform bike display –never happened though, because it started shitting it down and we didn't want to go out in the rain.'

De'Geer forced back a "fair weather rider" comment.

'But there was this rider there doing exhibition runs, had the same lean, identical,' Freeman said as he rifled through a drawer. 'Kept the programme somewhere, too. Ah, here you go.'

He pulled out a creased pamphlet, handing it over to De'Geer. The cover showed various stunt riders in mid-flight.

'James Kitson,' Freeman pointed to one of the names. 'Wasn't a big name or anything, but if you knew bikes, and I mean really knew them, you could tell he was something special. Had that same flair, that same unnecessary flourish in the corners. Worked with a partner, Stephen Mahoney, and genuinely, Mort, if I could have hired them instantly as motorcycle coppers, we'd have nailed every high-speed chase we ever did.'

'And you saw this flourish during the pursuit?'

'A couple of times, yeah. Clear as day. Same lean, same style. I would have bet my pension on it being him,' Freeman returned to his chair. 'But then they had an accident. I don't quite know what happened, I know it was at the exhibition centre we were supposed to do a show at. This was later on, not the same time that we were there, but it was a bad accident, one that killed his partner and did Kitson's legs in, but also gave him inner ear damage, I heard. Career-ending stuff.'

'Jesus. What happened?'

Freeman shrugged.

'There were rumours and all that,' he said. 'Mahoney was working with an injury, on pain meds, didn't want to let people down ... but I've got the report here.'

He rummaged in a drawer, pulling out a piece of paper, passing it to De'Geer.

'The centrepiece of the performance is a "crossover jump", where both riders accelerate towards opposite ramps, launch over an obstacle, and crisscross mid-air before landing,' Freeman explained.

'It says here the obstacle was a fuel tanker?' De'Geer looked up.

'Yeah,' Freeman's expression darkened. 'It gave a little "danger" to the jump. Officially, it was drained and safe after an earlier stunt, like it had been when they'd done the trick a dozen times before. I even saw it when we were there the first time.'

'So, what happened?' De'Geer was reading as he asked, likely by habit.

'Both riders sped up towards their ramps, like they'd done before. But something was off. Mahoney was a fraction late. According to witnesses, his body position was wrong – stiff, not fluid. Like he was compensating for something.'

'Pain meds?'

'Maybe. Kitson hit his ramp clean, but Mahoney ... he was just that little bit slow. It meant instead of clearing the tanker, he clipped the edge. The back wheel smacked off the top, sent the bike spinning, and Mahoney ... he went with it. Witnesses saw him roll across the tanker, arms flailing, before he dropped over the far side. Then the explosion went up; whole thing went to hell in a second. The blast knocked Kitson sideways mid-air; he was lucky, really. Broke his leg on the landing, but it could've been worse. By the time the crew got there, the fire had swallowed the entire area.'

'The tanker wasn't empty?'

'It was meant to be, but they'd cancelled an earlier stunt, the one that actually needed the fuel, so half of it was still in there. No one realised.'

'So, when Mahoney's bike hit, the impact must've ruptured something, and the heat from the engine or sparks from the metalwork ...' De'Geer trailed off as Freeman nodded.

'Boom. They found what was left of his bike, burnt to hell. Then his leathers, torn up, charred. Bits of them stuck to the tarmac, like he'd been right in the blast. Kitson was a mess after the crash; his leg was bent wrong, bone through the skin, and he was barely conscious. The blast had rattled his head too, left him dizzy, out of it. Kept trying to focus, but he couldn't even sit up without the world spinning. Paramedics said inner ear damage. He kept mumbling Mahoney's name, swearing he saw him moving before the flames took over. But in his state it's hard to say if he actually saw anything at all.'

'And the robberies ended after that?'

'Actually, no, and that's what's always bothered me,' Freeman's voice dropped slightly at the question. 'You see, there was one more time, about two days after the accident. So, when the rider turned up again, we were on him before he even realised. Same costume, same bike. But I tell you now, Mort, the riding was different. I can't explain how I knew, but it was technically perfect, but there didn't seem to be any flair. There was no signature lean. It was almost like someone else was wearing the costume, which made sense if Kitson was in hospital –'

'And Mahoney was dead.'

Freeman looked directly at De'Geer.

'Look, I never put that in any official report. What was I supposed to say? I thought it was a random stunt rider because of the way he took corners, and then maybe it wasn't, or maybe it was his ghost? They'd have laughed me out of the unit.'

De'Geer sipped at his tea for a moment.

'You might not have told anybody officially, but I'm guessing you kept notes?'

Freeman nodded at this, returning to the desk drawer and pulling out a battered notebook, its pages dog-eared and stained with what looked to be old coffee rings.

'Every pursuit, every detail I could remember. I've been waiting for someone to ask the right questions. This was the route he took that first night,' Freeman said, opening up a hand-drawn map. 'He went through Upper Loughton, then cut through the forest on the old trails. The bike he was using had to be altered. A standard machine wouldn't have handled those paths, not at those speeds. It was a Ducati Multistrada V4, upgraded and modified. I swear it.'

'These trails. Are they on regular maps?' De'Geer had placed the accident report down and was studying the map.

'Only as mountain bike trails. You know, the guys who cycle through the woods at speed. I don't think anybody expects people on motorcycles to go through them like banshees,' Freeman tapped the page. 'And that's what got me thinking. He knew the forest. Not just the main paths. He used the old tracks, the ones locals buggered around on with their dirt bikes. You know, the ones you know only if you've spent time there.'

He flipped to another page.

'He used the woods a couple of times, but the fifth pursuit was different. More showing off. He went through the Market Square in Waltham Abbey, right past the police station, like he was making a point. Little prick,' Freeman smiled as his finger traced the route. 'That's where I really saw the lean. Taking corners on the Ducati way harder than necessary. Throwing in little flourishes. At the time, we thought he was just being cocky. You know, dressed like Dick Turpin and acting like it. But now ...'

Freeman sat back in his chair.

'Now I wonder if he wanted us to see it, you know, to recognise it, like he was signing his work.'

'And the last one, after Kitson's accident?'

Here, Freeman turned his notebook page, revealing the final entry. The handwriting, however, was messier, more urgent, as if Freeman had been confused or trying to remember everything quickly before it went.

'It was a different route entirely. I mean, he still rode like an expert, however it was more precise. No showing off, no unnecessary risks. Went through Epping Forest again but stuck to wider paths. It didn't mean they were any easier to navigate at those speeds, but ...'

He trailed off, staring at his notes.

'But what?'

'But it felt like someone working from instructions. Kind of like they knew the route and knew the moves, but hadn't really lived through it,' Freeman closed the notebook. 'The first rider rode like they were dancing. This one, they rode like they were following a choreographed movement.'

He pushed the notebook across the desk.

'Go on, you might as well take it. It could help with the current case. Although I've got to ask, is he really back?'

'I don't know. I haven't seen him in action yet,' De'Geer picked up the notebook. 'But the level of planning and expertise needed, it feels connected. Could be copycats. Those old cases didn't get a ton of press due to the D-Notices being slammed down on the papers, but it still got out.'

Freeman rubbed his chin.

'You get a photo; I could tell you. We were close enough to see them several times.'

De'Geer paused, pulling out his phone, scanning through

to the image that had been taken by Matthews, turning and showing it. He watched as Freeman's face paled.

'Jesus,' he muttered, grabbing the phone and staring at it, zooming in to the image. 'That's the same bloody costume. That's the Essex Rider. Not sure about the bike, though. The headlight seems off for a Ducati. Maybe a Kawasaki Ninja?'

He looked back at De'Geer.

'So, he's back attacking city traders?'

'No,' De'Geer hesitated before replying. 'Our current target's not some random rich bloke. It's a high-ranking Treasury Minister.'

'Lord Carmody ...' Freeman passed the phone back, biting his lip as he considered that. 'You know what always bothered me about those old cases?'

'What?'

'The targets,' Freeman replied. 'Everyone assumed they were random, you know, rich people using country roads late at night, easy marks.'

He sipped at his tea, considering his words.

'But later, when I was reading the financial pages, every single one of them ended up in some kind of scandal. Market manipulation, insider trading, that sort of thing. The Essex Rider took their passwords and their accounts, their WhatsApp's and their texts, and then he outed their deals to the press. But there was never anything that showed him profiting from the thefts. It was just data. Sure, a little cash here and there, but he rode a bloody Ducati. That's twenty grand on a bike. This wasn't the "poor cheating the rich" people claimed.'

'You think the robberies were connected?'

'Oh, that's way above my pay grade,' Freeman shrugged, 'and probably way above my brother's, too. But it felt deliberate, you know? Like the riding skills were all just part of it. Like whoever was behind it knew exactly who they were targeting and why.'

He walked back to the filing cabinet and pulled out another file, holding it, staring at it for a long moment, as if internally deciding whether or not to pass it on, looking back at De'Geer with an odd expression.

'You know what's funny? Back then, this felt important, like I was on to something. Then Kitson had his accident, and suddenly nobody wanted to talk about any of it. After the final one, the robberies stopped, the investigation wound down, and this just gathered dust in my drawer.'

'But you kept it all.'

'Copper's instinct, I suppose. You spend a few years in the bike unit, you trust your gut, and my gut kept telling me that something wasn't right. Timing wasn't correct, the accident happening when it did, the last robbery feeling so different,' he opened the file, and spread the papers across the desk. 'Your new guy isn't the Essex Rider because the Essex Rider was Kitson, maybe even Mahoney before he died; I swear that on my heart. The last robbery, that was someone else. Possibly the same person you're hunting. Same basic setup, different target, same game. Look, take it all. Maybe you'll see something I missed. But Mort ...'

He fixed De'Geer with the same stern look he'd used during training.

'Be careful with this. Bike accidents, they can end careers.'

'Did you ever try to talk to Kitson?' De'Geer asked. 'After the accident?'

Freeman's expression tightened slightly.

'Once,' he said. 'About six months afterwards, he'd opened this little bike shop in Bethnal Green. Custom work, mainly, modifications. He could still work on bikes, even if he couldn't ride them any more.'

He sipped at his tea, staring at the images on the wall, reliving old days.

'It wasn't a social call, I had this theory about the modifications on the Ducati. It needed someone who knew custom work, someone who could recognise the specs, so I thought it'd be funny to ask him, pretend I didn't know he could have been the Essex Rider, see if he'd slip up. By that point, everyone had moved on and no one cared, but I kind of wanted to know for myself. However, the moment I walked in … Christ, Mort, you should have seen him. The man could barely stand straight. He had to keep one hand on the workbench just to stand upright.'

'The inner ear damage?'

'Vertigo, they said. Constant balance issues,' Freeman shook his head. 'You know what it's like being a rider. Your whole life is about balance. About knowing exactly where you are in space. And then suddenly …'

He made a gesture with his hand like a bike wobbling.

'Suddenly, everything's spinning and everything's uncertain. Couldn't even bring myself to ask him about the bike. Felt like rubbing salt in the wound. Bought some parts I didn't need and then left.'

Freeman's eyes softened as he thought back to the moment.

'But there was something in his eyes when he saw my uniform. Not guilt, exactly. More like resignation. Like he was waiting for someone to finally ask the questions.'

'But you never went back.'

'What was the point? The man had lost everything. His career, his balance, his whole identity. Even if he had been the Essex Rider,' Freeman spread his hands. 'Sometimes you have to know when to let things lie.'

'Could it be Mahoney? You said the body wasn't found, just burned leather. Could he have faked his death?'

Freeman's eyes narrowed.

'Some people reckon they saw him moving after, a figure limping away. Could've been smoke, could've been panic playing tricks. But if you're asking me? I don't know. I just know we never found a body. And until we do, I'd suggest not ruling anything out.'

He gathered all the papers together, the pursuit logs, the event flyers, the technical specs, and pushed them across the desk.

'Take them. Maybe they'll help with your case, but if you do ...' he fixed De'Geer with the training instructor glare again, 'if you do talk to Kitson, be careful how you approach it, yeah? The man suffered enough.'

De'Geer gathered the materials, tucking them carefully into his jacket. The floodlights outside caught the chrome of the training bikes, making them gleam.

'You still teaching people that trick with the clutch?' he asked, nodding towards the course.

'Still works, doesn't it?' Freeman managed a small smile. 'Although these days all they want to do is learn on those bloody automatic bikes. No feel for the machine.'

They walked over to De'Geer's Triumph Bonneville in silence, both aware that there was more to say, but neither quite willing to say it.

'You know,' Freeman said finally, as De'Geer straddled the bike, pulling on his helmet, 'there's one other thing that always bothered me about that last robbery.'

'Oh yeah?'

'The bike.' Freeman ran a hand along the Triumph's tank, appreciating its touch. 'First ones, you could hear the Ducati engine. You know, they were custom work, but they still had that recognisable growl, you know? The last one was different, quieter, like they modified the exhaust system somehow.'

'Why did that bother you?'

'Because it meant they were planning ahead, learning from our pursuits. They were adapting.' Freeman stepped back from the bike. 'Makes you wonder what else they learned and changed, and if they were planning more, why they stopped when they did. If you'd adapted and learned from the people pursuing you, you could carry on two, maybe three more times.'

'Maybe they just didn't want to get caught,' De'Geer kicked the bike to life, the engine's rumble filling the yard. As he pulled away, he caught sight of Freeman in his mirror, still standing there, looking thoughtful.

Or maybe they couldn't ride a motorbike any more.

10

PERSONAL TIME

Bullman and Monroe sat in a corner of *The Old Bank of England,* the low buzz of conversation filling the space. The pub, once the Law Courts branch of the Bank of England from 1888 to 1975 had fallen into disrepair, before being restored by Fuller's brewery two decades later, keeping its imposing grandeur. High ceilings with intricate plasterwork loomed overhead, while marble pillars and dark wood panelling gave the place a sense of history. Chandeliers cast just enough light to highlight the faded murals on the walls, but not so much as to make it feel less comfortable.

The bar stretched along one side of the room, polished brass taps and neatly stacked glasses catching the light. Tables were scattered across the floor, a mix of high-tops and booths, most of them already occupied by after-work crowds. The current owners, McMullen's brewery, had kept the place simple but inviting, the kind of pub that felt familiar after a long day.

'I still can't believe you're drinking that,' Monroe said, watching Bullman sip her pink gin and lemonade. 'All the decent Scottish whisky in the world, and you choose something that looks like mouthwash. They even do that hideous pear cider you like. You could have had some of that, instead of ... well, that bloody thing.'

'Bold words from a man adding ice into his scotch,' Bullman replied. 'Besides, I'm embracing change. New drink, new life choices, new ...'

She trailed off, staring quietly into her glass.

'He's an idiot,' Monroe said quietly.

'He's my boss.'

'Aye, and an idiot.' Monroe took a long drink. 'Though I suppose that's not mutually exclusive.'

Bullman managed a small smile.

'You know what the worst part is? I actually thought ...'

She shook her head.

'Doesn't matter. Ancient history now.'

'Two weeks isn't ancient.'

'In police years, it's practically geological. Anyway, enough about my disaster of a love life. What do you make of this Highwayman business?'

'Nice try.'

'What?'

'Changing the subject,' Monroe leaned back, studying her. 'You've been doing that all day. Every time someone asks how you are, suddenly there's something urgent about the case.'

'Because there *is* something urgent about the case.' Bullman's voice hardened slightly. 'We've got a Treasury Minister being robbed by someone in fancy dress, connections to old cases, and Charles bloody Baker breathing down our necks while he makes us his personal sodding task force. My personal life isn't exactly a priority.'

'Sophia ...'

'Don't.' She held up a hand. 'Just ... don't.'

As she commanded, however, the pub door opened, letting in a gust of evening air ... as well as Chivalry Fitzwarren. Several regulars turned to stare, but Chivalry seemed not to notice, as he finally appeared to recognise Monroe and Bullman.

'Ah,' he said, his usual booming voice dropping to something more measured. 'I do hope I'm not interrupting.'

'Not at all,' Monroe replied, though his tone suggested otherwise. 'Just having a quiet drink.'

'Splendid,' Chivalry approached their table but didn't sit. 'Detective Chief Superintendent Bullman. I trust you're well?'

Something in his manner made Bullman look up sharply; the theatrical flourishes were gone, replaced by genuine concern.

'I'm fine,' she said automatically.

Chivalry nodded, as if she'd answered a different question entirely.

'Fleet Street, historically one of London's main thoroughfares, was not a primary haunt for Highwaymen, who typically operated in more secluded areas such as Hounslow Heath, Bagshot Heath, and Shooter's Hill,' he said thoughtfully. 'However, during the reign of Queen Anne, Fleet Street was troubled by the "Mohocks," a gang of aristocratic ruffians known for terrorising citizens at night. These individuals would often assault passersby, adding to the area's notoriety during that period.'

'Fascinating,' Monroe muttered.

'Quite,' Chivalry's gaze hadn't left Bullman. 'Well, I should leave you to your evening. Though ...'

He hesitated.

'If you're interested in the history of highway robbery in London, I'm giving a lecture at the Guildhall Library next week. Purely academic, of course.'

Before either of them could respond, he turned and walked to the bar, soon deep in conversation with the landlord about the provenance of the copper fittings.

'Well,' Monroe said after a moment. 'That was different.'

'What was?'

'Him. Usually, he's all bombast and historical tangents. That was almost ...'

'Normal?'

'Aye.' Monroe frowned. 'Should we be worried?'

Bullman watched Chivalry gesturing enthusiastically at the beer pumps, apparently explaining their Victorian heritage to the increasingly confused landlord.

'Maybe he's just full of surprises,' she said quietly.

———

DECLAN HADN'T PLANNED ON STAYING LATE, BUT SOMETHING about today's revelations didn't sit right. The theatrical nature of the robbery felt like misdirection; almost like a classic magician's patter, getting the audience to watch the wrong hand as the other did the actual work. It wasn't the first time he'd faced someone doing this, hell, it probably wasn't in the top ten, but if there was one thing he'd learned over the years, it was to trust that nagging feeling that said you were missing something obvious.

So, when Billy had suggested working through dinner, Declan had agreed, but only on the premise that this wasn't Billy using work to avoid his social life again. Billy admitted that if he stayed in the office, he didn't have to go for a drink with Chivalry, and spend the evening being told why he needed to buck up and rejoin the family again. It also meant he didn't need to introduce Chivalry to Sam, his boyfriend – although Declan wondered whether this was more because Sam and Chivalry would likely hit it off incredibly well and Billy would sit at the side for the whole night while the two art experts tried to out-do each other.

Anjli had headed to Westminster, but Jess had invited herself to stay as well, claiming she could study just as easily here as at home; but given she'd spent the last hour high-lighting financial records instead of her English Lit notes, Declan suspected this wasn't strictly true. He wondered if she was doing similar to Billy, as Jess hadn't really mentioned Prisha, the girl she was dating lately, and wondered whether there was something wrong there. Also, he wondered whether, as a father, he should offer supportive advice, but realised very early on he didn't have a clue what to say.

They'd ordered from the Golden Palace – not because it was good, but because it was the only place that would still deliver to Temple Inn. Sure, there were probably others, but over the years, Doctor Marcos, usually the one ordering while on all-nighters in the morgue had alienated them all with her annoying habit of forensically analysing each meal and sending them detailed critiques of what was wrong with them. Therefore, empty containers of questionable sweet and sour chicken from the Golden Palace littered Billy's desk, competing for space with printouts of trading data and market reports, while Declan ate his chicken fried rice and crispy shredded beef, and Jess ate what looked to be a painfully hot, vegan Thai-style curry with no qualms whatsoever.

'If you're going to stare at that screen much longer,' he

said to Billy, 'you might want to actually blink occasionally. Your food's getting cold.'

Billy looked up from his computer, bleary-eyed. The faint glow of his monitors made him look almost spectral in the dimmed office lighting.

'Sorry,' he smiled, picking up his titanium chopsticks and tucking in – of *course* he had his own chopsticks in his desk drawer – as he turned back to Jess and Declan. 'These old Essex Rider cases ... there's got to be more to them.'

'I was thinking the same thing,' Declan agreed. 'But until we work out what it is –'

'I've worked out what it is,' Jess said from her current position on the floor, surrounded by printouts and food containers, and Declan almost wondered whether she'd been waiting for the right moment to say that. She'd been checking market data on her phone, flicking between apps with the casual expertise of a teenager, but Declan couldn't help but notice it also kept buzzing with texts she was clearly trying to ignore.

'You can answer those, you know,' Declan said quietly. 'I'm not going to tell you off for personal calls.'

'No point,' Jess sighed, tossing her phone aside as she tucked back into the food. 'Prisha's got mock exams tomorrow. She's probably just sending me revision panic messages again.'

'And you're not answering because ...?'

'Because I've got my own revision to do, and every time we talk lately it turns into this whole thing about how we never see each other, and then I feel guilty about being here, instead of studying, and ...'

She stopped, realising both Billy and her father were staring at her.

'What?'

'Nothing,' Declan said carefully. 'Just remembering what A-levels were like.'

'Yeah, well, at least you didn't have to juggle them with solving crimes.'

'No, I just had to juggle them with Kendis throwing things at me,' Declan grinned at her eyeroll. 'Seriously though, if you need to go –'

'Dad.' Jess fixed him with a look that was pure Elizabeth Farrow, her mother's eyes shining through. 'I'm fine. Besides, this is more interesting than romantic poetry. Look.'

She held up her phone, showing a trading chart.

'So, you know how back when you were working the Bernard Lau case, I was explaining about pump and dump schemes in crypto?'

'How does a then-fifteen-year-old know about pump and dump crypto schemes?' Billy paused, a mouthful of rice making him hard to understand.

'Sonya Hart came to my school and taught us.'

'Wait, *the* Sonya Hart? DCI Ford's little helper Sonya Hart?'

Jess grinned at Billy's obvious confusion, and Declan remembered back to the case. He'd been trying to work out random words on a note, and Jess had picked up on one of them.

'*It's a new Yield Farming coin, but it's aimed at helping people rather than just making money. It's called the Robin Hood Token.*'

'*HOOD?*'

'*Exactly. It rocketed up in price. Nobody expected it. Created by an unknown developer known as ScarletKitty.*'

She'd then explained to him how her school had attended an assembly called *policing the unpoliceable – staying safe in a world of rug pulls and crypto scammers,* and one of the officers had been DC Sonya Hart. Declan almost considered explaining this to Billy, but he was already staring back at the screen, lost in his own thoughts again.

'Anyway, when we were looking at the $HOOD coin back then, I saw the pattern,' Jess said. 'The way certain accounts would move just before a big price swing. Well, this is the same thing, just with boring grown-up stocks instead of altcoins; instead of Discord and Telegram channels pumping up some stupid coin, you've got theatrical robberies distracting everyone from the real action.'

She grinned.

'The principles are the same – it's just the scale that's different.'

'Like today,' Billy nodded, turning one of his screens. 'There's a ton of share prices, all connected to Infrastructure companies and conversations Baker's been having, bouncing all over the place.'

'How do you mean?'

'I mean over the last six months, Baker and his Government have been pushing for a new infrastructure deal in the UK, building massive data centres and going back to PFI deals with outside contractors, like both John Major and Tony Blair did,' Billy explained. 'Now, if a Treasury Minister – say, one with access to highly sensitive documents – was handed a briefcase full of delicate information, what do you reckon would be inside?'

'Probably government contracts connected to these upcoming agreements?'

'Exactly. We're talking multi-million, maybe even billion-pound deals, with all the prettiest companies lining up for a slice of the pie. If someone knew which firms were about to win those contracts before the announcements were made? Boom – you can buy shares before the news gets out, and the prices shoot up overnight. Likewise, get out of stocks that don't get considered for the dance.'

'Buy the rumour, sell the news,' Jess added.

'Exactly. That's insider trading gold,' Billy nodded at this. 'Then you've got policy changes. New tax breaks, incentives, regulations; things that could make or break a business. Say the government favours a certain sector, like renewable energy for data centres. Investors catch wind of that early. They'd pile in before the market even knew what was happening.'

Billy was on a roll now; it was fascinating to watch.

'Land acquisitions, that's another big one. If the government's buying up specific sites, property values in those areas will skyrocket. Some lucky bastard with the right intel could make a killing before anyone else even knows what's coming. And let's not forget funding; if they're throwing potential billions at this project, where's the money going? Who benefits? A little leak here, a strategic investment there – suddenly, someone's portfolio is looking very healthy.'

He turned back to Declan.

'Finally, we've got partnerships. If a small tech firm gets in bed with the government on this, their stock price will go through the roof. That kind of info in the wrong hands? It's a licence to print money. So, when I look at these numbers bouncing all over the place, tied to the exact conversations Baker's been having? Well, I don't believe in coincidences. Either someone's leaking, someone's trading, or someone's being very bloody stupid.'

'How do you know which ones to check?' Jess asked, and Declan wondered if this was less a case of her asking for the case, but more her asking so she could get a piece of the action too.

Billy let out a sharp breath, tapping a few keys and flipping between graphs on his screen.

'Alright, look, stocks don't just move on their own. Not like this. You get steady climbs, gradual dips, sure. But these?' He pointed at a jagged spike on the screen. 'This is someone getting a tip-off. This is money moving before anyone should officially know anything. I don't need to know what's in the briefcase. I just need to watch who Baker talks to and when. He meets with a Treasury official at two. By three, some obscure infrastructure firm suddenly sees a surge in investment. He's on a call with a telecoms CFO at three? By four, there's unusual trading activity in networking stocks. It's like watching dominos fall – someone always moves first.'

'But this isn't about Baker.'

'No, and it's not just one company. It's clusters,' Billy admitted. 'If it was a lucky guess, you'd see one or two trades. But as soon as the market opened today, I saw spikes across multiple sectors: construction, data storage, logistics. That means whatever Baker is working on is big, and someone's moving on it. The thing is, this kind of movement isn't normal. It's not retail traders getting excited. It's institutions – big money – buying in bulk before the news goes public because they know what's coming. And if *they* know, then someone, somewhere, is leaking. More importantly, if I can find this, then it won't be long before the finance journalists find it, too.'

'Do we know the companies?'

'They're shell companies, and there's a lot of red tape we need to unravel,' Billy grinned. 'And that always means ...'

'Dodgy things,' Jess smiled. 'See? I am listening to what you say, Dad.'

'But why go to all this trouble?' Declan asked. 'A theatrical highway robbery seems a bit extreme just to hide some dodgy trading. And it's not like the commission that was created the last time is still going.'

'True,' Billy said as he pulled up a webpage. 'But here's the weird thing – they never published any findings. The commission just ... stopped. Right when the robberies did.'

'How'd you find this?' Declan asked.

'Because they had a website,' Billy replied. 'Archived now, but still there if you know where to look. All very official – "Market Integrity Commission" and lots of stuff about transparency. But they only ever published interim reports. Never any conclusions.'

Jess's phone buzzed again. This time, the message preview caught Declan's eye.

miss you x

It was a simple message, but Declan saw it made his daughter's shoulders tense.

'Right,' he said, standing. 'Billy, keep digging into that. Jess, go home. Call your girlfriend. Remind yourself there's life outside this building.'

'But I've got more data to –'

'The case will still be here tomorrow. Your A-levels won't wait,' he smiled. 'Besides, if you fail English Lit, your mum will actually murder me this time.'

'That's emotional blackmail.'

'That's parenting.'

Jess gathered her things, trying to hide her annoyance at being "parented". At the door, she paused.

'Dad? That thing about you and Kendis Taylor during A-levels ... did you really –'

'Let's just say there's a reason I duck whenever someone holds a copy of *Wuthering Heights.'*

After she'd gone, Billy looked up from his screens.

'You know she'll be back first thing tomorrow?'

'Course she will.' Declan settled into a chair. 'She's her father's daughter. But for now, tell me more about this commission and their lack of findings. Maybe somebody was using the commission to find targets?'

'What do you mean?'

'Think about it. You're investigating suspicious trading. You find something dodgy. But instead of reporting it ...'

'You rob them,' Billy finished. 'Take whatever evidence they've got.'

'And make it look like a theatrical robbery so nobody looks too closely at the financial side.'

Billy nodded slowly.

'That's ... actually quite evil.'

'Question is,' Declan said, 'who was really pulling the strings? The Essex Rider? Lord Carmody? Or someone else entirely? And why did the robberies stop?'

His phone buzzed. A message from De'Geer.

Need to talk tomorrow. Think I've found something about the Rider.

Declan looked at the time; it was gone nine.

We could talk now?

> I need to check some old footage, Guv. It'll
> take a few hours. Need to be sure.

Declan grinned; the lessons De'Geer had picked up from Doctor Marcos had rubbed off, it seemed. Whatever he'd found would have to wait until morning.

'I'm checking if Anjli's finished in Westminster, and then I'm meeting her for dinner,' he said as he gathered the containers up. 'You should do the same.'

'Not until I know for certain Uncle Chivalry's gone too,' Billy grinned. 'And didn't you just have dinner?'

Declan looked guiltily back at the containers.

'Shit,' he muttered. 'Well, she can eat. I can –'

'Watch?' Billy grinned. 'Why Guv, I never realised you were into that –'

He didn't move quick enough to avoid a spring roll in the face.

11

THE STUNT RIDER

ALTHOUGH DECLAN HAD OFFERED TO HANDLE THE MATTER IN the meeting, it was Anjli who had instead travelled to the Houses of Parliament to meet Jennifer Farnham-Ewing. Partly, it was because she didn't trust Declan not to strangle the woman when he saw her, but there was also an element of jealousy. Not that Declan would ever do anything with Jennifer, no, Anjli wasn't jealous of that. It was the fact that Declan traversed the back rooms of the halls of power, something that Anjli, as a child, had always dreamed of doing herself.

She still remembered one of the first times she'd worked with Declan, standing in the octagonal Central Lobby, giving him an impromptu history lesson about the place. She'd kicked herself afterwards, convinced she'd completely ruined her first impression with her boss. As it turned out, years later, she now knew this was possibly one reason he'd fallen for her.

Still, it hadn't earned her the chance to walk around Westminster in her own right.

She'd called ahead, using Charles Baker's name with great abandon. If they were going to be classed as a government-sponsored task force for the moment, they might as well use that to *see* the government. And so, it was actually in Portcullis House, on the other side of the A302 and across from Big Ben itself, that Anjli now walked, heading towards the offices of the MP for Woodley in Berkshire, Jennifer Farnham-Ewing.

If she was being honest, Anjli would admit that the woman had been a bloody nightmare, and an absolute thorn in the side of the Last Chance Saloon over the years. Jennifer had first appeared on their radar as an aide to Charles Baker and had immediately felt that the Last Chance Saloon wielded some kind of undue influence over him. From the outset, she'd been a problem. She'd worked under Will Harrison – just a pair of legs and a decent typing ability back then – though, in a way, Anjli respected her for stepping up.

Jennifer could have stayed anonymous for the rest of her life, but once she'd gained Charles Baker's ear, she'd made waves. Not only did she have Westminster's security ban Declan's entrance on a crucial evening – when doing so nearly allowed a killer to poison the entire Cabinet, as well as the Queen, at a state dinner – but once brought back into the fold, she'd pushed for a ridiculous justice bill which hadn't just caused issues for one of the Last Chance Saloon's cases, but it had also relied on information she shouldn't have had access to in the first place, when a killer had provided her the GPS location of a body ... and she'd used it for her own advancement, rather than passing it on to the police.

That had been the last straw. She'd been banished deep into the bowels of Westminster until a kindly donor, using family connections, had arranged for her return via a by-election in a safe seat in Berkshire. Since then, Anjli knew Jennifer had been spending her time in Parliament boosting herself some right-wing alliances. The last time they'd spoken, Declan had even called her out on it, especially when it was discovered she'd been hacking into her old accounts to settle grudges, ones that blew up on her in a meeting with both Declan and Baker on the Members' terrace.

Declan had even recorded it for Anjli. She could hear Baker's threat as clear as day.

'I'm glad to have you in my party, and I expect you to be one of my most loyal MPs while I'm in power. In fact, I would expect you to dive in front of any bullets fired at me across that floor, or in the back rooms you've become so fond of frequenting. Because the moment you step out of line, you conniving little cow, I will make sure that everybody knows just how involved you were in all of this. How you made your play and failed on your first go.'

Charles Baker, though, saw Jennifer's influence as an asset rather than a threat; his own position in the party now becoming precarious, and with a couple of years left before he had to call an election, the vultures were already circling. Keeping someone like Jennifer close made strategic sense to him, and even though it was blackmail that kept her there, Anjli could see her staying for power's sake, and probably a chance to secure some ministerial position down the line.

Regardless, Jennifer had done Charles Baker's dirty work the previous day, and now Anjli wanted her to explain why.

Jennifer was sitting at a desk in a cramped office. She was only an MP, not a minister, so she didn't have a luxurious, open-plan workspace; most MPs ended up sharing offices in Westminster, as the expectation was they'd spend the majority of their time with their constituents, rather than in Parliament. She was surrounded by papers and empty coffee cups, and still looked exactly like her official parliamentary photo – long blonde hair that probably cost more than Anjli's monthly salary, careful makeup even at this hour and clothes that screamed Savile Row, or whoever did similar for women. However, it was also an austere look, as if the twenty-something was trying to look older than her real age, likely sick of the fact she was the "baby of the house" right now.

But there was something else, something beneath the polished surface. Tension, maybe. 'Detective Inspector Kapoor,' Jennifer's smile was pure PR training, as she looked up and saw Anjli. 'I wondered when someone would come asking questions.'

'Did you?' Anjli remained standing. 'Interesting. Most people would assume we'd be too busy investigating the actual robbery.'

'Please,' Jennifer gestured to a chair. 'I've been in politics long enough to know how these things work. Someone always follows the paper trail.'

'If there's anyone who should be worried about paper trails, it's you,' Anjli smiled darkly. 'Is that what this is? A paper trail?'

'That depends on what you're looking for,' Jennifer's smile didn't waver. 'Tea? Coffee? I'm afraid it's the machine stuff, but it's better than nothing.'

'I'm fine,' Anjli sat, noting how Jennifer's hand trembled slightly as she reached for her own cup beside her on the cluttered desk. 'Tell me about the briefcase.'

'What about it?'

'You handed it to Lord Carmody at the Dorchester. Why?'

'The Prime Minister needed him to review some documents.' Jennifer shrugged. 'I was merely the messenger.'

'He's still got you doing the shit jobs, then?'

Jennifer went to snap back a likely arrogant reply but then stopped herself.

'Yes,' she admitted. 'But I treat it as a learning experience.'

'Learning how to be a better member of the public?'

'Learning how to hide my tracks better.'

Anjli snorted. *At least she was being honest.*

'So, you did this at a charity event?'

'Government doesn't stop for fundraisers, Detective Inspector.'

'No,' Anjli agreed. 'But it usually follows basic security protocols. Sensitive documents aren't usually handed over at public events.'

Something flickered in Jennifer's expression.

'The Prime Minister has his own ways of doing things,' she said, and there was almost a slight tinge of irritation in her voice – Anjli couldn't tell if it was against her, or about being Baker's whipping-girl right now.

'Tell me, does Lord Carmody share your right-wing tendencies?'

'You're mistaken. I don't have any.'

'My mistake, let me rephrase that. Does Lord Carmody share your *friends*' right-wing tendencies?' Anjli smiled. 'You know, maybe share a WhatsApp group or two? I'd love to know what they think about people like me on there.'

'I'm afraid people like you don't even register on their radar –' Jennifer, realising what she'd just said, placed a hand in the air to pause Anjli. 'And by "people like you", I, of course, mean insufferable busybodies. Are you suggesting –'

'I'm not suggesting anything,' Anjli interrupted. 'But here's what interests me. You handed over that briefcase, but according to the event schedule, you weren't even supposed to be there.'

'Plans change.'

'They do,' Anjli agreed. 'Both calendar and personal. Did you arrange anything with Carmody to get back at Baker? Perhaps you decided to screw Carmody over to gain an ally elsewhere?'

This time, the reaction was unmistakable. Jennifer set her cup down carefully, precisely, like she was afraid it might explode.

'I think,' she whispered, 'that you should speak to my solicitor if you're going to accuse me of anything untoward.'

'Why? Have you done something untoward? Maybe something that requires legal counsel?'

'Detective Inspector,' Jennifer's voice was steady now, controlled. 'I handed Lord Carmody a briefcase containing documents the Prime Minister needed him to review. That's all. If you have questions about the contents, I suggest you ask Charles Baker. Though I doubt he'll tell you anything more than I have.'

She stood, smoothing her skirt.

'Now, if you'll excuse me, I have a late vote to attend.'

'I thought late votes were only on Mondays?'

'Sometimes we get to spend other evenings here, rather than going home,' Jennifer replied cooly. 'It's a "perk" of the job, if you like.'

The sarcasm wasn't wasted, but even though the obvious suggestion was for Anjli to leave as well, she remained seated.

'One more thing. The woman in the champagne dress. The one who left with Lord Carmody. Did you arrange that too?'

Jennifer paused at the door.

'I have no idea what you're talking about,' she said, and,

deciding Anjli wasn't going to be following her, turned to leave. 'I'll have security escort you out.'

'Look, if you're not involved, at least help me,' Anjli rose. 'What am I missing?'

'A Temple Inn officer? I'd say you'd miss –'

'Don't finish that,' Anjli growled. 'I might not be DCI Walsh, who we all know you hate, but you know damn well every time you've come at us, you've lost. You do it again? You'll only lose again. So, I repeat. What am I missing?'

Jennifer checked her watch and sighed.

'Let's be honest, Anjli – can I call you Anjli?' she asked. 'Charles Baker doesn't like Lord Carmody. He's never liked the man. He's nothing more than a holdover from a previous Prime Minister, and he's only in Parliament to keep some of the toffs in the House of Lords happy. If Baker could get his own way, he'd have him out on his arse as quick as possible. The man's nothing but a parasite.'

'How so?' Anjli asked.

'You become an MP, you get paid,' Jennifer explained. 'Cabinet Minister? More money. The more responsibility you get, the bigger your wage. But Lords, well, they don't get paid to be a Lord, it's part and parcel of being a Lord.'

'I thought they get an allowance?'

'True, but they'd actually have to keep attending to get that. And honestly? From what I hear about his debts, it just about breaks him even.'

'Debts?'

'Old houses and stately homes are notoriously expensive,' Jennifer replied. 'So, the only way that Carmody gets to make any money out of this is by being a Minister.'

She looked away for a second, as if deciding whether to continue.

'I mean, the only legal way, that is.'

'What would an illegal way be?'

'Well, I think Carmody realised quickly that if you're not drawing an additional MP salary, then the boost to Minister is less than he'd make as a Lord. But he'd also have learned that if you're in charge of a financial authority, especially one that deals with shares and institutions, you have advanced knowledge on a lot of different things. If you have contacts who can make trades for you, hypothetically you could make a lot of money. Enough to keep a crappy old house up north working on a far lower salary than you could claim.'

'That's quite specific.'

'I'm not saying anything,' Jennifer muttered stiffly. 'I'm just making a point that Carmody is a nightmare. Honestly, Charles has been trying to find a way of making him leave for ages.'

'And you think this ...?'

'Oh God, no.' Jennifer waved her hand dismissively. 'Baker's not that stupid. He wouldn't give details to Carmody, hoping to see them stolen. It's risky enough as it is, doing this. If word got out... No, he wanted them given to Carmody late at night to piss him off. He wanted him to be unprepared for the meeting the next day. Things like that could give him excuses to remove him at the next shuffle.'

'There's a cabinet reshuffle coming?'

'There's always a cabinet reshuffle coming,' Jennifer smiled. 'Add enough red to your ledger, and you're removed from the next batch. Carmody was on his way out. Someone else would probably take his place. Maybe a nice right-winger, as you said. Somebody against Joanna Karolides; she's currently Baker's major rival for Prime Minister. If the party starts sending letters into the 1922 committee, anyway.

Maybe even Tamara Banks – she's more Teflon coated than I am, it seems.'

She chuckled.

'And there Carmody is, getting caught in a highway robbery with a hooker by his side. It hasn't been announced to the press, but it will get leaked. He's not exactly the most liked person if it hasn't already been put out there.'

'I thought you didn't know about the woman.'

'Not the details, but people do talk,' Jennifer shrugged. 'Let's put it this way, it wouldn't surprise me if, in the next few days, Lord Carmody decided he wanted to step down from politics in order to "spend more time with his family". Although that would probably very much piss his wife off. I understand she's been learning how to play tennis recently.'

'You think his staying around the house would affect her game?'

'As long as he kept out of the bedroom while she's in there with her tennis instructor, I think she'd be fine with it,' Jennifer grinned warmly, showing genuine emotion. She was amused, and Anjli found it off-putting that her first real happiness was as she thought of something bad happening to somebody else.

'Look, I would say this has been a pleasure seeing you, but it hasn't been,' Jennifer checked her watch again. 'Baker has something over me, and he'll keep using it until he gets bored. My only options are to remove him, but if I do, then I could be thrown out with him. So, for the moment, it's option two, where I wait to play my cards. If you're clever, Detective Inspector Kapoor, you'll start making friends in Westminster who aren't Charles Baker.'

'With the best will in the world, Miss Farnham-Ewing,'

Anjli gave a warm smile in return. 'I never *was* friends with Charles Baker.'

'Well, that's a start then,' Jennifer nodded. 'Anyway, if I hear anything, I'll let you know. You should have a chat with Matthews, though.'

'The close protection officer? Really?' Anjli asked. 'He's been avoiding our calls.'

'Of course he has,' Jennifer nodded. 'I saw him last night at the party. That man was trashing more coke than Pepsi did in the nineties.'

With this passing comment, Jennifer Farnham-Ewing gave a brief nod, and left Anjli alone in the office.

Sighing, Anjli checked her watch, wondering whether the gift shop was still open, before heading off.

As she was about to walk out of the Portcullis House Atrium, however, she saw a man approaching from the left-hand side. He was in his late fifties, perhaps early sixties, but looked good with it. He was slim, muscled, and showed no sign of grey in his short, slightly messy brown hair. He had a smattering of stubble and the appearance of someone East European, his suit was bespoke, and his tie likely more expensive than her entire wardrobe.

'You,' he said. 'You are police, yes?'

The accent was indeed East European, and Anjli wondered whether this was the mysterious Mikhail Stefon.

'I am,' she replied. 'And you are?'

'I am Mikhail,' Stefon replied.

'Ah.' Anjli smiled. 'We've heard about you.'

'Nothing good, I hope.' Stefon gave a charming,

disarming smile at this, but Anjli wasn't in the mood to be charmed right now.

'Tell me, Mister Stefon,' she said, 'what exactly do you do in Westminster?'

'I work for people who are very important,' Stefon replied casually. 'I arrange events, sort out travel for various visits.'

'Really,' Anjli nodded, pulling out her notebook and noting this down. 'And I'm assuming that drugs and prostitutes are added into this?'

'I would never ...' Mikhail Stefon shook his head vigorously, but the smile stayed, as if he was playing a game and knew that she was part of it. '... never, do something like that, Detective Inspector Kapoor.'

Anjli looked up from her notes at this. *She hadn't given her name.* That he knew it, and had made his way over to her, showed that this was not an accidental meeting.

'So go on, then,' she said. 'Explain to me why you want to talk.'

'I think there is a confusion here.' Stefon frowned. 'I was given the impression that you wanted to talk to me.'

'And who would have given you that?' Anjli asked, looking back across the Atrium, and wondering whether Jennifer Farnham-Ewing had been passing messages out before she went to take her bill. Mikhail Stefon, after all, was exactly the kind of person Jennifer Farnham-Ewing would use.

Stefon moved to the side of the open space, allowing some civil servants to walk past as he turned and faced Anjli.

'You wish to talk to people about Lord Adrian Carmody,' he said. 'You are concerned about what happened last night. Whether I am somehow, in some way, involved, yes?'

'The thought had crossed our minds,' Anjli replied. 'Would you like to prove us wrong?'

'I would always like to prove people who believe I am the enemy wrong,' Stefon shrugged. 'But this is neither the time nor the place.'

'Really,' Anjli said. 'Perhaps we can make a different time and place? An interview room in Temple Inn. Tomorrow, ten o'clock.'

Stefon responded by pulling out his phone, opening a calendar app, and checking his schedule for the following day. There was a long, quiet minute of tapping on his phone before he looked back up.

'That is doable,' he said. 'But it would have to be ten-fifteen.'

'We're flexible,' Anjli replied, noting this down. 'Did you provide the woman for Lord Carmody?'

'I provide a lot of things for Lord Carmody,' Stefon replied. 'But if you want to know exactly what I procured for him last night, I am afraid you will have to speak to my solicitor.'

He checked his phone.

'I am very sorry,' he said. 'There is a bill being passed right now in Parliament, and I must speak to a couple of MPs before they go to take their vote.'

He turned to leave, but as he moved away Anjli paused him, grabbing his arm.

'I understand you're ex-Yugoslav military,' she said.

At the phrase, she saw Stefon tense and wondered whether he was surprised that they'd found out so much about him already.

'As a teenager, you were expected to provide one year of conscription in the Yugoslav People's Army,' he said. 'Luckily for me, it dissolved in 1992, following the breakup of Yugoslavia, and I was able to forge my own path after a year in service.'

'Yeah, yeah, whatever,' Anjli replied. 'Did they teach you explosives?'

At the question, Mikhail Stefon now turned to face her.

'Because I was in the military, you believe I understand explosives?' he asked. 'Is that how it works?'

'I don't know. You tell me.'

'Maybe you should ask Detective Chief Inspector Declan Walsh,' Stefon replied, the slightest of smiles creeping back onto his face. 'After all, he was in the army. Military police. Corporal, I believe. He would have received the same training I had, and more.'

With that, he carried on walking, leaving Anjli alone in the corridors of Westminster.

However, there was something off about the way he had gone. Something had thrown him, and it was something that Anjli knew, down the line, they'd be able to use somehow.

Could he have provided the explosives on the car?

Closing the notebook, Anjli looked back at the tunnel that led under the street and towards the Houses of Parliament, considering whether she wanted to speak to anybody else while she was here.

Then, eventually, deciding she'd rather have something to eat, she left.

12

LATE NIGHT OFFERS

DECLAN HAD APPARENTLY EATEN BUT WAS HAPPY TO SIT WITH Anjli while she grabbed a late night snack, and so they arranged to meet in Walkers of Whitehall, near Westminster and down Whitehall, where she could at least grab a hastily made toasted sandwich.

'I just don't get it,' Declan said, as they sat at a table by the window. 'I understand why you'd steal the briefcase, I'd understand why you'd want to disgrace Carmody, but why do it as a bloody Highwayman? What's the connection to six years ago?'

'Maybe it's the same people?' Anjli asked.

'I understand that,' Declan nodded, sipping at his Guinness. 'But surely, after six years, you don't want to drag things back. The last thing you want is to let people realise you're still around. The police had pretty much forgotten about these guys. It sounds like the moment Kitson had an accident, they stopped looking at them.'

'Possibly,' Anjli bit into the sandwich, chewing on it thoughtfully. 'Or maybe it wasn't them. Copycat, maybe.

Maybe it's somebody who admired what they did and decided they wanted to continue what had happened.'

'Or it's someone copycatting because he wants the blame to fall on the originals.'

'That's also an option,' Anjli nodded, reaching for her wine and taking a mouthful. 'Do you think Carmody knew what was in that briefcase?'

'Although he keeps saying he didn't, I think he's probably very aware of what was in the bloody thing,' Declan muttered. 'But we won't know until somebody somewhere can explain that to us.'

'Or let's hope Billy can get through with what's happening. What do you think about Farnham-Ewing's revelation of Matthews?'

Declan shrugged, leaning back in the chair.

'Honestly, it explains Harris' reticence to speak in the interview,' he stroked at his stubbled chin as he spoke. 'What was it he said? Matthews wasn't himself? Makes more sense if we know he'd been taking lines in the toilet. Or wherever.'

'It could also explain why Matthews is proving hard to find,' Anjli finished the first of the two toasted sandwiches, moving to the second. 'He knows we'll find out, and once we do ...'

She mimed a gun to the side of the head but then paused.

'So, what do you think's going on with Chivalry and Bullman?'

'God knows.' Declan shook his head. 'All I know is Bullman seems to be regretting her life choices. And Chivalry, well, I think anything to do with Chivalry Fitzwarren involves somebody regretting life choices.'

He was about to continue when a young man walked over. He was in his twenties, with slicked back blond hair and a cheap shiny suit – not a deliberate choice, probably the best he could get on whatever minimal salary he was on. He looked like a car salesman trying to move up in the world.

'DCI Walsh, DI Kapoor,' he said. 'I'm Craig Ellison. I work with Tamara Banks.'

Declan sighed.

'Look,' he said, 'we're not getting in the middle of any pissing contest between Banks and Baker. If you want –'

'No, I'm sorry, Mister Walsh, I wasn't here to speak to you,' Craig interrupted, glancing at Anjli. 'I was hoping to speak to you, ma'am.'

'And why exactly would you want to talk to me?'

'The Right Honourable Member of Parliament is a big fan of yours,' Craig shuffled on his feet, his shiny-blue suit wrinkling as he did so. 'We were hoping we could talk to you about becoming part of her team.'

'Her team?' Anjli frowned. 'I'm a police officer, mate. I don't join teams.'

'It's your police experience that makes you of interest,' Craig quickly added. 'I know the first thing you'll consider is that Miss Banks is using you as a pawn. But I promise you there's nothing further from the truth. She's a massive admirer of yours, ever since you saved her life at that dinner.'

'You know, all I seem to hear about is that bloody dinner right now,' Anjli looked back at Declan. 'We saved Carmody, we saved Banks, we saved Baker. Do you ever wonder how much easier life would've been if we'd just let Helen Gane win?'

Craig, unsure whether or not this was a joke, simply waited before continuing.

'Either way, ma'am, Tamara Banks would like to speak with you.'

'Well, you can tell Miss Banks that I'll have that conversation after I finish this case, yeah?' Anjli gave a warm smile back, but it didn't reach her eyes. 'Now, I'm in the middle of dinner, so please piss off, yeah?'

Craig, if he took any offence at this, didn't show it visibly, as he simply nodded, placed a business card silently on the table, and left.

Declan, watching him go, turned his attention back to his partner.

'You didn't have to be so rude,' he said. 'Poor sod was only doing his job.'

'He's one of Tamara Banks' minions,' Anjli replied, chewing thoughtfully on another piece of sandwich. 'Well, you know what she's like, so if you want to work with her, what do you think he's like? Probably goose-steps around the office and wonders how to put machine-gun nests on Dover cliffs to pick off migrants.'

'So the job offer isn't of interest?' Declan gave a smile, but Anjli, surprisingly, paused, the sandwich halfway to her mouth.

'Actually, I will take that meeting once this is over,' she said. 'But not because I want the job – because I want to see what her game plan is.'

At Declan's frown, she continued.

'Look, everyone's aware that Charles Baker has a connection with us. The running joke is that you're his pet copper.'

'You don't need to remind me of that,' Declan said. 'I'm very aware.'

'Now consider the fact that the other team is moving towards me,' Anjli said. 'Jennifer Farnham-Ewing said something to me today that struck a chord. Baker's going to be gone soon, and when he is, someone new will be in power.'

'Do you think it'll be Banks?'

'It's a possibility. Her, Karolides, a couple of other names I can't think of right now.' Anjli stared at her drink, looking through the glass, deep into the liquid itself.

'It's good to know who the enemy of your enemy is,' she explained. 'And whether they're going to be your enemy as well.'

She shrugged.

'And besides, what do I lose from doing it? Best-case scenario, we work out what her game plan is and what's going to happen to us next. Worst-case scenario, I might get a swanky new job.'

She punched Declan on the arm.

'Don't worry,' she said. 'When I hit the big time, I'll take you with me. You can be my assistant.'

'And Monroe?'

'He can come too,' Anjli grinned. 'And I'll call *him* "lassie" for a change.'

THE CITY OF LONDON WAS NEVER TRULY DARK, BUT THE Financial Conduct Authority's offices tried their best. Power-saving measures meant most floors were in darkness after hours – a fact Martin Reeves was counting on as he used his still-active pass card one last time.

Garden leave, they'd called it. A chance to "consider his options". But they hadn't disabled his access yet, which meant he had maybe an hour before someone in IT noticed the anomaly.

Just enough time to find the proof, again.

The trading floor was silent, his footsteps echoing

between empty desks. His old computer was already packed up – they'd been very thorough about that – but he knew the network backup was still accessible from any terminal. And right now, he needed those Market Integrity Commission files; the records that showed who'd really been pulling the strings six years ago. He'd found the information before, passed it on, even, but it'd been ignored. And the next time he checked into it? It was gone.

He'd sat on it for five years, but when Carmody returned, things had changed. The man was looking to gut services, gain data information. Reeves couldn't, no, *wouldn't* let him do that. He may have been a Treasury Minister, but he hadn't been elected by the British Public. He had an oversight that was beholden to no man, and Reeves needed to find the proof of his suspicions.

'Come on, come on,' he muttered, logging into a random workstation, and slogging through the archaic filing structure – the old case files were still there, buried in the archive system. Trading patterns, market movements, dates that lined up perfectly with each robbery. But more importantly, the commission's internal communications were in a folder with them, the ones that showed who'd known what, and when. He'd thought he'd been on the side of the angels when he'd spoken out about this. But then the commission was closed, and he was left out in the cold.

He plugged in a USB drive, hands shaking slightly as he started the transfer. If he was right about the connection between the Market Integrity Commission, the people who ran it and the current robbery ...

There was a sound behind him; what sounded like a polite cough. He turned, but a beam of light caught him directly in the eyes; a torchlight, the LED's brightness causing him to wince back. Through the afterimage, he made out a figure, their clothing a shadow of another century, a mask over the eyes and a scarf over the mouth.

The Highwayman had arrived.

'I wondered if you'd come,' Reeves said, trying to keep his voice steady.

'Did you indeed?' The figure's theatrical tone carried genuine amusement, and the voice modulator they used gave an almost robotic sound. 'And what, pray tell, did thy expect to find in these hallowed halls?'

'The truth,' Reeves glanced at the screen. The file transfer was still running. 'About what the commission was really doing with the findings. About who was using the robberies as cover. About what really happened to Stephen Mahoney.'

'Ah yes. Your fascinating theory about market manipulation.' The figure moved with what felt like liquid grace between the desks. 'Tell me, did you share these suspicions with Detective Chief Inspector Walsh?'

'I told him enough,' Reeves took a careful step sideways, keeping the desk between them. 'About the pattern. But I told him to look into Emma, just like you said to do.'

'I'm sure it was a compelling narrative.'

'I can prove everything I told him,' Reeves gestured at the screen. 'The trading data, the committee meetings, all of it. They weren't investigating market manipulation – they were coordinating it. Using your robberies to cover his tracks.'

'His tracks? Not Miss Thorne?'

'I ... I think she was involved, but she didn't make money from it like Carmody did. And she didn't blow up Mahoney.'

'And how, pray tell, did the illustrious Lord do that?'

'The explosion?'

'No, you fool. The money.'

Reeves looked abashed.

'Because ... because I told him about it.'

'Yes, Mister Reeves, you did, didn't you? And you believe this makes you valuable?' The Highwayman shook his head. 'It's nothing but dreams, and utterly incorrect.'

'It's not!' Reeves almost shouted, angrily. 'I know how it worked! The whole operation! How you chose the targets, how you used the theatrical robberies to hide what you were really after –'

'My dear fellow,' the figure interrupted, 'what makes you think *I* was the one doing the robberies?'

There was a long, awkward pause at this.

'Wait ... you're not him, are you?' Reeves stopped now, in silent realisation of his error. 'You're someone new. Did he bring you in for this? Did he ...'

The antique pistol caught the light, and if Reeves had seen the photo Matthews took, he would have known it was identical to the one from the recent robbery.

'You don't understand,' Reeves said quickly. 'If anything happens to me –'

'You'll what? Expose the truth from beyond the grave?' The theatrical voice hardened. 'Tell me something, my curious friend. Do you know why highway robbery persists in public memory?'

Reeves took another step back.

'The romance of it, I suppose. The drama.'

'No.' The figure advanced. 'It endures because the victims are forgotten. When you think of great criminals – the Krays, Jack the Ripper, the Great Train Robbers – you remember the names of those who hunted them. Detective Superintendent Leonard "Nipper" Read, Inspector Frederick Abberline, Detective Chief Superintendent Jack Slipper – also known as

"Slipper of the Yard"; their names live on beside the criminals they chased. But highway robbery? The pursuers are footnotes, irrelevant to the greater story. The focus is always ... on us.'

'Please,' Reeves said. 'I can help –'

'Just as you,' the figure continued as if he hadn't spoken, 'are irrelevant to this one.'

The shot was surprisingly quiet. Reeves had time for one last thought – that he should have told Walsh everything instead of playing safe – before the darkness became absolute, Reeves slumping onto the desk's surface, his chest blossoming blood onto his papers.

WHEN SECURITY FINALLY APPEARED, A FEW HOURS LATER AND on a regular security pass, they found only an empty office and Martin Reeves, sprawled across a desk he no longer had permission to use, dying with answers he'd never get to share.

Behind him, the computer screen still glowed, its file transfer frozen at ninety-eight percent complete.

13

FINANCIAL IRREGULARITIES

DECLAN HAD EXPECTED TO BE FIRST INTO THE OFFICE THE following morning; arriving early had become something of a habit since moving to Temple Inn, a chance to gather his thoughts before the day kicked in. He'd usually head in with Anjli when she wasn't using her own car or motorcycle. But he was alone this time, Anjli taking the car into Temple Inn on the off chance they'd need to split attention, and the radio in his car had put paid to any thoughts of, well, gathering thoughts.

'... and in our developing story this morning, questions are being asked after Lord Adrian Carmody was reportedly robbed at gunpoint in Essex two nights ago by what witnesses describe as a modern-day Highwayman ...'

'I know! Can you believe it! Stand and deliver! Dick Turpin's back!'

'We'll discuss this with today's guest, events organiser Derek McAfee, who's organising a Dick Turpin convention, after our next song – here's Adam Ant, and Stand an –'

Declan had turned the radio off after that.

The media scrum outside Temple Inn didn't help his mood.

Camera crews had already set up, reporters doing their early morning pieces to camera. Declan recognised Sean Ashby among them, looking far too pleased with himself for this time of morning.

'Detective Chief Inspector Walsh!' one journalist shouted as they spotted him. 'Any comment on Lord Carmody's female companion?'

'Can you tell us about the dandy Highwayman,' shouted another journalist. 'Or are you too scared to mention?'

Declan threw a weak smile back at that as he pushed through the crowd without responding, catching fragments of questions about theatrical robberies and ministerial security. The lobby wasn't much better; more press, more questions, and a very harassed-looking desk sergeant Mastakin trying to maintain order. Once past the main door, Declan walked through the now-empty corridor before pausing – he could see light glowing through the frosted glass of the morgue's door. It wasn't entirely unusual to find Doctor Marcos in there, having pulled an all-nighter, but De'Geer had recently started coming in early, too. Since his ordeal with Steve Cummings during the whole Reaper return, the sergeant had been throwing himself into work, spending more time examining crime scenes than riding his bike, or seeing Esme Cooper in their own time.

But this was different. As Declan pushed open the office door, he found De'Geer surrounded by paperwork, his usual neat desk covered in what looked like old case files, printouts, and a battered notebook that had clearly seen better days.

Two empty coffee cups suggested he'd been here a while.

'Morning, Guv,' De'Geer looked up, dark circles under his eyes suggesting he hadn't slept. 'Sorry about the mess.'

He held up the morning's edition of The Sun. The headline screamed:

STAND AND DELIVER, MINISTER!

And under it was the photo Matthews had taken; a silhouetted figure, haloed by a motorcycle headlight.

'It's everywhere,' De'Geer added. 'Every paper's running with it. They're claiming his protection detail failed basic security protocols.'

'New lead?' Declan asked, nodding at the rest of the paperwork spread across the desk.

'Maybe, but not from these bloody papers.' De'Geer set the newspaper aside. 'The Daily Mail is having a "list of suspects" betting pool. Names include Richard O'Sullivan and the comedian Noel Fielding, pretty much because they've both played Dick Turpin on TV.'

'We should bring Fielding in for questioning,' Declan suggested. 'Anjli's a massive fan of the *Great British Bake Off.*'

He sighed.

'Okay, so bollocks newspaper pieces aside, what do you have?'

'Remember I mentioned talking to someone about the Essex Rider yesterday?'

Declan nodded, leaning back on a chair. The morning light through Temple Inn's lower windows caught the dust motes in the air, giving the forensic office an almost ethereal quality, which felt at odds with the equipment inside.

'Danny Freeman,' De'Geer continued. 'He was my motorcycle instructor back in the day. Spent months chasing the Essex Rider.'

'DCI Freeman's brother, right?'

'Yeah ... and Guv, I think he might have spotted something everyone else missed.'

He picked up the notebook – its pages dog-eared and stained with coffee rings – and held it out.

'His pursuit logs. Every chase, every detail. But it's not just the routes, it's the way the rider changed over the chases. Started theatrical, ended practical.'

Declan took the notebook, noting the careful documentation of times, locations, even weather conditions. Danny Freeman had been thorough – the kind of thorough that came from someone who had become obsessed with something they couldn't quite catch. Which, if he was being honest, were most police officers he'd ever met.

'The first ones,' De'Geer explained, 'they were like performances. The rider wanted to be seen. There were small variances in style, but the last one. Clinical. Professional. Danny said it was like watching someone new, working from instructions rather than instinct.'

'Like they were following a script?'

'Exactly.' De'Geer shuffled through more papers. 'And there's something else. The bike changed too. First robberies, you could hear the engine – custom work on what he believes was a Ducati, distinctive sound. Last one was quieter, with a modified exhaust maybe.'

Before Declan could respond, his phone buzzed. It was Bullman.

'Yes, boss?' he answered, still studying the pursuit routes laid out before him.

'DCI Walsh.' The voice was crisp, official. 'You need to get to the Financial Conduct Authority building. Now.'

Something in her tone made Declan straighten. Bullman didn't make early morning calls without good reason, and she never called him by his rank unless there were people around.

'What's happened?'

'Martin Reeves was found dead in his office three hours ago.'

Declan felt his stomach tighten.

'Cause of death?'

'Single gunshot wound.'

There was a pause on the line.

'And Declan? Security cameras caught someone shooting him. Someone in period costume.'

'Christ,' Declan was already rising, De'Geer looking up at him quizzically, only hearing Declan's side. 'Have you called Monroe?'

'He's on his way. And I've got Doctor Marcos here now.'

Another pause.

'This isn't a coincidence, Declan. Reeves comes to see us, starts talking about market manipulation and old committees, and hours later he's dead?'

'Any signs of theft?'

'No, but apparently his computer was accessing old Treasury files when he died, ones he shouldn't have had access to, and something about the Market Integrity Commission.'

'I'll be there in ten,' Declan ended the call, turning to De'Geer. 'The motorcycle details will have to wait. You'd better come along as well. The man who came to see me yesterday's been shot and killed, possibly by the Highwayman. Marcos is on her way there. Or she's already arrived, appearing in a puff of smoke every time a crime scene is examined.'

De'Geer tidied up the files while Declan typed a message to Anjli; he needed to not only warn her about the press but also about this.

'Should we wait for the others?' De'Geer asked.

'No time.' Declan was already moving. 'Text Cooper, get her to meet us there. And call Doctor Marcos. She's already there, so find out what she's found.'

'You think this is connected to our theatrical friend?'

'Unsure, yet,' Declan pushed through the main doors. 'But if it is, something's changed.'

'How so?'

'Our Highwayman was content with threats and laser pointers when he faced Carmody. This is escalation.'

THE MORNING TRAFFIC WAS ALREADY BUILDING, DELIVERY VANS and early commuters clogging the narrow city streets. De'Geer's motorcycle would have made quick work of it, but in Declan's Audi, they were forced to stay in the traffic.

It didn't stop De'Geer muttering about this, though.

'What did Reeves actually tell you yesterday, Guv?' he asked.

'Not enough.' Declan pulled around a Luton van, muscle memory navigating the familiar streets. 'Kept talking about committees, about patterns they'd found. Said someone was using robberies to cover up financial crimes.'

Declan's phone buzzed again – Anjli this time. He gestured for De'Geer to answer it.

'Sergeant De'Geer here,' he said, putting it on speaker. 'You're with me and the Guv.'

'Matthews isn't answering his phone,' Anjli's voice carried an edge of frustration. 'After what Jennifer told me about his cocaine use, I wanted to talk to him, but he's gone dark. Harris too.'

'The protection officers?' De'Geer frowned. 'Both of them?'

'Both of them. And here's something else – I checked their duty logs. Neither of them signed in this morning.'

Declan exchanged glances with De'Geer.

'When Jennifer mentioned Matthews' habit,' Declan said carefully, 'did she say how long it had been going on?'

'No, but she implied it wasn't new. You think it could have affected his judgment that night?'

'I think we need to find him,' Declan turned onto Cannon Street. 'But for the moment, meet us at the FCA building.'

The Financial Conduct Authority building loomed ahead of them, all glass and steel modernity, completely at odds with the older buildings around it. Two City of London police cars were already parked outside, their lights reflecting off the building's mirrored surface, creating an odd strobe effect in the morning gloom.

Doctor Marcos stood at the entrance, already in her custom grey PPE overalls, speaking to a security guard who looked like he'd rather be anywhere else. She broke off the conversation as Declan pulled up.

'About bloody time,' she called out as they approached. 'I've got a dead financial investigator, a crime scene that's probably been trampled by half of London's "finest", and a security team who seems to think basic forensics protocol is optional.'

'That bad?' Declan asked.

'Worse,' she jerked her head towards the entrance. 'They tried to preserve the scene, but they also decided that pressing every bloody button on his computer would be a good idea, trying to see what he was looking at when he died.'

'Did they find anything?'

'Apart from destroying any chance of getting clean prints from the keyboard?' Doctor Marcos's tone could have stripped paint. 'Just that he was accessing something called *MIC files*. Mean anything to you?'

'Market Integrity Commission,' Declan replied. 'It's an old committee that looked into the Essex Rider, headed by Lord Carmody.'

'Well, whatever it was, someone didn't want him looking at it,' Doctor Marcos started walking towards the lifts. 'Body's on the sixth floor. Shot once, close range, probably with the same weapon used to threaten Lord Carmody. And before you ask, no, I haven't had time to do a proper examination because security keeps trying to tell me how to do my job. Boots, masks and gloves, guys.'

———————

THE LIFT STOPPED AT THE SIXTH FLOOR, DOORS OPENING ONTO A scene of controlled chaos. Forensics officers in white suits moved carefully between empty desks, photographing and cataloguing. A man in his fifties, suit rumpled like he'd been sleeping in it, was arguing with one of the forensics team.

'I'm telling you, these systems can't just be shut down,' he was saying. 'There are automatic trades running, compliance logs that need –'

'And I'm telling you this is a crime scene,' the forensics officer replied with practised patience.

'Peter,' Doctor Marcos's tone suggested this wasn't their first interaction of the morning. 'DCI Walsh, this is Peter Kendall, head of Market Oversight. He's been helping us understand the systems Reeves was accessing.'

'Trying to,' Kendall corrected, turning to face them. His face showed the strain of someone whose ordered world had suddenly become very complicated. 'But every time I offer to help, I get told not to touch anything or wear the booties and gloves you're wearing.'

'Because it's a crime scene,' Doctor Marcos repeated firmly.

'A crime scene with live trading systems,' Kendall insisted. 'Do you have any idea what happens if these go dark? The compliance implications alone –'

'Someone's dead, Peter,' Doctor Marcos cut in. 'I think compliance can wait.'

Kendall deflated slightly.

'Sorry. You're right, of course. It's just ...' He gestured at the covered body, illuminated by portable lights in the centre of the floor. 'I knew Martin. Worked with him for years. He was an excellent investigator. Thorough. Sometimes too thorough.'

'How do you mean?' Declan asked.

'He never let things go. Even after ...' Kendall caught himself. 'Well. Let's just say his fervour in tugging at threads, even when they went nowhere, ended up costing him his job.'

A white-suited forensics officer Declan didn't recognise approached them, carrying what looked like a crumpled receipt in an evidence bag.

'Doctor Marcos?' The young man held it out. 'Found this

in his jacket pocket. Time stamp's about two hours before death.'

Doctor Marcos took the bag, examining it through the plastic.

'Costa Coffee,' she read. 'Branch on Cannon Street.'

'He talked to me in reception yesterday evening, then vanished,' Declan mused. 'Must have wandered around, gone for coffee, then come back here afterwards, when he knew it was empty.'

'Coming back suggests he was looking for something specific,' De'Geer observed. 'Something that couldn't wait until morning.'

'I don't think they would have let him in once the doors opened,' Declan replied, looking at Kendall. 'He told me he was on Garden Leave.'

'That's shorthand for "piss off somewhere until your notice period is over",' Kendall muttered. 'But yes, you're right. He shouldn't have been back. His computer was locked down, so he used one here to get in through a back door in the system.'

Declan's phone buzzed. Motioning an apology, he turned and took the call.

'Walsh?'

'Got an update, Guv,' the voice of Billy Fitzwarren came through the phone now. 'Doctor Marcos sent me the list of files Reeves was looking at last night, but to do so, I had to be given access to the server.'

'Is that difficult?'

'No, not really, the FCA works with Cybercrime quite a lot, so we have a back-and-forth arrangement. Anyway, I could access Reeve's ID, mainly as he hadn't logged off, and checked the files.'

'And?'

'And nothing, they seem like spreadsheets. However, there *is* something odd. Early days, though. Someone else has been accessing these same files multiple times over the last week. Apparently, it's another name that keeps popping up – Emma Thorne.'

'Emma Thorne downloaded the files?' Declan was surprised.

'No, didn't download, but she did open them,' Billy replied. 'I'm running a database search to see what else she's looking at, but this could take a while, as she probably looks at loads of different files every day. I'll keep you in the loop.'

'Do so,' Declan disconnected the call, noting that Kendall's head had snapped up at the name when he mentioned it.

'Emma Thorne?' His voice carried a mix of recognition and something else. Concern, maybe.

'You know her?' Declan asked.

'Everyone in financial regulation knows Emma Thorne.' Kendall's earlier agitation about the systems had vanished, replaced by something closer to wariness. 'She was a force of nature a few years back. Youngest person ever appointed to a Treasury commission. Had a reputation for being utterly ruthless when she found something wrong, and was tied at the waist to Lord Carmody, on the Commission.'

'What exactly was the Market Integrity Commission investigating?'

Kendall glanced around the trading floor, as if the empty desks might be listening.

'Officially? Market manipulation. Share price fixing. The usual financial wrongdoing, but they'd pivoted to some robberies that seemed to be linked to them.'

He lowered his voice.

'But your man has to be wrong there, DCI. Those files were sealed when the commission ended. Even I can't access them any more.'

'But Reeves was.'

'No, he was downloading them, not opening,' Kendall shook his head. 'He probably wanted to spend time breaking into them.'

'Billy said she was reading them direct off the server,' Declan replied. 'That doesn't sound sealed to me.'

'She could've kept her credentials, I suppose,' Kendall replied. 'They never expire – something about maintaining institutional continuity, and as she was part of the commission that sealed them, maybe she had an override code?'

His expression darkened.

'But she shouldn't be anywhere near this. Not after what happened.'

'What happened?' Declan asked.

When they all turned to look at him, Kendall shifted uncomfortably.

'Look, Martin wasn't stupid. If he came back here at night, accessed those files … he must have had a reason.'

'And Emma Thorne's accessing the same files,' Declan said. 'That's not a coincidence.'

Kendall's phone buzzed, which seemed to surprise him more than anything else. He checked it, his face paling slightly.

'I have to take this,' he muttered, already moving away. 'Treasury calling. Probably wondering what the hell's going on here.'

They watched him hurry towards a quiet corner of the floor.

'Well,' Doctor Marcos said dryly. 'He's not nervous at all, is he?'

'Call Billy, see if we can get someone to track his call logs,' Declan said quietly to De'Geer. 'It's likely an FCA phone, so he might have a way to check quietly. Let's see who at Treasury is making early morning phone calls to a crime scene.'

'Already on it,' De'Geer was typing rapidly on his phone. 'Billy's going to –'

He was cut off by the sight of Kendall almost running towards the lifts, phone still pressed to his ear. The man jabbed frantically at the call button, glancing back at them before practically diving into the opening doors.

'That's not suspicious at all,' Doctor Marcos remarked.

'Get someone on him,' Declan said. 'But quietly. I want him intercepted downstairs.'

'Cooper's closest,' De'Geer replied, already dialling. 'She just pulled up.'

Declan turned back to the crime scene. The USB drive still protruded from Reeves' computer, its small LED blinking steadily. Whatever he'd found, whatever had brought him back here in the middle of the night, it had been important enough to get him killed, even if the download had corrupted somehow.

'Time scale?' he asked Doctor Marcos.

'From body temperature and lividity, somewhere between ten and one in the morning,' she crouched beside the corpse, gesturing at the entry wound. 'Close range, like I said. Weapon was almost against his chest when it was fired.'

'An execution.'

'More than that,' she pointed to powder burns on Reeves' shirt. 'See the pattern? Distinctive. We've seen similar before from the black powder guns used in the Peak District. You know, when they tried to blow you up and leave you to die in a cave. Good times.'

Declan waited patiently, forcing himself not to bite back.

'Anyway, I'd bet my next three months pay it matches the pistol from the Carmody robbery.'

'Same weapon?' he asked, walking back towards the bank of elevators, the second one now opening.

'Or its twin,' she straightened, calling out after him. 'Remember what Chivalry said? These pistols came in pairs.'

KENDALL BURST OUT OF THE REVOLVING DOORS INTO THE GREY morning light, nearly colliding with a newspaper stand. The press pack, who'd most likely followed Declan or Cooper from Temple Inn turned at the commotion, cameras swinging to capture his flight, but before they could react, a diminutive figure in police uniform seemed to appear from nowhere.

PC Esme Cooper moved with the fluid grace of someone who'd practised this moment countless times. Her shoulder caught Kendall at exactly the right point, using his own momentum to take him down. They hit the pavement together, Cooper controlling the fall so his head didn't crack against the concrete.

'Going somewhere?' she asked pleasantly, one knee pressed firmly into his back as she secured his hands.

'You don't understand!' Kendall's words came in a panicked rush. 'They were feeding me the evidence! Operation Highwayman – they used me as their whistleblower. Every robbery, I'd get an anonymous package. Trading records, bank statements, proof of manipulation ...'

He twisted his head, trying to look back at the building.

'I thought I was helping the commission expose corruption, but ...'

He trailed off, genuine terror in his voice. Then, quieter, he continued.

'But they weren't investigating it. They were profiting from it. God help me, I profited from it. They killed him. And now they're doing it again.'

'Who's doing what again?' Declan asked, having taken the next elevator, catching up with them at a far more leisurely pace, while De'Geer moved the officers outside into action, pushing the press away.

'The packages that went to the newspapers,' Kendall gasped. 'After each robbery. Everything the commission was supposed to be investigating. And that call just now ... it was the same voice. The same person who used to contact me about the drops.'

Declan exchanged glances with Cooper.

'Did you recognise it?'

'I never knew for sure,' Kendall had stopped struggling now. 'It's a machine voice. Could have been anyone on that commission. Martin must have figured it out. That's why ...'

He didn't finish the sentence. He didn't need to.

'Take him back to Temple Inn,' Declan growled, looking back at the press. 'And get these bloody vultures away from here!'

'DCI Walsh!' one cameraman shouted. 'How is this connected to Lord Carmody? Is he stepping down because of this?'

Declan stopped, frowning.

'What do you mean, stepping down?'

The cameraman paused, confused, maybe wondering if

Declan was playing with him, but then opened his phone, showing a press release.

'Lord Carmody's making a statement in an hour,' he said. 'Rumours are he's resigning before he's pushed.'

'Are you the one pushing him, DCI Walsh?' Another reporter shouted out. 'Are you removing him on orders from your real boss, Charles Baker?'

'I'm going back to Temple Inn,' Declan muttered to De'Geer. 'Before I start punching people.'

'I could do it for you, if you wanted?' De'Geer smiled.

'Honestly, Morten? Don't bloody tempt me,' Declan started back towards his car. 'Don't bloody tempt me.'

14

RESIGNATION

'NOW THIS IS A FINE KETTLE OF FISH AND NO MISTAKE,' MONROE muttered loudly as he stared up at the plasma screen, connected to Billy's laptop and broadcasting – through iPlayer – Lord Carmody's live resignation speech, currently on BBC News.

Monroe wasn't the only person in the briefing room; Declan and Anjli sat beside him, Bullman standing in her usual position by the door. Doctor Marcos was downstairs, checking into the Martin Reeves autopsy, and De'Geer had recently travelled off to Bethnal Green to speak to James Kitson. Only Cooper sat at the back, and Billy, working on a laptop, looked up, frowning.

'I've never understood that, Guv,' he said. 'Why would you have a kettle of fish?'

'There was a custom, laddie, where the gentry on the Scottish border with England would hold a picnic by the river Tweed,' Monroe explained. 'It was customary to entertain their neighbours and friends with a "Fete Champetre", which they called giving "a kettle of fish", because of live salmon being thrown into boiling kettles".

Billy grimaced.

'Um ... yum?' he muttered, unsure.

Declan glanced back at the door to the office. It was gone noon and Jess hadn't arrived. He was hoping she hadn't been grounded by her mum for staying out late.

'Oh, oh, here we go,' Bullman said, nodding at the screen, where, live, Lord Adrian Carmody walked out of the entrance to his Theydon Bois manor house, to stand at the gate, a sheet of paper in his hand, with his wife, Lady Claire Carmody, behind him and to the side.

'I wonder how much he had to promise her to stand beside him,' Monroe asked.

'I'm not sure what he's actually going to say,' Declan replied. 'Usually a resignation is just that. You don't need to do some kind of PR stunt.'

'Maybe he's aware of how thin the ice he's standing on is.'

On the screen, Lord Carmody, wearing a shirt under a crew neck jumper, as if to try to make him feel more human, looked at the various cameras that were pointed at him.

'Thank you for coming,' he said, as if it was some kind of personal invite party. Of course they'd be turning up. There was a chance to see a cabinet minister collapse in front of them. Perfect TV ... if you were into car crashes.

He cleared his throat and started to read.

'As many of you are aware,' he said, 'two nights ago my car, driving back from London, was held up in a robbery. There's been a lot of conversations about what exactly happened and I'd like to make a statement to put the record straight.'

'Do you think he's going to mention the briefcase?' Anjli

asked, but Declan didn't have time to reply as Carmody on screen had already continued.

'I have been a part of the Government, on and off now for many years, within the Treasury Department,' he continued. 'As such, I find myself attending many events and galas, speaking to various representatives and discussing financial irregularities and laws. I have done my best to uphold my levels of professionalism to the highest, something I expect of others, but two nights ago this did not happen.'

He looked up, and there was a slight glance at Lady Carmody.

Declan narrowed his eyes.

'He's not going to ...'

Again, Carmody had started talking, pausing Declan.

'At the Dorchester, at an event two nights ago, I made a grievous error,' Carmody continued. 'I offered to take an unknown woman home. My wife was in London, and I had imbibed too many drinks that night. It was a rash decision, and one I regret. In fact, we had already decided to take the poor woman to her own home instead – my mistake then realised – but, however, on the London New Road, we were stopped by a masked robber dressed in the guise of Dick Turpin.'

He now looked at the cameras.

'Several years ago, I ran a commission that investigated similar robberies in which a motorcyclist dressed in leathers representing Dick Turpin, including a tricorn hat, would target financial city folk. At the time, this was apparently done to reveal financial wrongdoings before we, and the police, found them and arrested them for their crimes. However, before this could happen, the criminal, who you named "The Essex Rider", disappeared. It is my belief that I have been targeted once more by the same rider, years later.'

Carmody returned to the statement.

'My close protection officers were second to none, but we knew that there were more people out there than we could defend against, with high-powered weapons aimed at us. They gained items of jewellery, government documentation I carried, and other items of worth. These were, however, not worth the lives of these brave men, and in doing so, I realise that through my actions that night I not only put the nation's finest officers in jeopardy but also the life of a woman who shouldn't have been in my car in the first place. I have therefore decided that it is time for me to resign from my position in the cabinet. I have sent my letter to the Prime Minister, Charles Baker, and he has accepted with grace. I intend to spend time now with my family.'

'Bingo!' Monroe shouted. '"Spending time with my family".'

There were questions being asked now, with Carmody folding up the sheet of paper. Declan expected the man to turn and walk away, but Carmody stayed, listening to several of the questions from the crowd of eager journalists.

'Yes, I do believe I was unfairly targeted,' he said. 'But I know also that the press, without full knowledge of the situation, has been having a field day at my expense.'

He gave a weak smile.

'I also understand a certain Highwayman-related song from the eighties is now number one in the UK streaming charts. So, I hope to gain a "thank you" from that.'

Questions were now being shouted to Lady Carmody, who stared, thin-lipped, at her husband.

'That's a divorce waiting to happen,' Monroe muttered.

Carmody had obviously decided he wasn't going to answer any more questions and held a hand up.

'Thank you for your time,' he said. 'I will now return to my previous life as a Lord, and city trader. I will not be working with the government unless requested, but my services will always be available. I am, as I always have been, a public servant.'

'What utter poppycock,' Monroe muttered as Billy turned the plasma screen image off.

'I don't get it,' Declan said. 'Why did he do that?'

'How do you mean?' Anjli asked. 'He had to get in front of it.'

'No, I get that,' Declan replied. 'But he had to know that sure, we'd have found the woman eventually, but he didn't have to step up and throw himself on a grenade like that.'

'Maybe that's what he wanted to do?' Bullman suggested.

'He's given his wife an opportunity to get rid of him,' Declan said, looking back at Bullman standing by the door. 'He's given her every piece of ammunition she needs. She'll gain half of what he owns.'

'Well, from what I can work out,' Billy looked up, 'all she'll get is a knackered old house up north. The Theydon Bois address, which by the way isn't in his name, was a rental apparently, from the Government. Added to that, she'll also get a ton of debt.'

He grinned.

'Also, I looked into the "private club bedroom" she stayed in two nights ago. Apparently she asked for the twin room they'd given her to be turned into a double.'

'Maybe she likes a larger bed?'

'And a second keycard to be coded.'

'Oh,' Monroe's eyes widened slightly. 'Looks like Lady

Carmody may have been playing a few sets of her own with her tennis instructor.'

'And if Carmody knows about this, maybe they're agreeing to just split and keep everything under wraps,' Anjli suggested.

'I feel sorry for the laddie,' Monroe mocked. 'Poor wee Lewis, watching his mummy and daddy break up.'

'Good,' Bullman growled. 'He probably needs the jolt of reality.'

Declan scratched at his head.

'Why am I feeling that we're seeing the wrong side of the story here?' he asked. 'Did you note when he said "government documentation I carried"? It was like he was stating he'd lost valuable data as an afterthought.'

'Maybe he was making sure the people who needed to know, well, *knew*, Guv?' Cooper spoke from the back. 'The government sees that – they know he means the briefcase. He could be covering his back?'

'Okay, so we know someone else is forcing the narrative, so let's look at this morning's addition,' Monroe said, while pacing the incident room. 'Kendall was receiving evidence packages after each robbery?'

'According to his statement.' Declan glanced through the interview notes Cooper had typed up. 'Anonymous drops, always after the Essex Rider struck. Trading records, bank statements – proof of financial manipulation by each victim.'

'Which he then passed on to ...?'

'Various regulatory bodies. Financial Times. Even Newsnight once, apparently.'

'So, he made himself a reputation.'

'Good enough to get promoted to Head of Market Oversight,' Declan confirmed. 'Must have looked great on his CV – the man who helped expose eight major trading scandals.'

'And nobody questioned where he was getting his information?'

'Different times. Pre-Leveson Enquiry. Papers weren't exactly checking their sources too carefully.'

Monroe stopped pacing and dropped into a chair.

'What exactly did he say about the voice on the phone?'

'That it was the same person who used to call about the drops. Someone from the commission.'

'Emma Thorne?'

'He wasn't sure. Said it could have been her, could have been Carmody, that they used some kind of voice modulator.'

'If we can get an audio of it, I can reverse it,' Billy looked up. 'The joy of a modulator is that it takes the original tone and uses one of several ways to alter it. So, the first step is figuring out how – whether it's been raised to sound higher or lowered to sound deeper. By analysing the frequencies, you can measure the exact change and then apply the reverse, bringing the pitch back to its natural range.'

'If it's that easy, why use one?'

'Well, it's not just about shifting the sound back,' Billy admitted. 'Voices have unique characteristics that might get distorted in the process, so you also have to restore the missing tones and balance the harmonics. Done correctly, you can strip away the disguise and recover the original voice, but to do so, it needs to be recorded.'

'Wait ... the security footage of Reeves' Murder, from the FCA would have that,' Declan said, realising. 'Let's just hope they have sound, too.'

'It should come anytime soon'. Billy checked in case an email had magically appeared. It hadn't.

'So, what was he on about when Cooper took him down?' Declan continued. 'Did he explain what he meant when he said he profited?'

'Apparently, our Mister Kendall was taking sneaky peeks at the information, and calling his broker.' Billy waved at the plasma screen, where a spreadsheet had just turned up. 'He did incredibly well from it – through fake corporations created by his broker, that is. He stopped making money shortly before the Essex Rider stopped.'

'Before, or after?'

'Before,' Billy confirmed. 'There doesn't seem to be any profits made after the last time the Rider appeared. Also, he wasn't sent the data.'

'Maybe the Rider realised he was skimming,' Declan pondered. 'Did he – or, rather his broker –make any money this week?'

'Not that I can find,' Billy admitted. 'Anyway, that aside –'

He paused as, through the main doors, Jess Walsh entered at speed.

'Sorry, sorry,' she said breathlessly.

'You don't work here,' Declan smiled. 'You can't apologise for being late if you don't have a starting time.'

Jess however was already beside Billy, their low conversation one of numbers and digits as she gave him a URL to open on his laptop.

'I'm late because I spent the morning going through more images at home, and I found something from the Dorchester,' she explained, sitting down in her usual spot with what looked to be the slightest hints of triumph.

'Your daughter's going through security footage now?' Monroe raised an eyebrow at Declan.

'Social media mostly,' Billy corrected, already pulling up

another window, using the URL she'd provided him to open up a cloud server page, which appeared on the plasma screen. 'You'd be amazed at what people post from charity events. Especially after a few drinks.'

There was a file in the cloud drive, and clicking it, Billy pulled up a shaky phone video, clearly shot by someone at the Dorchester event. The kind of social media post meant to show off that you were somewhere important.

'I found this on Instagram,' Jess explained. 'Some reality TV star decided they wanted to live stream the party and get a photo with Gary Barlow, but he wasn't having it.'

'And we care because?'

'Look behind them.'

As they watched the footage of Gary Barlow politely refusing a selfie or offer to give some kind of TikTok message, behind them, slightly blurred but visible, they could see Jennifer Farnham-Ewing walking up and handing Carmody the briefcase. He looked irritated at the interruption – he'd been deep in conversation with a striking blonde in a champagne-coloured cocktail dress as she did so.

'That's our mystery woman,' Monroe said. 'Got to admit, she doesn't look like someone who'd end up running through Epping Forest after dropping an earring.'

'Farnham-Ewing claimed she knew nothing about her,' Anjli growled. 'Impressive she missed her from three feet away.'

'Watch,' Jess said, and as the now-snubbed reality star wittered on about the charity, acting as if she was the royal correspondent for the BBC in the way she spoke, they could see in the background that the blonde stayed close to Carmody as he made his excuses to Jennifer, before heading towards the men's room, briefcase in hand.

Billy zoomed in despite the image quality suffering.

'And look who follows him in.'

'Matthews,' Monroe leaned closer to the screen. 'Makes sense, as he's the SEG. And he's ...'

'Taking something out of his pocket,' Billy finished, zooming along the timeline. In double speed the reality star now spoke to another man, obviously a friend, and someone who'd had a lot of poor work done to his face.

Billy sped up the footage at Jess's suggestion and after a moment, both men emerged again.

'Both men are in there for just over three minutes,' she explained as, on the screen, Matthews looked slightly unsteady, Carmody still carrying the briefcase.

'So his own protection officer's in the toilet doing lines, while Carmody's got sensitive Treasury documents,' Monroe shook his head. 'Question is, what was Carmody doing in there for three minutes with classified files?'

'If he knew the code to open them, he had time to check them over,' Declan said. 'Glean information from them.'

He slammed a hand on the table.

'That's why he used the "government documentation I carried" line,' he said. 'He's keeping the narrative that he didn't have time to see them. The blonde? She's not a floozy to be seduced, she's his bloody *alibi*!'

'How so?'

'Matthews? Harris? People could say he was coercing them to do what he said. That he spent the entire drive home going through the documents, and that they were forced by loyalty, official secrets, whatever, to keep quiet. But here's an outsider, a stranger. She'll be eventually found, and when she is, she'll admit the briefcase wasn't opened before it was stolen. Perfect witness. Meanwhile, Carmody moves on, his marriage likely over, his money-draining career finished, and his secret stock trades making millions.'

'We need to find this woman,' Monroe muttered. 'Any advances on her pimp? Mikhail Stefon?'

'He spoke to me last night,' Anjli spoke now. 'I think he was feeling us out, working out what we knew. Nothing was said, but I requested he come in this morning at ten and answer questions.'

Declan looked up at the clock, which showed it was past noon.

'I guess he forgot,' he said.

'No, he caught a late flight on a private jet to Prague,' Anjli muttered back irritably. 'Apparently he had a meeting there today he'd double booked, but he's back later today. We'll have officers waiting at City Airport.'

'Good,' Monroe nodded. 'In the meantime, I want this mystery woman's name, and then I want her bloody statement –'

Monroe paused, looking at Billy.

'You okay, laddie?'

'FCA sent the footage,' Billy looked up from the laptop. 'I'm loading it up for us to see.'

'The shooting?' Declan asked.

Billy nodded as the plasma screen flickered to life, showing the FCA's trading floor.

The timestamp read **22 : 47**

The figure that appeared on the bottom left walked with a calm efficiency, costume perfect in every detail. But there was something different about this performance.

'No theatrics,' Declan noted. 'Not like Carmody claimed.'

'Because this wasn't meant to be seen,' Monroe replied. 'At least, not by the public.'

The Highwayman moved through the trading floor like a ghost, no wasted movement, no dramatic flourishes. When Reeves appeared in frame, he was at a desk, scrolling through lines on his monitor screen, unaware of the danger until it was too late.

'Sound?' Monroe asked quietly.

Billy tapped on the keyboard.

'The file was compressed when they sent it,' he muttered. 'Amateurs. I might be able to adjust the codec as it goes along.'

'Whatever you can, laddie.'

On screen, Reeves finally noticed the intruder. Instead of panic or surprise, his posture suggested recognition. He even took a step forward, as if to speak. The two seemed to know each other, and it looked for all intents and purposes to be a casual conversation. Then, there was a loud SQWARK of noise and everyone flinched back.

'Sorry,' Billy replied sheepishly. 'I have sound from here.'

'... *what? Expose the truth?'* The theatrical and modulated voice spoke now. *'Tell me something, my curious friend. Do ... highway robbery ... in public memory?'*

'Codec's still corrupted,' Billy muttered as the scene continued. 'This is the best we'll get.'

'The romance of it, I suppose. The drama.'

'No. It ... the victims are forgotten. When ... great criminals – the Krays, Jack the ... Great Train Robbers – you ... those who hunted them. Detective ... "Nipper" Read ... known as "Slipper of the ... beside the criminals they chased. But highway robbery? The pursuers are footnotes, irrelevant ... focus is always ... on us.'

'Please, I can help –'

'Just ... irrelevant to this one.'

The shot, when it came, was brutally efficient. No

theatrical declaration, no "stand and deliver", just the flash of the antique pistol and Reeves crumpling across his desk. The Highwayman stared down at the body for a moment, as if checking Reeves wasn't faking, before leaving.

'Can you de-modulate from that?' Declan asked.

'Hopefully,' Billy mused. 'It's compressed, but I should be able to play with it.'

Declan was about to continue when his phone rang.

'Oh, Christ,' he muttered, noticing the ID before answering it. 'Are you okay to go onto speaker? I'm in the briefing room with the rest of your new task force.'

There was a moment of silence as Declan listened and then he pressed the button, ensuring that everybody could now hear the dulcet tones of Charles Baker.

'Hello, my loyal task force,' Baker replied. 'Daddy's here.'

15

SOCIAL MEDIA

'I'M GUESSING YOU SAW IT,' BAKER SAID.

'We did,' Declan replied, 'and I'm honoured you decided we were the first people you should call.'

'Regardless of whether you think you're our bloody "daddy" or not,' Monroe muttered.

'It's not a social call, Declan,' Baker snapped. 'I want to know what his sodding game is.'

'Funny enough, that's exactly what we were wondering,' Bullman said from the doorway.

'Prime Minister,' Declan started ... and paused as there was almost a guffaw of laughter down the line.

'Oh, I should have you talk to me on speakerphone more often,' Baker said, with humour in his voice. 'You're way politer to me when people are listening.'

'Prime Minister,' Declan continued, irritably. 'It would greatly help us if we knew for sure what was in that briefcase. We've got rumours, and we've got ideas ...'

There was a long pause.

'Tell me what you have, and I'll tell you if you're correct,' Baker replied.

Declan looked over at Billy, who pulled up a document on his computer.

'New tax breaks, incentives, regulations, based around a certain sector, like renewable energy for data centres,' he said. 'The data provided probably looked into the infrastructure too, as part of a revamped PFI initiative?'

'Bloody hell, you really are good,' Baker replied.

'To be honest, sir, I'm not pulling this data out of the air,' Billy replied. 'I've been watching market tradings. As soon as the market opened the day after the attack, companies connected to previous PFI deals but unconnected publicly to anything coming up, were starting to see significant rises in their stocks, bought by newer funds, especially shell companies where I've yet to work out who the owners are ... as if someone knows something big.'

'Christ,' Baker muttered. 'I didn't want bad news, Declan. I called to find out if you had anything good for me.'

'This is good, sir,' Declan replied. 'It means that whoever's seen the data is trying to make money off them. And that'll leave a trail, which'll come back to them.'

'As long as it's not bloody China or another enemy of the state, I suppose we can last a little longer,' Baker muttered. 'At least he didn't mention he'd been given a briefcase filled with top secret data.'

'Sir, I understand that the Theydon Bois address is a Government address that was provided to Lord Carmody?' Anjli asked.

'Yes,' Baker replied. 'It's a building owned by a donor of ours, a foreign business investor.'

'So basically, it's a rich billionaire who doesn't live in the country, who owns property and is quite happy to have someone house-sit it?'

'You might very well think that. I couldn't possibly comment,' Baker said, and there was an element again of humour in his voice.

'Please don't quote lines from *House of Cards* at us, sir,' Monroe replied. 'It makes you seem crass.'

There was a long pause down the line.

'You know, if just once, it'd be nice for the Scottish sod to treat me like a Prime Minister.'

'If I didn't know your past, sir, I think I probably would,' Monroe replied. 'That aside, we think Carmody is throwing himself under the bus in relation to his guest, so he can resign without mentioning he lost the sweetie jar.'

'So, he's actively hoping his wife'll divorce him? Ballsy.'

'I think he already knows the outcome, sir. We believe Lady Carmody is as likely to be having an affair as he is,' Anjli said. 'Also, I spoke to Jennifer Farnham-Ewing last night –'

'Oh God, I hope you washed yourself in bleach afterwards,' Baker muttered. 'Yes, we've heard the rumours too. Tennis coach or something, isn't it? If Carmody's clever, he's decided to throw himself to the mercy of the public, while secretly telling his wife he knows exactly about her own little peccadilloes. Which means that she'll quietly piss off back to wherever she came from, while he keeps his lordship and his manor up north. But he'll have to find some other way of earning money to keep the bloody place going, because he won't be staying in Essex any more.'

Declan frowned.

'I know we've already asked this,' he said, 'but there's no way that Carmody could have known in advance what the documents were, right?'

'No, I threw them on him at the last minute just to piss him off. I mean, he would have had an idea it was coming at some point, but no details.'

'And he did have the code to get into the briefcase?'

'It's the same code we always have, so he'd definitely know that.'

Declan glanced around the room.

'We have video footage of him at the Dorchester, entering the toilet.'

'Good God, what a great case-breaking video that must be, Declan,' Baker grumbled. 'Exactly explain to me why Lord Carmody taking a piss is so important here.'

'Because he went in with the briefcase, sir, and was out of sight for three minutes.'

There was another long silence.

'Well, *that* wasn't in his bloody resignation letter.'

'No,' Declan replied. 'Also, while we've got you here, do you recognise the name Martin Reeves?'

'Reeves? Yes, I do, actually,' Baker replied. 'He's been trying to get hold of the office. Used to work with a committee that Carmody was involved in. Is he worth talking to?'

'Only if you've got a Ouija board,' Monroe muttered. 'The man was shot dead by the Highwayman last night.'

'Goddammit! Who is this bloody Highwayman?'

'That's what we're trying to work out, sir,' Declan said. 'It isn't helped with Carmody doing something like this.'

'Anything else you get, let me know.'

'There is one more thing, sir,' Declan added. 'Another name. Emma Thorne?'

'Oh God, yes,' Baker muttered. 'She was one of Michelle Rose's favourites. Had every opportunity to become something big in the back rooms when Rose took over as Prime Minister. But as Rose only lasted about ten minutes, that never happened.'

There was a long pause, and for a moment Declan wondered if Baker had forgotten he was on a call.

'Oh God,' Baker eventually continued. 'She was always tied to Carmody's apron strings. We always assumed there was some kind of affair going on. I mean, he does like to go for the young ones … but if he's stepping down, I wonder if I'm about to get petitions for her to be involved in the next choice. What's your next plan?'

'Still working on it, sir.'

'Well work faster,' Baker snapped. 'You want to arrest someone? Great. Go wild. Offer a pardon if it helps the case? Sure, why not. Just do whatever you need to do.'

There was another break, and Declan waited for Baker to continue, but then when he looked at his phone, he realised Baker had actually just disconnected. No farewell speech, no orders for him to do something, Baker had simply decided he wasn't going to speak to them any more.

He looked up, surprised, from the phone to the others in the room.

'I think it was a bad signal,' he said almost mockingly.

Monroe was rubbing at his chin.

'Well, now we know why we're on the case,' he said. 'He's scared. You heard him, offering us pardons and arrest warrants willy nilly. He knows his pissing contest, deliberately screwing Carmody over has severely backfired on him.'

He looked around the room, considering the situation.

'Right then,' he said. 'Where are we on this? Give me a chronological situation. Tell me what I'm missing here. Six, almost seven years ago, there was a robber dressed like Dick

Turpin, and was seen eight times over the period of a year, but the motorcycle unit who chased him believed that the last time was a different rider, right?'

'Yeah, although that's Danny Freeman's opinion, and not proof,' Declan said. 'I mean, De'Geer vouches for him, but we can't take that as a fact for the moment.'

'Each robbery was targeting high-level city traders,' Billy continued the recap. 'Shortly after each robbery, a whistle-blower would provide data gained from that Highwayman. Data that was then used by the FCA and the treasury to place sanctions and criminal charges against some of the people. We're talking insider trading and other such things; market gouging, really dodgy crap. Treasury probably wanted to show the public that they were on the case.'

'And Kendall, he was the one who was the whistleblower, right, he made his own money from this?'

'I believe so, according to his statement.'

'Okay, so just under six years ago, the crimes stopped – possibly because the bike rider had some kind of accident,' Monroe finally stopped pacing.

'If it is James Kitson, his accident happened after the seventh,' Declan said. 'There would have been a second rider for the eighth.'

'So, Kitson had a backup.'

'Mahoney probably was, but he died that night as well.'

'The explosion,' Monroe muttered. 'Perhaps Mahoney was the Essex Rider instead?'

'We need more on the explosion that killed him,' Billy replied. 'Maybe it wasn't the accident people expected?'

'Hopefully, Kitson will be telling De'Geer all about that right now,' Declan replied. 'And give us an idea of who could be doing these attacks.'

'Maybe. But there are differences,' Bullman spoke from the door. 'For a start, Kitson – or Mahoney – never killed, never worked with others, never used laser sights and things like that. If it wasn't for the fact this new Highwayman dresses like Dick Turpin and attacked the man who hunted the first one, I would have said this was a completely different situation.'

'Maybe it is, lassie,' Monroe muttered. 'Anything else?'

'Possibly,' Billy leant back in his chair. 'It goes back to Carmody's comment just now about returning to his life as a Lord and city trader. He hadn't traded after he dropped out of Michelle Rose's cabinet, before Baker brought him back. In fact, he worked as a consultant and a public speaker. I checked into it, and his trading licence had been reinstated only a matter of weeks ago.'

'Trading licence?' Monroe frowned.

'To trade stocks in the city, you either need to use someone with a brokerage account or create your own,' Billy explained. 'But it's difficult for most, as you'd need to be regulated by the Financial Conduct Authority ...'

'Who just so happened to be controlled by Carmody until today,' Declan shook his head.

'Problem is, you can't trade when you're a minister,' Billy continued. 'He'd have to put all his businesses into a blind trust or something.'

'He's not a bloody minister now, though,' Monroe muttered.

'So, he knew he was about to be fired? Declan ignored Monroe's sour expression.

'I thought the timing seemed a little suss, so I started looking into it. Eight months ago, Carmody had a spat with his wife ... a very public one.'

'Yes,' Declan nodded. 'I remember Harris telling us about that.'

'Well, it seems this was the point that Carmody learned about the tennis instructor,' Billy replied.

'But he did nothing about this? He didn't petition for divorce?'

'No. Instead, he started creating a new company.' Billy opened up a document on the screen. 'That is, his son was. Just got the information back. As you can see here, *Carmody Holdings* was created about six months back.'

'Another shell company?'

'Quite public, actually,' Billy replied. 'His son, Lewis Carmody went into it with three other men – Carmody senior, but only on the basis he'd become a shareholder once his government tenure was up, an Essex entrepreneur and business owner named Ryan Boyask, and ... Mikhail Stefon.'

It was Monroe who slammed his fist on the desk.

'Carmody played Baker,' he snarled. 'And this random meeting with Stefon and the girl – Sophia – doesn't look so random any more.'

'On that note, we have something on her as well,' Billy grinned. 'Police report. Uniformed officers found a woman walking down the side of the road towards Epping, about two in the morning on the night of the robbery. She claimed she'd got lost, but there was a comment made about how her clothing was a little too mud stained and torn for a woman who claimed she'd simply left a nightclub, although her shoes were clean.'

Monroe swept at his beard with his fingers, clicking his tongue against the back of his teeth as he considered this.

'Tell me,' he asked, 'while looking into this, have you found any details of how long our illustrious Prime Minister has been talking about this PFI infrastructure agreement thing behind closed doors?'

'Since the start of the year. No, wait ... about eight months. Probably since just before the budget,' Billy read the documents again. 'The companies that Stefon lobbies for, and is likely a partner in – a couple of them are connected to this new Government plan. Chances are this is how Carmody found out about it, maybe even before the briefcase was given to him.'

'Chances are Carmody and Mikhail discussed this, but there's nothing illegal about creating a company,' Declan replied. 'However, Mikhail Stefon is sounding more and more connected to this as we go along. And eight months ago is becoming a very interesting time for Lord Carmody. Can we check into this new company and see what's been going on for the last week?'

Billy nodded.

'I'll have to get permission and go through the regulatory committees,' he replied.

'But that shouldn't be difficult, considering the fact that it's one of their own they're worried about,' Bullman suggested.

'I was thinking more about the fact we had the Prime Minister's personal thumbprint,' Billy grinned. 'I've already ordered half a dozen new items.'

'Is that where the bloody monitor came from?' Declan shook his head. 'He might ask for it all back, you know.'

'Let him try,' Billy replied. 'Let him try.'

Monroe went to chide his young officer, but then grimaced as, through the doors, the mismatched tweed of Chivalry Fitzwarren became visible.

'Good, you're all here,' he said, walking in. 'You got my message.'

Declan raised his eyebrows, noticing that everybody else in the room seemed just as surprised.

Billy, however, reddened.

'Sorry, I forgot to mention,' he said sheepishly. 'Uncle Chivalry's turning up again.'

Chivalry glared at his nephew before turning to face the rest of the room.

'I have news. I spoke to my gunsmith friend last night. After I saw you both,' he said, looking at Monroe and Bullman. 'And I apologise, my lady, for interrupting your evening, and this meeting.'

Again, his tone seemed to change and Declan wished he had some popcorn to eat as Bullman's face flushed.

'It's okay, we were discussing the case,' Bullman replied awkwardly. 'And Monroe was explaining to Billy where the term "kettle of fish" came from.'

'Aha!' Chivalry smiled, as across the room Billy groaned. 'The good old kettle is probably derived from Latin *catillus*, which means a "deep pan or dish for cooking". The inherited English form would have been "chettle" due to palatalisation –'

'Pallete-what?' Declan frowned.

'Palatalisation is a phonetic process, where a consonant sound shifts closer to the hard palate because of the influence of a neighbouring front vowel or "j" sound, often changing its pronunciation, as seen in the evolution of "kirk" to "church" in English,' Chivalry explained. 'But the initial consonant in chettle was changed back to a "k" in around 1300, probably under the influence of its Old Norse cognate, "ketil".'

'I have no idea what the bloody hell he just said,' Monroe grumbled. 'Can we talk about the bloody gun, please?'

'Well, of course,' Chivalry continued, unabashed. 'I showed Marius Blake the gun, and he agreed that it was definitely a Griffin & Tow duelling pistol from 1730 ... and that it had been altered to fit a nine-millimetre bullet.'

'And how would he know that from a picture?' Declan asked.

'Oh dear boy, it wasn't from a blasted picture he learned that. He's good, but he isn't that good,' Chivalry laughed. 'No, he knew because he was the one who did it. He was told it was going to be for competition shooting.'

'Wait,' Declan frowned. 'Marius Blake made the gun? In that case, he knows who owned it.'

'Yes, he does ... well, at least he did.' Chivalry smiled. 'You see, the gun, the original, was part of a pair bought at auction in 2003. They went for a pretty penny as well. The winning bid?'

He paused, allowing the moment to build for dramatic intent.

'Lord Adrian Carmody.'

'Son of a bitch,' Monroe muttered. 'He had to know we were going to find this out. This is why he stepped down, did the big PR piece.'

'Possibly not,' Chivalry added. 'You see, a year ago, Carmody claimed he sold them on. Apparently, he had to fix a roof or something and needed the money. The guns brought in close to ten thousand pounds, which, to be honest, I think is actually less than he paid at auction almost twenty years earlier.'

'Who did he sell to?'

'Unfortunately, the sale was private, and I'm yet to find

this out, but dear Marius said the new owners, who bought from Carmody then asked for the guns to be upgraded,' Chivalry said. 'Marius was paid a large amount of money to do this, and when he looked into the accounts, as one would, he was paid through a corporate account of a holding company used for such trades. But the interesting thing was the name of the man who arrived to *give* him the guns.'

'If it's Martin Reeves or James Kitson –'

'God no, nothing so pedestrian,' Chivalry laughed. 'The name of the man who asked for the guns to be altered to fit a nine-millimetre round was *John Palmer*.'

Billy instantly started to type, but Anjli held her hand up to stop him.

'I wouldn't bother,' she said, 'it's fake.'

'And how would you know that?' Billy almost pouted at being stopped from using his computer.

Chivalry grinned as he looked over at Anjli.

'Pray tell, my lady, inform them of who John Palmer was. I'm guessing you know.'

'John Palmer was the name that Dick Turpin was arrested under, and finally hanged,' Anjli gave a small bow to the briefing room as she continued. 'It's the name he used when he tried to change his identity.'

'Makes sense. If someone dressing like Turpin wants a gun that fires a special bullet, they're going to use a Turpin identity,' Declan nodded. 'Still doesn't help us.'

'It does, in a particular way,' Chivalry pulled out a shiny CD. 'On this disc is security footage from the day in question. You will see the man who paid for the gun to be altered for competition shooting.'

'Blake keeps things like this?'

'Blake keeps things when he knows he's adapting a

working firearm,' Chivalry smiled. 'I provide it to you of my own free will.'

He turned and placed it in both hands, almost bowing as he presented it to Bullman.

'My lady,' he said. 'I only hope my work has helped you in solving this case.'

'Okay, are you dying?' Bullman asked. 'Seriously? Is this some kind of brain disease that we don't know about?'

Chivalry stood up, looking shocked at the accusation.

'My lady ...' he said.

'I'm not your lady. Last time we saw each other, I was "Detective Chief Superintendent Bullman". Where has "my lady" come from?' Bullman was getting frustrated now.

'Because he's got a crush on you,' Anjli said, smiling. 'I thought you'd be a detective and understand it.'

'Pish and tosh,' Chivalry waggled his finger. 'I simply claim names for beauty.'

'Christ,' Bullman muttered, mostly to herself as she left the room. Chivalry, to his credit, simply shrugged and replaced her, leaning in the doorway, as Monroe nodded at the disc.

'Go on then, laddie, stick it in your laptop and let's see who this man is,' he said.

However, Billy reddened at the comment.

'I'm afraid I'm unable to do that,' he mumbled. 'Laptops these days don't actually come with CDs.'

'So, how do we do this?'

'I didn't say all my computers don't have CDs, Guv. Just this one,' Billy muttered as he examined the disc. 'Give me ten minutes. I'll have a look on the main computer.'

Monroe sighed, checking his watch.

'I just hope De'Geer's doing better,' he said.

16

WORKSHOP VISIT

THE SHOP SIGN READ "KITSON CUSTOM MOTORCYCLES" BUT from the layer of dust on the window, it hadn't seen any customers for a while. A cardboard "Back in 5" sign hung crookedly in the glass, its edges curled and faded from long exposure to sunlight.

Bethnal Green had changed since De'Geer's last visit – more coffee shops, more street art, more signs of creeping gentrification – but this stretch of railway arches seemed to remain stubbornly resistant to update. Oil stains marked the pavement outside each arch, fighting back at industrial cleaning fluids, mechanical ghosts of decades of repairs and modifications.

He was about to try the door when movement through the window caught his eye. A man had emerged from the shadows at the back of the shop, one hand gripping the edge of a workbench for support. Even in the dim light, De'Geer could see how much effort it took him to stay upright.

'We're closed,' James Kitson – at least De'Geer assumed it was Kitson – called out. His voice carried the strain of someone fighting to maintain balance. 'Workshop's shut till further notice.'

'Detective Sergeant De'Geer,' he held up his warrant card. 'City of London Police. I really need to talk.'

'All my work's above board, and if someone's had an accident, then it's likely user error.'

'Look, I'm not here to confront you on anything,' De'Greer responded, keeping his tone polite. 'I was actually hoping to ask you a few questions about the Essex Rider?'

Kitson's grip on the workbench tightened.

'That was a long time ago.'

'Not as long as you might think, if you read the papers.'

Kitson gave a bitter laugh that turned into something closer to a grimace as he shifted position. The movement sent a stack of magazines sliding off the workbench, their pages splaying across the oil-stained floor, as he waved De'Geer to enter.

'Six years, two months, sixteen days.' He nodded towards a chair as De'Geer entered. 'If you're going to interrogate me about ancient history, you might as well sit. And shut the door – draught plays hell with my balance.'

'How?'

'It makes me cold, I get pissed off, and I fall over.'

De'Geer closed the door but remained standing, taking in the workshop properly now. Despite the apparent neglect of the shopfront, the space was meticulously organised. Tools hung in careful order on wall-mounted boards, each outline carefully marked. Spare parts filled labelled shelves. In the corner, a partially dismantled Norton gleamed under work lights.

'Still doing custom work?' he asked.

'When I can,' Kitson gestured at his own unsteady stance.

'Have to take breaks these days. Inner ear's shot to hell, and I have more metal in my legs than a Suzuki fork – some days I can barely stand, let alone work on bikes.'

He studied De'Geer carefully.

'But you didn't come here to discuss my medical history. Maybe you're here to pillage my womenfolk? You'd be shit out of luck if you are.'

'No, nothing like that,' De'Geer pulled out the battered notebook. 'I'm here about the recent robbery on the London New Road, and as part of the enquiries, I've been talking to Sergeant Dan Freeman, who was one of the police motor-cycle team pursuing the Essex Rider. He suggested I speak with you.'

Something flickered across Kitson's face; recognition, maybe concern. But it was gone as quickly as it appeared.

'Danny bloody Freeman,' he shook his head. 'Should have known he'd never let it go. Man's like a dog with a bone when he thinks he's on to something.'

He slowly made his way over to a high barstool chair, leaning against it with a sigh.

'So, he thinks I'm up to my heinous old tricks again?'

'I don't think anyone thinks that, Mister Kitson.'

'He thinks Mahoney's back from the dead, then? You know it was never proven that I was the bloody Essex Rider, right?'

'I know, sir,' De'Geer moved closer and leaned against the workbench. 'But he said you have a particular style, a way of taking corners, that matched the Rider's style.'

'Had.' Kitson's smile was sharp-edged. 'Past tense. These days I can barely walk in a straight line. So what's Danny been telling you? That I was the Essex Rider? That my accident was convenient timing?'

'Was it?'

'Exhibition centre was cursed.' Kitson's laugh was hollow. 'Place had dodgy electrics; we had issues every bloody week. Water got into the system during a show, fused half the lights earlier in the show, and they lost time. Decided to scrap a stunt, but it meant they didn't drain a fuel tank. They also didn't expect us to clip it. Could have happened to anyone.'

'But it happened to you.'

'Yeah,' Kitson's hand went unconsciously to his head. 'During the explosion, the bike went one way, I went another. Doctors said I was lucky; I could have been paralysed. Instead, I just got this – constant vertigo, random dizzy spells. Try riding a bike when the world won't stay still.'

His voice took on a darker tone.

'But Mahoney was the one who was cursed that night. I landed bad, but he went straight into the tanker. They say he died on impact, but if he didn't, the explosion would have made it instantaneous.'

'Must have been hard,' De'Geer said. 'To move on from that.'

'Harder than you'd think,' Kitson's gaze drifted to a framed poster on the wall – himself in mid-stunt, suspended against a twilight sky. 'Stephen was a brother to me. I had to be there for his parents while trying to keep my own head above water. It was tough ... but that's not why you're here, is it? Someone's playing Highwayman again, and Danny's got you chasing old ghosts.'

Interesting choice of words,' De'Geer said. 'Ghosts.'

'Figure of speech,' Kitson's hand had found the work-bench behind him again, knuckles white against the metal edge. 'Though I heard about Lord Carmody. Theatrical stuff. Almost like someone's trying to make a point.'

'Like someone's copying the Essex Rider?'

'Nobody copies the Essex Rider.' The words came out sharper than Kitson seemed to intend. He took a breath, steadying himself. 'Look, I know what Danny thinks. That I was some kind of modern-day Dick Turpin, targeting the rich and corrupt. But I was just a stunt rider. The accident proved that.'

'Did it?' De'Geer moved closer to the partially dismantled Norton bike at the side of the workshop. 'Because Sergeant Freeman showed me the pursuit logs. Showed me how the riding style changed after your accident. Became more precise. Less theatrical.'

'What are you suggesting?'

'That maybe someone else took over, someone who learned from watching you, or maybe Mahoney?'

Kitson's laugh had an edge of genuine amusement now.

'You think I trained my replacement? In between operations and lying in a bed, morphine'd out of my brain?' He shook his head, then immediately regretted it, grabbing the bench tighter. 'Christ. Do you have any idea what it's like? Spending your whole life in perfect balance, knowing exactly where you are in space, then suddenly ...'

He gestured at his white-knuckled grip on the workbench.

'This is me on a good day. Some mornings I can't even get out of bed without the room spinning. You try planning elaborate robberies when you can't tell up from down.'

'But you still work on bikes.'

'Because I understand them,' Kitson's voice softened. 'Even if I can't ride any more, I know every part, every modification. People bring me their machines; I make them better. That's all.'

He looked up at De'Geer now, fury in his eyes.

'Also, your "Sergeant Freeman", the one with the bone to gnaw on? He was so desperate to prove I was the Rider, going on about my sodding "turning style", he didn't check all the dates. Of the eight the Rider did? Sure, one was after my accident, but two of them were at the same time I was performing at shows, the other end of the country. I know Dick Turpin's "ride to York" is a romanticised load of crap, but even I can't manage three hundred miles in an hour to turn up in Forest Hill.'

For a moment, De'Geer thought Kitson might actually fall from his precarious perch on the stool, but he caught himself, possibly because of years of muscle memory keeping him upright despite his damaged balance.

'Mahoney –'

'Stephen Mahoney is dead, officer,' Kitson snapped. 'I'll not have you sully his name, especially in connection with the people who killed him.'

De'Geer looked up in surprise.

'I'm sorry?'

Kitson swore softly.

'Wanna hear a cool conspiracy?' he muttered, his eyes closed. 'There's no way, even half full, that the tanker would have exploded on a clip from a bike. Someone detonated it. Someone who wanted us dead.'

'And why would that be?'

'Because just like you, they thought I – or Stephen – was the Essex Rider, and they wanted us dead,' Kitson snapped. 'Set up a detonator, but Mahoney was late and screwed the stunt. Saved my life in the process.'

De'Geer wrote this down.

'Why didn't you say anything?' he asked, confused. 'You always claimed it was an accident.'

'As I said, it's a conspiracy. That's what you call things you can't prove, right?' Kitson spat. 'Everything was cleaned up fast, I couldn't prove it if I wanted. And at the time I was in a hospital bed, you know?'

'Do you know who it could have been?'

Kitson shook his head.

'I think,' he said carefully, 'you should leave now –'

The crash from the back room cut through their conversation like a gunshot. Kitson's eyes widened; genuine surprise, not acted.

'You bring backup?' he asked.

'No,' De'Geer rose from the workbench he'd been leaning against. 'I'm guessing you're alone?'

'Nobody else is here,' Kitson said quietly. 'Workshop's been closed all week.'

De'Geer was moving before Kitson finished speaking, pushing through the door and entering the back room, a maze of partially stripped bikes and diagnostic equipment, all meticulously organised. But papers were scattered across the floor, drawers pulled open, and the rear door was swinging in the breeze.

'Bollocks,' he muttered. 'You keep your room like this usually?'

'Christ, no!' Kitson looked through the door in horror, as De'Geer headed towards the rear door. Through the opening, he caught a flash of black leather, a motorcycle rider, already moving towards a bike. It wasn't the full theatrical costume from the Carmody robbery, there was no flowing cape, no tricorn hat; just professional-grade leathers and a helmet that concealed any identifying features. But there was stitching that matched the witness reports; it was as if the High-wayman was here and going "undercover".

Surprisingly, there was something in the way they moved, a fast-moving grace that spoke of an inner calmness.

The Highwayman didn't expect to be caught, even though they'd been seen.

The bike itself was a Ducati Multistrada V4, matte-black, heavily modified – the same bike Freeman had claimed he'd chased, and the kind of machine that could outrun anything the police had, if ridden in the right hands. As De'Geer burst through the door, the rider was already throwing their leg over, the engine catching with a sound that suggested extensive custom work.

His own bike – a police-spec BMW R1250RT – was parked in front and, so he turned quickly and ran back through the workshop, grabbing his helmet as he did so – with Kitson staring in shock at him as he passed. By the time he reached his bike the Ducati was already accelerating down Three Colts Lane, weaving through traffic with supernatural precision.

The radio headset in his helmet crackled to life as he fired up the engine.

'Control, Sergeant De'Geer, City of London Police, in pursuit of suspect on a Ducati Multistrada V4, matte-black, heading east on Three Colts Lane towards Cambridge Heath Road. Requesting air support.'

He knew he wouldn't likely get it, but there was no way he wasn't going to ask for it. If this was the same rider as before, he'd outsmarted an entire unit of motorcycle coppers. De'Geer was one man.

That said, they weren't going through woodlands this time.

The BMW's siren cut through the morning air as he

launched after the disappearing rider. Even with years of police pursuit training, De'Geer knew this wouldn't be easy. The Ducati was a monster of a machine, and whoever was riding it knew exactly how to handle its power. They took the corner onto Cambridge Heath Road at an angle that should have been impossible, their knee almost brushing the tarmac. De'Geer recognised it – the move was pure track racing, the kind of instinctive motion you only learned from years of, well, turning corners at great speed, or from someone who had the experience of it to teach.

A double-decker bus pulled out ahead of them – the Ducati didn't even slow, threading the needle between the bus and a line of parked cars. Resisting the urge to wince and close his eyes, De'Geer followed, the BMW's fairing barely clearing the gap, sirens blaring, earning a blast of the bus's horn.

Traffic scattered at the sound of his sirens, but the Ducati was already a couple of hundred yards ahead, slicing through gaps that barely existed. A taxi cut across their path; the Ducati's rider dropped a gear and bunny-hopped the bike over its bonnet, landing with perfect precision. De'Geer had to brake hard and swerve around, losing precious seconds as the taxi driver stared open-mouthed at what he'd just witnessed. They hit the railway bridge at speed, and as they did so, the Ducati's rider shifted their weight somehow in a way that made De'Geer's breath catch. He'd seen that movement before, in videos he'd watched on YouTube the previous night while going through Freeman's logs. A signature shift that preceded ...

The Ducati launched off a loading ramp outside the builder's merchants, sailing over a line of parked cars in a perfect arc.

De'Geer spotted a gap in the traffic – a harder route, but one that might let him catch up. He swung the BMW hard right, accelerating down a narrow service road parallel to the main street; the bigger bike shouldn't have been able to handle it at this speed, but years of riding had taught him exactly how far he could push the machine ... and then how much *more* he could pressure until the bike gave up on him.

He emerged onto Bethnal Green Road just as the matte-black Ducati passed, close enough now to see the custom work on the bike's fairings. But they were already disappearing east towards Globe Town, weaving through traffic like mercury through cracks. He almost considered calling Johnny Lucas and getting him to throw spike strips out on the road, or something; however, the chase had now moved on as the Ducati cut through the heart of Bethnal Green, past a delivery van as it reversed out of a side street – the Ducati lifted its front wheel, shifting trajectory mid-wheelie to avoid it. De'Geer countered with his own expertise, dropping the BMW into a controlled slide that took him around the obstacle, clipping the side of the delivery van in the process. The moves were different but did the same thing ... even if it cost more time for De'Geer, and a chunk of scratched paintwork.

They hit Roman Road Market at full speed, stallholders diving for cover as the Ducati threaded between market stalls. A large crate filled with soil and flowers, placed there to stop cars driving along the now pedestrian walkway appeared in their path – the rider bunny-hopped again, this time using a market table as a launch ramp. De'Geer had to slow, watching helplessly as the rider approached the canal bridge. He knew what was coming and had seen it in the YouTube videos – even read Danny Freeman's description of it in his notes.

The Ducati's front wheel lifted as they hit the bridge's apex. It was a perfect balance point; the bike rotating back until it was almost vertical. Then, impossibly, they held it there, riding a wheelie across the entire bridge, avoiding the crate before taking the ramp and twisting the bike in the air as it turned lazily, dropping back to both wheels and disappearing down, past the bridge's view of sight.

De'Geer killed his siren, pulling to a stop as, beneath him he heard the Ducati speeding off down the far side canal path. There was no point continuing as by the time he got down there the rider would be long gone.

But he'd seen enough.

That wheelie across the bridge ... it was a signature move. The sort of stunt that only a handful of riders could master.

More importantly, it was one he knew was familiar to James Kitson.

THE WORKSHOP WAS EERILY QUIET WHEN DE'GEER RETURNED. Kitson hadn't moved from his position by the workbench, but his face was tight with tension.

'Did you see who it was?' he asked.

'No.' De'Geer was still breathing hard from the chase. 'But I saw how they rode. There was this move on the canal bridge – a wheelie, but not just any wheelie. Jumped the barrier, landed on the canal path.'

Something shifted in Kitson's expression.

'Describe it.'

'Front wheel up at the apex. Bike almost vertical, like they were walking it on the back wheel. Caught the makeshift ramp perfectly, allowed the momentum to take them over and across, turning to land on both wheels below.'

Kitson's grip on the workbench tightened, knuckles white against the metal.

'The Spider's Walk,' he breathed.

'I saw you do it, Mister Kitson,' De'Geer replied. 'In a show video from seven years back, in Southend.'

'It was a signature move,' Kitson nodded as he reached for a framed photo on the wall. Two riders in matching leathers, bikes balanced impossibly on their rear wheels. 'You have to absolutely commit to the move, or you'll overbalance. Me and Stephen developed it together.'

He shook his head as he stared at the photo.

'Point is, only two people ever did that move, because the insurers kicked up a stink, said we couldn't do it in shows. But it can't be us, as I can't ride any more, and Stephen's dead.'

De'Geer looked at the photo, then back at Kitson.

'So, how does our friend in black know it? Or at least do it so well?'

James Kitson didn't answer, and after a moment's silence, De'Geer walked back through the workshop, checking his phone. He needed to call this in, report what had happened – both with the chase and with the conversation he'd had with Kitson.

But there was something else, something nagging at him.

What had the Highwayman been looking for?

Through the rear door again, De'Geer walked back into the small yard behind the workshop, looking around, almost expecting to see the mysterious rider again. Stacks of old tyres lined one wall, organised by size, while back in the building tools hung on boards, outlines carefully marked, the kind of precision you'd expect from someone who lived and breathed machines.

And, to the left, a skip. Not unusual, given the amount of debris a workshop like this would generate, but it looked off ...

Especially as it looked like there'd been a fire in there recently.

His recent months of working crime scenes next to Doctor Marcos had taught De'Geer to trust his instincts, and he leant over the lip of the skip, his seven-foot frame working to his advantage here.

At first, he saw nothing but workshop detritus – old rags, metal shavings, discarded parts. But, as he shifted position, light caught something beneath the surface debris.

Dark leather, gleaming despite a coating of grime. A briefcase –although fire had warped and twisted its shape, opening it. Scattered around it were charred fragments of paper – remnants of documents someone had tried to destroy.

His hand was already reaching for his radio when he heard a movement behind him. Kitson stood in the doorway, steadying himself against the frame.

'Find something interesting?' he asked.

De'Geer turned slowly. The genuine confusion in Kitson's expression as he saw De'Geer's own told him everything he needed to know.

Either Kitson was a good actor, or he genuinely didn't know what De'Geer had found.

'You been at the skip recently?' he asked.

'Not for a few days,' Kitson frowned. 'Although I think someone had a bonfire in there, smoke smell was bloody awful. Had to ask next door to check it though as I was having a "moment" around then, couldn't make it across. Why?'

De'Geer looked back at the contents of the skip and narrowed his eyes. Someone had gone to a lot of trouble to make this look right.

Too right.

'James Kitson,' he said quietly, genuine regret in his voice. 'I'm arresting you for suspicion of theft of government property ...'

He continued with the caution, watching Kitson's face shift from confusion to shock to something closer to anger. Whatever game was being played here, someone had just changed all the rules.

And De'Geer had a feeling they were going to change again, real soon.

17

ADDICTION

BILLY'D BEEN STARING AT THE SCREEN FOR SO LONG THAT THE grainy security footage had started to blur, with black and white shapes melting into each other like some kind of twisted Rorschach test. The figure on the screen moved with careful precision through Marius Blake's workshop, baseball cap pulled low, face always turned just enough to evade clear identification. Billy had tried every enhancement technique he knew, but the image quality fought back, refusing to give up its secrets, as Monroe, in the office behind him tutted like an ADHD backseat driver.

'Bugger this,' he muttered, reaching for his fourth coffee of the day, grimacing at the taste. 'Urgh. How did it get cold?'

'Because you've been staring at the screen for close to an hour now without moving, laddie,' Monroe's voice carried a hint of amusement. The Scotsman had been prowling the office like a caged animal since Baker's phone call, as if physical movement could somehow speed up the process of solving the case. 'Any joy with our camera-shy friend?'

'About as much joy as you'd get from a kick in the balls,

Guv,' Billy replied, ignoring Monroe's mock disapproval of his language. 'I mean, not *you* you, but more a *generic* you.'

He zoomed in on the figure again; the image breaking down into blocky pixels.

'Whoever it was, they knew exactly what they were doing. Look at this –'

He tapped a key, cycling through frames.

'See how they always keep their head at this angle? That's no accident, that's –'

'Someone who knows which cameras to avoid when they're doing something they shouldn't.' Monroe went to continue, but the sound of footsteps in the corridor outside made them both turn.

Sergeant Mastakin appeared in the doorway, his expression suggesting he'd rather be anywhere else right now, possibly already pining for the reception desk.

'Guv,' he said, nodding at Monroe. 'Got someone downstairs you might want to talk to.'

'Thank god,' Monroe smiled darkly. 'De'Geer's arrived with –'

'Not De'Geer, Guv.'

'If it's another bloody journalist –'

'It's Matthews.'

Monroe's eyebrows rose sharply.

'Matthews? As in Detective Chief Inspector Matthews?'

'Same one,' Mastakin shifted uncomfortably. 'Says he wants to make a statement. He's ... well, he's not in a good way.'

'Define "not in a good way"?' Monroe's voice had shifted, the casual tone replaced by something harder.

'Let's just say I've put him in Interview Room One,

sending him up on the back route, and I've got Cooper watching the door. Best if you see for yourself.'

Monroe glanced at Billy, then back at the frozen image on the screen.

'Keep digging,' he said. 'I want to know who our friend in the baseball cap is. And get Declan. If Matthews is ready to talk ...'

He didn't finish the sentence. He didn't need to. Billy was already reaching for his phone as Monroe headed towards the interview room.

———

DETECTIVE CHIEF INSPECTOR MATTHEWS LOOKED LIKE A MAN who'd been broken and badly reassembled. His shirt was crumpled, like he'd been sleeping in it, and spots of dried blood on the collar suggested a nosebleed. Declan had seen enough office bathroom lines in his time on duty to know what had likely caused that.

The interview room was its usual self; a table, three chairs, one occupied by Matthews, a mug of coffee in front of him, and the other two chairs empty, waiting for Declan and Monroe's arrival.

'Was starting to think you weren't coming,' Matthews muttered as Declan and Monroe entered. 'Have to say, didn't expect both of you.'

'Aye, well, we're full service here at Temple Inn,' Monroe replied, pulling out a chair. 'Although I notice you didn't go to your own unit.'

'My own unit wouldn't understand.'

'About the cocaine?'

Matthews gave a bitter laugh that turned into a rattling cough.

'You knew?'

'We were told by a Member of Parliament,' Declan said diplomatically. 'But from what we hear, Carmody seemed to know, too.'

'Carmody knew everything,' Matthews replied. 'Well, almost everything. At least, that's what he liked to think.'

Declan watched as Matthews drummed his fingers on the desk, the movement betraying tension, maybe withdrawal. His pupils were still wide, despite the harsh light above them.

'I need to make a statement,' Matthews continued. 'About what happened that night. About what I saw.'

'What you *think* you saw?' Monroe asked. 'Because I'm guessing your perception might have been slightly affected by –'

'Don't.' Matthews held up a hand. 'Just ... don't. I know what I did. I know what I am. But that's not what this is about.'

'Then what is it about?'

'It's about Carmody. About how he changed.'

'Changed how?'

Matthews shifted in his seat, his fingers still drumming that nervous rhythm.

'Week before it happened, he was in pieces. Money was tight. Really tight. You know what they pay ministers these days?'

'I believe it's around thirty-one grand,' Declan replied, and saw Matthews look up, surprised he knew. 'We already know Carmody wasn't making as much as he felt he should, and also that he couldn't claim the Lords's allowance while in Cabinet.'

'Thirty grand. Barely enough to keep the lights on in that bloody house of his up north,' Matthew muttered bitterly. 'Oh, how the other half lives.'

'Must be a big house.'

'Big enough to drain every penny. And that's before the wife's tennis lessons,' Matthews gave another bitter laugh. 'Three times a week. Private tuition. Probably cost more than my annual salary. But Carmody didn't care about that, he just cared that he wasn't making what he thought he was worth.'

'Which was?'

'According to him? What he'd make in the private sector. High six figures minimum. Didn't help he was hanging around with millionaire lobbyists and entrepreneurs. But he couldn't leave the Treasury role – said he needed the position, needed the influence.'

Declan caught Monroe's eye. They both knew where this was going.

'Then something changed,' Matthews continued. 'About a week before ... before that night. Suddenly he's not complaining any more. Suddenly he's almost happy.'

'Any idea what caused this change in mood?' Declan asked.

'Heard him on the phone to his son, Lewis. Something about everything being sorted.' Matthews rubbed at his nose, wincing. 'Thought little of it at the time. Was too busy ...'

He trailed off.

'Too busy trying to score?' Monroe suggested.

'Too busy trying to stay functional,' Matthews corrected. 'Do you know what it's like? Being that close to power and knowing you're just ...'

He shook his head.

'Doesn't matter. What matters is what happened at the Dorchester.'

'When Jennifer gave him the briefcase?'

'No,' Matthews looked up, his eyes suddenly sharp despite their previous chemical dilation. 'When he took it into the bathroom. Standard procedure is I check the facilities first, make sure it's clear. So I do.'

'But you didn't,' Monroe added. 'We saw video footage. You follow him in.'

Matthews nodded as he closed his eyes.

'I screwed up. I wasn't straight, I needed a line. Just to stay focused, you understand. Just to keep functioning. So, I'm buggering around outside longer than I should be. And Carmody goes in right before me. With the briefcase and his phone.'

'What happened then?'

Matthews ran a hand through his unkempt hair, his fingers shaking worse now, the movement dislodging a few strands that fell across his forehead, making him look even more dishevelled. He stared at the table for a long moment, as if gathering his thoughts, or maybe just trying to sort reality from cocaine-addled memory.

'You have to understand something,' he said finally, his voice quiet but intense. 'Protection work, it's not just about keeping people safe. It's about watching. Observing. Even when you're not quite, well, yourself, you notice things. Patterns. Changes. And Carmody had changed. A week before, he's barely holding it together – talking about re-mortgaging the estate up north, cutting back on expenses, even muttering about selling some family heirlooms. Then suddenly he's calm. Controlled. Like a man who knows exactly what's coming.'

He looked up at Declan.

'The bathroom at the Dorchester, it's all marble and brass. Old school luxury. Sound echoes. So, I follow him in, see there's nobody else in there, thank God and go to the end cubicle, decide to sort myself out. So, I'm in there, in the cubicle, trying to get my head straight, and I hear the click of the combination lock. Three numbers – I remember thinking it was strange he knew them already, didn't even have to check. Then paper rustling. Not just glancing through them – proper reading. Taking his time. And his phone ...'

Matthews mimicked a camera sound, his hands miming holding a phone.

'Click. Click. Click. Must have been twenty, thirty photos. Then I hear him on the phone. Speaking quiet, but like I said – marble walls. Everything echoes. He's talking to someone – "It's all here," he says. "Everything we need. Infrastructure contracts, development zones, the whole bloody lot." Then something about trading patterns, about moving fast. And a name – Lewis.'

'What exactly did he say about Lewis?' Monroe asked.

Matthews shook his head, frustration evident in his expression.

'That's where it gets ... fuzzy. The coke, it does things to your memory. Fragments everything. I remember him talking about preparations. About everything being in place. But it's like ... like trying to remember a dream. The more you focus on it, the more it slips away.'

He drummed his fingers on the table, that same nervous rhythm from before.

'But I remember what happened next. Clear as day. Because that's when Harris knocks on the door. Says the car's ready. And Carmody ... he laughs, like actually laughs. Then he's gone. Left me there, still hiding in the cubicle like some bloody teenager.'

'And you followed him out? Continued your protection duty?' Declan kept his voice neutral, professional.

'What choice did I have? I was his SEG. Even if I'd wanted to report what I'd heard, who'd believe me? Coked-up officer imagining conspiracies?'

Matthews gave that bitter laugh again.

'Besides, by then I was so far gone ... the drive is just fragments. Flashes. The woman in the champagne dress. Carmody insisting on that specific route. The motorcycle appearing out of nowhere.'

He stopped, his expression darkening.

'The laser sights.'

'What about them?'

'They weren't right.' Matthews leaned forward, his voice dropping. 'Twenty years in protection. I've seen laser sights before. Real ones. These were ... different. Too steady. Too perfect. Like ...'

'Like what?'

'Like they were fixed in place.' His hands were really shaking now. 'I didn't realise it at the time. Too busy trying to keep my head straight. But afterward, thinking about it ... they wavered, danced on my chest, but it was a set routine, you get what I mean? Like a small figure of eight. Real snipers, their sights drift. Breathe in, breathe out – you see it in the dot. These were fixed. Like they were mounted on something and made to look like they were human.'

Monroe and Declan exchanged glances.

'Why are you telling us this now?' Monroe asked.

Matthews slumped back in his chair, suddenly looking every one of his years and then some.

'Because yesterday, Carmody calls me. Says he's planning to resign. Says he needs to "clear the air" about what happened. Tells me I should do the same. Makes it sound like he's doing me a favour, giving me a chance to admit to the cocaine before it all comes out. But the way he said it ...'

He shuddered.

'I've heard that tone before. From Lords, from Ministers. It's the tone they use when they're about to throw someone under the bus. And I realised – I'm the perfect fall guy, aren't I? The coked-up protection officer who missed all the signs. Who let his Minister get robbed. Who was too high to see what was really happening.'

'And what do you think was really happening?' Declan asked quietly.

Matthews met his gaze steadily for the first time since they'd entered the room.

'I think I was watching a performance,' he said. 'A show. Everything perfectly staged – the route, the timing, even the woman in the car. All of it designed to hide what was really going on. And now Carmody needs someone to blame when it all falls apart. Might as well be the junkie cop who couldn't keep his nose clean, right?'

Declan leant back in the chair.

'I might not be the addict you are, but I've tried cocaine,' he said quietly. 'Back in the Military Police. And I have to say, what you're stating as a cocaine high really wasn't what I remember it being like.'

Matthews looked up.

'I know,' he said, almost as if he was looking at Declan for salvation. 'It wasn't. Trust me, I know a coke high, and this was worse. Broken. Like ...'

'Like someone spiked your line?' Monroe suggested. 'Who gave you it?'

'One of the guests,' Matthews admitted. 'One of the millionaires I mentioned. Mikhail Stefon. He's good at getting anything, and he ... well, "provided" me.'

Declan sighed.

'Yeah, I can pretty much state for the record you were spiked,' he said. 'We think Mikhail Stefon was involved in the robbery somehow. Makes sense he provides you doctored drugs. As you said, he thought you were the perfect fall guy.'

Matthews stared at his shaking hands.

'So, even my addiction was part of their game,' he whispered. 'Christ. Twenty years' service. Twenty years of keeping these bastards safe.'

'And now they're trying to destroy you,' Monroe replied. 'Unless ...'

'Unless I help destroy them first.' Matthews looked up, and Declan thought he saw something of the close protection officer's old steel returning to his eyes. 'I'll make a full statement. Everything I remember. Everything I saw. But you have to understand – some of it might not have happened. Some of it might be the drugs. And some of it ...'

'Might be exactly what they wanted you to see,' Declan finished.

Matthews nodded.

'One more thing,' he said. 'The woman. Sophia. When she ran into the woods that night – she didn't run away from us.'

'No?'

'No,' Matthews' voice was barely a whisper now. 'She ran *towards* something. Like she knew exactly where she was going. Like it was all part of the plan. And I'll swear I saw a light in the forest, like a bike was waiting. But ...'

'But it could be the drugs,' Declan gave an almost sympathetic smile now, but as he did so, he ran through what Billy had said. *If Sophia had climbed on a bike, maybe even the Highwayman's, and ridden off, then why appear, walking down the side of the road towards Epping ... unless she wanted to be found?*

Declan was about to comment on this, but his phone buzzed. Looking down at it, he saw a message from De'Geer.

> We've got Kitson, but you're not going to believe what we found in his skip.

Monroe must have received the same message, as he was already rising.

'Right then,' he said. 'Let's get someone in to take your full statement. And DCI Matthews?'

'Sir?'

'Get yourself clean,' Monroe snarled. 'Because when this goes to court? I want you clearheaded enough to nail these bastards to the wall.'

18

EVIDENCE

The forensics offices always smelled of cleaning fluid and coffee at this time of day.

Doctor Marcos had started her third cup – of coffee, not cleaning fluid – since lunch, the paper one from the coffee shop around the corner on Fleet Street. It was sitting beside pieces of the scattered remains of the briefcase; the rest having been sent to Lambeth for the scientists to examine.

'You can try all you like,' she muttered at the remains in front of her, as if having some kind of one-sided conversation. 'But paper always keeps secrets.'

She'd been photographing and documenting for a couple of hours now, enjoying the aloneness while De'Geer, in another room in the building, was going through ANPR traffic cameras in some desperate way to prove a theory he'd had, following his recent confrontation with the Highwayman. The remains in front of her told a story; accelerant patterns suggested a controlled burn, not a panicked destruction. Someone had taken their time, and made sure the most important parts were destroyed first.

But they'd missed things. They *always* missed things.

So far she'd barely scratched the surface, and in an ideal world would have a good couple more hours to work through this, but she knew that wasn't an option right now. They needed answers; primarily whether this was Carmody's stolen briefcase, whether it'd been opened and examined after the theft, and finally, whether any of the charred and burned papers were still of worth.

The door opened behind her; Billy, probably, asking if she'd found anything that could help with his trading-pattern theories. But the footsteps were wrong – lighter, more hesitant.

'We're closed,' she said without turning. 'Unless you're actually dead, in which case take a ticket and wait your turn.'

'I'm here about James Kitson.'

Doctor Marcos turned at that. The woman in the doorway was probably in her early thirties, in a professional dress that suggested Civil Service, but there was something in her expression – concern, perhaps, mixed with a little trepidation. But her face was familiar, having been shown on a plasma screen in the briefing room the previous day.

'Emma Thorne?' Doctor Marcos asked, although she already knew the answer. 'Last time I checked, James Kitson wasn't dead. Although given what De'Geer found in his skip ...'

She shrugged, looking back at the workbench where the charred pieces lay.

'You're in the wrong office, anyway,' she continued. 'You want upstairs.'

'Yeah, sorry, I just entered the first door I found,' Emma replied sheepishly. 'I've never been here before. I thought it was a storage facility, if I'm being honest.'

'It was, until a couple of years back,' Doctor Marcos frowned. 'How did you get through the main door?'

'I waved my Treasury ID card, mentioned Charles Baker's name a couple of times,' Emma shrugged. 'Helped that two of your colleagues, Monroe and Bullman, came to see me yesterday, so I could use that as an excuse. They assumed I was expected, and I ...'

Emma didn't need to continue as she moved into the room slowly, her heels clicking against the tile floor, but there was a tension in her movements, like someone trying very hard to appear calm.

'He didn't do this,' she whispered, stopping at the examination table. Her eyes fixed on the burned briefcase, widening slightly. 'James ... he couldn't.'

'Really?' Doctor Marcos watched her carefully, noting the way Emma's hands clenched at her sides. 'Because right now, the evidence isn't exactly in his favour.'

'Well, then the evidence is wrong.'

'Is it?' Doctor Marcos picked up one of the larger fragments of paper, holding it under the light. 'Someone went to a lot of trouble to burn these documents. Used an accelerant. Knew exactly what they were doing. But they were careful about it – controlled the burn, made sure it didn't spread. Almost like ...'

'Someone who understands fire, or how to control it.'

'And Mister Kitson did use fire in his stunts, and I'm guessing the accelerant, when identified, will be something commonly found in a garage or bike shop.'

'I know how it looks,' Emma snapped. 'And if I didn't know him, I'd think the same.'

'But?'

'But James can barely stand most days,' Emma's voice

carried genuine pain now. 'The vertigo – some mornings he can't even walk straight. You think he could have pulled off something like this?'

'You don't need to be able to walk, to set something on fire,' Doctor Marcos watched as Emma's eyes tracked over the evidence. *Professional interest, or something else?* The Treasury advisor's fingers twitched, as if fighting the urge to touch something.

'You knew him before the accident,' Doctor Marcos said finally. It wasn't a question.

'Yes.'

'How well?' Doctor Marcos continued. 'Was it through the commission, or was it something different?'

Emma's laugh was hollow.

'Before the commission, and well enough to know he didn't do this.'

She looked up, meeting Doctor Marcos' gaze.

'I was dating his partner.'

'Sorry?'

'Stephen Mahoney, the stunt rider, we'd been seeing each other for almost two years, before ... before everything went wrong.'

'The accident.'

'If that's what you want to call it.' Emma's voice hardened. 'Stephen was an expert rider. The best. He wouldn't have made that kind of mistake. Not unless ...'

She trailed off, but Doctor Marcos caught the implication.

'Unless he wasn't in the right state?' she asked. 'We heard rumours, that –'

'Pain killers and opiates?' Emma glared back at Doctor Marcos now. 'Yeah, that's what I heard, every bloody time someone looked into it. Stephen had a meds problem, and he wasn't right when he did the stunt. Everyone took this at face value, but accepted that it could have been an accident. The problems earlier made the ramp slippy, they didn't empty the tanker ... but sure, let's blame the rider.'

Doctor Marcos turned to face Emma now.

'My sergeant told me that Mister Kitson believes an explosive was used.'

'Yeah, well, they never found evidence of that, did they?' Emma muttered. 'They were too clever.'

'The thing about evidence, though,' Doctor Marcos said carefully, 'is that it tells stories. Not just about what happened, but about the people involved. Take this briefcase, for example.'

She gestured at the burned leather.

'High-end. Expensive. The kind of thing a government minister might carry. But look at the burn patterns.'

She pointed to where the fire had eaten through the leather.

'Whoever did this, they wanted it found with just enough evidence still visible to confirm what it was, while making sure any passing dumpster diver didn't find themselves with a bonus payout, insider knowledge-wise. The skip behind Kitson's workshop – it was too obvious. Too perfect.'

'Like someone was trying to frame him.' Emma's voice was barely a whisper.

'The question is, why? Why frame a man who can barely walk?' Doctor Marcos asked, watching Emma. 'Anything you'd like to add?'

Emma Thorne stared at the briefcase for a long moment.

'I think I need to speak to someone,' she eventually said.

'Yes,' Doctor Marcos smiled. 'I think you really do.'

THE MAIN OFFICE HAD GONE QUIET; MOST OF THE TEAM WERE
out following leads or up in the interview rooms. Billy's desk,
usually a fortress of screens and paperwork, had been
invaded by Jess, who'd commandeered his spare keyboard
and was methodically working through Essex traffic camera
footage.

'This is pointless,' she muttered. 'Half the bloody cameras
were down that night.'

'Language,' Billy replied automatically, although his heart
wasn't in it. They'd been trying to piece together the movements of vehicles around the time of the robbery, hunting
anything that revealed the vans that had blocked the street.
'Anyway, it's not the traffic cameras we need.'

He stopped as De'Geer entered the office, his eyes
narrowed.

'Everything okay?' Billy asked, a little concerned that
somehow he'd managed to piss off the seven-foot-tall Viking
and this was dangerous bloody retribution returning.

De'Geer slumped in what was usually Anjli's chair.

'I have spent hours checking every Essex traffic camera,'
De'Geer muttered. 'I've gone through the photo that
Matthews took, that you enhanced. I've compared it to time-
stamps ... all I can find are two or three possibly grainy
images of a figure on a motorcycle heading south from what
looks to be either Loughton or Epping.'

He scratched at his beard absently.

'I can't tell you if it was a Highwayman or not,' he
mumbled, 'but what I can tell you, having based my deduc-
tions on both image and cameras, is that the man who held

Lord Carmody at gunpoint is not the same man that took me on a chase through Bethnal Green.'

'How do you know?' Jess asked, curious.

'I checked the bodycam footage from the original chases,' De'Geer replied. 'Freeman passed what he had across to me earlier today. There's not much, mainly a couple of files, but enough to show the bike as they rode through the woods. It matched the bike I saw today – a Ducati Multistrada V4. The bike on the ANPR I found, the one that Matthews took a photo of, it's more angular. Going through the files and pretty much every bike sales site I could find to try and match the bike, the closest I can find – and believe me it's pretty bloody exact – is a Kawasaki Versys 1000. The Versys has a more angular bodywork design compared to the Multistrada's flowing lines.'

'Could someone mistake one for the other?' Billy was already pulling up bike images.

'At a distance, maybe. But the engine configuration is all wrong – inline-four versus the Ducati's V4.'

'What about handling?' Jess asked.

'Less sophisticated suspension system on the Kawasaki.'

'And the sound?'

'Different exhaust note entirely. The Kawasaki lacks the Ducati's distinctive rumble,' De'Geer shook his head. 'It's a close match, don't get me wrong; close enough for people not to realise, and can probably do the same sort of job that a Ducati can in the woods. But it means that if our High-wayman was really trying to pin this on the Essex Rider from six-years-ago, they didn't know them, because they didn't know the bike.'

'Or they couldn't source one they could use in time,' Billy suggested.

De'Geer nodded.

'Either way, it's not the same bike, so it's probably not the same rider,' he muttered. 'Although how that helps us, I've no bloody idea, as the traffic cams are rubbish.'

'Yeah, that's the same problem we have right now –' Billy started, but his eyes widened as a realisation crossed his mind.

'God, of course. Think about it – middle of the night, quiet road ...'

'Yeah?'

'What do most people have in their cars these days?'

Jess's own eyes widened now.

'Dashcams.'

'Exactly.' Billy pulled up another window. 'There was a witness, the one who said they saw Sophia running. Maybe they had a dashcam, perhaps took an image ...'

He tapped on the keyboard, running searches through an automation he had running in the background, and after a minute or two he smiled, bringing up an Instagram Reel. The quality was poor – cheap dashcam in low light – but it clearly showed the side of a white van, hazard lights blinking as it'd spun, blocking both lanes.

Over the image was text.

STOPPED AS THE HIGHWAYMAN APPEARS!!!

WAS THIS VAN INVOLVED???

#DickTurpinLives

'This was the car directly behind one of the broken down vans,' Billy said as, on the screen the driver, cap low over his eyes waved at the car, opening up the engine bonnet, waving hands in a "what can I do" manner. 'It seems that rather than send us this when they gave their witness statement, they decided instead to gain social media clout with it. Look at the side.'

De'Geer and Jess both leant closer as Billy pulled the video into an editing program, raising the contrast and brightness.

'Premium Fleet Rentals,' she read. 'The number starts with 01992.'

'That's an Epping number,' Billy had pulled the number onto his browser, where an address, number and website for Premium Fleet Rentals was already up, Billy already dialling.

After three rings, a woman answered, Billy placed the phone on speaker.

'Premium Fleet Rentals, Sandra speaking, how can I help?'

'Hi Sandra, this is Detective Sergeant Fitzwarren, City of London Police,' Billy replied, typing and emailing as he did so. 'I need to check some vehicle movements from two nights back. Are you able to do that?'

'I'd need proof of identity first –'

'I've just sent that to the email on your website,' Billy added. 'If you check, you'll see my full name, rank, badge number, and the police department I'm affiliated with. There's also a number you can redial and call me back on, if you want, and it's a number you can find easily online by checking for the City of London Temple Inn Unit.'

'Give me a sec ... right ...' The voice named Sandra paused, obviously checking the emails, reading the email Billy had sent, and likely noting the email address it'd been sent from. 'So, do I call you back on this?'

'You can do, if you're concerned about being scammed.'

'No, I trust you,' Sandra replied. 'You have a kind voice.'

'Thanks, but I'd still like you to feel secure here.'

'I'm good, Detective Sergeant. What time are we talking?'

'Between midnight and two am, two nights ago.'

'The Highwayman night?'

'Yes, the Highwayman night.'

'Is this about the Highwayman?' Sandra sounded excited. 'Can you tell me?'

'Well, what I can tell you is we believe two of your vans were used in the robbery,' Billy replied, tiring of this. 'Is *that* what you wanted me to tell you?'

'Oh. No, not really,' Sandra's voice had dropped in enthusiasm now. 'Okay ... looks like we had seven vans out that night. Two long-term hires to building firms, three to private individuals, and ...'

There was a pause.

'Hang on, that's weird.'

'What is?'

'Says here two vans were listed as "in service" but there's no record of them going anywhere.'

Billy's fingers were already moving across his keyboard.

'Could you give me the registration numbers of those two?'

As Sandra read them out, Jess watched Billy's screen fill with company records.

'How could this happen?' he asked. 'To be in service but still be in the lot?'

'Usually it's when they're on hold for something, but they weren't,' Sandra replied. 'I have the night logs if you want?'

'Please, just reply to my email with them attached, that'd

be most helpful. In fact, if you could add the other five as well that'd be appreciated.'

'I'll do it right now.'

'Thanks Sandra, you're a star,' Billy said, ending the call and noting down the two license numbers on a pad to his side.

'Premium Fleet Rentals,' he muttered, looking at the data that had appeared on the screen during his call. 'Epping rental company, owned by Sovereign Transport Solutions, who apparently run the yard's infrastructure and rent two shipping containers on the site. Who are owned by Apex Holdings. Who are owned by ...'

His eyes widened.

'Got you, you bastard.'

'What?' De'Geer couldn't see what Billy was seeing in the data, and this obviously irritated him.

'Look,' Billy pointed at his screen. 'Apex Holdings is owned by RB Enterprises. And RB Enterprises is owned by Ryan Boyask. One of the millionaire directors of the brand new Carmody Holdings.'

Jess was already reaching for her phone.

'I'll text Dad,' she said. 'He'll want to see this.'

Billy went to reply, but paused as the main doors opened, and Chivalry Fitzwarren entered like a man on a mission. Billy went to pre-empt whatever he was going to say, explain that *this wasn't the time for any shenanigans about guns,* but almost felt a little hurt as Chivalry walked past them both without even a sideways glance, heading for Monroe's – currently Bullman's office.

De'Geer grinned as he looked at Jess.

'I think your dad might want to know about that, too,' he said.

M0NROE'S OFFICE ALWAYS FELT DIFFERENT WITH BULLMAN behind the desk. Maybe it was the fact she'd actually tidied it, filed away the piles of paper that usually lurked in corners. She'd even removed the lingering smell of whatever Monroe usually ate for lunch, replacing it with something that might have been lavender air freshener.

Change was good, she told herself. *Change meant moving forward.*

Of course, returning to the office that was once hers and turfing Monroe out temporarily wasn't exactly moving in a forward direction, but change was best made in baby steps. Which was probably why, when Chivalry Fitzwarren appeared in the doorway like a mismatched explosion in tweed, she felt her heart sink. He was clutching a manila folder that probably contained something relevant to the case, but his usual bombastic entrance seemed somehow muted.

'My lady,' he said, hovering in the doorway. 'I trust I'm not interrupting?'

'You are,' she replied, not looking up from her paperwork. 'But since when has that stopped you?'

He moved into the office, his usual energetic stride somewhat hesitant. The folder in his hands appeared to be trembling slightly.

'I've been examining the historical records of the Griffin & Tow pistols,' he said, his voice lacking its usual theatrical flair. 'Fascinating really, how they moved through various collections over the centuries. Did you know that in 1842, one pair was actually used in the last recorded noble duel in –'

'Chivalry.'

He stopped, surprised by her use of his first name.

'Yes?'

'What are you really doing here?'

He shifted uncomfortably.

'I merely thought ... that is to say ... the historical context of these weapons might prove invaluable to –'

'You've been in and out of this office six times today,' Bullman said quietly. 'Each time with some new historical fact that could have waited. So I'll ask again ... what are you *really* doing here?'

The silence that followed felt heavy with what felt like unspoken words. Chivalry looked down at his folder as if seeing it for the first time.

'There's an exhibition,' he said finally. 'At the Wallace Collection. Medieval and Renaissance arms and armour. Next Thursday evening. Private viewing.'

'Chivalry –'

'I have two tickets,' he continued quickly. 'And I thought, perhaps, given your interest in historical weaponry ...'

'I've never expressed any interest in historical weaponry.'

'No, but you expressed an interest in that quarterstaff technique I showed young De'Geer during the re-enactor case.'

'If I recall, he showed you it.'

'Maybe, anyway, I thought ... well ...'

Bullman put down her pen.

'Are you asking me on a date?'

'Good Lord, no!' Chivalry's voice carried genuine horror, but his eyes said something different. 'Merely a professional consultation. About the case. Obviously.'

'Obviously,' she echoed.

He clutched the folder tighter.

'Although,' he added, 'they do serve rather excellent canapés. And the wine is usually quite tolerable.'

Bullman fought back a smile.

'I'll think about it,' she said.

'You will?' His face lit up, then quickly settled back into something more composed. 'I mean, yes, of course. Take all the time you need. Though they do need final numbers by tomorrow morning.'

'Chivalry? The folder you're crushing – does it actually contain anything about the case?'

He looked down at the now-crumpled manila paper.

'Ah.' His face reddened slightly. 'Actually, it's empty. I thought it might make me look more professional.'

This time, she couldn't help the smile.

'Get out,' she said. 'I'll let you know about next Thursday.'

He backed towards the door, already reaching for his hat to doff, which, to his surprise, wasn't on his head.

'Until then, my lady,' he said, and was gone in a swirl of mismatched tweed.

Bullman stared at the doorway for a long moment, then shook her head and returned to her paperwork.

But try as she might, she couldn't quite shake the smile from her face.

DECLAN ALWAYS FELT INTERVIEW ROOMS HAD THEIR OWN particular smell. Not unpleasant, exactly, but institutional, like schools or hospitals, places where hope came to die under fluorescent lighting. This one carried extra tension today, the kind of tension that came with interviewing someone who clearly knew more than they were saying.

James Kitson sat opposite them, somehow diminished by the harsh overhead lights. One hand gripped the edge of the table – not nerves, Declan noted, but balance. Even sitting down, the vertigo that had ended his career seemed to affect him now and then. For almost ten minutes they'd bounced back and forth about nothing, allowing the interview to settle into a rhythm, but now it was time to turn the pressure up a little.

'Where were you two nights ago?' Declan asked.

'I was out,' Kitson replied.

'Out where?'

'Just out.'

'Home by what time?'

Kitson hesitated, just for a moment.

'About ten.'

'Really?' Anjli's voice carried polite scepticism. 'Because while checking through your workshop, we chatted to your neighbours, including Mister Asif, from the shop next door to you.'

Something shifted in Kitson's expression.

'What did you talk about?'

'His surprise at you not being around two nights back,' Anjli continued. 'Apparently, he tried to drop off a package for you, which a delivery driver had asked him to hold when you didn't answer the door earlier. Said he knocked, but your workshop was locked up. Completely dark. No answer. He was stock checking his other shop the following day, so kept checking in case you'd returned. Gave up past midnight.'

Kitson said nothing, but his fingers tightened on the table edge.

'I must have misread my watch,' Kitson admitted, his voice quiet but firm.

'Yes,' Declan agreed. 'You must have. So, where were you?'

Kitson stared at the table, his jaw working as if fighting some internal battle.

'I can't ... I wasn't there.'

'That's not an answer, Mister Kitson.'

'It's the only one I can give you.' The words seemed to pain him. 'Look, I know how this looks. The briefcase, the documents, all conveniently found in my skip. But I didn't put them there.'

'Someone went to a lot of trouble to make it look like you did.'

'Story of my life.' Kitson's bitter laugh held no humour, grimacing as a wave of vertigo hit him. His knuckles whitened on the table edge.

'James,' Declan kept his voice gentle. 'We're trying to help. But you need to give us something.'

'I can't.'

'Can't? Or won't?'

'Both.' Kitson looked up at them, genuine pain in his expression. 'Some secrets aren't mine to tell –'

As he said this, the door opened; Doctor Marcos stood there, and behind her ...

'Emma?' Kitson's voice carried equal measures of relief and concern. 'You shouldn't be here!'

'Yes, I should.' Emma Thorne moved into the room, Doctor Marcos following. 'You don't have to protect me, James. Not any more.'

She turned to Declan, giving an enormous sigh.

'James Kitson isn't the Essex Rider,' she explained. 'I am.'

19

THE "WOMAN"

Detective Sergeant Rachel Thwaites hated airport duty. City Airport's terminal always felt too bright, too sterile, all glass and steel trying too hard to look modern. The morning crowd moved in predictable patterns – business travellers with carry-on luggage, heading for early evening flights to Frankfurt or Amsterdam, their shoes clicking against polished floors.

She'd been stationed in the City of London's Bishopsgate police for three years now, but today's assignment felt different. The Temple Inn Unit didn't usually request outside assistance, and when they did, it usually meant something big was brewing.

PC Webb stood beside her, a reassuring presence in his crisp uniform. They'd been here since lunchtime, watching every arrival from Prague, running through the same routine with each landing – check manifests, scan faces, report nothing.

'Last flight's due in ten minutes,' Webb checked his phone. 'Flight OK681.'

Thwaites nodded, scanning the arrivals board. The fluorescent glare made her eyes ache. They'd been told Mikhail Stefon was booked on this flight; his name was on the manifest, his seat assigned. Business class, window seat, meal pre-ordered. Everything arranged perfectly.

But, considering the fact this was the last flight of the day, Thwaites had that terrible feeling in the pit of her stomach.

'Check with the desk again,' she said. 'See if they've had any updates.'

Webb moved towards the CityJet counter, where a tired-looking woman in corporate blue was tapping at her computer. Sarah, according to her name badge, looked like she'd already handled too many complaints that day.

Thwaites watched their interaction: Webb's polite inquiry, Sarah's growing frown as she checked something on her screen, the slight shake of her head.

Shit. He's not on it.

'Mind if I verify what was just seen?' she asked, joining them at the counter.

'Of course,' Sarah the receptionist turned her monitor slightly. 'Passenger manifest for OK681. Stefon, M, seat 3A. But look ...'

She highlighted a column.

'No baggage. He checked in – not at Prague airport; he gained his boarding pass online but never arrived at the gate.'

'Could he have switched flights?' Webb asked.

Sarah tapped a few more keys.

'Nothing showing on our system. The ticket was paid for but ...' she shrugged. 'He just didn't show.'

Thwaites pulled out her phone, scrolling to the Temple Inn number she'd been given. Detective Chief Inspector

Monroe answered on the second ring, his Scottish accent carrying clearly despite the airport's background noise.

'Aye?'

'DS Thwaites, sir. We've been waiting at City Airport for Mikhail Stefon.'

'And?'

'He didn't board in Prague, sir. Ticket was purchased but never used.'

There was a long pause on the line. Thwaites could almost hear Monroe processing the implications.

'Interesting,' his voice carried careful neutrality. 'Any indication of where he might have gone instead?'

'Not yet, sir. Want us to check other London airports?'

'No, we'll handle that. Get back to your unit, grab some food, lassie. Sorry for leading you on a sodding goose chase.'

Thwaites ended the call, turning to Webb.

'He called me lassie.'

'He does that. It means he likes you.'

'Could he do that without calling me lassie?'

Webb shrugged.

'Ask him,' he smiled. 'What's the worst that can happen?'

Thwaites wasn't sure, as Webb continued.

'Anyway, what's the plan?'

'Get food. They're taking it from here.'

'Think Mikhail Stefon knew we'd be waiting?' Webb asked, watching another wave of travellers emerge from customs, each focused on their own routines, none of them the man they'd been waiting for.

'Oh, he knew,' Thwaites said quietly, as she looked back at the arrivals board, where OK681 from Prague had just switched to LANDED.

'Question is, who warned him?'

.   .   .

PC ESME COOPER ALWAYS FOUND IT STRANGE HOW THE MORE expensive a London apartment building was, the less its concierge seemed to care about security. The man behind the marble-topped desk barely glanced at her warrant card, waving her through to the lifts with the bored indifference of someone who'd seen too many celebrities to be impressed by a police uniform.

The building itself screamed money; all glass and steel and carefully cultivated emptiness. The kind of place where people paid astronomical rents to pretend they lived some-where exclusive, even if half the flats stood empty most of the year.

Sophia's apartment was on the eighth floor. According to the report from the officers who'd found her walking towards Epping that night, she'd given them this address without hesitation.

Almost like she'd wanted it on record.

The woman who opened the door looked nothing like the composed escort from the Dorchester images. No designer dress, no careful makeup, just yoga pants and an oversized sweater that probably cost more than Cooper felt it was worth. Her eyes widened slightly at Cooper's uniform.

'Can I help you?' Her voice carried a curated, careful neutrality.

'PC Cooper, City of London Police,' Cooper kept her own tone professional. 'Following up on your statement from the other night. Mind if I come in?'

Sophia hesitated just long enough to be noticeable.

'Of course,' she stepped aside, gesturing Cooper into a

living room that looked like it had been staged for a property magazine. 'Though I'm not sure what else I can add.'

'Just confirming a few details about that night.' Cooper remained standing as Sophia perched on the edge of an expensive-looking, grey, leather sofa. 'You said you left a nightclub, but we know for a fact you were picked up by Lord Carmody at the Dorchester.'

'Yes.' Sophia's fingers played with the edge of her sleeve. 'I know I should have said something, but I was scared of him coming after me, you know, demanding my silence. He offered me a lift home.'

Cooper watched her for a moment; DCI Walsh had been right, the moment the story was examined, she folded to the real one. She'd probably been waiting all day to give this rehearsed performance.

'Directly from the event?' she continued.

'Yes,' Sophia gave a slight frown. 'Am I in trouble?'

Cooper noted this down; Sophia would have been told what to say, but even then she couldn't be a hundred percent sure on what would be asked.

'Not from me,' Cooper smiled. 'Just sorting the timeline. Was he walking out of the party when you were offered the lift?'

'Yes, I'd spoken to his officer, Matthews,' Sophia was back to the calm, rehearsed script now. 'He was the one that offered. Between us, I think he was on something.'

'On something?' Cooper pulled out her notebook, as if about to write this down. She'd already heard from Temple Inn; Matthews was there, having admitted to doing cocaine. However, it was also suggested he might have been spiked – *was Sophia the person who did this?*

'Drugs,' Sophia said with a horror that felt straight from a cheesy Hammer Horror movie, but also hammering the point home. 'Definitely.'

'Ah,' Cooper replied, relaxing the pen.

'Aren't you going to write that down?'

'No,' Cooper replied calmly. 'And you needn't concern yourself. We gave DCI Matthews a full toxicology test the following day. It was completely clean of any traces of pharmaceuticals.'

'Really?' Sophia hadn't expected this, and her face caught in surprise. 'Are you sure? Did you test again?'

'We're happy with Matthews, but I am a little concerned you believed he offered this lift to you as they were leaving,' Cooper continued the lie matter-of-factly. 'It's just that the footage from the Dorchester shows you were there earlier. When Lord Carmody received the briefcase.'

Something flickered in Sophia's expression.

'There was no CCTV there.'

'Yes, but there were cameras.'

'Well, in that case, I don't remember a briefcase.'

'No?' Cooper pulled out her phone, showing the footage Jess had found. 'Because you were standing right there when someone handed it over.'

She leant closer.

'Maybe Matthews wasn't the one partaking in recreational pharmaceuticals that night?'

'No, it's just that I ... I wasn't paying attention.'

'Really?' Cooper kept her voice neutral. 'Because you seem to be watching pretty carefully here. I can play it again if you want.'

Sophia's fingers had stopped fidgeting.

'I was hired as company,' she said carefully. 'Nothing more.'

'By Mikhail Stefon.'

Another flicker.

'I don't know that name.'

'Look Sophia, you seem to be a clever woman, and you've done well to have a place like this, so let's cut to the chase, yeah?' Cooper moved slightly, positioning herself between Sophia and the door. 'You'll notice that I already know every answer you're giving, because we know what Stefon told you to say. And it was Mikhail Stefon, wasn't it? Who arranged everything? The dress, the timing, even the route home?'

'I told you; Lord Carmody offered me a lift.'

'No, you said the SEG officer did, who you also believed was on drugs,' Cooper watched Sophia's face. 'But let me also ask, did Carmody also insist on taking that specific road? The same road where, coincidentally, someone was waiting with a motorcycle?'

Sophia's eyes darted towards the door.

'I don't know what you mean.'

'The officers who found you said you were walking towards Epping,' Cooper continued. 'But you weren't lost, were you? You were looking for someone. Someone who was supposed to pick you up after you ran into the woods. Or did someone pick you up and take you somewhere you could be found, somewhere you could give your statement?'

'I was scared,' Sophia's voice hardened. 'I just ran.'

'Towards a pre-arranged meeting point?'

'You can't prove that.'

'No,' Cooper agreed. 'But I can prove you were part of it. The briefcase, the timing, the specific route – all of it planned. You ran down a path into Epping Forest, where a partner waited. Perhaps one of the people in the vans, maybe the Highwayman himself, before riding north to a car park near Epping, where, after ten minutes of walking down the road, you were found.'

'Because I ran through the woods!'

'You see, that's where I have the issue,' Cooper relaxed the notebook as she stared at Sophia. 'You see, I've been in those woods. Recently, in fact. And, at the sides of the road, there's leaves all over the place. But for you to run through the woods to get to where you were found. You'd have gotten mud –'

'I did!' Sophia protested. 'Check the statement! I was mud stained and my dress was torn from brambles!'

'But weirdly, your shoes weren't,' Cooper continued. 'And before you say you took them off, your stockings were clean on your feet, so you didn't run barefoot. You looked like someone who'd mainly gained some splatter from the wheels of a bike, maybe rubbed some on the dress for extra points ... but forgot to do the shoes.'

Something changed in Sophia's expression – fear, maybe, or realisation.

'I want a solicitor,' she said, rising.

'Of course,' Cooper didn't move. 'Though it might be worth knowing that the man who organised all this for you, Mikhail Stefon, hasn't returned from his last-minute trip to Prague.'

This time, the fear was unmistakable.

'What?'

'Missed his flight back. Phone's dead. Almost like he's disappeared.'

Sophia's composure cracked. She lunged for the door, but Cooper was already moving, years of training taking over. The takedown was textbook and with absolutely no unnecessary force. As Cooper secured the cuffs, Sophia finally broke.

'He promised,' she whispered. 'He promised he wouldn't leave me. That I'd be the woman who brought Carmody down, that I'd get my newspaper money.'

'Who promised?' Cooper asked quietly. 'Mikhail?'

Sophia started to laugh, but it held no humour.

'You don't understand,' she said. 'None of you understand what's really happening.'

'Then help us understand.'

Sophia was quiet for a long moment.

'Get me somewhere safe,' she said finally. 'Then we'll talk about what really happened that night.'

Cooper pulled out her radio.

'Control, PC Cooper. You might want to let DCI Walsh know we've got ourselves a witness.'

———

Billy had been working with audio software since his teens, the product of a well-spent youth, but this was different. Every change to the modulation revealed new layers, like peeling an onion made of white noise and electronic distortion.

'The thing about voice modulators,' he explained to no one in particular, though he knew Jess was still somewhere behind him, 'is they work in predictable ways. Raise or lower pitch, add distortion, maybe some reverb. But the base pattern stays the same.'

On his screen, the security footage played silently; the Highwayman confronting Reeves, the theatrical posturing, the final gunshot. Billy had watched it so many times he could lip read the dialogue – if he knew how to lip read, that was.

'My uncle gave me the clue when he talked about palatalisation,' he said. 'Most people think changing their voice means making it deeper. But that's actually harder to maintain. The overtones get muddy.'

He adjusted another setting, watching the waveform shift. 'So if we take the base frequency ...'

The sound kicked in, still distorted but clearer. The Highwayman's theatrical declaration echoed through the office.

'... *When ... great criminals – the Krays, Jack the ... Great Train Robbers ...*'

Billy tweaked the algorithm again. The mechanical edge faded slightly.

'... *those who hunted them. Detective ...*'

Another adjustment. The voice was normalising, becoming more natural. Behind him, he heard Bullman enter the office, probably drawn by the sound.

'... *But highway robbery? The pursuers are footnotes, irrelevant ...*'

Billy tapped out a key combination, and suddenly the modulation stripped away completely. The voice that emerged was younger, cultured, with the slight edge of someone trying to sound more important than they were.

'... *focus is always ... on us ...*'

Bullman's sharp intake of breath made Billy jump and turn. Her face had gone pale.

'Play that again,' she breathed.

Billy reversed the footage, adjusting the final filter.

'... *focus is always ... on us ...*'

'I know that voice,' Bullman's fingers gripped the back of Billy's chair. 'From Carmody's house. That's his bloody son.'

'Lewis? The one who tried to stop you from seeing his father?' Billy started scanning through YouTube.

'Sorry, are we diverting you from something else?' Bullman asked with a wry smile.

'We don't have Lewis on record,' Billy explained. 'But his father's important, so I bet he's in a news report, or something …'

He paused.

'Here we are. Lewis Carmody arguing with a hunt sabo-teur, two years ago,' he said, zooming through the footage, until a young man with floppy hair was seen shouting.

'… *think you own the bloody land! But you don't! I own the bloody land and I can kill whatever the hell I want on it –*'

Billy lined up both audio tracks and played them one after the other. It was unmistakable; the same voice, one trying to sound authoritative, the other hidden behind elec-tronics, but unmistakably the same speech pattern, the same slight emphasis on certain words.

'Got you, you little shit,' Bullman smiled grimly. 'Billy, can you clean this up enough for court?'

'Already on it.' His fingers flew across the keyboard. 'Though we might have a problem.'

'What?' Before she continued though, Bullman's phone buzzed. She checked it, her expression shifting from concern to something closer to satisfaction.

'Get that analysis to Monroe,' she said. 'Cooper's just found us a witness. Looks like your voice match isn't the only piece falling into place.'

She stared at the screen, the slightest of smiles on her face.

'Got him,' she muttered. 'That's going to sink them.'

'Yeah … not exactly,' Billy replied reluctantly as his fingers moved across the keyboard, pulling up a complex waveform display. 'We can't use this in evidence.'

'What do you mean?' Bullman looked horrified at this. 'Why the hell not?'

'The problem with voice modulation is it's all mathematical,' Billy explained almost apologetically. 'Frequency shifting, harmonics, overtones – they're just numbers. And numbers can be changed.'

He highlighted a section of the waveform.

'See this pattern here? It's the base frequency of the voice; what we'd call the fundamental. When someone uses a modulator, they're just shifting these numbers up or down.'

His fingers flitted across the keys, adjusting parameters.

'First, we strip out the electronic artefacts – the bits that make it sound robotic,' he said, and as they listened the harsh edge of the modulation faded. 'Then we look at the harmonic structure.'

On a second screen, a spectral analysis displayed complex patterns of sound.

'Everyone's voice has specific overtones, like a fingerprint. But ...' Billy tweaked another setting. 'If I shift these patterns, adjust the resonance ...'

The Highwayman's voice emerged again, but now it carried distinctly different tones – older, authoritative, with more than a hint of Glasgow in the vowels.

'... *focus is always ... on us ...*'

Bullman's eyes widened.

'That's unmistakably Monroe.'

'Or we can adjust the formant structure,' Billy said as, pausing the revised sounds, he continued typing. 'Shift the resonant frequencies that make voices sound unique.'

Now it was Declan's voice – same words, same intensity, but with his characteristic cadence.

'Change the pitch modulation ...'

Another adjustment. The words now came in something incredibly similar to Anjli's precise tones.

'Modify the spectral envelope ...'

His own voice emerged.

'And if we really want to have fun ...'

He combined several adjustments, and Doctor Marcos's sardonic drawl filled the room.

Billy closed the program, saving his work but knowing it'd never see a courtroom.

'Any halfway-decent defence solicitor would show exactly what I just did,' he said. 'Demonstrate how easily it can be manipulated. All we'd be proving is that someone used a voice modulator, and that we chose Lewis Carmody's voice to be the finished product.'

Bullman's earlier triumph had deflated visibly.

'But we know it's him.'

'We know,' Billy agreed. 'But knowing and proving are different things. Especially when you're dealing with digital evidence. At least we're certain now, though.'

'Certain enough to set a trap?' Bullman asked.

'Maybe,' Billy replied, turning to face her. 'But we'll need something more concrete than voices to make it stick.'

Bullman nodded, already thinking ahead to their next move. They had the knowledge – now they just needed the evidence to support it.

'So, can we do that with any voice?' she asked, a gleam in her eye. 'I really want to see Monroe's eyes, when we play audio of him arguing against Scottish Independence.'

Billy smiled at this.

'Actually, before that, we might have something we can use,' he said. 'The security guard reckons he saw no one come in or out, right?'

'Lewis Carmody isn't a sodding ghost, Billy.'

'Exactly. The shooting happened on FCA property. If Lewis Carmody was there, how did he get in?'

Bullman scratched at her lip.

'Does Lord Carmody have a pass?'

'To the FCA? Probably.' Billy was already typing. 'And he would come in through one of the back entrances too, to avoid press. So there might be multiple ways in. FCA isn't exactly Number Ten, in the list of "most secure building in London".'

'If Lewis used his father's card to gain access, there'll be a log,' Bullman considered this. 'We can link Lewis to the card, then the card to Lord Carmody, and then Lord Carmody to Reeves' murder.'

'Which means this gets a lot more dangerous,' Billy added quietly.

20

CONFESSIONS

In the interview room, Declan waited for the tension to settle. Emma had moved to stand beside Kitson, one hand resting protectively on his shoulder. Doctor Marcos leaned against the wall by the door, her expression suggesting she'd expected this.

'You were the Rider?' Anjli asked, her voice carrying genuine surprise.

'For all of it,' Emma replied firmly. 'The whole time.'

Declan noticed Kitson's slight flinch at this, though he tried to hide it.

'Stephen helped me learn,' Emma continued. 'I was dating him, and he taught me to ride like they did.'

'You rode before?'

'Since I was a kid, on dirt bikes,' Emma nodded. 'He taught me the stunts, the technique – everything.'

Kitson went to speak, but Emma shook her head.

'I worked in the City when we met, and I saw firsthand what was happening with the traders.'

'The corruption?'

'Yeah. I couldn't take it, so I quit. But, when I joined the Market Integrity Commission, I also realised nobody was going to do anything about it.'

'So, you became a Highwayman?' Declan kept his voice neutral.

'More of a modern folk hero.' As Emma said this, the faintest ghost of a smile crossed her face. 'The theatrical element helped hide what I was really doing.'

'Which was?'

'Gathering evidence. Documents. Passwords, when we could get them, although half the time they'd just get changed. I wanted proof of market manipulation.'

She squeezed Kitson's shoulder.

'James helped change the bike. Made it perfect for what I needed. But the riding ... that was all me.'

'Even after the accident?' Declan watched her carefully. 'After Stephen died?'

Emma's expression didn't waver.

'All of it,' she repeated. 'Every robbery. Every ride.'

Declan glanced at Doctor Marcos, who raised an eyebrow slightly. They both knew Emma was lying – protecting someone. Maybe multiple someones, people in the room, perhaps.

'The last robbery, six years back. It was different. More precise, less theatrical,' Declan watched her face. 'Danny Freeman noticed it. Said the riding style had changed.'

'I was tired,' Emma replied smoothly. 'Eight robberies in, the adrenaline wasn't quite the same.'

She smiled, and for the first time, it was genuine.

'Ask your stupidly tall bike-riding friend if my riding style wasn't tight enough, especially after I left him on the canal bridge.'

Declan paused his next response. *She had to have been the rider to know that. But was she the rider six years ago?*

'Tell us about the night Stephen died,' Doctor Marcos said.

'I wasn't there.'

'No?' Declan glanced at Doctor Marcos. 'Where were you?'

'Home. In bed.' Emma's voice was steady, but her hand had tightened on Kitson's shoulder. 'I heard about it the next morning.'

'Must have been hard. Losing him like that.'

'It was.'

'But you kept going. Did the last robbery anyway.'

'Yes.'

'Why?'

'Because someone had to.' Now Emma's voice carried real passion. 'Because what we'd – *I'd* – found ... it was too important to stop.'

'We?' Declan caught the slip.

'I.' Emma repeated quickly. 'I meant what I'd found.'

Declan sat back, studying her.

'You know what I think?' he said finally. 'I think you're protecting people. Dead and alive.'

'I've told you everything.'

'No. You've told us what you want us to hear. A story that wraps everything up neatly. Takes all the blame.'

'It's the truth.'

'Parts of it, maybe.' Declan's voice softened. 'But not all of it.'

'I rode that bike earlier today,' Emma said quietly. 'Ask your sergeant. I led him on quite the chase.'

'And why were you there?'

'To check on James.' Emma's voice softened. 'I was worried.'

'Worried enough to go through his paperwork?' Declan said. 'If you were such a good friend, why the theatrics? Why not just ask him what you wanted to know?'

He rose now, facing her.

'You knew we were coming for him. You knew we believed he was the Essex Rider – or at least one of them. When Monroe and Bullman spoke to you, you realised things were closer than you believed. So, I think you deliberately dressed as the Rider, waited until one of us was there at Kitson's workshop, and then made an appearance, purely to lead us away, to make us believe Kitson wasn't the Rider.'

Emma's face darkened.

'He isn't the Rider.'

'Are you the new Rider?' Anjli asked. 'Did you rob Carmody? Did you burn the briefcase in a skip behind James Kitson's workshop?'

'I couldn't have as I wasn't in town –' Emma started, but then stopped, quickly changing tack. 'No.'

'No?' Declan frowned. 'So you weren't around two nights ago ... James wasn't around two nights ago, either. Care to share where you were? Maybe where you both were?'

For the first time, Emma smiled properly.

'Actually, that's why I originally came here,' she said. 'To tell you where we were. Manchester Royal Infirmary. James had an appointment with a specialist about the vertigo.'

'That's a long way to go for a doctor.'

'He's the best,' Emma's hand hadn't left Kitson's shoulder. 'We stayed at the Midland Hotel. Separate rooms. Had dinner in the restaurant. Breakfast too. You can check my credit card receipts. But it means that when someone was burning documents in James's skip, we were a hundred and eighty miles away.'

'You always go with him to these appointments?'

'Since the accident.' Something flickered in Emma's eyes. 'Since Stephen.'

'Because you feel guilty?' Declan asked softly.

'Because he's my friend.' Emma's voice hardened. 'And someone's trying to destroy him. Like they destroyed Stephen.'

There was a long moment of uncomfortable silence. Declan looked over at Kitson.

'Let me guess,' he said. 'You didn't tell us where you were because you were trying to keep Miss Thorne out of the enquiry.'

Kitson said nothing, but his body language spoke the words for him. This seemingly confirmed, Declan nodded to himself and then returned his attention to Emma.

'We all know you're lying,' he said quietly. 'About being the Rider. About all of it.'

'Maybe ... but can you prove that?' Emma gave the slightest of smiles.

'No. And that's rather the point, isn't it?' Declan sighed.

'I've told you the truth.'

'Parts of it.' Declan glanced at Kitson. 'The Manchester trip, for example. That's real. But the rest? You're protecting people.'

'I'm confessing to multiple crimes,' Emma replied. 'Isn't that enough? Who else is going to solve your case?'

'Peter Kendall's down the hall,' Anjli said. 'He's been telling us about anonymous packages. Evidence that arrived after each robbery. Maybe he can tell us something.'

Something shifted in Emma's expression.

'Peter Kendall,' she said carefully. 'Yeah, alright. I chose him. He worked at the FCA, had a reputation for exposing things. A bit bitter, a bit angry at the system. Perfect for what we needed.'

'You sent him the evidence?'

'After each robbery. Everything I found. Documents, passwords, trading records,' she gave a small shrug. 'He did what we – I – expected. Took it to the papers, made himself look good. Started making money on the side too, though that wasn't part of the plan.'

'And now he's terrified,' Anjli said. 'Because someone's using the same method, the same theatrical distraction. But this time it's not about exposing corruption.'

'No,' Emma agreed. 'This time it's about profiting from it.'

'Did you kill Martin Reeves?'

'No,' Emma shook her head, then held out her hands. 'I genuinely don't know who the new Rider is. But I will state, on oath, it isn't James. Let him get on with his life; the poor man's suffered enough.'

Declan waited a moment.

'The last ride,' he said. 'Did you know Kendall had been making money on the side? That he'd created some fake accounts for his broker to use?'

'Not at the time,' Emma shook her head. 'But there was a committee hearing, and I learned that someone was making money from it. And Peter's not exactly a mastermind; I worked out it was him very quickly, but I couldn't prove it. So I threw a Trojan Horse into the last load of details, sending them to Kendall, and watched to see if the random stocks I'd suggested rose or not.'

She sighed.

'You see, if it was a normal heist, the data could have been out there. But with the fake data, nobody else would look.'

'And did you see it move?'

Emma nodded.

'Yes,' she said. 'But it wasn't Kendall's stock accounts that fluctuated. It was Adrian Carmody.'

'Carmody made money from this?'

'No, he lost it, because it was fake stock information,' Emma chuckled. 'I checked into him, but I couldn't make anything stick. He wasn't making money, and claimed he'd been given the tips from friends who also bought in – and lost out on – stocks.'

'Do you remember who?'

'The lobbyist, Mikhail Stefon, an Essex entrepreneur –'

'Ryan Boyask?'

'Yeah, that's the one.'

Declan frowned.

'Then if it was Carmody, how did they get the tips?'

'You might want to ask Kendall that,' Emma smiled, but then the smile faded as she realised her predicament right now.

Declan went to continue but then stopped as a thought crossed his mind.

'What were you looking for?' he asked. 'In the spreadsheets?'

'What spreadsheets?' Emma replied, confused.

'Martin Reeves died last night. And when he did, he was trying to download FCA files. Ones connected to the Essex Rider case. And ones that, apparently, you'd been looking at recently as well.'

'It's not a crime to look at files,' Emma replied defensively.

'I never said it was,' Declan countered. 'But if you're now

claiming that you were the Essex Rider, it does become a bit of a conflict, doesn't it?'

Emma sighed and nodded.

'When I heard about what happened to Carmody, I wanted to check something,' she said.

'What exactly did you want to check?'

'Whether he was being a lying sack of shit, if I'm being honest.'

'Why would you think he was anything but?'

'Have you spoken to Kendall yet about the money he was making?' Emma asked.

'In part,' Declan admitted. 'Is there something more that you know we should be asking?'

'You should ask where it went,' Emma gave a dark, humourless smile. 'You should ask where the money he made disappeared to, and why it disappeared shortly after he ended up having a chat with Carmody.'

Declan bit his lip as he thought through the statement.

'So what,' he said. 'Carmody finds out that Kitson here – I'm sorry, *you* – were the Essex Rider. Talk me through this, explain to me what I'm missing.'

Emma sighed a second time.

'Look,' she said. 'I told you I did one last job after the explosion. I had to prove to myself that Carmody knew. Martin Reeves told Carmody everything, trying to prove his worth, but then instead of being arrested, James and Stephen were targeted. But Kendall – the money he made – he should have had millions in his bank account. Yet, when we looked into him six months later, he didn't have a penny. He'd withdrawn it all, placed it into other stocks, which had then been bought by other companies and other brokers. Basically, it was a very long money-laundering route that left Kendall with nothing.'

'You think Carmody blackmailed him?'

'I think Reeves told Carmody everything he knew, including who the Essex Rider was, and who the whistle-blower was,' Emma nodded. 'I think Carmody confronted him, demanded the money and, more importantly, demanded the stolen files if it ever happened again. And when I sent my Trojan horse out, Kendall immediately gave it to Lord Carmody, who passed it out to his friends.'

'But, if Lord Carmody knew who the Essex Rider was and kept the case unsolved –'

'Well, they didn't, did they?' Emma shook her head. 'They swept it under the carpet, pretended it never happened. Remember, we were investigating the financial irregularities, not the thefts.'

She shifted her stance.

'Look, all I can tell you is that when we started looking into the companies that had profited – ones that had been targeted during my run – several of them turned out to be connected to Carmody. Sovereign Holdings was one.'

'Ryan Boyask,' Declan said.

'And a couple that were connected to Mikhail Stefon.'

'So, if the Essex Rider was targeting Carmody's friends, it made sense that once he was known, Carmody and his friends would target the Essex Rider,' Declan trailed off into silence.

The moment of quiet didn't last long, however.

'I was the Essex Rider,' Kitson said quietly, almost as a whisper.

'James –' Emma started, but Kitson looked up at her. His eyes flashing.

'No,' he interrupted. 'You've done a lot for me over the years, but I'm not having you throw your life away.'

He turned back to face Declan.

'Me and Stephen, we were both the Rider,' he explained. 'It was mainly me, but Stephen did it twice so I could gain an alibi. But we were reckless in what we did, and Emma heard rumours we were on the police's radar, thanks to Martin Reeves, who reckoned he was a better investigator.'

He chuckled wearily.

'Who, sadly, was better, as Emma hadn't realised in time to divert him,' he continued. 'Then, there was the accident ...'

He looked away, and Declan knew what was going through his mind; that Stephen Mahoney could have died because of his identity as the Essex Rider.

'And Emma?' Anjli asked.

'She helped us, gave the information, and passed what we gained to Kendall,' Kitson admitted. 'But she wasn't the Rider. Well, maybe once, after the accident.'

Emma looked furiously at Kitson, but he glared back resolutely.

'You've done so much for me,' he said calmly. 'I won't let you do this.'

He looked back at Declan.

'They knew,' he said. 'They worked it out, and they sabotaged the jump to kill us both. When I told Emma, she tried to find proof, but the lobbyist, Stefon? He'd cleaned the place. Interestingly, we learnt later he'd been there that day, too.'

'When the electrics went out?'

Kitson nodded.

'Nothing that can be proven, though,' he said. 'They thought they'd stopped us, and then we heard Reeves had told Carmody everything before that happened. Got himself a pat on the back and a promotion, Kendall was dragged in to see headteacher and ... boom.'

Another uniformed officer had arrived by now, and Declan nodded at Emma.

'Please take Miss Thorne into custody,' he said, glancing back at Kitson. 'If you can wait here, I think you can see we have a lot to discuss before we return to your questioning.'

Kitson nodded and, as the officer took Emma away, Declan followed, Anjli and Doctor Marcos beside him. They stopped to face each other in the corridor, the door to the interview room closed.

'I don't like this,' Doctor Marcos muttered.

'You think we're missing something?'

'No, I mean we're spending time on people who shouldn't be our focus,' Doctor Marcos replied irritably. 'All these guys are guilty of is exposing corruption and giving some justice.'

'And the actual thefts, and the –'

'I get they broke the law,' Doctor Marcos snapped back at Declan. 'But nobody was hurt. Nobody died. And they didn't really profit, did they? From what I see, them doing this effectively caused the accident that killed Mahoney and injured Kitson.'

She looked back at the door, where behind now sat a broken and dejected James Kitson.

'She lost her love, and he lost his career – technically his own love,' she muttered. 'I just think they've paid enough.'

Declan didn't answer this; if he was being honest, he actually agreed, and they'd seen far worse swept to the side.

'So, what's your solution?' he asked. 'Because I'm all ears.'

'We're here to solve a crime, so let's solve it,' Doctor Marcos straightened. 'And if either James Kitson or Emma

Thorne can help in the process, surely that could go towards their defence.'

Declan considered this.

'You're right,' he admitted. 'Let's solve the current problem first.'

'They'll likely get involved anyway,' Anjli admitted as they started down the corridor, back towards the main office area downstairs. 'You don't burn a briefcase in someone's skip unless you want to give a message to them.'

'True,' Declan smiled, an idea coming to mind. 'So let's show we got it, and see what comes out of the woodwork?'

21

HALLOWED HALLS

Monroe hadn't been as welcoming to the idea of letting Emma Thorne and James Kitson off but understood the reasoning. And so, it was decided that as they were technically under Charles Baker's remit right now, perhaps it would be Charles Baker that could, like Solomon, cut this Gordian knot in two.

Declan had expected to go alone to Westminster, but Monroe had insisted on coming with him. Declan wondered whether it was because he'd walked in to hearing his own voice speaking out about Scotland never leaving the loving bosom of the Westminster elite, informed afterwards that not only was this the same software that proved Lewis Carmody was the Highwayman, but also proved that they couldn't use it to *show* a court that Lewis Carmody was the Highwayman.

Monroe had needed air, and so he joined Declan in his "wee little trip to the devil's lair" as he called it.

Usually, Baker would have been in Number Ten – it seemed an art gallery meeting was out of the question this time – but, on checking, they saw he was currently in a meeting in Portcullis House and would meet them in a small office there. It was made to sound as if he was helping them, but Declan knew it was really a case of Baker not wanting anyone to know about the meeting, especially Jennifer Farnham-Ewing.

And so, it was in a small office, down a nondescript backroom corridor that Declan and Monroe debriefed the current Prime Minister of the United Kingdom.

'OK THEN,' CHARLES BAKER SAID AS HE LEANT BACK AGAINST his chair, watching the two men in front of him. 'What do you have for me?'

'Well, we're zeroing in on the suspect for the robberies, and we should have a response for you in the next few hours,' Monroe replied, struggling to find a comfortable position in the chair he now sat upon.

'And what exactly does that police speak mean?' Baker asked, a smile on his face. 'Because that could mean that you've found somebody, you don't know if you've found somebody, or you're still looking for somebody.'

Declan stepped in.

'Cards on the table?' he asked. 'We think we've worked out who the Essex Rider was six years ago, and we –'

'I don't give a toss about someone six years ago,' Baker snapped. 'I brought you in because I wanted you to sort out who stole our secrets.'

'I was getting to that, sir,' Declan said, forcing the "sir" out pointedly. 'I get that you're annoyed, but we also believe that the people who did this were using the Essex Rider as their alibi.'

'Fine, fine,' Baker sighed, waving a hand to move things

along. 'But seriously, I don't care about some crimes that happened with city folks six years ago. Nobody was hurt. But this modern-day Turpin's already killed someone.'

Declan noted this down in his notebook, nodding as he did so.

'Yes,' Monroe agreed. 'In that case, we'll cut to the chase. We believe the Highwayman is Lewis Carmody, the son of Lord Adrian Carmody.'

Baker's eyebrows rose in surprise.

'The son did it? So what? Are you saying that Carmody didn't know?'

'Oh no, sir, we believe it was all part of the same plan,' Monroe continued. 'You see, a few months ago, Carmody got wind that he was about to be removed from office. I believe you were unhappy with him about something. You're always unhappy with people, so this feels like a solid guess.'

Baker didn't respond to this, but his curt nod was all they needed.

'Anyway,' Monroe continued, aware he was on the right track now. 'He also had some large payments to make, some kind of debt he had to clear. We understand this was when he started to plan some kind of split from his wife, maybe a divorce, and possibly because of the latter, he also created and set up a new company. The partners in it were his son, Mikhail Stefon, and Ryan Boyask.'

'Stefon I've heard of,' Baker nodded. 'We'll come to him in a moment. But Boyask?'

'We know little about him,' Declan said. 'One thing we can prove is that he owns a variety of businesses, including a company that leases vans to the public – two of which were used in the heist a couple of nights back.'

'So, Lewis Carmody was the Highwayman, and Ryan

Boyask was the man who supplied the vans,' Baker mused. 'How is Lord Carmody still involved?'

'We think he knew something was coming,' Declan explained. 'We think he was given warning that he might get a package that night. So, when you thought you were surprising him, in effect, you weren't.'

'And how would he know that?' Baker shook his head. 'No, don't bother answering. Westminster is a leaky bloody sieve. Somebody somewhere would have told him. I wouldn't put it past Jennifer Farnham-Ewing to do it just to screw me over. So what, Carmody knows about it, then has somebody steal it so he can read it at his leisure?'

'No, sir,' Monroe shook his head. 'We believe he followed through with what they promised ... which was to steal the case and then set fire to it, destroying the items inside, and giving him public deniability on whether he saw the information or not, as the timeline showed the papers were destroyed soon after the theft, which also showed he simply didn't have the time. However, we have a witness statement saying that after being given the briefcase, Carmody entered the men's toilets, where he stayed in a cubicle for three minutes.'

'And this is great detective work?' Baker scoffed.

'Sir, Detective Chief Inspector Matthews claims he was in there with Carmody and could hear him taking photos. We're hoping he wasn't taking photos of, well, what he was doing, but more of what he was *doing*,' Monroe added.

Baker nodded, understanding the emphasis.

'So, you think he opened the case, took photos of everything, and then had it burned to give himself plausible deniability.'

'Yes, sir, I believe we just stated that,' Declan confirmed.

'Now, we're assuming he didn't use a Government phone, so we're looking into his personal one. We believe that during the event, Mikhail Stefon gave Matthews some drugs – what he thought was just normal cocaine but was actually spiked. It put him off his game and made him paranoid and nervous when the Highwayman approached, which meant he wouldn't confront him.'

'There was a micro-explosive in the car under the wheel arch, which detonated and took out the front wheel,' Monroe continued. 'We don't know for sure yet, and we're questioning her right now, but we believe this was done either by the Highwayman, or possibly by Sophia, the "passenger" Carmody picked up, who was sitting in the back.'

'This is great,' Baker laughed. 'Carmody ... we can nail him to the wall with this. So why haven't you arrested him?'

'Because everything is still circumstantial, sir,' Declan replied. 'We believe Lewis is the Highwayman, because we have video footage of him killing Martin Reeves. He uses a voice modulator, and our cyber expert, Detective Sergeant Fitzwarren, could reverse-engineer it to reveal Lewis Carmody's voice.'

'But it's not something that can be used as evidence in a court of law,' Monroe continued. 'You can alter that modulation to sound like anybody. A good solicitor would tear that apart.'

'Bullshit,' Baker snapped.

'Sir, we can play you a tape of you saying how much you love Michelle Rose right now,' Monroe smiled. 'We thought you'd think this, and we made sure we had a wee something to show you.'

'Christ no, I don't want to hear that,' Baker shivered. 'And feel free to delete it completely. So, what else?'

'Boyask's secretary claims his vans were stolen, so we can't prove that he provided them that night,' Declan continued. 'Carmody wasn't seen in public holding the documents, so we can't prove he took them. All we can prove is that his company made money, but companies are made to make money. That it was profitable isn't helpful here, especially as he can claim he's out of the loop while in the ministry, and with it effectively blind-trust hidden from him. We intend to call him in, however, and see if we can –'

'No.' Baker shook his head, sighing. 'If you're not sure and you're scrabbling in the dark to prove him guilty, we're not going that way. I want this so airtight there's no way he can breathe. I want this nailed to him. I want him caught in the act. I don't care what you need to do, gentlemen, but we are not acting like police here. You are God's bloody vengeance on this man. If you believe he stole secrets and used them, forcing me to U-turn on several policies, then I want you to catch Carmody in the sodding Highwayman mask with the gun in his hand.'

'Sir, that means we might have to pardon people from the earlier case –'

'I don't care what you have to do!' Baker exploded. 'I will not have this go through the courts only to be thrown out! That would kill my career!'

'I'm sorry,' Monroe replied, stone-faced. 'I didn't realise we were that concerned about your career right now.'

'Of course we're worried about my bloody career, Monroe!' Baker continued angrily. 'Anybody would be. Don't be a bloody fool.'

He leant forward.

'I'm grateful that you've worked out who did this, but let's be honest, it wasn't that difficult. We've had our eye on

Carmody for a while. You work out exactly how he did it, when he did it, why he did it, who did what, and how you can prove it. Because unless you've got Carmody literally standing there with the gun in his hand saying "yes, I did this", we won't be able to put this through. He has too many high-level friends who will cause me problems.'

There was a long moment of silence before Monroe nodded.

'Okay, Charlie, what's the actual issue here?' he asked. 'Is it connected to the man hovering outside the door for the last five minutes?'

Baker muttered to himself and waved for the man to enter the office. He was in his fifties, slim, and seemed familiar.

'This is Alex Curtis,' Baker explained. 'He runs the London desk.'

'Of?'

'Of something above your bloody pay grade,' Baker muttered, but Monroe simply narrowed his eyes as he examined the new arrival.

'We've met, right?'

'Yes,' Curtis nodded. 'I worked with your nephew, Tom Marlowe, a couple of times.'

Monroe smiled.

'You're the one who reinstated him into MI5,' he exclaimed. 'We like you. Why are you talking to us?'

'Mikhail Stefon,' Curtis replied. 'What do you know of him?'

'Lobbyist, rich, was a conscript in the Yugoslav army before it turned to shite,' Monroe frowned. 'Why, what should we know?'

Curtis looked back at Baker, who nodded.

'Officially, he's an Eastern European entrepreneur,' he

began. 'Unofficially, he's a former Yugoslav People's Army conscript who walked out of the ruins of the JNA in 1992 and disappeared for a decade. We know he enlisted at eighteen, trained as a combat engineer – explosives, demolitions, sabotage. When the army collapsed, he didn't go home. He went to Serbia.'

'Serbia?'

'The Yugoslav Wars were in full swing by then – ethnic conflicts, state breakups, massacres. Serbia wasn't officially at war, but its paramilitary units were fighting in Bosnia and Croatia, later in Kosovo. Best intelligence puts him in one of those units – Red Berets, Scorpions, something like that. That means black ops, deep cover work, urban warfare. More importantly, bomb-making.'

At this, Declan glanced at Monroe and saw he was thinking the same thing.

'Small or large?'

'Whatever it needed,' Curtis shrugged. 'These weren't just battlefield demolitions; they were assassinations, infrastructure sabotage, car bombs, false flag operations. He was in Bosnia; he was in Kosovo. He was on the wrong side of the NATO airstrikes in '99. He survived, which tells you something. By the time the wars ended, he had a skillset someone was willing to pay for.'

'There's a big jump from that to what he is now,' Monroe replied. 'How did you miss this?'

Curtis reddened at the comment.

'Honestly? We lost track of him after the Kosovo conflict,' he admitted. 'By 2002, he resurfaces in Brussels, cleaned up, and respectable. He's moving money, lobbying for Eastern European energy firms, advising on security. On paper, he's a self-made entrepreneur. In reality, he's got ties to Serbian intelligence, Russian FSB, and a laundry list of former war criminals turned entrepreneurs. He doesn't pull triggers any more, but he knows where the bodies are buried, some of which he probably put there himself.'

Baker watched Declan as Curtis spoke, and Declan realised this wasn't the first time the Prime Minister had heard this.

'Post-Brexit, he shifts operations to London. A fixer, a strategist, a go-between. He plays power games in Whitehall, greases wheels in the City, and keeps his hands in certain – let's say off-the-books – ventures.'

'Christ, he's a Russian spy,' Monroe muttered.

'No, what he is, is useful, and we've made sure he knows it,' Baker replied. 'He's not one of ours, but he's an asset. A reluctant one.'

'One that's now screwing around with your secret financial documents,' Declan said softly. 'No wonder you needed this fast and secret. If this gets out, that you gave a potential Russian ally our deepest financial plans in a pissing contest with a Lord you hated ...'

'Yes, well, hindsight is always great, isn't it?' Baker snapped. 'The question isn't what we do about it, but what *you* do about it.'

Declan considered this.

'Would you like us to tell you what we'll do about it?' he asked.

'Yes, I bloody would,' Baker finally relaxed back into the chair, his anger dissipating. 'Please, for the love of God, tell me.'

Quietly, and with a smile on his face, sitting in an unknown office on a nondescript corridor, Declan told him.

BILLY RUBBED HIS EYES, THE GLOW OF MULTIPLE SCREENS making patterns dance in his vision. He'd been cross-referencing private airfield manifests since the City Airport team reported Mikhail's no-show, each dead end leading to three more possibilities.

'This is bloody ridiculous,' he muttered, pulling up another terminal window. 'How many shell companies does one person need?'

On his left screen, a complex web of corporate ownership diagrams sprawled like some demented family tree. On the right, flight manifests from every private airfield within fifty miles of London scrolled past. The centre screen showed his custom search algorithm, methodically connecting company names to known aliases.

'Talk to me, my pretty little computer genius,' Bullman called from Monroe's office. 'Tell me you've found something.'

'Working on it, Guv.' Billy's fingers flew across the keyboard. 'But these aren't normal shell companies. Each one owns part of another, which owns part of a third ... it's like someone's played corporate Jenga with the registers.'

He highlighted another connection, adding it to his growing diagram.

'Sovereign Asset Management owned forty percent of Premium Fleet Rentals, which owned shares in a dozen other companies, each of which ... hang on.'

Something caught his eye – a pattern in the noise. He typed faster, pulling up registration details.

'What is it?'

'Sovereign Asset Management. They're not just connected

to the van company.' Billy's screen filled with financial records. 'They've got fingers in everything. Including ...'

He paused, double-checking his findings.

'Including what?'

'A private aviation firm. The one, in fact, that flew Mikhail Stefon to Prague last night,' Billy was already diving deeper into the records. 'And they've just chartered a jet.'

The booking request had been buried in Biggin Hill's system; a last-minute arrangement through three different shell companies. But the payment trail hadn't been hidden, probably because they didn't expect someone to look into it. Billy's fingers flickered across the keys, following the electronic breadcrumbs.

'Got you, you sneaky bastard.'

'Billy?' Anjli appeared behind him, peering at the screens. 'Want to share with the class?'

'Look at this,' Billy pulled up the flight plan. 'Private jet, arriving from Prague in ...'

He checked his watch.

'Forty minutes. Scheduled one-hour turnaround, then continuing to Zagreb.'

'Zagreb?'

'Capital of Croatia,' Billy explained, still typing. 'Zagreb's not a typical destination for British fugitives, and that's probably why it's attractive. It allows someone to avoid the heightened scrutiny you'd get on routes to places like Spain or the Netherlands, and it's a quieter route, easier to slip through unnoticed.'

'Does it have extradition?'

'It's in place, of course, but the process in Croatia can be slower and more bureaucratic compared to Western Europe.' Billy continued to scan the screens. 'That can buy a fugitive, especially one with Stefon's connections, valuable time to reorganise or move on. Because that's the other thing – Zagreb is a gateway. From there, it's an easy step into Serbia, Bosnia, or Montenegro – countries where enforcement cooperation can be slower, and it's far easier to disappear.'

He shrugged.

'Or maybe his mum lives there,' he finished. 'But either way, he slipped up with the payment.'

He highlighted a transaction record.

'See? Look at the passenger manifest – just says "private party". But the catering order's for one person.'

'What kind of catering?' De'Geer asked from the back of the room.

'Seriously?' Billy turned to stare at him. 'That's what you focus on?'

'Details matter,' De'Geer shrugged. 'And I'm hungry.'

'Children,' Bullman interrupted. 'Focus. Billy, you're sure about this?'

'He's running, Guv.' Billy pulled up more data. 'The charter was booked two hours after Thwaites called in about him missing his commercial flight. And look, he's paid for fuel stops all the way to Montenegro.'

'No extradition treaty,' Anjli noted.

'Exactly.' Billy highlighted another transaction. 'He's been moving money too, over the last twenty-four hours. Large transfers from London accounts, all just under reporting thresholds.'

'He's clearing out,' Bullman muttered. 'Getting ready to vanish.'

'Not if we can help it,' Anjli was already reaching for her jacket. 'How long till the plane lands?'

'Thirty-five minutes. But you'll need to move fast. One hour turnaround means he won't want to hang around.'

'Take backup,' Bullman ordered. 'If he's running, he's desperate. And desperate people do stupid things.'

Anjli nodded at De'Geer, and the two of them left the office at speed. Billy watched them leave, then turned back to his screens. An email had just arrived from Monroe about new information on Mikhail Stefon.

'Oh, shit,' he muttered as he read it, turning to face Bullman. 'We need more backup there! Way more backup!'

22

FUGITIVE

THE PRIVATE AIRSTRIP WAS ALL SHADOWS AND TALL SECURITY lights, and Anjli felt it was the kind of place that specialised in discretion at premium rates. When you flew to a private airfield, you were either super rich or, in this case, didn't want the attention that an international hub would give you.

A sign at the entrance announced "Biggin Hill Private Aviation Services" in a brushed-steel style of lettering that probably cost more than the Temple Inn's monthly budget. Her car sat dark near the perimeter fence, while De'Geer, who had ridden his bike rather than a squad car, was hidden behind the maintenance shed. It had been decided before they even left that they didn't want to spook Mikhail Stefon from flying off. After all, a plane landing could easily carry on and rise back up, and squad cars with blue flashing lights were likely to be a bit of a red flag for the man.

If she was being honest, Anjli wondered whether De'Geer, having been bettered by Emma Thorne as the High-wayman, was trying to prove that he really *was* a very good motorcycle rider, although the last thing Anjli wanted to see was De'Geer riding his motorcycle in some kind of "chicken" competition against a private jet. Of course, if you could afford a private jet, you were richer than Croesus or you didn't want customs to see what you were bringing with you. And that Mikhail Stefon had turned down an already paid for several-hundred-pound ticket on a commercial jet to pay out the money for this private flight, meant that he was desperate not to be seen.

Shame that wasn't happening.

'Flight's ten minutes out,' De'Geer's voice came through the car speaker, her phone connected through to him at the moment. Even whispered, his voice betrayed his Scandinavian heritage.

'If he's even on the bloody thing,' Anjli checked her watch. The information that Billy had gathered suggested that this was definitely Mikhail Stefon's escape route. But until the plane landed, it was very much a Schrödinger's plane – he was either on it or he wasn't. There was every chance even that he knew they'd find this and had gone by train somewhere – Prague itself being quite a good travel hub.

'Are we sure he's even coming back here?' she muttered. 'If you're in Prague and you want to go to Zagreb, there's plenty of overland ways.'

'Maybe he needed to pick something up here,' De'Geer suggested. 'He left in a hurry. He's probably not coming back …'

He trailed off, and Anjli knew what he meant. There was every chance he could have asked someone to pick something important up for him, something he'd left behind, and drop it off to the airstrip while he was waiting for the plane. This meant there'd be some kind of handover, very much likely in the terminal of the private charter company. And, following the email they'd both received about his illustrious past, that handover could involve anything.

'Has anybody turned up?'

'Not yet,' De'Geer replied. 'I've got an eye on the road. I'll see if any cars arrive. Billy said that the company reckoned it'd take half an hour at least to refuel and get the plane ready to turn around, so they could be turning up before he goes. The ground crew's getting ready right now.'

Anjli saw them, too. Three figures moving near the fuel depot, preparing for the quick turnaround. Everything about this place screamed efficiency, but then if you were paying the money, you expected the service.

'Do you think he knows about Sophia turning on him?' De'Geer asked.

'It's probably why he's running. Although, that said, I don't really have any proof of this.'

They'd positioned their vehicles in locations able to view both entrance roads, but Anjli knew it was overkill. Mikhail would exit straight from his plane to the terminal, and those places specialised in avoiding official attention. He'd then wait around, probably drinking expensive champagne, until the plane was ready to go again, possibly gaining a briefcase full of private knick-knacks, spy stuff or personal items before leaving.

The sound of jet engines cut through the night, growing louder. Up in the sky, landing lights appeared over the trees, the twin beams sweeping the runway.

'Moment of truth,' De'Geer muttered through the speaker.

As they watched, the plane, an Embraer Phenom 300 – modern, fast, and one of the best-selling light jets globally –

began its landing run. As she exited her car, she saw it touch down smoothly, taxiing across the short runways, moving its way slowly towards the private terminal and lounge. At the side of the car, Anjli watched through binoculars as, once it had stopped, the plane's door opened, steps extending out.

After a moment, a figure emerged – a familiar man in an expensive suit, moving with the confidence of someone used to private aviation, a figure familiar from a meeting he'd had with Anjli the previous evening.

Mikhail Stefon descended the steps, phone already in hand.

'Got him,' Anjli murmured quietly as he left the steps to the plane. She could see that Stefon was trying to make a call as he walked, probably checking his next connection was ready.

'Now?' De'Geer asked.

'Wait,' Anjli watched Stefon move towards the terminal. 'Let him think he's made it. He's on a call right now. If he's able to cry out that he's been captured, whoever he's talking to could cause a problem.'

Anjli watched with interest. For a few moments longer, Stefon finished whatever he was doing and then placed his phone back in his pocket. In fact, he'd almost reached the door when De'Geer moved. For someone his size, De'Geer could be remarkably stealthy when needed. One moment Mikhail Stefon was reaching for the handle, the next he was face down on the tarmac, De'Geer's knee in his back. It had been a sneak attack, as recent information on Stefon had shown he could have fought his way out of a confrontation, but not a tackle from a seven-foot Viking.

Out of the car and running across the tarmac, Anjli

approached with her warrant card already out, the runway lights casting long shadows as she did so.

'Mikhail Stefon,' she kept her voice professional as she shouted out. 'I think we need to have a little chat about Lord Carmody.'

At the name, Mikhail's face showed pure panic, the look of a man whose careful and well-thought-out plans had just proven to be *not* so careful and *definitely not* well-thought-out as they collapsed around his feet.

'DI Kapoor,' he said, a quaver in his voice betraying the forced calmness. 'If this is about the missed meeting, I can happily reschedule.'

Through the terminal windows, Anjli could see the ground crew pretending not to watch, waiting to see what happened before going out to finish the job of refuelling the plane.

Pulled to his feet, handcuffs keeping his wrists behind his back, Mikhail Stefon looked around calmly.

'Lawyer,' he muttered. 'Lawyer.'

'You know what? That's a really good idea,' Anjli smiled. 'You're definitely going to need one, especially since your friend Sophia's been really chatty about what happened that night, and MI6 has gone into great detail about your history in black ops paramilitary organisations. And it's only a matter of time before Mister Boyask explains more about your plans at Carmody Holding. Oh, and I'd really be careful if you see Detective Chief Inspector Matthews anytime soon. He has a real issue with the fact you tried to spike his drugs.'

These comments got his attention; a slight flinch crossing his face that had nothing to do with De'Geer's grip on his arm.

'You've got nothing on me.'

'Everyone talks eventually,' Anjli nodded to De'Geer, who started walking him towards the car. 'The question is, where do you want to be when it happens? Do you want to be the one sitting in the cell waiting to be nailed to the wall, or do you want to get ahead of this?'

Behind them, the jet's engines were still cooling, the sound of ticking in the night air.

Stefon's expression shifted from calm arrogance to something closer to resignation.

'We never looked in the briefcase,' he murmured. 'It was set fire to. Although Carmody promised me the photos, if I put in some good words with my oligarch friends.'

'Were you the one who set fire to it?' Anjli continued. 'We know where it was torched, why it was torched there, and we're working through the forensics right now. We're also comparing the detonator we found under the Range Rover's wheel arch with explosives you would have used in the Yugoslav wars, as well as reopening the murder of Stephen Mahoney.'

She leant closer.

'You see, we think that might have been an explosive, too. Funny that you were there the same day.'

Mikhail Stefon's expression definitely soured at this.

'Lawyer,' he said.

'Of course,' Anjli gestured towards her car. 'Although it might be after you spend some time in an MI6 black site. You've pissed a lot of people off. That okay?'

She watched the comment land as De'Geer led him away. Through the terminal windows, she could see the pilot emerging, confusion evident as he watched his passenger now being led away in handcuffs. The ground crew had already given up, pretending not to stare.

'Tell them to fuel it anyway,' she said to a ground crew officer who had appeared at her shoulder. 'Is it paid for?'

'Yes.'

'Good.' Anjli grinned. 'In a minute, that Viking-looking officer there is going to have a quick peek inside the airplane and see if anything's been left. Once he's finished, why don't you continue to Zagreb?'

'Empty?'

'Empty.' Anjli nodded. She knew someone would be waiting at the other end. Someone who'd now be wondering why their carefully planned escape route has suddenly gone quiet.

Inside her pocket, her phone buzzed; Monroe, probably wanting an update. She took a moment to look over at her car, Mikhail Stefon's silhouette visible in the back seat.

'How much is one of these flights?' she asked the pilot as he emerged from the terminal building. 'And could I get a police discount?'

ROOM THREE FELT COLDER THAN USUAL, THOUGH ANJLI KNEW the temperature never changed. Sophia sat opposite her, still in designer yoga wear, though the composed escort from the Dorchester was long gone. Her fingers played with the edge of a paper cup of interview room coffee, going cold.

Bullman, sitting to the side, had just turned on the recorder and given their names and time, and now leant back, letting the younger detective take lead.

'Sorry we took so long to start this,' Anjli smiled. 'I had to catch a plane. Well, someone on a plane, anyway.'

If Sophia understood this, she said nothing, simply staring at the coffee cup.

'Let's go through this again,' Bullman said. 'From the beginning.'

'I've told you what happened.'

'You've told us what you were told to tell us.' Anjli kept her voice neutral. 'About running into the woods. About being lost.'

'I was scared.'

'Of the Highwayman?' Bullman smiled. 'Or of the bike not being where it was supposed to be?'

Something flickered in Sophia's expression.

'I don't know what you mean.'

'The officers who found you?' Anjli checked her notes, though she knew them by heart. 'You were walking towards Epping. But you weren't lost, were you? You were looking for them.'

Sophia's fingers tightened on the cup.

'Mikhail Stefon arranged everything, didn't he?' Anjli continued. 'The dress, the timing, the specific route home.'

'I was just hired company.'

'Hired by Mikhail Stefon.' Bullman watched the name land. 'Who, by the way, we just arrested trying to flee the country on what looks to be espionage charges.'

That got a reaction – genuine surprise, maybe fear.

'What?'

'Private jet at Biggin Hill. Heading for Zagreb.' Anjli leant forward. 'He was running. Leaving everyone else to take the fall.'

'He wouldn't.'

'He did, and now he's in an MI6 black site, waiting for us to chat to him after we finish here.' Anjli pulled out her phone, showing the booking details Billy had found before they even drove to pick up the fugitive. 'Single passenger. One-way ticket. Doesn't look good, does it?'

Sophia stared at the screen, her carefully maintained composure cracking.

'He promised.'

'Men like that promise a lot of things.' Anjli put the phone away. 'Just like Lord Carmody promised to look after you if anything went wrong, right?'

'I don't –'

'Know what my colleague means?' Bullman finished the statement for her. 'What did you tell PC Cooper when she took you in? Oh yes. "Get me somewhere safe, then we'll talk about what really happened that night".'

Sophia's face had gone pale as Bullman looked around the interview room before turning to Anjli.

'This room looks safe, right?' she asked. 'I think this is safe.'

'Very safe, Guv.'

'Good.' Bullman returned her attention to Sophia. 'So, let's cut the crap and just get on with this, right?'

'It wasn't supposed to happen like this.' The words were barely a whisper.

'No?' Anjli kept her voice gentle. 'How was it supposed to happen?'

'I was just meant to be there. To be seen.' The words came faster now. 'So when he was robbed, there'd be a witness. Someone who'd run away, be found later. Make it look real.'

'And the bike in the woods?'

'Mikhail said it would be waiting. That someone would pick me up, take me somewhere safe until it was over,' Sophia's laugh held no humour. 'But when I got there ...'

'No bike.'

'No, there was a bike.' She wrapped her arms around herself, suddenly looking very young. 'But only when I got on did I learn I was going to be left in the dark to be found. They drove me to some roundabout, literally threw me off. Then I started walking.'

'Who rode the bike?'

'The Highwayman.'

'Did you know who it was?'

'No, they never told me,' Sophia admitted. 'But if I heard his voice I'd recognise it.'

'That can be arranged,' Bullman was already texting Billy. 'So, you were left to find the police, give the "official" story to everyone ...'

'And now people are dead, and Mikhail tried running.' Anjli watched her carefully. 'Leaving you to handle the fallout.'

Sophia said nothing for a long moment, and Anjli wondered if she'd even known people were dead. Of course, if she hadn't, Anjli would have expected a bigger reaction.

'What do you want to know?'

'I believe you promised us everything.' Anjli pulled out her notebook. 'Starting with the planning meetings. Who was there? What was discussed?'

'Mikhail arranged it all.' Sophia's fingers twisted the paper cup. 'But the Highwayman ... he was so particular about everything. Made me practice my reactions over and over.'

'Practice?'

'How to act scared, where to run,' she gave a bitter laugh. 'Like some twisted theatre rehearsal. He'd appear in full costume, often using that weird voice modulator thing, although he didn't a couple of times. I never saw his face –'

'Definitely a he?'

'Oh yeah, he was definitely male. He was a prick, constantly saying I was a distraction, nothing more, and I had to get my reaction just right, and usually these were the times he wasn't modulating. The timing, the fear – everything had to be perfect. Mikhail said it was better if I didn't know who he was. Plausible deniability, he called it.'

'What was he like?'

'Obsessed with getting the details right. Would go mental if anyone used the wrong historical terms.' She took a sip of cold coffee. 'Called it "maintaining theatrical authenticity" or something.'

Anjli made a note.

'And Lord Carmody?'

'Never there. But Mikhail was always on the phone to someone.' Sophia's voice had steadied now, anger replacing fear. 'They used me, didn't they? Set me up to take the fall if anything went wrong.'

'Pretty much.' Anjli made a note to check Lewis's theatrical background. 'Want to make a formal statement?'

'Will it help?'

'Might help you, especially if there's any kind of paper trail.' Anjli closed her notebook. 'And, more importantly, especially since Mikhail seems to have forgotten all about you.'

Sophia stared at her coffee for a long moment.

'Get me a solicitor,' she said finally. 'Then we'll talk about everything. About the rehearsals, the plans, what they said about some stunt performer dying years ago ... and about why someone went to all this trouble just to steal a briefcase.'

WALKING OUT OF THE INTERVIEW ROOM, ANJLI LOOKED BACK AT Bullman.

'This isn't working,' she said irritably. 'She'll give a statement, sure, and it might help, but she never saw Lewis, or his dad.'

'She could identify his voice, but as Billy's already shown me, a good defence solicitor for the Carmodys could tear through her statement in minutes,' Bullman nodded, rubbing the back of her neck absently. 'Same as before. We know who did it, but can't prove who did it. Stefon?'

'According to Monroe's ex-wife Wintergreen, who happily seems to be on talking terms again, he clammed up the moment he arrived in a Thames House basement room,' Anjli said as they started down the stairs towards the office. 'He won't say a thing until he's truly screwed.'

She glanced back up the corridor.

'We've got Sophia, James Kitson, Emma Thorne, Peter Kendall and Mikhail Stefon all in custody and not one of them can help us,' she said, shaking her head in resignation. 'And Baker wants us to have Carmody holding the smoking gun? This is impossible.'

'Maybe not,' Bullman smiled.

'Not impossible?'

'No, they can't help us,' Bullman replied as they carried on. 'Maybe it's time to take Baker's words literally, and see what that gives us.'

She looked back up the corridor, as if seeing through walls, her mind far away as she worked through some kind of unspoken question. There was a buzz, and she checked her phone.

'Oh,' she said, showing the message. 'Billy just gained

Martin Reeves' phone records. Seems he deleted a text conversation before he died.'

Anjli took the phone, reading it.

> Did you do what we asked you to?

> I mentioned her name.

> Good man. Now forget about this, and we'll forget about you.

'Shit,' she whispered. 'Reeves was being told to give us Emma Thorne.'

'What's to bet it was by bloody Carmody?' Bullman took the phone back.

'Again though, if it's a burner, we won't know without a seance,' Anjli muttered.

Bullman, however, stared at the message and smiled.

'Do we know if the Ducati was ridden by Kitson and Thorne?' she asked. 'Mahoney too?'

'Most likely,' Anjli replied. 'Why?'

'Because I think I might just ask Emma Thorne if there was more than one Highwayman bike,' Bullman smiled darkly. 'I have a plan, and I think it'll work very nicely with Declan's.'

23

FAMILY VISIT

MONROE WANTED TO DRAW STRAWS TO SEE WHO WOULD GO TO visit Carmody at his Theydon Bois address but, in the end, Declan had pointed out that the last time Monroe had spoken to Carmody, he'd been quite belligerent; if they were to have Carmody believe them, it needed to be somebody a little more earnest.

And so it was Declan, alone, who knocked on Carmody's door this time.

The door was opened by Lewis Carmody, and Declan had to force himself not to say anything. He'd seen the man on video, had heard his unmodulated voice, but he'd never met him in person, and had to pretend that he didn't know who the man was.

'Can I help you?' Lewis asked.

Declan frowned, as if confused by this new appearance.

'I'm looking for Lord Carmody.'

'He's my father. And you are?'

'DCI Declan Walsh, City of London Police.'

Lewis glanced behind Declan, and Declan wondered for

a moment whether he was looking to see if Monroe was hiding in the bushes.

'Don't worry, my boss isn't with me,' he said. 'I understand you've met him before.'

'Your boss is a prick,' Lewis replied coldly. Declan didn't answer, mentally noting that everybody's opinion of Lewis so far seemed to be correct. There was a long pause, and then Lewis sniffed, shrugged, and stepped to the side.

'I suppose you'd better come in, then,' he said. 'I hope you've got good news.'

'That'll be up for Lord Carmody to decide,' Declan replied as he entered, the door being closed behind him.

He couldn't help himself, however, and glanced around.

'I thought you'd be packing by now,' he said.

'What's that supposed to mean?'

'Well, I was under the assumption this was a Conservative Party donor's house,' Declan shrugged, looking back to stare straight at Lewis. 'From what I hear, Lord Carmody has resigned. Therefore ...'

He let the question tail off. Lewis wrinkled his nose, his eyes narrowing as he stared at the detective in front of him.

'We'll leave in our own time,' he snapped. 'Besides, politics is a strange business. You never know what could happen tomorrow. Baker could be out, someone else could be in, and maybe my father will be back at Westminster.'

'Maybe,' Declan said. 'Maybe we'll even find the briefcase he managed to lose while having a hooker in his car.'

The words shocked Lewis, but Declan wasn't sure if it was faked or not. After all, Lewis *knew* there was a "hooker" in the car. He'd arranged it. He also knew that Sophia had been paid to tell people she'd *been* in the car. Currently, Declan was giving him everything he wanted ... but he obviously couldn't show that. So, instead, Declan gained the bad acting of Lewis Carmody.

Lewis had walked him across the hallway by this point, pausing at a large wooden door, knocking on it and then opening it.

'Dad, the police are here,' he said into the room. 'DCI someone or the other.'

'Not the Scot?' The voice of Lord Adrian Carmody came out.

'No, not the bloody Scot.'

'Good, send him in.'

Declan entered to see Carmody looking up from his desk, obviously unsurprised to see him, sipping at a whisky glass while *playing* at being incredibly surprised. And, seemingly, the Carmody acting ability had been passed from father to son. The curtains were pulled now; the night drawing in outside, as Carmody rose from his chair, hand outstretched, his smile warm and quite obviously fake.

'Detective Chief Inspector Walsh,' he said smoothly. 'Come to give me back my briefcase? Or maybe you're here to arrest me?'

'Actually, I came to apologise on behalf of our department,' Declan moved into the study, shaking Carmody's hand, noting how his expression had shifted from controlled disdain to careful interest after the statement. The study felt different to most he'd been in, emptier perhaps. He wondered whether it was the fact that Lady Carmody's presence was missing.

'Claire's staying with friends,' Carmody said, as if psychically guessing what Declan was thinking, but his glancing around, as if looking for someone might have given that away. 'Ransacked the knick-knacks in here, I'm afraid. All rather awkward, really, although I suppose that's what the papers wanted.'

'They do like scandalous stories,' Declan replied, keeping his tone neutral. 'Your resignation speech was ... interesting.'

'Damage control, Detective Chief Inspector, something I've become rather good at over the years,' Carmody gestured to a chair. 'Although I suspect that's not why you're here.'

'No,' Declan replied, remaining standing. 'We found Sophia.'

That got a reaction. Subtle, but there. A slight tightening around the eyes, which was surprising. Surely Lord Carmody *wanted* that to happen. The address had been left with the report. *Was he still playing the game? Or was this something, perhaps, that had been planned without Carmody's advice?*

'Ah, yes,' he said. 'The young lady from the car. I trust she's well?'

'Quite well. Very helpful, actually. Especially about Mikhail Stefon.'

Now, there was a second tightness, and this felt way more genuine. Sophia wouldn't have been told to mention Stefon. The fact Declan and his team knew this meant they'd gone in a different direction to the one Carmody had laid out for them.

'The name means nothing to me,' Carmody replied.

'No?' Declan moved over towards the window, examining one of the ornate standing lamps at the side, keeping moving, stopping Carmody from controlling the space. 'Interesting, because he seems to know you well. You even started a company with him. Carmody Holdings.'

'That's a blind trust, I don't know who the other investors are.'

'Oh, well, that explains how you don't realise you're working with an agent of an enemy state.'

'What?'

Yeah, you bastard, you didn't expect that, did you, Declan thought to himself.

'He's been on MI6's watch list for years, apparently. Lots of war crimes and espionage accusations ... although he's been quite busy in other ways lately.'

'Has he?'

'Well, allegedly. Let's just say we have him arranging escorts and providing certain substances to protection officers.'

Carmody said nothing and his expression gave nothing away. Declan was leading him down an alternative path; one where Stefon was believed to be working with Matthews, and this worked with his narrative again.

'You mean Matthews' cocaine habit?' he nodded sadly. 'Yes, it's a very unfortunate business. I've known for several years, but he's a good officer, you see. I didn't feel it was my place to, what's the term, "dob him in". The man would have lost his job, and he never caused me any problems.'

'I do mean his cocaine habits, and it is indeed a very unfortunate business,' Declan replied as he turned back to examine the flock wallpaper. 'Especially since it seems someone deliberately spiked his supply that night. It made him incredibly unreliable, almost like someone wanted him compromised.'

Again, something else Carmody hadn't expected them to realise.

'Are you accusing anyone of this?' Carmody asked, almost matter-of-factly, and Declan wondered if he was leading to an "are you accusing me" question. 'This East European agent, perhaps?'

Instead, Declan shook his head.

'I never said he was an East European agent, Lord Carmody. Actually, we've been looking in completely the opposite direction,' Declan kept his voice carefully neutral as he continued. If Carmody wasn't going to give him anything, he sure as hell wasn't going to give anything back.

Well, until the moment he needed to.

'I believe you used to work with a woman named Emma Thorne?'

'Yes, at the commission. What about her?'

'Well, believe it or not, she's confessed to being the Essex Rider, the Highwayman your commission was hunting. She and James Kitson, that is, although getting charges to stick ...' Declan shrugged, letting his frustration show through his expression.

'Did she now?' Carmody's tone was almost amused. 'How fascinating, though I am rather curious why you're telling me this. The Essex Rider was six years ago, and the man who attacked me was definitely *not* Emma Thorne. For a start, he was male. Unless you're telling me that Emma has "transitioned", or whatever they like to call it these days?'

'No, nothing like that, I just felt you should know,' Declan replied, ignoring the fact that the text messages on Martin Reeves' phone not only showed that Carmody likely *knew* this already, but had planned this. 'We've been brought on this case at Charles Baker's request, but if you've read anything about us, you know that Charles Baker's not exactly our favourite person. I can't help but feel you've been set up.'

'And why would you think that?' Carmody asked, turning to face him fully.

'Well, the whole thing seems pointless,' Declan continued. 'Especially since the documents were worthless, anyway.'

That got Carmody's attention. He had sat back down behind his desk, but now there was a slight shift in his chair, barely noticeable. He picked up the whisky glass from his desk, a small amount left inside it and downed it before placing it down.

'Worthless?' It was asked so casually, so innocently, that Declan almost started laughing.

'Apparently so,' Declan started looking around the study once more, examining the books on the bookshelf, making sure that he didn't catch Carmody's eye.

'Why?'

'Well, Farnham-Ewing was working for Baker when she gave you that briefcase, and apparently Baker changed everything before he gave it to you,' Declan said, letting real irritation enter his voice. 'New contracts, different from the ones he claimed were in it. Apparently, he'd been planning it for weeks. The data that was stolen? Completely outdated.'

'Why would he do this?'

Declan turned and faced Carmody.

'Matthews,' he explained. 'Apparently, Mikhail Stefon was working with Thorne, providing certain "services" for her, including making sure any protection detail there would be compromised. Somehow Baker had gained information, probably through Farnham-Ewing and her friends, that Matthews was untrustworthy, and decided to test him. Unfortunately for *you*, Lord Carmody, Matthews worked for you. So, therefore, *you* were the one who gained the briefcase.'

'That's ... unfortunate,' Carmody's fingers drummed on

his desk as he paused between words. 'So, Thorne stole the briefcase?'

'We're still looking into that,' Declan replied. 'We can't work out how she was able to do such a thing, though. She has an alibi for the night. But we believe it's her, somehow. Or, possibly James Kitson isn't as ill as he claims to be, or his onetime stunt partner Stephen Mahoney faked his death. The thing is ...'

Declan now paced, as if thinking aloud.

'We've been talking to Peter Kendall, one of her colleagues. He was the one who tried to make money from the Essex Rider six years ago. And when interviewed, he mentioned something interesting about MI6 interviewing him six years ago, asking if he'd dealt with Stefon. Seems Kendall's been working for MI6 ever since.'

'How exciting for him.' Carmody's voice remained steady, but his fingers had stopped drumming, the empty whisky glass sitting forgotten. 'Has he spoken of anything else?'

'No, he clammed up and asked for a solicitor as soon as we sat him down, but before he realised we were on to him, he had mentioned this meeting,' Declan shrugged. 'It's probably nothing, although with Mikhail Stefon vanishing like that ...'

'Mikhail's vanished?' the question came back too quickly, Carmody forcing himself to calm down.

'Never made his flight back from Prague,' Declan replied, pretending to have not noticed this, 'although that fits the pattern from what I can work out. We believe he's chartered a private plane, landed at Biggin Hill, grabbed some supplies and flew off to Zagreb, where his East European handlers are. You know he has East European handlers, right? I mean, you had to know that, or else you'd not have gone into business with him.'

'How do you mean?' Carmody was getting flustered now. 'I'm not –'

'Of course, you're not working together,' Declan nodded sagely. 'Lucky really. Apparently, he also provided the explosive that killed Stephen Mahoney and critically injured James Kitson, the two stunt riders Reeves told you about six years back when you ran the commission. I'm sure you remember looking into them. I'd definitely remember if suspects *blew up* when I was looking into them.'

'You seem very well informed,' Carmody said, rising from the chair.

'Yes, Sophia's been quite thorough in her statement,' Declan smiled. 'It's amazing what people remember when they realise they've been abandoned. Stefon really confided in her.'

There was a long, quiet moment, and Declan watched Carmody carefully.

'She said Stefon also knew about the real value, and wanted it for himself.'

'The real value?' Carmody was trying too hard now, his practised aristocratic indifference beginning to slip.

'The new contracts. The ones that actually matter,' Declan moved towards the door, pausing to examine a framed photo of Lewis at some rowing event; the photo looked about ten years old. 'As I said, Baker wanted to screw over Matthews, Stefon and Thorne, in the process catching you as collateral damage.'

He turned back, looking back at Carmody.

'You know he never liked you, right?' he continued. 'From

what we could work out, he felt he had to keep you, but had a grudge from the time Stephen Holland was Prime Minister.'

He sighed, a real tension release groan.

'But anyway, I'm sure you've got better things to do than listen to me think out loud.'

Carmody was still standing, his face carefully composed, but his hands had tightened on the edge of the desk.

'What do you think will happen to these documents?' he asked.

'I don't really care, to be perfectly honest,' Declan replied. 'We've been sent on a wild goose chase to find a Highwayman who doesn't really exist, and who stole items that were fake and worthless. If anything, I think we're pretty much going to claim it as a loss before they try to throw us under the bus they ran *you* over with. Matthews will lose his job, probably be found to be connected. Stefon will be hunted, and when we find him, he'll eventually tell MI6 what really happened while having electrodes strapped to his balls.'

Carmody's face remained neutral still, but something was flickering in his eyes. Calculations. A cunningness.

He was already planning ahead.

'Indeed,' he breathed. 'Thank you for keeping me informed, Detective Chief Inspector Walsh.'

'Of course,' Declan replied. 'Although, I would advise you to keep off any country lanes for the moment. Roads are dangerous at night, especially with motorcyclists.'

He reached for the door handle and then paused as if remembering something.

'You have a good night, sir,' he said. 'I thought I'd just let you know what was happening as I was on my way to High Beech.'

'High Beech? The other side of Epping Forest?'

Declan froze.

'I shouldn't have said anything,' he replied, admonished. 'Please don't tell Monroe.'

'Don't worry, Detective Chief Inspector,' Carmody replied. His hands loosening from the desk. 'We're all friends here.'

'Are we, sir?' Declan asked, still keeping his professionalism.

'You don't like Baker, and I don't like Baker,' Carmody replied. 'But if there's a way for me to perhaps regain his trust, though, I could possibly regain my job. After all, as you said, the briefcase that I fell on my sword for seems to be a decoy.'

Declan considered this.

'All I know, sir, is that Harris, the driver that took you home and was on your detail before you resigned, will be driving Jennifer Farnham-Lewis tonight, back to her family home in High Beech, near Holy Innocents Church. She's leaving from the Commons about nine, and I believe she has a certain briefcase with her, to pass on to whoever Baker's naming as your replacement tomorrow.'

Declan considered this.

'We're putting it out that she's heading to Stansted, and we hope to catch Thorne somewhere near Bishops Stortford, where we're setting up a base camp. Once Thorne learns the papers she burnt were fake, she'll want another go.'

'And Farnham-Ewing?'

'Perhaps you might be able to call her, meet her at her family home, ask her to assist you? After all, I know she's not exactly Baker's greatest ally either. She's more stuck with him until he, well ...'

Declan grinned.

'Leadership battles are always a nightmare.'

Declan nodded a quick farewell and left before the Lord could respond any more, hoping he'd planted just enough seeds of doubt.

Now they just had to wait and see which ones grew.

As he walked through the hallway, away from the study, he saw Lewis watching him from the bay windows at the back, his phone suddenly buzzing.

Right on cue. Daddy was probably calling the son in to tell him to put his leathers back on.

At least Declan hoped so. Stefon was in custody, and now it was time to gain the others and give Baker exactly what he wanted ...

A smoking gun in either Lewis, or Adrian Carmody's hand.

Declan just hoped it wouldn't be smoking because whichever Carmody was holding it, had just *fired* it.

24

THE HIGHWAYMAN

THE FOREST SEEMED PARTICULARLY DARK, AS LEWIS CARMODY checked his watch for the fifth time, the luminous dial of his Rolex glowing faintly beneath his sleeve, shown through the gap between the sleeve and his leather glove. The rural roads between Theydon Bois and High Beech stretched out before him, like unlit black ribbons between the ancient trees of Epping Forest, occasionally illuminated by the headlights of a passing car, or the smattering of homes and businesses that still lit up in the distance. Each time a car passed, Lewis would shrink further back into the shadows, the weight of the modified Griffin & Tow pistol somehow reassuring.

His father's instructions earlier that evening had been very precise; he was to wait until the Essex Rider, now apparently outed as Emma Thorne, appeared and stole the briefcase from Jennifer Farnham-Ewing's car as it approached High Beech. He was to let her take it, allowing the authorities to hunt the wrong person, but then follow her to a secluded location somewhere in the woods where she could be "dealt with permanently".

His father's exact words.

Lewis shivered despite the warmth of the leather biker costume he was wearing. The theatrical aspect of it had been his idea originally, taking elements from the Essex Rider and adding his own, but his father had embraced it with a disturbing enthusiasm, once he'd understood its potential.

Nervously, Lewis checked the bike he sat upon. It was a Kawasaki Versys 1000, a bike he'd mistakenly believed was the same as the one the Essex Rider had travelled on years earlier. He'd been in his first year at university when it had happened, his father informing him gleefully of the new committee role he had under Stephen Holland's government. But as the university year continued, he'd heard nothing else, and it was actually only when he returned for a break that he saw how much it irritated his father. The rider had been hard to find, but then one suspect had had some kind of accident, and his father closed the case, stating that they believed the Essex Rider was gone and it was up to the police now, while the financial side of the situation had been paused with no proof that anybody was benefiting from this ... apart from the newspapers, who were nailing some of his father's closest friends to the wall.

Lewis still remembered the day he arrived to see his father in incredibly high spirits. He had been taken aside and sat down and informed that one of the FCA, a man named Reeves, had come to Carmody, explaining he'd discovered a colleague, Peter Kendall, had been the one sending the information. But not before checking the data and making trades, effectively skimming from the top, in the process making several million pounds, an amount that had been eventually blackmailed back to Carmody once Kendall was dragged in for a "chat", one that included Mikhail Stefon and his terrifying interrogation methods.

Lewis had felt sorry for Kendall at the time, but back then he was just a university student, and he didn't understand the ways of business. Now, six years later and currently involved in several of his father's businesses, he understood that you needed to kill, sometimes, to make a killing.

Although he understood *why* it needed to happen, Lewis hadn't been happy with becoming the Highwayman. For a start, it was incredibly risky, something he hadn't been ecstatic about, but more importantly, apart from some dirt bike riding in his teens through the north of England, Lewis hadn't really ridden a motorcycle. This, however, according to his father, was the reason why he'd be perfect. No one would expect Lewis Carmody would be the Highwayman, and so he'd spent weeks practising in secret, thanks to motorcycle riders hired off books by his father. As far as they were concerned, Lewis was practising for his Direct Access test – or whatever they called the bloody thing – the licence that allows you to ride one of these things legally. Lewis, however, didn't feel he needed such a licence to show he could ride a bike. He was Lord Carmody's son, and he could do what he damn well wanted.

He also felt that if he was captured by the police while escaping, the last thing they'd be thinking about was whether he was legally allowed to ride the motorcycle. Surprisingly, he'd been more worried about riding the motorcycle than he had been about killing Martin Reeves. As far as Lewis was concerned, Martin was a parasite, someone who needed to be removed, and Lewis Carmody had no problems firing his weapon that night. In fact, there was a detached coldness and a curiosity to it.

Could he do it again?

In a second.

The sound of an approaching car cut through his thoughts. Checking his watch, he saw it was roughly the time Jennifer's car, a grey or silver Mercedes, was expected.

Showtime.

He adjusted his mask and pulled the tricorn hat lower, deciding that this time he wouldn't need a helmet, and although he wasn't intending to speak to anybody who'd survive to name his voice, he still made sure the voice modulator was secured beneath the scarf covering the lower half of his face. After all, you never knew what would happen, especially as the headlights of a silver Mercedes, likely Jennifer Farnham-Ewing's car, swept around the bend of the road, the government-issued vehicle moving at a cautious speed.

As he watched, Lewis recognised Harris at the wheel, his profile illuminated briefly as they passed beneath a gap in the trees. It was perfect, and just as that idiot detective had said.

Lewis held his position, waiting, daring not to turn on the engine in case he spooked anyone. According to his father's intelligence, Emma Thorne would make her move any minute now. He'd let Thorne take the bait if she was indeed the Essex Rider and then eliminate her, removing both a troublesome witness and retrieving the genuine documents in one elegant manoeuvre. His father had already sold the shares he had bought from the fake papers at a small profit, luckily, and was preparing to make more money once the correct ones were through.

The distant growl of a motorcycle engine now echoed through the trees, and Lewis tensed, watching, as a single headlight appeared around the bend, approaching Farnham-

Ewing's car from the opposite direction. The rider's silhouette was unmistakable; it was the same leather outfit that had
become synonymous with the Essex Rider years ago, one
almost exactly the same as the outfit that Lewis wore too.

Lewis almost wanted to complain about Thorne wearing
the costume – after all, he felt it was his now to wear, rather
than hers.

Perhaps he'd tell her right before he killed her.

The motorcycle overtook Farnham-Ewing's car in the
same way that he had to his father's car a matter of days
earlier, and then swerved sharply, forcing Harris to brake.
The government car skidded to a halt, nose almost angled
into   the   verge,   and   the   Highwayman   dismounted,
approaching the driver's door with the theatrical flair Lewis
recognised from rehearsing his own performances. He'd
never seen footage of the Essex Rider performing, just being
chased, and there was a part of him that wondered whether
she had learnt this from *him*. From his vantage point, Lewis
couldn't hear the exchange, but he could see it, and he
watched Harris' hands raised in surrender as the rider
motioned with what appeared to be a gun. It probably wasn't
the same as the Griffin & Tow that he wore; Emma Thorne
would be far less imaginative, and the double of the one on
his hip was in the family safe just in case they needed it.

The passenger door opened, and the rider reached in,
emerging out moments later with the distinctive leather
briefcase. There was no resistance, and no surprise, almost as
if it had been expected.

The thought had niggled at Lewis, but he pushed it aside.
The plan was unfolding perfectly. The rider, likely Thorne, was
definitely female as she remounted, secured the briefcase,
and accelerated away, headlight disappearing into the forest.

Harris, meanwhile, was on his phone, and Lewis almost pitied the man. Two Highwayman heists in less than a week meant Harris would never get another job again, and likely be accused of being connected to this for the rest of his career.

He counted slowly to ten, giving Thorne enough of a head start to believe she succeeded, and then he kick-started his Kawasaki, the engine's roar shattering the forest silence as he pulled onto the road, passing Farnham-Ewing's car without a glance, focused entirely on the fading taillight ahead.

THE PURSUIT, SUCH AS IT WAS, TOOK THEM DEEPER INTO Epping Forest, away from the main roads and onto narrower tracks. Lewis knew from her riding that Thorne wasn't aware she was likely being followed right now, although she must have assumed that somebody would have been watching. The Highwayman, after all, was a wanted man.

Lewis frowned behind his mask; Thorne was taking a familiar route, one of the old Essex Rider paths documented in that idiot Sergeant Freeman's police reports from years ago. It was, however, a strange choice for someone trying to make a clean getaway. If Lewis had done it, he would have kept to the main roads, moved into the built-up areas like Waltham Abbey, and dumped the bike as quickly as he could, swapping into a car or van.

The path he followed widened into a small clearing, Lewis almost falling off the bike, struggling to keep it straight. When he practised his riding, he had spent little time in forests, and it was only his teenage dirt bike skills that had kept him secured to the seat.

However, unexpectedly, the rider also slowed ahead. Lewis narrowed the gap, wondering whether they too had had problems with the path, caution warring with the opportunity of what was about to happen. *Was Thorne's bike developing mechanical problems?* If so, this would be easier than anticipated.

The Essex Rider came to a complete stop in the middle of a clearing, dismounting smoothly. As Lewis pulled up behind, headlight shining on Thorne, the briefcase was clutched against her chest. Lewis stopped twenty feet or so away, keeping the bike's engine running as he dismounted, drawing his pistol.

'You know, I never thought I'd meet the Essex Rider,' he muttered with a smile, 'but you've done me a great service, especially now when you take the blame for everything I've done, your identity revealed to the world when they find your body.'

'Ah, but identity is just a mask we wear,' the rider called out, her voice muffled by the helmet. 'You should know that better than most, shouldn't you, *Lewis?*'

At the name, Lewis froze.

Something was wrong here.

The woman's voice, even distorted through the helmet, carried a challenging tone, one he hadn't expected to find.

'Take the helmet off,' he demanded, his own voice transformed by the modulator into something mechanical and cold.

'Masks and modulators are useful things,' the rider continued, reaching up with deliberate slowness, 'but they always come off eventually.'

The helmet lifted away, and Lewis's eyes widened. The face behind it wasn't Emma Thorne's, but the coolly professional expression of an Indian lady, most likely the Detective Inspector that worked with that annoying Scot and DCI Walsh. He'd seen photos of Anjli Kapoor, but never met her close up, and the realisation hit Lewis like a physical blow.

He'd been set up.

'Where's Emma Thorne?' he demanded.

'Where you'll be very soon,' Anjli replied calmly, placing the briefcase on the seat of her bike. 'In custody.'

Lewis raised the pistol, desperation clouding his judgement, but before he could say another word or even pull the trigger, the surrounding forest seemed to come alive with lights and sound. Cars and bikes, hidden in a circle around them lit up, and Lewis realised that in the same way that he'd sat in the darkness waiting for a car to appear, they had done the same ... but instead, they'd been waiting for motorbikes.

His motorbike.

As the realisation hit him, Lewis groaned as he saw DCI Walsh step from behind a massive oak tree to the right, and several officers aimed tasers squarely at Lewis's chest. There was every chance that if he fired his weapon, they'd take him out.

'I wouldn't,' Walsh spoke quietly, as if reading Lewis's mind.

The rumble of another motorcycle engine now shattered the momentary stillness, as a large, seven-foot-tall motorcycle sergeant emerged from a side path, his imposing frame astride a police-issued BMW, effectively blocking his most obvious escape route.

'Just like old times,' another voice called out from the shadows, and Sergeant Freeman, one of the motorcycle officers who had been chasing the Essex Rider six years earlier, seemed to materialise at the edge of the clearing, his own police bike lit and aimed at Lewis, the veteran officer's expression grimly satisfied. 'Except this time you're not getting away.'

Lewis spun wildly, his fight or flight instinct overwhelming rational thought. *They were going to pin the Essex Rider's crimes on him? Hell no.*

He needed to get out. There – a narrow gap between the trees leading deeper into the forest.

He lunged for his bike, desperation lending him speed before anybody could stop him. The Kawasaki's wheels spun in the loose soil as he sped up towards the gap, branches whipping past his face. Behind him, he heard engines roaring to life; Kapoor, Freeman, and the Viking sergeant giving chase, their motorcycles as good as his in the forest terrain.

Lewis had no choice. The race was on.

25

SIDESWIPED

HALF A MILE DEEPER INTO EPPING FOREST, BULLMAN CHECKED her watch for the third time in as many minutes, and the vintage Land Rover Defender they'd positioned across the narrow track creaked as Chivalry Fitzwarren shifted in the driver's seat beside her.

'Are you sure you want to be here?' she asked.

'My lady, there's every chance that your officers might destroy a valuable duelling pistol,' Chivalry replied as if it was the most obvious point in the world. 'At least by being here I can make sure that the right hands regain it.'

'The right hands will be the forensics team,' Bullman replied calmly. 'Doctor Marcos needs to confirm it's the same weapon that killed Martin Reeves, remember?'

'Yes, but after that, after that, it –'

'Will become evidence in a murder case.' Bullman couldn't help herself. 'Chivalry, I know you're here for the equipment and for the history, but you're not gaining this gun any time soon.'

Chivalry didn't reply, adjusting his driving gloves with meticulous care, his tweed jacket strangely formal against the utilitarian interior of the Defender, as Bullman looked around the interior.

'You know, I never thought you'd be a driver of one of these,' she said. 'I assumed you were far more a Bentley driver, or maybe a Rolls-Royce.'

'Really?' Chivalry smiled. 'Then perhaps you don't know me as well as you feel.'

The radio crackled, Declan's voice.

'He should be coming through any minute now,' he said, as Bullman strained to hear the approaching motorcycles over the wind through ancient trees.

'Remember, Baker wants him literally with a gun in his hand,' she muttered. 'So perhaps don't try anything stupid, in case that gun goes off?'

Chivalry, however, was staring out of the window.

'The forest paths haven't really changed much since the days of actual highwaymen here, you know,' he remarked conversationally. 'The Earl of Essex used to hunt in here in the sixteen hundreds. There's even a hunting lodge they'd made for Henry the Eighth down the road. Fascinating historical continuity, wouldn't you say?'

'Fascinating,' Bullman replied dryly, fighting the urge to check her watch again. 'Just remember the plan, yes? Block the path, nothing more.'

'My dear lady,' Chivalry said, reaching into his jacket pocket and pulling out a Webley Mark IV pistol. 'I shall perform my role with historical accuracy and modern restraint.'

'Where the hell did you get *that?*' Bullman snapped, grabbing at the weapon. 'You're not supposed to be armed! Do you know the paperwork this'll give us –'

'It's deactivated,' Chivalry interrupted with a mildly theatrical wave. 'Purely for theatre. And you didn't complain the last time I used it.'

'I wasn't there the last time you bloody used this,' Bullman sighed, checking the weapon and then passing it back to Chivalry. 'And if I remember right, it *wasn't* deactivated back then. You only use it as defence, okay? Because if he tries to shoot you and you pretend to shoot him, he's going to win.'

The radio crackled to life again.

'Target approaching your position,' this time it was De'Geer's voice that came through, slightly distorted by static and surrounding noise. 'He's moving. Going fast.'

'Ready?' Bullman asked her driver, suddenly all business, the weapon forgotten for the moment. Chivalry's eyes gleamed with excitement as he started the engine, the Defender's diesel rumble cutting through the night.

'Absolutely,' he said, 'I haven't had this much fun since –'

'I don't care,' Bullman said, as the distinctive sound of at least three motorcycle engines grew louder. And suddenly, without notice, Lewis Carmody, in his Highwayman leathers, burst from the tree line, sweeping across their position. Seeing the Land Rover blocking his path, he swerved sharply, the manoeuvre forcing him onto a sidetrack where the ground was less stable, slowing him momentarily.

'Bollocks,' Chivalry muttered, throwing the Defender into reverse. 'Don't worry, we can get him –'

Suddenly, a white van exploded from a concealed position off to their right. Bullman recognised it immediately; it bore the same "Premium Fleet Rentals" logo they had identified from Billy's research, likely one of the two "missing" vans.

'It's Boyask,' she shouted, reaching for the radio. 'Monroe, we've got company. Ryan Boyask is in a white van, moving to intercept.'

The van accelerated towards the approaching motorcycles – De'Geer, Anjli and Freeman – clearly attempting to cut them off and provide Lewis Carmody with an escape route. Chivalry, however, watching the situation unfold with an alarming calm, wrenched his hand on the gears.

'Hold tight, my lady,' he shouted, jerking the wheel with surprising strength, and the Defender lurched forward, its substantial bulk gathering momentum down the hill as Chivalry aimed directly for the approaching van's side panel. Bullman grabbed at the dashboard, bracing for impact, very aware that a vehicle this old *didn't* have airbags.

'This wasn't the plan,' she shouted as the Defender connected with the van's rear quarter, sending it into an almost uncontrolled skid that ended with its front wheels in a roadside ditch.

'Improvisation has always been the soul of incredible tactical success,' Chivalry replied, looking thoroughly pleased with himself as he straightened the Defender. 'Wellington would have approved.'

Before Bullman could reply, Chivalry was out of the Defender, striding towards the front driver's side, his Webley in hand and aimed at the window.

'Stay where you are, Mister Boyask,' he said to the driver. 'I would really hate you to see what I can do with this weapon.'

Bullman laughed. It was accurate, yet at the same time a complete bluff.

'We've got Boyask,' she said into the radio. 'Now get that bloody motorcyclist.'

THE DEFENDER HAD BEEN A SURPRISE, BUT ONCE HE'D REALISED it was a set-up, Lewis had expected something more, and had leant into the curve, the Kawasaki responding instantly to his touch. The forest now seemed to blur around him, the sliver of remaining moonlight filtering through the canopy to cast patterns across his narrow, leaf-strewn path. The Griffin & Tow's weight at his hip felt strangely heavy as he sped up away from the Defender, putting distance between himself and the police.

'I won't go to bloody jail,' he muttered behind his mask, the voice modulator transforming the words into something mechanical and cold. He might not have ridden them, but he knew these paths; he'd been studying them meticulously while preparing for the previous robbery. These were the same routes the original Essex rider had used years earlier. His father had some of the bodycam footage and he'd watched while simulating the journey, seeing the same tricks, the same escape plans. Lewis had memorised every turn, every shortcut through Epping Forest's labyrinth trails, but what he hadn't counted on was Sergeant De'Geer.

He'd realised it was De'Geer the moment he'd seen him, a giant Viking on a bike; it could only be that man. His father had made a point of learning everything he could about the Last Chance Saloon, as they were called, after the Scottish prick and his assistant – or boss, or whatever she was – had appeared at their house, and in his mirrors Lewis could see the hulking police officer gaining ground, his BMW eating up the distance between them. Which was confusing really, because there was no way a police issue BMW should have been able to do the things it was doing. All he could assume was that somehow, De'Geer had upgraded his own bike. Which wasn't following police rules and *simply wasn't fair.*

De'Geer rode with an economy of movement; there was no wasted energy, no theatrical flourishes, just pure professional pursuit. The BMW's headlight cut through the darkness, illuminating the path behind Lewis and giving clarity to the two bikes beside him; one being Emma Thorne's onetime Ducati – Lewis was absolutely sure of it – ridden by Kapoor, the other another police-issue bike, but strangely older, as if the person riding it had forgotten to update the bloody thing.

Lewis twisted the throttle, pushing the Kawasaki harder, and the engine squealed in response, catapulting him down a steep incline towards a narrow wooden bridge that spanned what looked to be some kind of seasonal creek. Hopefully, this would be where he'd lose any pursuit, as the bridge was barely wide enough for a motorcycle, and the downward slopes, connected with various tree branches and roots that had now emerged out through the ground beneath, gave a treacherous approach that required perfect timing, or, in Lewis's case, a desperation that meant he'd try anything.

He hit the approach at speed, the Kawasaki's front wheel lifting as he executed the transition onto the wooden planks. For a heart-stopping moment, he felt the rear wheel slide on the slick wood, but then somehow the bike corrected the drift before it became unrecoverable. In his mirrors, he saw De'Geer pause at the bridge's approach, assessing the risk, and the delay bought Lewis precious seconds as he sped into the deeper forest, but in front the path narrowed further, ancient oak roots creating natural obstacles that required constant attention. Lewis was forced to slow as he weaved between them, the Kawasaki suspension absorbing most of the terrain, the custom exhaust system muffling the engine's roar to little more than a whisper.

This was another detail that had been borrowed from the original Essex Rider's modifications, and Lewis was happy about this, because it meant that over the roar of their own bikes, they couldn't likely hear him.

Lewis allowed himself a moment of triumph. He was pulling away, the distance between him and his pursuers widening with each passing second. There was a single lane road a mile or so ahead that lead towards the M25, and then Waltham Abbey, to the northwest. If he could disappear into the network of lanes that surrounded the forest, and abandon the distinctive motorcycle for some nondescript car, he could escape. The plan was unravelling, but not beyond salvation. He still had options. All he had to do was prove that he wasn't here, in the woods, being chased. An alibi would be perfect right now, and he was already working through a list of options when a flash of movement to his left was his only warning before another motorcycle burst from a side trail, cutting across his path at a forty-five-degree angle.

Lewis swerved instinctively, the Kawasaki's tyres scrabbling for purchase on the loose soil. For a terrifying moment, he thought he'd lose control, but the bike responded to his corrections, skidding to a halt mere inches from collision. This new rider, riding *another* bloody Ducati blocked his path completely, however, their own machine positioned sideways across the narrow trail.

'You should move,' he called out, the modulator distorting his voice as he went to pull his pistol, but he paused as the rider removed their helmet, revealing Emma Thorne's face.

'Surprised?' she asked, dismounting smoothly. 'You shouldn't be. You think you could take my role, kill people, and put the blame on me? This is the Essex Rider's territory. Babies of Lords need not apply.'

The clearing lit up, and furiously, Lewis glanced behind him. De'Geer, Kapoor, and Freeman had caught up, the Viking's massive frame blocking the path back the way they'd come. They remained on their bikes, engines idling, ready to give chase if Lewis attempted to escape.

He calculated his options. The woods were too dense on either side for the Kawasaki to navigate at speed. All the officers and even Thorne were experienced riders, and they wouldn't be shaken in a prolonged chase, especially with his limited amount of trail skill. His only advantage was his knowledge of the forest paths, but even that edge was diminished as he realised Thorne had intercepted him by using a shortcut he thought was known only to him and the Essex Rider.

You bloody fool. She is the sodding Essex Rider, remember? You should have guessed she would join the police to stop you.

'This doesn't end here,' Lewis said, the modulator hiding his nervousness.

'It does,' Kapoor spoke simply from behind. 'By now, your father will already be in handcuffs. We have Boyask, too, and Mikhail Stefon's talking to MI6 to save himself. It's over, Lewis.'

But Lewis Carmody, son of Lord Adrian Carmody, refused to accept defeat. With a sudden desperate movement, he gunned his Kawasaki's engine and veered off the path entirely, aiming for a narrow gap between two old oak trees. It was reckless, borderline suicidal at the speed he'd forced, but if he could slip through, he might still escape. The

Kawasaki's front wheel bounced over more exposed roots, the suspension bottoming out as Lewis fought to maintain control. Tree branches whipped past his tricorn hat, one taking it off fully, as leaves and twigs created a natural curtain he had to navigate through blindly. Behind him, he heard both De'Geer's BMW and Thorne's Ducati roaring in pursuit, the larger officer somehow squeezing his frame through the same gap.

Their skill was undeniable. Where Lewis fought against the forest, De'Geer seemed to flow with it, anticipating obstacles rather than reacting to them. The trees thinned slightly in front, revealing a stretch of relatively open ground, and Lewis realised that this was freedom, and accelerated hard, the Kawasaki leaping forward like a living thing.

If he could cross this clearing and reach the road beyond, he might still escape –

However, he was halfway across when Thorne's motorcycle emerged from the tree line to his right. She executed a perfect intercept trajectory, her bike angling across his escape route once more, and Lewis swerved to avoid her, the Kawasaki's tyres losing traction on the damp grass. He overcompensated, the bike fishtailing wildly as he fought to regain control, but the Kawasaki went down, sliding across the clearing in a shower of sparks and torn vegetation. Lewis tumbled free, instinct taking over as he rolled to absorb the impact, coming to rest against a fallen log. Before he could recover, however, Emma Thorne had dismounted, approaching with caution, likely understanding the danger he still represented with the pistol at his hip. As he looked around, he saw the other three motorcyclists converging from different directions, creating a square of containment.

'You shouldn't have come,' Lewis spat at her. 'This isn't your fight.'

'You made it my fight,' Emma replied calmly, 'when you framed James, when you burned evidence in his skip, when you killed Martin Reeves, and when you perverted everything we tried to accomplish six years ago – including killing Stephen Mahoney.'

'I wasn't anything to do with that!' Lewis struggled to his feet, his right leg protesting with a sharp stab of pain. It wasn't broken, but he could tell it was definitely sprained. 'That was Dad and Mikhail! They realised they were in the crosshairs so removed them!'

'And Reeves?'

'I don't know what you mean! I don't have a pass to get into the office!'

'But your Dad has,' Anjli smiled. 'And we have records of you using it.'

'Bullshit! My father said it wasn't placed on the records if we used the back entrance –' Lewis started but then stopped, realising he'd said too much.

'Good to know, thanks for telling us,' De'Geer patted his own bodycam, which had annoyingly picked up every word Lewis had said. Glancing around, Lewis saw the pistol had also come loose in the fall, lying in the grass several yards away.

As he saw it, the Viking sergeant tracked his gaze.

'Don't,' he advised quietly.

For a long, uncomfortable moment, the clearing was silent, save for the idle rumble of engines and Lewis's ragged breathing. Then, from the surrounding forest, more vehicle lights appeared; uniformed officers who'd been following the chase, arriving from more conventional routes, moving in to secure the scene.

'Tell me one thing,' he said, addressing Emma, as De'Geer moved forward. 'How did you know I'd take this route?'

Emma's expression softened slightly.

'Because it's the route I would've taken,' she explained. 'And apparently you so desperately want to be me.'

As De'Geer secured the handcuffs, Lewis's mind raced through the implications, the revelations and betrayals.

'He'll deny everything,' Lewis mumbled, a last desperate attempt to salvage something from the disaster. 'My father, he'll say I acted alone.'

'He might try,' Kapoor agreed, turning off her motorcycle. 'But unlike you, Lewis, we came prepared. Your father's already walked into a trap of his own, one he set for himself the moment he took those photos in a Dorchester hotel toilet.'

As the officers led him towards the waiting vehicles, Lewis looked back at the battered Kawasaki lying on the side of the clearing. It had reached the end of its journey, much like the theatrical persona he had adopted and corrupted. Emma Thorne, however, remained by her bike, likely the original Ducati the Essex Rider had used six years ago, a double of the one Kapoor rode, watching the procession with some kind of unreadable expression.

Lewis didn't understand why she'd done what she did. She'd risked everything, her freedom, her future, all to help catch him –

To right a wrong they'd committed against motorcycle riders six years earlier.

In that moment, Lewis Carmody understood something his father never had; that true power came not from manipulation and self-interest but from conviction. She'd been willing to sacrifice herself for what she believed in, and he had only ever been willing to sacrifice others.

As the police-van doors closed behind him, Lewis realised sadly that the theatrical Highwayman he'd played was finished.

And the real riders, those who understood the forest and its secrets, remained free.

26

CLEAN UP

At the clearing, De'Geer looked back at Sergeant Danny Freeman.

'I'm glad you were here,' he said.

'I wouldn't miss it for the world,' Danny smiled. 'You know, I might even go back to the force. It's one thing to teach people how to do this, but when you get to do it yourself ... oh, there's no feeling like it.'

As De'Geer and Freeman walked off, likely to discuss motorcycles, Bullman, having arrived by squad car, surveyed the scene with no small amount of satisfaction. Lewis Carmody sat handcuffed in the back of a police van, his weapon and costume bagged as evidence. Deeper into the forest, beside a wrecked van and Land Rover Defender, paramedics were checking Ryan Boyask for injuries; nothing serious, just a bruised ego, and a sprained wrist from the impact, while Cooper waited to drag him into custody.

'Quite the evening's work,' Monroe remarked, joining her at the edge of the clearing. 'Though I'm still not convinced we'll get Lord Carmody with what we have.'

'We've got the son dead to rights,' Bullman replied. 'The gun, costume, and Boyask, which connect him to the vans used in the original robbery. Add Mikhail Stefon to that –'

'Aye, but the old man's crafty,' Monroe's expression darkened. 'The wee bairn might be guilty, but Carmody will have made sure there's nothing linking him directly to any of this. Plausible deniability, as young Lewis has so helpfully pointed out.'

As he looked up, he saw Declan approach, phone in hand, having finished a call at the edge of the clearing.

'That was Baker,' he said. 'He's been updated, and he's pleased with the progress, but he wants Carmody Senior as well. What do you think Stefon will do? Any chance he'll talk now that Lewis is in custody?'

'He might,' Bullman replied. 'Especially if he believes Carmody's hanging him out to dry. They'll all turn on each other with a bit of luck, but we still need something concrete to connect Carmody to the planning.'

Monroe's eyes narrowed thoughtfully.

'Well, we've just bagged the son,' he said, 'and we've got officers watching the old man's house. What do you think Carmody will do when he realises his wee bairn has been arrested?'

Declan caught on immediately.

'He'll want to remove any evidence linking him to the operation.'

'Exactly,' Monroe nodded. 'And the most dangerous piece of evidence?'

'The photos he took of the original documents,' Declan finished. 'He'll want to destroy them before we can get a warrant.'

As he considered this, though, he shook his head.

'He'll just delete them from his phone.'

'Laddie, I believe he's probably already done that,' Monroe said. 'If I were him, that would have been the first thing I'd do. Make sure there's no record on the cloud or anywhere else. But Carmody's old school. He's arrogant. He believes he deserves this. I'll bet you a pound to a penny that somewhere in his house, or somewhere nearby, Lord Carmody has a little collection of printed out pictures, or a USB flash drive that he's now going to have to destroy. So, we watch him, wait, he'll lead us to where he's hidden them.'

'He's not left the house, though,' Declan frowned. 'He's been holed up there since the resignation, and we would have seen him leave.'

'Aye, so we might need to wait until we can get that warrant to search the bloody place. Or, maybe he wasn't the one who took them,' Monroe gave a pointed glance back at the squad car holding Lewis. 'Maybe he took them?'

'But all he'd have done is take them to wherever the bike was hidden,' Bullman said, before brightening. 'He would have taken them to wherever the bike was hidden! We just get the location from him.'

'Already lawyered up,' Declan replied morosely. 'By the time we get it from him ...'

'I've got a better idea,' Monroe smiled, the expression somehow making him look years younger, although that could have been the delight of taking down one of the ruling class. 'Let's create a situation where he has no choice but to go after them himself.'

Bullman raised an eyebrow at this.

'What do you have in mind?'

'Well, we've just arrested his son for murder, theft and conspiracy, right? The first thing any good solicitor will do is advise to cooperate, perhaps by providing evidence against those higher up the chain.'

'You want to convince Lord Carmody that his son is about to flip on him?' Declan asked.

'I want Carmody to believe his son already has, laddie,' Monroe corrected. 'And that we're about to execute a search warrant on a specific location where the evidence is hidden.'

Bullman considered this.

'It's a bit far-fetched,' she replied. 'We don't usually operate that way.'

'Aye, but he won't know that. He'll believe whatever we say if it's pressed correctly.'

'It's risky if Carmody doesn't bite.'

'Oh, he'll bite,' Monroe said confidently. 'Men like Lord Adrian Carmody don't survive in politics or business without a healthy sense of self-preservation. The moment he thinks Lewis has betrayed him; he'll move to protect himself.'

'And when he does, we'll be waiting,' Declan added. 'But how do we know he doesn't have them at the house in Theydon Bois?'

'Because he's been told to leave it,' Monroe replied. 'It's a donor's house, not Carmody's. The last thing he'll want is to be kicked out before he can dispose of them. No. He would have placed them somewhere. Try to work out where Lewis would have gone tonight. See if there's anything we can use.'

As Declan considered this, and officers began processing the scene, Chivalry Fitzwarren approached, somehow looking entirely unruffled, despite having just executed a precision vehicle manoeuvre that would have made a stunt driver proud.

'I say,' he said, addressing Bullman, 'my lady, I was wondering if our arrangement for Thursday is still ...'

'The Wallace Collection?' Bullman asked, her expression softening slightly as she replied. 'Medieval and Renaissance arms and armours, yes?'

'Indeed,' Chivalry looked pleased she'd remembered, 'although after tonight's excitement it might seem rather tame by comparison.'

'Actually, a little bit of tame sounds perfectly right about now.' She held out a hand. 'But we will need your weapon.'

'Of course,' Chivalry smiled a beaming grin as he knelt to one knee and provided up the weapon with two hands, as if proffering his lady with a sword. 'Anything for you.'

With this said, he turned and walked away, leaving Bullman shaking her head.

'I can't work out if he's taking the piss or not,' she said.

Monroe, smiling at the scene, paused.

'You know, lassie, as fun as it is to watch him and you have your little tete-a-tetes, there is something I think you need to know about Chivalry Fitzwarren,' he said.

'And what is that exactly?'

Watching the man leave, and unsure whether he should be talking or not, Monroe told her.

DE'GEER AND FREEMAN STOOD OVER THE ABANDONED Kawasaki, the veteran motorcycle officer pointing out the modifications to the engine with what felt to be a professional appreciation.

'Custom exhaust system,' he said, 'near silent when it needs to be. Same set-up the original rider used. Nowhere near as good, though.'

De'Geer nodded as he crouched down, taking a closer look.

'You think Emma Thorne was telling the truth?' he asked, 'About being the Rider?'

Freeman shrugged.

'Parts of it, maybe. The original rider was definitely Kitson, at least for most of the jobs. Your Detective Inspector claims Stephen Mahoney had done a couple, and I can see that too. But when she admitted that last one after his accident was her, you could see it had Emma Thorne written all over it. I just wish I'd thought of it at the time, but hindsight is always twenty-twenty.'

'If you two Bampots have finished admiring the pretty wee motorcycle, we've got a trap to set,' Monroe's voice interrupted their discussion, and as they looked up, they saw Declan was gathering the team around the bonnet of one police car, where he'd spread out a map of Epping Forest and Essex.

'We don't have much time, and we have a lot to do,' he began. 'We need Adrian Carmody to believe his son's betrayed him, and we need him to act on that belief.'

'How do we make that happen?' Anjli asked.

'We use what we know about him,' Declan replied. 'His pride, his sense of entitlement, and most importantly, his fear of exposure.'

He looked to his phone, placed on the bonnet, partly as a weight, but also to link through the speaker to Billy and Jess at the office.

'Any clues, Billy?'

'Actually, I might have,' Billy replied down the line. 'The van company.'

'Boyask?'

There was a pause, and then Jess replied.

'Billy forgot he was on a phone and just nodded,' she continued. 'When he spoke to Premium Fleet Rentals, Billy was told that one of the shell companies that owned it rented two shipping containers on site. Checking into it, we saw that only Boyask, Carmody and Carmody Junior have keys to them.'

'A shipping container can hold bikes,' De'Geer replied. 'Danny here does that with the police ones.'

'Okay then,' Declan smiled. 'Let's find a way to check this, and then aim Carmody in the wrong direction.'

ADRIAN CARMODY PACED THE STUDY OF HIS THEYDON BOIS house, phone pressed to his ear.

Lewis should have checked in by now. It had been over an hour since he'd left.

The operation had been meticulously planned: intercept Farnham Ewing's car, retrieve the briefcase, eliminate Emma Thorne if she appeared, and return home. It was simple, elegant, and foolproof, so why wasn't Lewis answering his sodding phone? And why did an empty plane land at Zagreb? Was Stefon playing silly bastards? Had he turned on his master, too? Were Walsh's stories of Stefon being a bloody foreign spy potentially true?

The house around him felt oppressively silent. Claire had left for her sister's early in the afternoon, taking most of her possessions with her, and any staff remaining had been given the night off; Carmody couldn't risk witnesses to Lewis's return. Now, however, the emptiness of the rooms seemed to amplify his growing unease.

Suddenly his phone rang, and jerking at the noise before reacting, Carmody grabbed it, but then paused as he saw the screen displayed an unknown number.

He hesitated but then answered. *Maybe Lewis was on the run.*

'Carmody?'

'Lord Carmody!' The voice was familiar, irritating and Scottish, belonging to Detective Superintendent Monroe, his accent unmistakable. 'I thought you'd like to know we've arrested your wee son.'

'Son?' Carmody's blood ran cold, but somehow he managed to maintain composure under the pressure. 'I beg your pardon?'

'Lewis Carmody was apprehended thirty minutes ago near High Beech,' Monroe continued. 'And would you believe it? He was in a full Highwayman costume, on a modified motorcycle and carrying the exact same antique pistol used to murder Martin Reeves – which, by the way, we believe he stole your Treasury ID card to enter the building with, unless you let the wee laddie borrow it?'

Carmody's mind was racing as Monroe spoke, calculating angles, assessing damage, formulating any kind of response. There wasn't much that didn't burn Lewis, but he was a big boy. He'd understand the greater good here.

'I'm afraid I have no idea what you're talking about, Detective Superintendent. My son is a grown man who makes his own decisions. If there's anything he's done here, or any ID of mine he stole, it is without my knowledge –'

'Aye, that's exactly what he said you'd say,' Monroe interrupted, and Carmody could hear the smile in his voice. 'Right before he started telling us about those photos you took of the documents in the Dorchester bathroom. It was sad, really, because he really thought he was giving up something big, but we'd already been told about that by Matthews. It seems when you took those wee photos, you forgot to turn your phone's "camera click" sound off.'

Carmody's grip on the phone tightened.

'This is preposterous and insulting. I demand to speak to my son immediately.'

'I thought you'd think that, but he's rather busy at the moment,' Monroe said. 'He's currently giving a detailed statement about your involvement in the robbery, the marketing integrity commission, the death of Stephen Mahoney six years ago, and several other matters we found quite interesting.'

'Whatever Lewis has told you, I can assure you –'

'I think you need to save whatever you're going to say for court, Lord Carmody,' Monroe interrupted again. 'We're executing a search warrant on your Theydon Bois house in thirty minutes. Lewis was quite specific about where we'd find the original photos, so don't go anywhere.'

The call ended before Carmody could respond. He stood frozen for several seconds, his mind racing through possible implications, possibilities, escapes.

Lewis wouldn't betray him.

He couldn't ... unless the police had convinced him it was his only option.

Lewis would betray him.

There was one hope here, though. The photos wouldn't be there, but they weren't in the house either. They were in a lock-up container on Ryan Boyask's van lot, on a USB drive dropped off by Carmody before he "resigned". It was the same container that held the bike and the costume of the

Highwayman, making sure nobody would find them, and Lewis hadn't been told.

And both Ryan and Lewis knew about the container. It'd be the next place the police looked.

The photos themselves weren't incriminating, he could claim they were documents that legally came into his possession after the fact, but the metadata on the RAW files would reveal the timing of their creation, proving he'd taken them before the robbery.

He grabbed his keys and hesitated. *If they were watching the house ...*

Carmody moved to the window, peering carefully through the curtains. It seemed empty outside, but that meant nothing. Modern surveillance didn't require visible officers. The Jaguar would be too conspicuous, and he didn't have a Minister's car any more, but Claire's Mini was still in the garage; she'd taken the Mercedes to her sister's. This was good, as the smaller car was less noticeable, especially at night.

Decision made, Carmody moved through the house quickly, grabbing the Mini's keys from the hook in the kitchen, and slipping out through the conservatory, crossing the garden to the rear entrance of the garage, where any security cameras wouldn't track his movement.

The Mini started quietly, its engine barely audible as Carmody eased it down the gravel driveway and onto the road.

He took a back route towards the M11, avoiding the main roads where police might be watching. All the while, his mind was calculating his options. He could afford to lose some money, but he couldn't afford to lose everything, and more than that, his reputation was worth more than anything else.

Ten minutes to reach the van yard.

Five minutes to retrieve the photos and destroy them.

Another ten, maybe fifteen, to return.

If he was lucky, he could be back before anyone realised he was gone.

THE TRAFFIC THINNED AS HE REACHED THE SOUTHERN outskirts of Epping, allowing him to push the Mini well above the speed limit. The irony wasn't lost on him; a Lord and former Cabinet Minister thrashing through the night like a common criminal, all because that pompous fool Baker couldn't keep his documents secure.

Carmody allowed himself a bitter smile at this. At least there was one thing coming out of this; once he'd destroyed the photos, there would be nothing connecting him to any of the night's shenanigans. Lewis might talk, but it would be his word against his father's, and Carmody had spent decades cultivating relationships with the people who mattered – judges, senior police officials, newspaper editors. He could claim that Lewis was always his mother's son and had done this deliberately to get his father back for having an affair. He'd even bring out his wife's affair, probably save himself a lengthy divorce case, and still come out as a hero in the end. Mikhail Stefon? Boyask's friend. He'd simply kill that friendship, play the victim.

He'd weather this storm as he'd weathered others before it.

He parked two streets away from the van lot at Bell Common, approaching on foot. There was a doorman at the yard's gate who nodded respectfully as Carmody entered. He knew Lord Carmody was connected to his boss and knew better than to comment on the coming and goings of anyone, especially at unusual hours. Once in the yard, Carmody moved swiftly down the edge, jogging up to a large red shipping container, unlocking the padlock on the front and stepping inside.

Everything appeared untouched.

It was a minimalist space, if he was being honest; enough room for a motorcycle, some items, and in a drawer within a desk at the back there would be photos that could end his career, stored on an encrypted USB drive, among a variety of pencils, pens and highlighters.

Making his way to the desk and opening the drawer, though, he saw the pens and highlighters had been moved, and even worse – the USB drive wasn't there. As he fumbled around on the desk, turning on his phone as a torchlight, he realised the familiar shape of the drive was missing. He tried again, his hand moving more frantically now, exploring every inch of the desk.

The drive was gone.

Had Boyask taken it? Had Lewis seen and taken the drive himself as a "get out of jail free" card?

'Looking for this?'

Carmody spun around at the voice and saw Declan Walsh standing in the doorway to the shipping container, holding up a small black USB drive.

'How –'

'We've been here for ages,' Declan spoke conversationally. 'Nice hideaway. Bit minimalistic for my taste, but I'm sure the view's spectacular – well, if you had windows at least.'

Carmody's mind raced.

'This is private property. You have no right –'

'Actually, we do,' Declan interrupted. 'You see, we have Ryan Boyask in custody, so he gave us permission to do whatever we wanted on any of his land. I believe he thinks it'll help him in his upcoming court case.'

'This is absurd,' Carmody blustered, falling back on decades of political and aristocratic training. 'I demand to speak to my solicitor immediately.'

'Of course,' Declan nodded. 'You'll have that opportunity at the station. But first –'

He was interrupted by Monroe appearing at the door behind him.

'Got everything?' Monroe asked.

'USB drive with the photos, financial records linking him to Boyask's companies, and a rather interesting journal detailing meetings with Stefon,' Declan confirmed. 'Plus, of course, the fact he's here at all when he's supposed to be at home in Theydon Bois.'

Carmody's shoulders sagged as the full implications hit him.

'Lewis didn't talk, did he?'

'Not a word,' Monroe confirmed with apparent satisfaction. 'It seems the laddie is definitely his father's son. Although, I suspect he *might* talk, now he knows his father was willing to let him take the fall alone.'

'Adrian Carmody –' Declan started formally.

'Lord Adrian Carmody,' Carmody protested, almost automatically.

'*Lord* Adrian Carmody, I'm arresting you for conspiracy to commit theft, perverting the course of justice, and conspiracy to murder. You do not have to say anything, but it may harm your defence if you do not mention when questioned something that you may rely on later in court. Everything you do say may be given in evidence.'

As Monroe moved forward with handcuffs, Carmody's carefully constructed exterior finally crumbled. The arrogance that had defined his career gave way to something smaller, more pitiful.

'Baker set me up,' he whispered. 'The briefcase, the documents, all of it. He wanted me gone.'

'Maybe,' Declan conceded. 'But he didn't make you steal state secrets, and he certainly didn't make you order your son to kill witnesses.'

'Is there anything I can do to get out of this?'

'No,' Monroe replied. 'But, to make this easier for you … there is one thing.'

'What?' Carmody asked, suddenly realising there was a possible lifeline here. 'What do you need?'

'I want you to shout loudly, and in your best Scottish accent, one word,' Monroe said.

'*Freedom*.'

27

DINNER DATE

CHARLES BAKER TUCKED INTO HIS POACHED EGG ON sourdough bread.

'Well, I have to admit, this isn't exactly how I expected you to end it,' he remarked, 'but I did ask you to literally find him with the gun in his hand. You did the next best thing you could.'

Declan, sitting opposite him, shrugged.

'Carmody was never going to be there himself,' he explained. 'It was quite surprising he gave up his son in the process. Carmody, Stefon, Boyask and Lewis are all in custody, and the paperwork they stole was destroyed in a skip – although we did find copies of the images on Carmody's USB drive, and we can make a case he'd profited from them. That said, how many people were told about this, and how many others profited, we can't yet –'

'It's fine,' Baker sighed. 'If anything, we can use this as an excuse to remove a project I was never a fan of.'

'Very good, sir,' Declan smiled.

Charles Baker placed his cutlery down and glared at Declan.

'I'm not sure I like this new you,' he muttered, 'all bowing and scraping and "yes sirs" and "no sirs".'

'Well, you are now my boss,' Declan replied.

'I'm the Prime Minister of the country,' Baker replied haughtily. 'I'm everyone's bloody boss, Declan.'

'Well, since you made us your own personal unit, it's become a little more official,' Declan stated.

'You disapprove of my leadership?' Baker asked with a dark smile.

'Not at all,' Declan replied impassively. 'It's your decision to do whatever you want.'

'Damn right it is,' Baker took another mouthful as he spoke. 'But you do have a point. I can't take you from the streets or pull you away whenever I get a boo-boo. So let's make a deal. As far as I'm concerned, your unit provides an excellent service to the people of London. Your record over the last couple of years has proven this. I'll provide you with a remit that gives you more scope –'

'Actually, Charles,' Declan said, 'we were kind of hoping you'd free us from that, instead.'

'You don't want to have a private remit?' Baker asked. 'Or you don't want to have a private remit from *me*?'

'It's more the first, if I'm being honest,' Declan admitted. 'We're police, not a private security firm. We felt we'd gone a little grey in the last few days. There was less clarification of what we should or shouldn't do. Also, down the line, you're opening yourself up to press inquiries and articles about your own private police force. I don't know if you've read history much, but leaders who have their own private police forces often turn out to be dictators.'

Baker carried on eating his food, and Declan assumed, correctly, that Baker had expected this from him.

'I'll still call on you when I need you,' he said. 'And I'll expect you to come running.'

'We're the City of London Police,' Declan replied. 'When *anybody* calls us, we come running. If we're done now, sir? I have a briefing I need to attend.'

'Why, me too,' Baker said. 'Although I'm guessing my briefing is going to be far more world-changing than yours.'

'As it should be,' Declan rose now. 'Do you know who's going to replace Lord Carmody?'

'Oh, I have ideas,' Baker sighed. 'We're sounding out a few people right now. Farnham-Ewing has her own suggestions, as well, from the right-wing boys' club. It's not perfect, but it keeps me in power for another month or two.'

'Things are that bad?' Declan asked.

'Let's just say I'm staying very friendly with the 1922 committee right now,' Baker shrugged, 'I've seen a couple of letters come in, but nothing that makes me concerned.'

He smiled.

'And if I do, DCI Walsh, I'm sure I'll react accordingly, and not send my private police force in to arrest my enemies, for *that* would be the work of a dictator.'

'Yes, sir, it would,' Declan smiled.

'Hey, what happened to Emma Thorpe, and that whole Essex Rider thing?'

Declan shrugged.

'Wasn't our case,' he said, his face impassive. 'And as you said, Carmody was the target. Luckily for us, we worked for you on this case, not the law, it seems.'

Baker almost choked on his toast.

'You're letting a thief go free?'

'Not at all,' Declan replied calmly. 'Carmody and his son could have been guilty of the cases six years ago, too.'

'Not James Kitson, Stephen Mahoney or Emma Thorne?'

Declan waited a moment and then leant closer.

'I don't know if you heard, sir, but James Kitson and Stephen Mahoney were in a terrible accident, one that killed Mahoney and retired Kitson,' he explained softly. 'And Thorne? She was on Carmody's staff, nothing more.'

'So you believe,' Baker chuckled.

'So we believe,' Declan nodded. 'And luckily for us, we had a carte blanch blessing from the Prime Minister himself to arrest whoever we wanted ... and to *pardon* whoever we wanted. So, thank you for that. Sir.'

Baker choked on a mouthful of egg as Declan, with a little wink, left the members' terrace.

There was every chance Emma Thorne would have to pay for her time as the Essex Rider down the line, but today was not one of those days.

As HE EXITED THE ROOM, HEADING DOWN THE CORRIDORS towards the back entrance of Westminster, he saw Jennifer Farnham-Ewing waiting for him, arms folded as she leant against one of the ornate wooden doorways.

'He knows his time is ending,' she said. 'It's very sad. It's like an old dog waiting to be taken to "the farm".'

'As a fan of dogs, I'd prefer it if you didn't state it like that,' Declan replied irritably, looking around. 'Should you be speaking to us?'

Jennifer grinned.

'You were there when he told you. Of course I'm going to

stand and talk to you. We're back in the same sodding role; in debt to a Prime Minister that we both hate.'

'I think "hate" is a bold term,' Declan smiled. 'I think "mildly dislike" or "are irritated by" are possibly better options.'

Jennifer shrugged.

'Look, Walsh, we've had our problems in the past, I'm aware of that,' she said. 'But how about this time we keep an alliance going, yeah? If you have any problems with Baker, maybe I can help, and if I have any problems with Baker, maybe you can.'

'Are you expected to have problems with Baker?' Declan asked innocently.

Jennifer pondered her words.

'Carmody wasn't working alone. There were others in Parliament with their own agendas. Keep a weather ear open.'

'Well, it's appreciated,' Declan smiled, nodding, and then carrying on past her. 'I'll see you around, Miss Farnham-Ewing.'

'Not if I see you first, Walsh,' Jennifer said as she turned and walked back towards the Houses of Parliament.

Declan stopped, watching her leave. When he first came into the force, the last thing he wanted was politics in his life, but now this seemed to be the way forward.

Sighing, he continued down the corridor and eventually out of the building.

There was a long day ahead, and already there was talk of a new case.

CHIVALRY FITZWARREN HAD JUST SEATED HIMSELF AT HIS TABLE in *Hawksmoor* Canary Wharf, and was checking his phone, sipping at the water he'd been provided before examining the menu ... as Bullman walked over and sat opposite him.

He looked up and was about to say something, believing her to be someone else, then froze as he stared at her.

'Hello, Chivalry,' Bullman smiled. 'Lovely place you've brought us.'

'My lady, I'm afraid I'm a bit confused,' Chivalry spluttered, placing his phone down and looking around the restaurant nervously. 'I was expecting –'

'Your girlfriend,' Bullman smiled. 'Although, do you call Jeanette your girlfriend still? I mean, you've been with her for close to fifteen years now.'

She leant back in her chair, watching Chivalry.

'It's not exactly a secret either, is it?' she continued. 'Billy mentioned you'd been seeing this woman on and off for years, although he didn't know what the current status was. A quick check on the society pages of the *Mail Online* had shown a couple of times where there you are, Jeanette on your arm. She's quite striking, you know. I'm almost jealous.'

Chivalry blushed.

'I'm a very lucky man,' he said. 'And I'm afraid it's Jeanette I'm meeting tonight.'

'Oh, I know,' Bullman smiled. 'I had Billy check your diary. That's how I knew you were here.'

She leant forward.

'What I can't work out is why Chivalry Fitzwarren, a man with a long-term love who has expressed no interest in me for years, has spent the last couple of days acting like a love-struck fool around me. It's caused quite a distraction, and I'd like to know what was going on.'

Chivalry smiled himself.

'And there I was thinking you were the detective,' he said, sipping at his water.

Bullman narrowed her eyes once more.

'This was all a distraction?'

Chivalry nodded.

'Billy had informed me how you and the Commander had split,' he said. 'When I came into the room, I saw instantly that you were still struggling with this. I felt it was my duty to assist you in getting over it ...'

'By trying to date me?'

'By trying to court you in the most confusing and haphazard manner possible,' Chivalry grinned. 'Bumbling, rambunctious, and completely out of his depth, poor Chivalry Fitzwarren, failing miserably to seduce the Lady Bullman.'

'So all of your flustered performances were basically to make me feel better about myself?'

'That, and perhaps convince you to reconsider your possibly rash decision. Did it make you feel better?'

Bullman chuckled.

'Actually, it did,' she nodded. 'I mean, don't get me wrong, I never thought of you in that kind of way, but it did feel nice, in a strange, twisted, Chivalry Fitzwarren way.'

In response, Chivalry waved over to the server, before returning his attention to Bullman.

'The event at the Wallace Collection I invited you to? It's still open if you're interested, but as a friend, not a love interest.'

'I can deal with that,' Bullman replied as the server walked over.

'Are you ready to order?' she asked.

'No, my partner hasn't arrived yet,' Chivalry explained. 'But can we lay out the table for one more, please?'

'Oh no,' Bullman said. 'I wasn't here to interrupt.'

'My dear lady,' Chivalry said. 'As you said, Jeanette and I have been together for many years now. This was nothing more than a meal. No anniversary, no underlying reason. She will be as happy as I am to turn it into a dinner with fine friends. My treat, of course.'

Bullman leant back in the chair.

'You know what, Fitzwarren,' she said. 'Your family never fails to surprise me.'

'We've been told that before,' Chivalry nodded. 'Look, I can't claim to know you better than my nephew does, or the others in the Last Chance Saloon. But what I can tell you is the woman I've seen over the years, is a strong and independent, ferocious woman, who in the past seems to have grabbed life by the horns and wrestled it to the ground, while the woman I've seen for the last couple of days has been, well, *lacking*. Whatever happened between you and Mister Bradbury, it shouldn't sully who you are, who you were, and what you can become. You're an exquisite woman, Miss Bullman, and out there is a very good-looking man just waiting for you to find him. Or a very good-looking woman, I'm not going to judge you. Or maybe it's Bradbury still, and you're just too bloody stubborn to admit it.'

The server returned with cutlery and glasses and began to create a third space on the table. Chivalry raised his water in a mock toast.

'Who knows,' he said, 'maybe he'll even come back on his hands and knees *begging* to be returned to your bosom. But until then, perhaps you should just enjoy being yourself for a while.'

'Thank you,' Bullman flushed as she nodded, but rose from the table, pausing the server. 'But I won't be joining you.'

'Are you sure?'

Bullman looked around the restaurant, and for a moment Chivalry wondered if she was weighing up the options of a free steak meal compared to what she was about to say, but then she nodded, looking back.

'I'm an independent, free-thinking woman,' she said. 'I need to start remembering how that is. Thank you, Chivalry. Don't be a stranger.'

'I couldn't if I wanted to, my dear,' Chivalry grinned, his arms now out, as if baring his chest to the world. 'Every person I meet is a friend, and every time I leave, it is a sad farewell for them.'

'By the way,' Bullman said as she turned to leave. 'Did I see that you've made an offer to Lord Carmody for his guns? They *are* a murder weapon, you're aware of this, right? You're not going to get them for a very long time, even if at all.'

'I know,' Chivalry shrugged, 'but a deal is still a deal, and I can't resist a challenge. And they only killed someone with *one* of them.'

As Bullman left the restaurant, she found herself smiling, laughing even. She'd walked into the restaurant with a completely different impression of what was going on, and now, strangely, she felt like a weight had lifted from her heart. But it wasn't the weight that Chivalry thought he'd saved her from.

Pulling out her phone, she dialled a number.

It answered on the second ring.

'David,' she said. 'It's me. I think we need to have a chat.'

EPILOGUE

Of course, Lord Carmody didn't go quietly and continued to claim that he was set up by the Prime Minister – which, in a way, he was. Although, in Charles Baker's defence, he'd only expected Carmody to use the information gathered to his own advantage, maybe a little insider trading – he hadn't expected him to make his son wear a Highwayman's costume and shoot a witness.

As soon as everyone was arrested, people started pushing to make deals. Mikhail Stefon immediately began throwing everyone under the bus, aware very quickly that his position in Westminster was diminishing by the minute and doing anything to stop being thrown permanently into a black site, even confessing to the murder of Stephen Mahoney – although he claimed it was on Lord Carmody's orders. However, within a matter of hours, various people had pressured Baker to enquire on Stefon's behalf if he could be removed from the case. They claimed Stefon was nothing more than a provider of drugs, assuming that he hadn't been aware of what had happened and as he'd placed Sophia into the car – a woman who, by her own admission, had used a tracker to let Lewis Carmody know they were approaching – this was a little farfetched and argued this was assistance he could have given unknowingly.

Baker, of course, couldn't tell them the truth.

Either way, the evidence was becoming circumstantial at this point, and Declan knew that once out, Mikhail Stefon could finally catch that private flight to Zagreb, whether on his own steam or as an asset for MI6, and there was nothing they could do.

The other two, however, were a little more solid. Ryan Boyask had been arrested while trying to hinder the police, in a hire van matching the same registration number as one involved in the original heist on Carmody, whereas Lewis, caught in full Highwayman gear, and with the weapon that killed Martin Reeves in his hand, hadn't managed to explain a way to get out of this, and was now making deals on taking down his father, using the paper trails he'd created while working as the executive trustee for the "blind trust" his father had claimed to have.

Lord Carmody, still refusing to speak and bunkered down with expensive solicitors while he burnt every favour he was owed to give him more time, would most likely find some way to wheedle out down the line, but his reputation was in tatters, his finances were frozen, and not only was he now evicted forcibly from his Theydon Bois house, he was likely about to lose his mansion up north as well.

As for the others? Well, Declan knew there was a valid argument to be made to say that Peter Kendall, although skimming money originally six years ago, had been a victim himself of Lord Carmody. Martin Reeves was dead, Sophia was nothing more than a paid actor, so to speak, and both

James Kitson and Emma Thorne, although both effectively outed as the original Essex Rider, were not involved with this second theft. Declan had no problem with people bringing the rich to justice, and he'd only have really cared if it had been his case – which, luckily for Declan, the Essex Rider case of six years earlier *wasn't*.

Declan only hoped that the truth of Stephen Mahoney's death coming out would give them both some closure.

DANNY FREEMAN ARRIVED AT HIS MOTORCYCLE SCHOOL EARLY on his last day as an instructor.

It was a bittersweet morning; after the chase through Epping Forest a couple of weeks earlier, he had applied back to the Met, asking if he could return to active duty. Training coppers to ride bikes was all well and good, but he wanted to get back out in the field. He felt he was finally ready.

What he wasn't ready for was seeing Morten De'Geer in full bike leathers, waiting at the entrance.

'If I recall correctly, Mort, I've already done you,' he said. 'You've got a certificate and everything.'

'I'm not here as a student,' De'Geer shrugged. 'I understand today's your last day. They're bringing somebody in to replace you.'

Danny looked around the car park area.

'Yeah, it's a guy from Surrey,' he replied. 'He's good enough. I gave him a refresher when he came back after an injury. He'll be able to teach them.'

He smiled.

'And there's a new consultant, coming in once, maybe

twice a week to let them pick his brain, while also sorting out the bikes for us.'

'Kitson?'

'Yeah. If anyone knows what we need to do better, it's him,' Freeman shrugged. 'And it's the least we can do. Also, it means we can help get him some more treatment for the vertigo. Who knows, in a year or two, he might be able to ride again. Not to the levels he did before, but Christ, having that would only be good for us if he was on our side.'

'How many have you got today?' De'Geer asked.

Freeman had by now opened the container door and stepped into his makeshift office, picking up a clipboard and checking it.

'Eight,' he said. 'Two brand new, six carrying on from a previous set of lessons. Why?'

De'Geer smiled.

'Thought I'd give you some assistance today,' he said. 'If you're up for it.'

'You teaching people how to ride bikes?' Freeman grinned. 'God help them, Morten De'Geer. God help them all.'

CHARLES BAKER HATED CABINET RESHUFFLES. IT ALWAYS seemed to be a case of finally getting people to follow his beat and then swapping them all out for new ones when he realised just how corrupt and useless the ones he'd picked were.

This, however, was an important Cabinet reshuffle; the people he picked this time would either make or break his premiership. He knew there were a handful of letters that had been sent in to the 1922 Committee – votes of no confidence in his abilities. He also knew that the more centrist members of his party were starting to turn against him, which was amusing considering he'd once been a Labour MP, and had almost been deemed too centrist to lead the party.

And so, he was forced to make a deal with the devil as he sat in his Number Ten office, facing Tamara Banks. She was a true-blue right-wing Conservative, and more than one person, including himself, had likened her, over the years, to the *bastard daughter of Cruella De Vil and Heinrick Himmler.* Which was hilarious considering a few months back she'd had to resign from a Cabinet position after a diary containing secrets about her had been leaked to the *Daily Mail,* claiming she'd joined the National Front in the nineties, had dressed like Eva Braun for a party once, owned a copy of *Mein Kampf,* first edition no less, and attended a Hen Party at the Eagles Nest.

Everyone had expected her to shrivel up and die, but Tamara Banks wasn't that kind of person. She'd sued the paper, demanding conclusive proof of these attacks or a retraction, and as the "witness" that claimed to have seen her in fancy dress and in questionable locations never appeared, these were reluctantly classed as rumours. Nobody could ever prove she'd bought the bloody book, and she hand-waved aside the National Front membership as "a mistake she'd learnt from, but had also been because of an abusive, racist boyfriend who'd gaslit her, while an impressionable student, into his way of thinking."

She even did an apology tour, and her sodding rating went up. Apparently, being a onetime Nazi *wasn't* the terrible thing it once was, no matter what Baker thought.

She had once gone against him for Prime Minister in the past but hadn't quite had the votes. But now, with this new following – including actual racists who believed she was "their girl" – Baker knew that if she went for him again, she'd take him out like a sniper.

This time, he had to find a way to get around that.

'So, I understand you want to offer me a job?' Tamara smiled, giving the impression of a shark looking for more babies to munch. Actually, as far as Baker was concerned, she didn't need to be a shark to want more babies to munch. He genuinely believed this was something Tamara did on her weekends.

'As you know, with Lord Carmody resigning, we had an opportunity to shuffle the deck,' he said. 'We'll be keeping Joanna Karolides as Home Secretary. She's got too many irons in the fire to pull her out right now. We were thinking about bringing Malik Abiola in as Treasury Minister.'

He watched, looking for distaste, but Tamara was clever enough to keep her face impassive.

'Opening up Defence,' she nodded. 'Is this why I'm here?'

'It is.' Baker leant back in his plush leather chair, watching Tamara for a moment, almost wondering whether he could simply say "I've changed my mind, we're not hiring bastards today", but instead, he gave a smile and held out his hand.

'I'd like to offer you the role of Defence Secretary,' he said.

Tamara leant forward, grabbing his hand and shaking it, perhaps a little too ambitiously. He thought she would have argued, maybe tried to push for a better role; Defence was good, but it wasn't as high up as, say, Chancellor or even Home Secretary. She had a right to challenge Karolides, even with the last year's worth of controversies around her neck. But it seemed that Tamara Banks was happy with her new role.

'Of course, with this comes loyalty,' he said. 'I'd expect you to back me on any plays that are made by the Conservative Party.'

'I'll back you as long as I believe in you,' Tamara replied.

'Do you believe in me right now?'

Tamara watched Baker for an uncomfortably long moment, and Baker remembered that years earlier, the two of them had been on a Star Chamber – one that would make decisions politicians couldn't. He'd had to step down when he became Prime Minister, but he knew very well that Tamara was still on it, even though it'd been another thing outed by the press, and she'd claimed publicly it'd now been closed down.

Which was a lie, of course.

Either way, she still had the power of God, and giving her Defence made her, in a way, more powerful than he was.

'I know how many letters have gone in,' she said matter-of-factly. 'I also know who they're from, why they were sent, and what you can do about it.'

'And will you help me?'

Tamara considered the question, then nodded.

'Of course, Prime Minister,' she said. 'To not do so would be incredibly unpatriotic.'

After the meeting, and when Tamara had left – presumably to get her subordinates to leak the news to the press before he made an announcement – Charles Baker headed towards the Members' Terrace at Westminster. Even though he was Prime Minister and expected to do most of his work in Number Ten, he still liked to come here. It was a chance to gain some composure, and to consider events while sitting in the heart of everything.

There was another reason for his journey today, though.

Jennifer Farnham-Ewing sat amongst a group of middle-aged men, all laughing as she told some mediocre joke. It wasn't that she was hilarious, it was that she was young and pretty, and they were all in their sixties and incredibly misogynistic, probably living out their daddy fantasies or, in some cases, *granddaddy* fantasies while talking to her.

Baker didn't care. Jennifer Farnham-Ewing had made it very clear where she stood on power. It was absolute, and she would use whoever she could to get there. If she courted the right-wing grandfathers to get into position, that was fine with her. And currently, if she was willing to help him, that was fine with Charles Baker.

She saw him enter, made her excuses, and walked over, giving a respectful nod.

'Prime Minister,' she said. 'How grateful we are that you would grace us with your presence. I can't remember ... am I supposed to kiss your ring?'

'You can keep the hell away from my ring,' Baker muttered. 'It's done. Tamara is the new Defence Secretary.'

Jennifer said nothing, simply giving a short, simple nod.

'Any pushback?'

'There will be, as people hate wannabe Nazis and all that, but I'll wave it down,' Baker said. 'I've done you this favour, Jennifer, to give you clout. You'd better make sure that clout works for me.'

'Hey,' Jennifer patted Baker on the shoulder, a familiar motion that threw him for a moment. 'I told you how to remove Carmody, right?'

'You didn't tell me there'd be a line of bodies once I started.'

Jennifer considered this.

'True,' she said. 'But, let's be honest, Charles, this isn't the first time your road to power has been littered with dead bodies, is it? I keep a list. You never know when it'll come in handy.'

She glanced back at the others, who were now watching their conversation with interest.

'Anyway, great to see you, Prime Minister,' she exclaimed. 'I totally understand I can't be in the Cabinet yet, but if there are any roles you need to fill, or junior Cabinet Minister positions, you know you have my utmost loyalty ... for as long as you're in power.'

And with this ominous line spoken, Jennifer Farnham-Ewing walked off.

Baker watched her, wondering whether he should have let Declan Walsh and his team return to the City of London after all. There was a chance he'd be needing their help soon – if only to help him hide another murder ... that of Jennifer Farnham-sodding-Ewing.

She hadn't been wrong, though. The Devonshire Affair had meant he'd spent twenty years believing he'd committed murder; the things he'd promised to Frankie Pearce over that time weighed heavy on his soul. Then there was Malcolm Gladwell, and the deaths of Kendis Taylor and Nasir Gill, even his own poor wife, Donna, who committed suicide, God rest her troubled soul.

And that was before he even came into power.

Charles Baker kept a list as well, and he was very aware that one day, someone would come looking for payment.

'But today is not the day,' he muttered to himself, as with

a smile, he wandered back to his car, and his SEG close protection officers. As he did so, he caught sight of someone out of the corner of his eye – standing in one corridor, guarding a low-level door.

DCI Matthews. No longer in the role he had been in for many years, and lucky he even had a job, still.

Some people simply aren't built for pressure, Baker thought to himself, as he carried on past.

Some people could never be king.

———

ANJLI WAS SITTING AT HER DESK, READING A NOVEL WHEN Declan returned with three coffees, one for him, one for Anjli and one for Jess, currently sitting at Billy's monitor station, doing homework. Although the canteen upstairs had a working coffee machine, sometimes it felt good just to get out of the building.

'What are you reading?' he asked.

It was an old leather-bound book, and Anjli smiled as she looked up.

'*Rookwood,*' she said. 'Chivalry lent it to me.'

'Haven't you had enough Dick Turpin for a while?' Declan asked, placing her coffee down.

She leant back in her chair.

'I just don't get it,' she muttered. 'I mean, I'm sure there's a reason, but Highwaymen were scumbags. They stole from people, they murdered people. The victims were usually battered or threatened. These were muggers, carjackers, yet we treat them like heroes. Dick Turpin, Sixteen-String Jack, Tom King –'

'Don't forget Claude Duval, he danced with a lady rather

than taking her items once, or "Swift Nick" Nevison, who supposedly rode from Kent to York in a single day to establish an alibi for a robbery,' Jess added. Declan wasn't sure how, or even why, she knew this. *Was knowing Highwaymen a teenage thing these days?*

'Wasn't that Turpin riding to York?' Declan asked.

'It is now, ever since Ainsworth stole it and used it in *Rookwood*,' Anjli waggled the book. 'But look at your daughter, Declan. Look at her wide, sparkling eyes. To her, they're not scumbag criminals. To her, and people like her for centuries, they're folk heroes.'

Declan sat on the desk, looking down at Anjli as he sipped his coffee.

'You have to remember that it was a different time,' he replied. 'There wasn't really a police force as such back then, and people who could ride in carriages and travel how the victims did, well, they were often members of the higher gentry – effectively the one-percenters of today. People were poor, living conditions were squalid and usually massively substandard. They saw Highwaymen –'

'And Highwaywomen,' Jess added, sipping her coffee.

'Indeed, they saw these as people who were getting one back against "the man", so to speak. Standing up for the common folk, even if the Highwaymen themselves weren't really passing the money around.'

'Sixteen-String Jack was apparently generous with his friends and mistresses,' Jess muttered.

'Oh, that's okay then,' Declan smiled.

Anjli looked back at her book, quoting from the novel.

'*With our hearts ready rifled, each pocket we rifle, with the pure flame of chivalry stirring our breasts.*'

She shook her head.

'Pure flame of chivalry. I mean, come on.'

'In a way, Emma Thorne and James Kitson, I suppose even Stephen Mahoney, were folk heroes for a modern generation,' Jess mused. 'Stealing from the rich and giving to the poor.'

'How do you work that out?'

Jess shrugged.

'They never took money.'

'They took information.'

'True, but once they had it, they took down the rich with it – passing it to newspapers, effectively telling the story.'

'But, at least with Emma Thorne, we didn't get any bloody songs,' Anjli chuckled.

'Don't tell Chivalry that,' Declan replied with a smile. 'He'll be bereft.'

'Where is he, by the way?' Anjli asked, looking around. 'I've kind of got used to him being here.'

'He finally caught Billy,' Jess sipped from her coffee, returning to her homework. 'He's taken him out for lunch. Apparently, there's a family discussion that needs to be had.'

'Are they finally welcoming him back into their bosom?'

Declan shook his head.

'From what I can work out, it's something worse … but I'm sure we'll be told at some point.'

'And all that faff with Bullman?'

'Apparently, Chivalry was doing it all as some kind of learning exercise … showing Bullman the path she needed to take,' Declan replied. 'From what I can work out, she's back with Bradbury. How long that lasts, I've no idea.'

Anjli sipped at her coffee.

'I'm glad they're back together,' she added. 'When you work that close, it must be really hard if you break up.'

She looked up at Declan.

'We're not doing that anytime soon, right?'

'Are you kidding?' Declan laughed. 'If anybody's leaving someone here, it's you leaving me.'

Anjli placed her coffee down and stared intently at Declan.

'You know what,' she said, 'you're absolutely right, Walsh, it will be me that leaves you. But not until you've won the lottery. I've got to get *something* from this relationship.'

Declan rose from the desk, patting Anjli on the shoulder as he began heading to his office.

'And that, my friends, is love,' he quipped, and was about to continue, but Anjli's phone buzzed with a new message. She checked the message, then frowned.

'Tamara Banks is the new Defence Secretary,' she said, coldly.

'Only a matter of time before Baker welcomed her back,' Declan shrugged.

'That was Craig, her assistant,' Anjli continued, looking up. 'God knows how he got my number, but she wants to speak to me tomorrow.'

Declan thought back to the meeting in the pub.

'You going to take that meeting?' he asked, concerned.

After a moment, Anjli reluctantly nodded.

'She's up to something, and I think it'd be better to know what it is than to learn it on the news,' she said. 'Besides, it might make her actually lose points with her team if she's seen with someone of, well, my ethnic persuasion.'

Declan snorted as Monroe walked into the office, plonking himself down between Anjli and Declan.

'Did I hear you talking about folk heroes?' he asked, pointing at the leather-bound novel on Anjli's desk. 'Aye, that's a nice wee book you've got there, and I'm sure the fictional Dick Turpin is way more exciting than the real one.'

He leant in slightly, lowering his voice in mock secrecy.

'But how about I show you a real folk hero? A film that is *exact and true* to the history that happened before?'

'And what would that be?' Declan asked.

Monroe gave a conspiratorial wink.

'How about we take a moment, fill our hearts with Scottish pride ... and watch Mel Gibson in *Braveheart*?' he suggested, retreating into his office quickly, laughing hard as Anjli rose, leather book in her hand like a weapon. '*Freeeee-dommmmmm!!!*'

Want the next Declan Walsh novel? CLICK HERE, or turn the page...

DCI Walsh and the team of the *Last Chance Saloon* will return in their next thriller

Order Now at Amazon:

www.mybook.to/weplaywithdeath

ACKNOWLEDGEMENTS

When you write a series of books, you find that there are a ton of people out there who help you, sometimes without even realising, and so I wanted to say thanks.

There are people I need to thank, and they know who they are, including my brother Chris Lee, Jacqueline Beard MBE, who has copyedited all my books since the very beginning, and editor Sian Phillips, all of whom have made my books way better than they have every right to be.

Also, I couldn't have done this without my growing army of ARC and beta readers, who not only show me where I falter, but also raise awareness of me in the social media world, ensuring that other people learn of my books.

I also thank Fosco, my Cocker Spaniel of twelve years, who sat, or walked beside be during the creation of every Jack Gatland book. She unfortunately passed during the creation of this book, but I truly believe she still sits beside me as I write this.

But mainly, I tip my hat and thank you. *The reader.* Who once took a chance on an unknown author in a pile of Kindle books, and thought you'd give them a go, and who has carried on this far with them, as well as the spin off books I now release.

I write Declan Walsh for you. He (and his team) solves crimes for you. And with luck, he'll keep on solving them for a very long time.

Jack Gatland / Tony Lee,
London, March 2025

ABOUT THE AUTHOR

Jack Gatland is the pen name of *#1 New York Times Bestselling Author* Tony Lee, who has been writing in all media for thirty-five years, including comics, graphic novels, middle grade books, audio drama, TV and film for *DC Comics, Marvel, BBC, ITV, Random House, Penguin USA, Hachette* and a ton of other publishers and broadcasters.

These have included licences such as *Doctor Who, Spider Man, X-Men, Star Trek, Battlestar Galactica, MacGyver,* BBC's *Doctors, Wallace and Gromit* and *Shrek*, as well as work created with musicians such as *Ozzy Osbourne, Joe Satriani, Beartooth, Pantera, Megadeth, Iron Maiden* and *Bruce Dickinson.*

As Tony, he's toured the world talking to reluctant readers with his 'Change The Channel' school tours, and lectures on screenwriting, story craft and comic scripting for festivals and conferences such as *Raindance* in London and *Author Nation, The Global Publishing Summit* and *20Books* globally.

An introvert West Londoner by heart, he lives with his wife Tracy, just outside London.

Locations In The Book

The locations and items I use in my books are real, if altered slightly for dramatic intent.

London New Road is a real stretch through Epping Forest, between Buckhurst Hill and the Wake Arms roundabout, and has just the right mix of quiet and unsettling. I've driven it more times than I should've, usually at night, and it never feels entirely normal.

Ambresbury Banks is a genuine Iron Age earthwork nearby, sometimes linked (dubiously) to Boudica's last stand. The forest itself has more solid folklore — Dick Turpin, the high-wayman, is said to have used this area as a hideout and ambush spot. None of that's confirmed, of course, but it all adds to the atmosphere, which is why it earned its place in the book.

The Fenchurch Street Vaults: There are no known underground vaults exactly like the ones in the book beneath Fenchurch Street — or if there are, they're doing an excellent job staying hidden. The version I describe is fictional, but inspired by a mix of real underground spaces across London.

The closest real-world comparison would be the abandoned *Kingsway telephone exchange* — a Cold War-era bunker beneath Holborn once used as a secure communications hub. That, combined with the old *railway mail tunnels* and various bank vaults hidden beneath the City, helped shape the layout in my head.

As with most things in this world: if it *shouldn't* exist, there's a good chance it probably does.

The Guildhall Art Gallery is the official gallery of the City of London, tucked just behind the historic Guildhall itself. It's best known for housing a remarkable collection of Victorian art — and something even older underneath.

Beneath the gallery is the preserved remains of London's Roman amphitheatre, discovered in 1988. You can still see the outline of the arena embedded into the floors of the lower level — a detail too good not to use in a scene. The mix of art, politics, and ancient history makes it one of the more surreal corners of the City, which is exactly why it appears in the book.

Theydon Bois is a real village on the edge of Epping Forest, one of those Central Line stops where London quietly turns into countryside. It has a village green, a duck pond, and more Range Rovers than seems strictly necessary.

It's the sort of place where everything looks peaceful, but the trees are always just a bit too close, and the forest never quite lets go of the edges.

The Dorchester Hotel is very much real — a Park Lane landmark since the 1930s, and still one of London's most exclusive hotels. It's the kind of place where heads of state arrive through discreet side entrances, where the carpets are deeper than some bathtubs, and where the staff can summon a dry martini with a glance.

It has that particular old-world glamour: all polished brass, grand chandeliers, and hushed conversations over high-backed chairs. The Grill is famous. The bar is low-lit and excellent. The clientele is... exactly who you think it is.

You don't stumble into The Dorchester. You arrive there, probably in something blacked-out, probably not on your own name.

The Great Hall of Middle Temple is very real, and very old — completed in 1573, it's one of the four Inns of Court, still used by barristers today. It has everything you want from a place like this: hammerbeam roof, stained glass windows, portraits of dead men with excellent posture, and that slightly intimidating stillness that settles in buildings where power has lived a long time.

It also has a working gas fireplace that's been burning almost non-stop since 1919, and the hall itself was supposedly where Shakespeare's *Twelfth Night* was first performed. There's a library, a set of cloisters, and a private garden hidden behind its stone walls — the sort of garden no one talks in loudly, and where the Wars of the Roses was believed to have started, with people picking coloured roses to choose their side.

I actually use this location far more in *The Lionheart Curse*, if you're interested!

The Old Bank of England pub is real, and the description and the history written in the book explain more than I could here, although one thing I don't mention, which was until recently true is that in their 'sun garden' is a double decker bus that you can drink in.

The Houses of Parliament — officially the Palace of Westminster — are as real as they are surreal. On the outside, all gothic drama and spires. On the inside, endless corridors, fading carpets, and a quiet hum of paperwork, whispered favours, and unspoken rivalries.

It's not just a government building. It's a maze. Offices and chambers sit next to bars and dining rooms, while signs point to things like "The Crypt Chapel" or "The Stranger's Gallery" with no sense of irony. There's a rifle range in the basement. A hairdresser. A shooting club. MPs vote by physically walking into rooms marked "Aye" or "No", which feels charming until it isn't.

Every corner of the place feels heavy with history, and a little too comfortable with power. It's both exactly what you'd expect — and somehow, stranger.

Finally, **High Beech** is a very real part of Epping Forest, sitting between Loughton and Waltham Abbey, and it's one of the oldest, most storied corners of the woodland. It's a mix of tangled oaks, twisting trails and unexpected glades, with trees that lean like they've been whispering to each other for centuries.

The area has been part of Epping Forest since before it was even called that — this was royal hunting ground as far back as the Norman period. High Beech itself became a popular Victorian destination after the arrival of the railway, and some say it's where Alfred, Lord Tennyson wrote part of *In*

Memoriam while staying at a nearby cottage. Whether that's true or just local legend depends on how romantic you're feeling.

There's also the famous tea hut — technically *The Original Tea Hut*, opened in 1930 — which still serves bikers, hikers, and the occasional slightly shaken detective. There was once a grand hotel here too, long gone now, and during both world wars, parts of the forest around High Beech were used for military training.

Like much of Epping Forest, it feels ancient and quietly alive — the sort of place where you can be alone, but never unobserved.

If you're interested in seeing what the *real* locations look like, I occasionally post 'behind the scenes' location images on my Instagram feed. This will continue through all the books, after leaving a suitable amount of time to avoid spoilers, and I suggest you follow it.

In fact, feel free to follow me on all my social media by clicking on the links below. Over time these can be places where we can engage, discuss Declan and put the world to rights.

www.jackgatland.com
www.hoodemanmedia.com

Visit Jack and Tony's Reader's Group Page
(Mainly for fans to discuss his books):
https://www.facebook.com/groups/jackgatland

Subscribe to Jack's Readers List:
https://bit.ly/jackgatlandVIP

www.facebook.com/jackgatlandbooks
www.twitter.com/jackgatlandbook
ww.instagram.com/jackgatland

Want more books by Jack Gatland? Turn the page...

THEY TRIED TO KILL HIM...
NOW HE'S OUT FOR **REVENGE.**

NEW YORK TIMES #1 BESTSELLER **TONY LEE** WRITING AS

JACK GATLAND

THE MURDER OF AN **MI5 AGENT**...
A BURNED SPY **ON THE RUN** FROM HIS OWN PEOPLE...
AN ENEMY OUT TO **STOP HIM** AT ANY COST...
AND A **PRESIDENT** ABOUT TO BE **ASSASSINATED**...

SLEEPING SOLDIERS

A **TOM MARLOWE** THRILLER

BOOK 1 IN A NEW SERIES OF THRILLERS IN THE STYLE OF
JASON BOURNE, JOHN MILTON OR **BURN NOTICE,** AND
SPINNING OUT OF THE **DECLAN WALSH** SERIES OF BOOKS

AVAILABLE ON AMAZON / KINDLE UNLIMITED

THE THEFT OF A **PRICELESS** PAINTING...
A GANGSTER WITH A **CRIPPLING DEBT**...
A **BODY COUNT** RISING BY THE HOUR...

AND ELLIE RECKLESS IS CAUGHT IN THE MIDDLE.

JACK GATLAND

PAINT
— THE —
DEAD

A 'COP FOR CRIMINALS' ELLIE RECKLESS NOVEL

A NEW PROCEDURAL CRIME SERIES WITH
A TWIST - FROM THE CREATOR OF THE
BESTSELLING 'DI DECLAN WALSH' SERIES

AVAILABLE ON AMAZON / KINDLE UNLIMITED

EIGHT PEOPLE. EIGHT SECRETS.
ONE SNIPER.

THE
BOARD
ROOM

HOW FAR WOULD YOU GO TO GAIN JUSTICE?

NEW YORK TIMES #1 BESTSELLER TONY LEE WRITING AS

JACK GATLAND

A NEW STANDALONE THRILLER WITH
A TWIST - FROM THE CREATOR OF THE
BESTSELLING 'DI DECLAN WALSH' SERIES

AVAILABLE ON AMAZON / KINDLE UNLIMITED

"★★★★★ AN EXCELLENT 'INDIANA JONES' STYLE FAST PACED CHARGE AROUND ENGLAND THAT WAS RIVETING AND CAPTIVATING."

"★★★★★ AN ACTION-PACKED YARN... I REALLY ENJOYED THIS AND LOOK FORWARD TO THE NEXT BOOK IN THE SERIES."

JACK GATLAND

THE LIONHEART CURSE

HUNT THE GREATEST TREASURES
PAY THE GREATEST PRICE

BOOK 1 IN A NEW SERIES OF ADVENTURES IN THE STYLE OF 'THE DA VINCI CODE' FROM THE CREATOR OF DECLAN WALSH

AVAILABLE ON AMAZON / KINDLEUNLIMITED

PICK A CARD. PICK A SIDE.

TAROT QUEENS. IMMORTAL ACES.
EXILED JOKERS. FAERIE COURTS.
RYDER WAITES FORGOT THEM ALL.

BUT NOW HE REMEMBERS...

AND NOW... HE WANTS ANSWERS.

NEW YORK TIMES #1 BESTSELLER

TONY LEE

KNAVE
SPADES OF

THE PLAYING CARD WAR 1

THE PLAYING CARD WAR BEGINS JAN 2025
AVAILABLE ON AMAZON / KINDLEUNLIMITED

Made in the USA
Columbia, SC
22 April 2025

57002464R00240